No Harm Can Come to a Good Man

to a Good Man

James Smythe

W F HOWES LTD

This large print edition published in 2015 by
W F Howes Ltd
Unit 4, Rearsby Business Park, Gaddesby Lane,
Rearsby, Leicester LE7 4YH

1 3 5 7 9 10 8 6 4 2

First published in the United Kingdom in 2014
by The Borough Press

A CIP catalogue record for this book is available
from the British Library

ISBN 978 1 47128 551 6

Typeset by Palimpsest Book Production Limited,
Falkirk, Stirlingshire
Printed and bound by
www.printondeman   d-world   ugh, England

This book is ma   materials

To my family

What is now proved was once only imagined.

William Blake

When catastrophe strikes, we look for the signal in the noise – anything that might explain the chaos that we see all around us and bring order to the world again.

Nate Silver, *The Signal And The Noise*

PROLOGUE

Laurence Walker presses play and the video begins.

On it, he is standing in a seemingly blank room. He is looking straight into the camera lens, or the facsimile of him is; a broken version, created from photographs and screen grabs. It looks like him, but only barely. There is something about the version of his face that the software has created – so blank and expressionless – that makes him feel sick to his stomach. Behind him he can see similarly wrong versions of his family, of his wife and daughters. This created version of him isn't looking at them, his body language barely even acknowledging their presence. He wonders why they are so scared. Deanna and the girls are huddled together, clinging onto one another, terrified, backing away from him. Their faces are approximations of what that would actually look like: twisted and distorted and not at all real.

In the background, he hears a noise, a rustle that he cannot put his finger on; and then another noise, quieter in the mix. *Sobbing*. And then, finally, he notices that the version of him is holding something.

It's a gun. He knows the thick black metal. The digital version's thumb is on the trigger. The screen version of Laurence seems to shudder. More than a shiver: it seems uncontrollable.

Then the video cuts to black and a noise rings out that he knows can only be one thing: the crack, solid and sharp, the sound of a bullet leaving the chamber of a gun. The sobbing stops and turns into a scream, ringing through the darkness.

PART I

CHAPTER 1

Deanna wakes up. She lies perfectly still at first, because she loves these moments of being awake, of being in control of everything for just a second, before the day allows itself to interrupt. She can hear Laurence breathing, a harsh snore that's developed over the past few years into something akin to a growl. She can feel the slow rise and fall of his chest travelling through the mattress. After a while she rolls over and looks at him. He's still propped up as he was when she was falling asleep, his back against the giant pillows that they have taken to using as a headboard. His reading glasses are hanging off his face and his tablet is on his lap, his hands clutching it. He doesn't move much when he sleeps these days, she thinks, not since he became a senator. He tends to sleep so heavily that he stays perfectly still. The world could shift around him and he would somehow stay static.

She doesn't want to wake him yet – the alarm isn't set to go off for another half an hour, and he needs his sleep for today – so she turns away from him and slides to the edge of the bed. The floor is freezing cold on her feet, the house so draughty, always carrying a breeze up through the floorboards. She pads to the bedroom door and he doesn't even shift slightly as she opens it and sneaks out.

She heads downstairs, turning the lights on as she goes, straight into the kitchen. The glass along the back wall, looking out onto the garden, is darkened and she flicks the switches on the counter to bring it back to a clear state; no glare from the rising sun, just the light pouring in. She loves the feeling of the warmth of it coming through the glass, heating up the kitchen while she makes the coffee, selecting pods for the machine – they each take a different flavor, and she has to do nothing past setting the thing going. She stands at the counter, both hands on the marble, propping herself up; and she basks for a few seconds. All is silence.

Laurence wakes up as she comes back into the room, because she's not trying to be quiet now. He feels his glasses on his face and swats them away, a knee-jerk reaction; and then he opens his eyes and looks at Deanna front on. He sleepily smirks at her. This isn't the first time it's happened.

'I slept like this?' he asks.

'You did.'

'I'm so tired. I *was* so tired. You know.'

'I know,' she replies. 'You need to get dressed. The car will be here soon. I'll get the shower going for you.'

'You let me sleep, curse you.' He reaches for her and pulls her close, kisses her. 'I wish they'd let me drive myself,' he says. 'I feel like such a prick in that thing.'

Staunton is a small town, and Laurence has worked hard to win its people over. He came from the city but Deanna grew up here. When they left college, Deanna pregnant, they came back here at her behest, and he did his best to persuade the townsfolk – who knew her, who had known her parents before they moved away, before he got her knocked up and forced a retreat, law degree between his legs – that he was a good man. He's spent the best part of the last seventeen years earning their trust. The showmanship of politics sets that trust back a good decade, he thinks. Because New York City is drivable, if there's ever a TV show appearance they send tinted-window town cars, and that always makes Laurence embarrassed. Every time Deanna has to remind him that he has to get used to it; that if he gets what he wants from his career, he'll have an armed escort everywhere he goes. Soon he won't be allowed to drive anywhere by himself. He rubs his face and clambers out of bed. He stretches. 'What tie, do you think?'

'The lemon one.'

'Lemon? Jesus. You want the crowd to turn on me? Start some riot about fence-sitting with my colors?'

'It's smart. It's bright. You want potential voters

7

to think you are as well, don't you? At least, until they know you as well as I do.'

'Ha ha.' She kisses him as she leaves the en suite, and he strips his boxers off. She looks back at him: slightly looser around the edges than he used to be, but not totally out of shape; love handles, a slight belly, a sagging of his chest. It's only the effects of age, of a more sedentary lifestyle, of being comfortable. 'You want to come in?' he asks. 'I might not wash myself properly.'

'I'm sure you'll manage,' she says. 'I have to wake the girls.'

She goes to the twins' room first. Alyx, their youngest daughter, is curled up on her bed, her feet hanging off the side, her arms splayed into a position not far off that of a crucifixion: spread out, extended from the shoulders. Sean, their only son, is almost textbook fetal on the other bed, rolled up as small as possible. Deanna thinks how curiously defensive it is. She wonders if he had bad dreams.

'Hey, campers,' Deanna says, 'it's morning – rise and shine.' She raises the blinds and stands out of the way of the window, so that the light can hit her daughter in the face. Alyx giggles, and wriggles herself under the duvet. 'Nope, not today,' her mother says, pulling it away from her, 'you've got school.'

'I don't want to,' Alyx says. She's stubborn and defiant, in that way that kids can be. All three of the children are, something that they get from their father. Sean pulls himself to sitting and then to the floor where he stands in front of the bed, swaying slightly, like a zombie. Deanna goes to him and prods him with her finger, making it rigid, and he tumbles backwards to his bed, collapsing into laughter.

'You guys have got five minutes to get up and in that shower, or I'll be back, and I'll be mad as all get out,' Deanna says. She tugs on Alyx's ankle as she leaves the room, and the girl slides down the bed, giggling again; and then Deanna lets her go, and she tumbles gently to the floor.

The next room on her rounds is the bathroom that the kids all share. Deanna flicks the switch for the shower, letting it warm up, and then heads down the corridor to Lane's door. She knocks on it once, a single, solid rap, but there's no answer; so she turns the handle. The room is dark, but she can see the clutter through it. The clothes thrown everywhere, the books and vinyl sleeves scattered around the place, her daughter in bed still.

'I'm awake,' Lane says. 'It's fine, I'm awake.'

'Just checking,' Deanna says. The room is painted dark, grays and blacks, because that's what Lane is into. Deanna opens the door wide and steps in, tapping Lane's leg through the blanket. 'Your dad's got his thing today, so stress-free morning, please.'

'Fine.'

'You know what I'm saying. You want eggs?'

'Sure.'

'Straight home tonight as well. Like I say, no crap today, okay?'

'Jesus, okay.' Lane doesn't stick her head up to look at Deanna the whole exchange; but she reaches up, to itch her head as it stays still on the pillow. She scratches at the bit where the neck meets the skull, through her hair; and Deanna sees the tattoo on the inside of her wrist, the logo of one of the bands that Lane is obsessed with: three intersecting geometric shapes, a block of symmetrical color in the center of them. It looks like a puzzle, but it's not (or at least, it's not one that Deanna's been able to solve). The tattoo was the first real mark of rebellion from Lane: the lie that she told to be able to get it, and the months of hiding it to pretend that it didn't exist. But, she promised no more.

Deanna hears the bathroom door slam shut, meaning that one of the twins is doing as they've been told, and she tells Lane that she's next. Lane won't shower: she's started cutting back on that now, letting her hair get greasy. It's a thing, and Deanna knows it's only a matter of time before she cuts it off. That's what the kids in her school are doing now, her friends: shaving their hair right back. Deanna's begged Lane not to, simply because of Laurence's impending campaign. They have a deal: she won't be made to wear floral dresses as long as she covers up the tattoo and does her hair for the cameras every once in a while; and as long as she smiles when the cameras

10

are out. It won't be forever, but Deanna used the words *consideration* and *family* a lot, and eventually Lane agreed. Still, her second act of rebellion was to shave the underside of her hair on the sides over the summer, and then argue that she could hide it by wearing her hair down if she was ever at a public event. Besides which, Laurence – she calls her parents by their first names, a stupid and totally forced gesture which makes Deanna's skin prickle – hasn't formally announced yet. They have spoken about holidays and the cabin that they have bought and spending time with the children. There's no press to worry about for just yet, she reasons. Another few months, they can have that argument all over again. I'll even pay for the dresses we end up forcing her to wear, Deanna thinks.

She goes to the kitchen and puts the eggs into the poacher and starts the cycle. She hears the crack of their shells, the splash as they hit the water. Perfect every single time: no shell in there, no mess. It does it all for her.

'Television,' she says loudly. The set reveals itself in the corner of the room, the screen turning from its camouflaged setting – matching the wallpaper behind it, making it as inconspicuous as possible – and automatically boots onto the news channels, showing the four that Laurence watches most in its different corners. They'll all be covering the announcement; they're already hyping it, talking about what they can expect. They know, of course

11

they know; there's an embargoed press release already gone out, she's sure. She hears everything from here, because you do in these old houses: the sound of the showers switching off; of feet padding across the floors; of drawers and wardrobes opening and shutting. And still, there is that feeling of the sun on her face; still, something that she will never ever tire of.

Alyx is first down, and she walks to the refrigerator and takes out a bottle of juice. Deanna passes her a glass from the cupboard, and she puts it on the breakfast bar before climbing onto a stool and pouring the juice for herself. She watches the news (not understanding it, necessarily, but it's something to occupy her) while Deanna puts bread into the toaster and pops it early so that it's barely browned. She puts the eggs directly onto one slice for Alyx and deposits it in front of her. The little girl breaks one with her knife and the yolk sluices down onto the bread, soaking through it. She tugs it apart with her nearly blunt kids' cutlery, using the spork to scoop the sodden bread and egg into her mouth.

'You're so messy,' Deanna says. She gives her a paper kitchen towel, and Alyx wipes her mouth with it, and her hands. 'Mucky pup.' Sean runs in then and sits next to Alyx. No ceremony: he just waits to be fed.

'I don't want eggs,' he says.

'No? So what do you want?' Deanna asks.

'Can I have a Pop-Tart?'

12

'Fine. But if you have that today, you have eggs tomorrow. Deal?'

'Deal,' he says. There's a trade-off in the house, Laurence and Deanna constantly trying to do what's right by the kids, to balance and manage their food, their exposure to TV shows and music. They want to do this right – that's their motto. She puts the pastries in the toaster and clicks it down. She stands and looks at the kids, both of them watching the news now, as if the world is something that they even comprehend yet. The toaster pops, and she puts the tarts on a plate.

'They're hot,' she says, so Sean blows on them. She thinks about how cute he is; how she should relish these moments. Everybody tells her: this is all too fleeting.

'Deanna?' Laurence calls, from the top of the stairs. She finishes loading the dishwasher and heads out to the hallway. He's wearing the suit that he had custom-made earlier this year; the first outing for it, having saved it for a special occasion.

'How is it?' he asks, raising a leg as if he's a catalogue model. It's something he's always done when he should be taking himself seriously, a deflection. And it's always made her smile. He opens the jacket at the sides, to show off the shirt that he's wearing, and the lemon tie, and he twirls, posing again at the end. He sucks in his cheeks. She'd bought the tie for him, knowing how good it would look; how it would complement his complexion, his salt-and-pepper hair, the almost gray core of his eyes. He walks down and towards her and stands on the first step, even taller than usual next to her.

'Perfect,' Deanna says. 'The tie is lovely.'

'You would say that.'

'It's joyous. It makes me happy. It'll make other people happy, and that will make them want to vote for you.'

'Good. I'm stressing and I need to not stress.'

'This is true,' Deanna says. 'Not-stress is always better.' She reaches up and straightens the tie for him. She thinks about what she's doing, and how many times she has done this. How many more times there will be, if the future that they are working towards all goes to plan. 'You're going to be amazing,' she tells him.

'You always say that.'

'That's because it's always true.' Lane comes down behind him, and he steps aside to let her through, pulling a face at her as she goes. She is wearing one of the band tees that she near-as lives in and jeans that Deanna's never seen before, and she's got a beanie carefully balanced on her head, her hair tucked up inside it. 'Right,' Deanna says to Laurence, beckoning him down, 'food time. In there, sit down. Today, you relax.' She stands and points, watches as they both go into the kitchen, then follows them. Sean finishes his breakfast and gets down from the table, and Deanna sends him to get his bag. 'Leaving in three,' she says.

'I hate school on days like this,' he says.

'Only a few weeks until the summer,' she reminds him. 'Then you can have days like this over and over and over, until I'm sick to death of you.'

'Mom!' Alyx says. 'You won't get sick of us.'

'I will. I'll be on Xanax by the time you go back.'

'What's Xanax?'

'It's nothing,' she says. 'And you,' she says to Alyx, 'bag, now.' They disappear, and Lane walks off, clutching an apple in her hand. Deanna turns to Laurence as he eats his toast. 'I love you,' she says. 'Knock 'em dead, you hear?'

'If they're dead they can't vote for me,' he replies.

'Then knock 'em into a coma until the election.'

'Better.' She kisses him, and she tastes the butter, the marmalade. The same taste every morning for eighteen years.

'Right,' she says, pushing away from him. 'Time to go. Call me.' She shouts for the kids and Laurence leans to one side and watches down the hallway as they all leave. They wave at him from the front door and wish him luck, and he smiles and waves back. He watches them as they get into the car. The Hendersons are walking on the other side and Deanna talks to them, as she always does, every single morning. She tells them that she'll be along later to pick up one of their fresh loaves. They tell her that they'll put one aside. She laughs, because every conversation about anything here is somehow gently amusing. Laurence watches it

15

happen; he's seen this a thousand times before. His car is waiting as well, and he grabs his jacket and briefcase. As he gets into the car he asks which way they're going because there's probably going to be traffic going into the city their usual way. The driver tells him a route.

'You want me to go a different way?' he asks. Laurence brings up the *ClearVista* app and searches the route finder. All the options are just as likely to get messy at this time of day.

'It's fine,' Laurence says, 'whatever you think is best.' He watches as the driver lets the app pick the route for them. Hell or high water, it's what's easiest.

Deanna is at home and writing – or rather, the laptop is open, along with document that's meant to be her new book; and she has reread what she wrote the last time, deciding that it's fine and can stay, for now, when she hears Laurence's name mentioned on the news, saying that it's time for the live coverage of the press conference. She turns the volume up and watches him at the podium, surrounded by blue banners and badges. And his tie has been replaced with one that matches the color of everything else, a blunt-force sign of unity and support for the party that he seems so estranged from, at least on paper. He's a new breed, a potential future. These are the words that he's introduced with by the ex-President who stands by him, who is diametrically opposed to so many of his policies, but is tucking that behind them for the sake of what Laurence could do. This is an opportunity, they all know.

'So – and I realize that I am getting ahead of myself, but what the hell, that never did me any harm before in life – let me introduce you to the future candidate for the Democratic party, and the next President of the United States, Laurence Irving Walker!' He stands to one side and applauds so loudly that it's all that can be heard for a beat over the microphones on the podium. Laurence looks slightly sheepish, humbled by the words, and he shakes the ex-President's hand, almost cupping it, a gesture that's focus tested and proven to show security, strength and power. He stands up at the front, and he smiles. The crowd cheer and he works it like a comedian; letting them have their moment, stepping back as the applause overwhelms him. He nods, and he laughs, and he steps back.

'You're too kind,' he says. 'I haven't done anything yet.' That gets a laugh, and he puts a hand on the podium, the other into his trouser pocket, which brushes back his jacket. Deanna can hear Amit telling him the things he can do, the gestures and phrases that will work in this situation. Humble, but not too humble; strong, but also showing that he's human; a leader, but not unable to listen. She recognizes these things as being a part of Laurence, but not like this. This way they're exaggerated, offered up like evidence. 'But I hope to. And that's what today is all about, really: hope. That's something that the people who live in New York State tell me all the time. They say: we feel like our hopes for our children, our health, our homes – our hopes for the future – they're being lost in the chaos of life. You wouldn't believe how common it is to hear that.' Everyman, but not too casual. The camera focuses on him, shows him in a good light. He's got make-up on, Deanna thinks, and his hair has been coiffed, like something from that old TV show about advertising, a slick and neat look that's pushed back from his face. It says he's a family man, but not *too* married.

She's heard the speech, and she knows he won't fumble it. He's never fumbled a speech in his life. He's going to slyly announce his intentions, set this all up. This is how it works, now. It's all about starting a quiet storm. She shuts off the TV and walks around the kitchen, thinks about what happens next. This house will be gone, sold to somebody else. They'll start a family in it, and the place will get its own memories. And Deanna and the family will live . . . where? An apartment in Georgetown until they move. She doesn't want to think about the end of this: a giant house where their every movement is monitored, where they can't go for a walk without somebody wondering if they're okay; what they're doing; if somebody might make some foolish attempt on their lives.

She sits at her laptop and minimizes her book, and she opens a browser window. She types *www. ClearVista.com* into the window, and the site loads.

Will Laurence Walker ever be President? she asks. The site does its thing, the little icon spinning and folding itself into itself, a perpetual loop of folding and unfolding, and then spits out an answer. *There is a sixty-three percent chance of Laurence Walker becoming President.*

She stares at the screen. That's based on today. It's based on right now, the data mining – she hates the idea of it, as if thoughts, emotions, journalism and tweets and whatever else can be broken down into something that's utterly tangible and totally immutable – having trawled the latest reactions to Laurence's statement. She imagines that *Twitter* is full of #*Walker2020* advocates, buying into both the message and the man.

For a second she hates this. For a second, she wonders what might have happened if she'd given a different answer when he told that her wanted to run; when he asked her if she thought it was a good idea. She had said, 'It's what you've always wanted', and now she thinks that saying that wasn't really an answer at all.

Laurence's team takes a detour to Nassawa after the speech is done, already arranged but spontaneous-seeming. This is the start of the process: a meeting with Laurence's current constituents, the beginning of the handshaking and baby kissing. They stop off at the town hall, and they walk in, unannounced, and the people working there laugh and smile and take photos. Somebody from the *Nassawa Tribune*

19

comes down and writes an article, takes a short interview with Laurence.

'Earlier on, your speech? Seemed like you were hinting at a bigger platform for your message. Any chance you can confirm, absolutely, your intentions of running for office?' the interviewer asks, and Laurence almost laughs at their moxie, at their attempt to get an answer far bigger than their paper probably would usually get. Despite what others are saying, he hasn't shown his hand yet. Everyone in the room smiles; they all know what the reporter is asking.

'Not a chance am I answering that one,' Laurence says, with a smile, and that gets a laugh; and he shakes the journalist's hand and grins for another photograph. They move on, to a local café, and they eat lunch with the locals there, and Laurence fields questions about the current government, the policies being pushed through. He takes his platform stands: he believes in free healthcare for all, and he believes in the right to a free education that stands head-to-toe with the best that private education can offer. That's where money should be going. He wants to siphon off far more money from the richest 0.5% – this isn't about the 1%, he says, it's those earners who manage to somehow take in the bulk of the country's income in one fell swoop – and put that back into the country itself. 'If you've got an income that would allow us to give everybody in the country a personal doctor and teacher, why shouldn't we be taking more from you? If you've got money you won't miss, that you won't even notice is gone from your accounts, why shouldn't you help where you can?' That gets applause, the people cheering over their sandwiches and salads. When they're done they go to the local high school, and there's a buzz because this doesn't happen often – Nassawa isn't big on the map, one school and one hospital – so there's an impromptu assembly, all the kids brought into the gym for the chance to ask Laurence questions. He's one of them, and he sells it like that. He grew up in the city, sure, but he lives in the sticks now – 'The boonies,' he says, and that gets a laugh, because he's old and he's using language like that – and he answers more questions. One younger boy asks if he wants to be President somebody. 'Someday, sure,' Laurence says. 'That, and an astronaut. But President most of all.'

When he's done, Laurence calls home.

'How did it go?' Deanna asks.

'Good,' he says. 'Met some people. All very nice.'

'That's what it's about,' she says.

'It is. Love you.'

'Good luck tomorrow,' she says.

'With the big shots? They'll take what they can get, I'm sure.' He breaks everything down to casual dismissals. 'We should go out for dinner when I get back. A proper night: dinner and drinks. A hotel. Maybe a weekend away, before this goes insane.'

'It's not insane already?'

'It'll get worse.'

'I don't even know who you are any more,' she jokes.

'Probably for the best,' he replies. 'We have a party tonight, for the team.'

'Party hearty,' she says, 'then get some sleep.'

'Yes, boss,' he replies.

The party runs all night. Laurence's people have hired a bar in Midtown, taken the entire place over, and they've had a cocktail created for the occasion, some luridly blue thing called the *Walker All Over 'em*, that tastes like Jolly Ranchers and the cheap flavored wine that teenagers drink. Laurence necks two before he's even found a seat, and then is handed a third when he's asked to make a speech. This, he's told, is the speech for them. Not self-aggrandizing: boosting the troops. He drinks faster as he starts to slur his words ('Couldn't have done this all without all of you,' he says, letting the façade slip only slightly) and then a fourth. There's an area at the back with a dance floor and somebody puts on some new song that's been a huge hit pretty much across the world, music made for memes, and he's dragged out to dance, which he does. Amit stands at the side and watches and laughs, and he takes a photo – expressly banned at the party, because this stuff lingers on the Internet, and there's always some-body on one of the political blogs who's desperate to print anything that looks as if it could be the start of a scandal – and shouts that he'll use it as leverage.

'You ever fuck up, guess what's being sent to *TMZ*?' he says, and his whole team laughs.

Deanna has trouble sleeping. It begins to rain, and the weather's so close that she can barely stand it, even with the air-con jacked up as high as it will go. It's something about the sort of humidity they get here, because at its worst it's a warm breeze off the top of the lake, dragging along whatever from the base of the mountains, the warm smell of somewhere else entirely, somewhere with a logging industry and factories and a whole other way of life.

She gets out of bed and goes downstairs, and she opens her laptop and the file for what's meant to be her new novel, years in the making. It's a book that's three years late already, if only by her own deadlines rather than those of a publisher that it doesn't yet have, and she's so behind. It used to be that she could sit at a table and just write the things, and the words would come out exactly as they were always meant to: from her head to the page, in the right order, the way that she had imagined them (for better or worse). But this one has become stuck, and she can't move past it until it's done. She can't abandon it, that's for sure. She never gives up on anything. When she first hit the wall she was frustrated: a year of struggling against certain words, of rearranging sentences until they fit the best they could into what was inside her head. After a while, she almost got used to being blocked. The wall was there every time she tried to write, and it never left. Some writers she knows have cats that sit with them while they work; she has the wall.

She tells herself to not rush, because there's no contract. She never had a real audience, the previous books appearing on shelves one day and then slowly fading from them, until you had to go online to track them down; and how would you even know to? Her agent emails every so often, asking how the book is, how life is, if she's still writing, and she says that she is. She tells him that she's working on it, that it'll be worth it when she's done. But then she hits send and looks at the word count: not quite static, but close. A few words here and there, up and down. She thinks that she should give up almost every day of her life. Laurence tells her that it'll be different when he's done whatever it is he's going to do. He laughs that people will be desperate for a novel written by the First Lady. It's only half a joke. She wonders if that's the pressure that she needs: that maybe the scrutiny of her earlier books, people tearing them apart, looking for truth between the words, might actually drive her to finish this one. And maybe that's why this book has been so hard, she thinks. It's more personal than anything else she's ever written. It's part of her, in places: of her childhood, and about her sister Peggy, who has been missing ever since she was a small child. It's about family, mostly, and she knows what will happen to it. The women will be read as proxy for her, the men for Laurence. She wonders if that's why she's so hesitant to get any further with it. She began it when Laurence first mentioned running, back when he was doing a talking-head spot during the previous election, and it's been written in the shadow of his career ever since.

She writes the same sentence over and over, tweaking words. She tweets – which she does anonymously, because these things never die on the Internet and one day some of things she's said could really bite her in the ass. She exercises on the floor of the kitchen, lying flat on the dark slate tiles, the moon outside, the blinds left up, doing push ups and sit ups until she leaves a patch of sweat the breadth of her body on the tiles themselves.

Twenty-three words. She counts them, and reads them, and tries to evaluate them, two sentences that she knows can't live up to, and that can't actually mean anything, not taken like this. She reads them so many times that they start to disintegrate, ceasing to look like actual words any more, starting to be just shapes on the page that she happened to type.

In his hotel room, Laurence dreams: of his children and his wife. And there's a pale room, pale because the light is so bright, and pale because it's not a place that he knows. Maybe that's how dreams are, he thinks through it, because he knows that he's dreaming. If they're not grounded, if they're not somehow stolen from what is actually real, maybe they're just faded before they even begin. So Deanna and the kids are clear as day, but the room, the background – it's not a thing that exists and they are taken away from him. They're pulled backwards into the pale, and there's nothing that Laurence can do to stop it.

When he wakes up, the dream is a memory that is barely there.

The representatives from the party's higher echelons all stand to shake Laurence's hand, and they smile and laugh and pat him on the back.

'You ready for this?' one of them asks. 'You ready for what's going to happen to your life, son?'

'Not especially,' Laurence says, moving around the room, 'but I'll do my best.' They grin, waiting for him to speak more. This is him as a show-pony: put him in front of a crowd and watch him perform. 'I'm highly adaptable, that's my thing. That's always been my thing. Adapt, don't stop talking, don't let the others get a word in edgeways.'

'It's his major skill,' Amit says, 'and it means that he never ends up listening to me as well.' That gets a laugh, because they know it's not true. Amit knows his own reputation, and he knows what he's worth to the campaign. Everybody in the room does.

There are two empty spaces at the table, the chairs already pulled out for them, the glasses already filled with water, and the two men take them and sit down. The smiling doesn't stop, nor the gentle laughs that accompany the comfort of the situation for the panel.

'So, you're going to be formally announcing Monday,' an older woman at the far end of the table says, 'making sure that we get the full week's cycle. Are you ready for that?'

'Yes,' Laurence says.

'Of course, it'll mean you'll have to slightly scale back your day-to-day work, but you'll still be working for them for a good while yet.'

'And there's no race? No contest?' Amit asks.

'Nobody with any weight,' another man says. 'A few senators are batting their lashes, but your man here tests off the scale.'

'What about Homme?'

'He's thrown his hat into the ring, sure. But you throw a hat onto the floor, it's likely to get trodden on.'

Another of the old guard interrupts him. 'Senator Walker, you have our full support. You go out there, you work the states you have to work, shake the hands and kiss the babies. That's a cliché, Laurence, but clichés exist for a reason. There's always truth packed inside them.'

'How long are we talking?'

'Usually it's a twelve, fifteen-month race from announcing the intent. This time, we're winding

27

it back. Let's try for six before anybody else concedes and then we can concentrate on putting the pressure on POTUS, see if we can't get him a little scared about what we're bringing to the table.' The man who says this, who once ran for President himself, back in the latter part of the last decade, grins. 'Laurence, you're a threat. You're what the party needs, let's be honest. You're going to shake this up. You're going to drag voters in by their bootstraps and coat tails, and you're going to win this thing.'

'Thanks for your faith,' Laurence says, looking around at them all. He makes eye contact with every single one of them; he wants them to know that he's serious, that their support means something to him. That's been one of his major arguments the last few years: politics has become about empty words and even emptier eyes, promises made that are made for self-aggrandizing reasons rather than because somebody believes that they are the right thing to do. This is how he's become popular, a man of the people.

'There's paperwork, of course, and we have to talk strategy.'

'What sort of strategy?' Amit asks.

'Well, for one thing, the very reason that you were hired,' the ex-nominee replies. 'We're going to have to talk about *ClearVista*.'

The bar is in a hotel that's full of people who shouldn't be there at a quarter of four in the afternoon, so nobody bats an eyelid when Laurence and Amit take a table. Laurence orders an Old Fashioned, Amit lemonade. He and Amit don't talk until the drinks arrive, brought by a waiter, brandishing them on a polished silver tray, like some service from a time long before this. Laurence sips; the drink is sharp enough, and good. The meetings with the higher echelons of the party always terrify him; they bring out the prospects of the future, and the reality of what this all could mean over time. Amit brings out the paperwork and the contracts.

'They're footing the bills,' he says.

'But this feels like bullshit,' Laurence argues.

'Necessary bullshit,' Amit says. 'Look, they want this, and everybody's going to be using it. You know that POTUS's team have some *Here's what Four More Years will mean* stuff prepared, and you know that if they don't, the press will. Anybody can use these stats; better we're first out of the gate with them.'

'So I fill this in, and then it tells me if I should be President?'

'In theory.' Amit flicks through the pages. 'All this stuff, it's all designed to use as a jumping-off point, that's all. You answer this stuff honestly, the data miner verifies it – and then the concept of you as an honest candidate rises. It's not rocket science, not like people think it is.'

'It's numbers.'

'It's math; they're different things.' Amit turns

to various questions. '*I have never cheated on my wife*. You tick the *True* box, and you move on.' He leans in close. 'That *is* true, right?'

'Of course it's true.'

'Just checking. Because this is when there's no chance for secrets, Laurence. This is when you have to be honest. All those things people hide, they come out. Clinton never inhaled, remember? But Obama did. And that stuff *seeps*.' He finds more questions and picks them out. 'These are easy wins. *I have fought in a war. I have been honest about my policies. I have never lied about my sexual preferences*. These are so easy, Larry.'

'What's the deadline? Realistically.'

'No more than a couple of weeks: this is new tech; you get to be the first up to bat with the new, more polished algorithm.'

'How different can it be?'

Amit smiles and leans forward. 'When I stopped working for them, what we were doing was small fry. Compared to that . . . I mean, Jesus, Larry, the software will *know* you. That's how it works. It finds out everything about you, and it learns you, and it predicts you. That's the next wave.'

'It's ridiculous. So my word means nothing?'

'Of course it does. But this reinforces that. You know their slogan? *The Numbers Don't Lie*, Larry. Never have, never will. The public believes math. They believe computers. People? People are harder to believe.' He looks down at Laurence's hands, which are shaking, the ice rattling in the bottom of the glass. He raises his hand at the waiter walking by. 'One more,' he says, pointing to Laurence's glass. 'Listen: you can't lie, though. Seriously, I know you're full of integrity and all that stuff, so whatever. But we all lie. You lie on that, you'll get caught. What I've heard about the algorithm now, the data mining? That thing will find out any secrets you've got.' He finishes his own drink. 'Look, this is fine. It's totally fine. It's you and answers and some bullshit video that's going to run and run because it's the first of its kind. We do this, we win the election. That's what you want, right?'

'Yes,' Laurence says. The drink is put in front of him and he gulps it in the way that you shouldn't. 'That's what I want.'

Laurence's hotel room is functional. He lies on the bed, his head slightly swimming, and switches on the news. There's a picture of him on the screen, between the two anchors: the shining, smiling one that's on the front page of his website. The hosts are discussing the rumors.

'I think it's safe to say that they don't qualify as rumor any more,' one of them says, 'because, come on. Look who he's hired. Look where he's been. And his answers to questions about it have been—'

'So who'll run against him?' the other anchor asks. 'Because, for my money, there's only one other viable candidate, unless we're dredging up one of the failures from last time.'

31

'Which they won't do.'

'So, Homme?'

'Makes a lot of sense. Good profile. Family man – I mean, they're both family men, but still . . . and maybe more inclined to appeal to the more traditional members of the party.' Laurence thinks about how little he likes or trusts Homme: they've met a few times and their politics do not have many natural points of intersection. His would-be opponent is as red as the Democrats get, he's wavering on choice, healthcare, war. Everything is structured as a response to the last few governments, a way of suggesting that the soft touch that has been taken hasn't been enough. His platform is a return to more old-school values. 'But I don't think he's got a chance. Walker's going to take this. He's going to take the White House back, and maybe he's what's needed. You know, he's got some real guts.'

Laurence switches the set off. He thinks about sleep, but instead he takes up his phone and searches for his name on *Twitter*, on *Google*, on *Facebook*. He reads all the comments, and he tries to let the negative ones slide away from him.

Deanna shouts at the twins to stay quiet and they do. She has a voice that she uses to get the desired effect – total, gently terrified silence – and she engages it only rarely, because otherwise it will lose its effectiveness. But she snaps at them, and she peers out of the windscreen at the streetlamp-lit junction, trying to see Lane coming from one of the directions. She's already an hour late and she's not answering her phone or tweets or messages. She said it was a party somewhere around here. Deanna thinks about driving the streets to look for it. She knows what teenagers are like when they're Lane's age: they can't help but turn the music up a little too loud which makes them much easier to find from the sidewalk, at least. There aren't many streets in this town – Parkslide being only a little bigger than Staunton is – but she worries about Lane coming here to find her and having to wait around on the corner. She knows what it will look like; she saw what Lane was wearing when she left the house, an outfit that Laurence would have freaked out about. She tries to call Lane again, and talks to the twins as she holds the phone to her ear.

'Guys, Mommy needs silence for a little while. This is important, okay?' It's an apology for what she said. She wants to scare them, but not that much.

'Okay,' Sean says. 'Mom, where's Lane?'

'I don't know, sport,' she says. 'She's on her way, I'm sure.' The cell goes to Lane's answering service, but Deanna doesn't leave a message. She sees somebody walking in the distance, a girl – the figure is slim enough to be Lane, certainly – but as they get closer she sees that she is tottering along on heels. Lane wouldn't be caught dead outside her boots, even at a thing like this. The girl is drunk, swaying and swerving along the sidewalk, stepping into the road every so often, stumbling down the lip between the pavement and the gutter.

'Excuse me,' she shouts at the girl. 'Hey, excuse me?' The girl stops and looks up at Deanna from across the road. 'Have you been to a party?'

'Sure,' the girl says. She looks Lane's age – actually, Deanna thinks, she looks younger, because Lane doesn't wear make-up that looks as if it's been put on by a child playing dress-up with her mother's beauty products – and there's a good chance it's the same one.

'Could you tell me where?' Deanna asks.

'Tim's house. I mean, Tim's *parents*' house,' she says, seemingly angry, as if there was ever any chance of Tim owning the place, and how could Deanna not know that? 'They came back early, so . . . whatever.'

'And where do they live?'

The girl waves behind her. 'Just down there,' she says. She belches under her breath and sits down by a streetlamp, pulling a packet of cigarettes from her bag – Deanna stretches her brain to think when she last saw somebody with this brand – and fumbles to light one.

'Guys,' Deanna says to the twins, 'your sister is in so much trouble.' The twins laugh at this, a shared secret. They understand: Deanna will use her angry voice on Lane. They drive in the direction that the girl indicated and soon Deanna sees

34

where the party was: a large house, shining white with the lights that are turned on inside it, a flood of teenage bodies outside it, milling around in the front yard. She pulls over and rings Lane's phone again, winding down the window and hearing it ringing, the tinny echo of a song that Lane loves cutting through the hubbub. Lane cancels the call, so Deanna steps out of the car. She turns back to the twins. 'I warned her,' she says.

She shouts Lane's name, her full name: Lane Alexandra Walker.

'Oh shit!' comes Lane's reply. The crowd seems to part like it's a trick, and there stands Lane. She drops something as Deanna gets closer; a bottle of some cheap, sweet-smelling liquor. She reeks of pot, that sweet, sweaty smell that Deanna remembers from her own youth.

'Get in the car,' Deanna says. She isn't even putting the voice on this time.

They drive home in silence, even the twins. When they're parked, Deanna tells Lane to get inside and to take her brother and sister with her. Lane does as she's told. The car smells of smoke and alcohol and sweat and Lane's hair products, used to push her hair into something that makes Deanna think of the punk hairstyles that she used to toy with in the nineties. This, she thinks, is cyclical: teenagers do this. I did it, she tells herself. I was exactly like this, living in Staunton and rebelling in my own little ways. She stays in the car while they all go inside and watches the lights flick on throughout the house. The twins are well past their bedtime, which means tomorrow she's going to have two seven-year-old nightmares on her hands. Better a weekend than a school day, she thinks.

She gets out and goes to the downstairs bathroom, finding air freshener, and she sprays the inside of the car with it, almost pushing it into the fabric of the seats. She thinks of bug bombs, and filling a space with something to purify. When she's got a good cloud of the stuff going she shuts the doors and goes into the house. The twins are in the living room, Alyx on the iPad, Sean on the Xbox.

'No,' Deanna says. 'Well past bedtime.'

'Mo-o-om . . .' Alyx says.

'Come on,' Sean pleads.

'Don't screw with me tonight, you guys. Bed!' They both sigh – the same sound of exhalation, the same exasperation – and they put down their games and march past her. 'You guys go to sleep, you get to pick what we have for dinner tomorrow.'

'Can we get pizza?' Sean asks.

'Sure. Pizza. Deal. Clean your teeth and get to bed.' She stands at the bottom of the stairs and listens to them doing their routine, finely tuned as it is. Always Sean into the bathroom first, then he cleans his teeth in the hallway while Alyx goes in. Then she cleans her teeth and both of them stand at the sink. They spit the toothpaste out at the same time. They get into bed, and she tucks them in, kisses them on their foreheads. 'Pizza – if I don't hear a peep from you,' she says. 'That's the deal.' They both do the same gesture: zipping their mouths shut with invisible zips, and they smile. She doesn't understand them, not all the time, because there's something she simply can't get close to there, that only they share. She worried, when she knew that she was having twins, because she was older than she thought she would be when having another child, and because she thought that they might be too much for her to cope with. But now, eyes shut, they're what she wants, two perfect halves of a perfect whole. She wonders if they'll always be like this.

The sound of music, wafting down the corridor from Lane's room, stops her daydreaming and reminds her what's gone on here. She pulls the twins' door shut and strides down the corridor. All the tricks that they've learned over the years about how to make the kids respect them – or, at least slightly, fear them – come into play now. Lane is almost too old for them, but still, they're worth a shot; and residual feelings of what they used to inspire in her might just swing it in Deanna's favor.

She opens the door wide, letting it swing until it hits the stopper. It thuds, and the whole door shakes. Lane is on the bed, lying back, staring at the ceiling of her room. There are still the remnants of the pale stars there that they put up when they moved in, when Lane was the same age as the twins are now. She wanted the stars because she'd had them in the old house. Laurence and Deanna relented, even though she was too old for them, maybe. It was easier.

'What the hell are you doing?' Deanna asks. Lane doesn't look at her. 'Lane, you *know* the rules.' She walks over, stands next to the bed. 'You know that we don't want you drinking, and we don't want you smoking. You *know* about your father's career – you get yourself arrested, and God only knows what that does to him, the sort of questions he'll have to answer about that.'

'Fuck that,' Lane says.

Deanna steps back. 'Okay, you're done. Lockdown for the next week.'

'You can't do that!' Lane retorts.

'Can and will. Watch me.' She leaves the room, slamming the door shut behind her, and she goes to the bedroom and takes her cellphone from her pocket. She starts writing a text to Laurence, explaining what has happened, telling him that he's going to need to talk to Lane when he gets home; that she always listens to *him*, or pretends to. Something about the father-daughter relationship works while Deanna and Lane have always had this wall between them when it comes to basic levels of respect. She writes all of that out, and then thinks. She doesn't press *Send*. Instead, she goes downstairs and she brings up the calendars on the screen embedded in the door of the refrigerator, and looks at Laurence's. The next few weeks are brutal for him: back tomorrow morning,

Sunday working in DC on policy, then leaving first thing Monday for the announcement, then on to LA, Seattle, back to DC, home for three days, then NYC for a week. She taps through the following weeks and months, looking for a break, but there's nothing. He's barely hers, barely part of the family with his schedule the way that it is.

She clears the text. This is hers to deal with.

CHAPTER 2

Laurence sits up in bed holding the tablet. He scrolls through the questions while Deanna reads, and he sighs exaggeratedly at them. She puts her book down and laughs at his face, a mock-grimace at the task ahead of him.

'These fucking questions,' he says.

'How many are there?'

'A thousand; a thousand questions. Which is, what, nine hundred and fifty more than for a citizen ID?' Deanna puts the coffee down on the table at his side of the bed and leans in. She pulls the laptop away from him and turns it around to face her.

'*Aged eighteen, where did you see yourself aged thirty?*' she reads. 'You've only made it to eighteen years old?'

'Which is about a third of the way through. Because, apparently, they can tell if I would be a good president based on whether I ever gave some kid a wedgie when I was in high school.'

'It's not a science,' Deanna says.

'Probably not,' Laurence tells her, 'but *ClearVista* sure as hell acts as if it is.' He collapses backwards in mock anguish. 'It's fine. I have to do it.'

'Says who?' Deanna touches his chest. He's so warm, she thinks.

'*They* do. Shadowy *they*. The would-be Illuminati of America. And Amit.'

'Of course Amit does. He probably still has shares in the company.'

'He says that it's the future of politics.'

She leans in and kisses him. 'And there was me thinking that the future of politics would be you,' she says. 'You ready for today?'

'Barely.'

'Did you sleep?'

'Barely.'

'Barely?'

'Barely.' He smiles. 'It'll be fine.'

'All you have to do is dance, monkey.' She leans in to kiss him, and he pushes his tongue behind his lip, imitating the animal. She grins as she feels it, and he pulls her towards him, onto the bed. She rests her head in the nook between his chin and his shoulder. 'You'll be fine.'

'I know.'

'I'm going to the house, to try and make a start on stuff. Cleaning it.'

'I'll come and join you when I'm done.'

'There's no party?'

'Don't care if there is.' He thinks about what happens after this, and how busy he suddenly becomes. He's seen the effect that it's had, his slight withdrawal from them all in the wake of his career. This is, he thinks, important.

41

'I'll wake the kids,' she tells him, and then he hears her go down the corridor and into the twins' room. He hears them giggling. They've been waiting for her. Laurence gets out of bed and goes to the bathroom. He looks at his face. He thinks about how old he looks and wonders how old he will look at the end of this, what sort of effect even running for the role will have on him. He pulls at gray hairs, and he examines the lines on his mouth and eyes, the slight jowl underneath his chin. He rubs at his temples, and the spots on his head where the hair will start to go. It's in his family, or it was; and it feels like an inevitability to him. He'll turn forty and his stress levels will be off the charts, and then he'll just be clinging to whatever aspects of youth feel like letting him off the hook for the longest.

Deanna reappears in the doorway. 'Lane isn't coming,' she says. 'I told her she can have lockdown here or there, but she chose here.'

'Foolish girl.'

'I'm going to call her every hour, check she's not gone out.'

'We can trust her,' Laurence says.

'I wouldn't have trusted myself when I was her age,' Deanna replies. 'Anyway, the twins are getting dressed. What time are you on?'

'Ten,' he tells her. He goes to the wardrobe and pulls his suit out – the gray suit, the lemon-yellow tie – and as he dresses himself he hears her go downstairs and switch on the TV. He hears his name mentioned, and then the set goes quiet.

'Can we go swimming?' Sean asks.

'Later,' Deanna says. 'Maybe we can go in later.' She's packed all the cleaning supplies and the toolkit, and she pulls them both out of the trunk of the car. She wants to start clearing the house out, getting rid of the crap that's been left, making sure that there are no splinters. There is furniture in the house; wooden tables and chairs that match the walls and floors and make it feel like the set of a horror movie. She pulls up outside the front, driving as close to the house as she can. There's no real space for the car, just the dirt and gravel ground. 'Watch yourselves,' she says. 'No running, no picking up anything that looks as if you shouldn't pick it up, okay?' She looks at the twins. 'And stick close,' she says, 'No idea what's waiting to bite you in this place.' She snaps her teeth at them, and they both laugh.

The front door sticks and she has to shoulder it as hard as she can, really putting all of her weight into forcing it open. It finally swings, a hard arc that makes it smack into the wall and kick up clouds of dust. To Deanna's eyes the house looks as if it's barely holding itself up. It's a building of pencil-drawn monochrome, the walls slightly askew, in need of a ruler. Rays of light hit the dust that seems to fill every part of the place, the light coming from not only the windows, but also through the cracks in the walls. There's a smell inside that she struggles to recognize, that's not totally unpleasant. It's on that fine line, and it needs such a clean. They should have hired somebody, she thinks.

'Right,' she says, and she opens her bag, pulling out cloths and disinfectant sprays. 'We need to get this place a little more habitable.' She holds a cloth out for each of the kids. 'Help me today, maybe we think about buying you guys a video-game later in the week. Deal?' The kids snatch the cloths from her hands, and she shows them how to use the spray on the work surfaces in the kitchen, and how to wipe them down. She knows she'll have to go over it again, but this is fun, the three of them working on this. She knows that when this is done, the place might feel like more of a home.

There's no water from the taps; she writes it into her phone as something for Laurence to sort out when he arrives.

The delegates usher him onto the stage. 'This is official,' one of them says, 'so treat it with some goddamn respect, you hear?' He's smiling while he talks, so Laurence smiles too; but it sounds, for a second, like an actual threat. 'You do us proud,' the man says. Not, 'Do the party proud,' Laurence notices. He takes Laurence's hand, reaching for it and forcing the handshake.

Laurence reaches the stage and the flashbulbs

go, the cameras all pointing at him. He's got a speech that was prepared for him and he uses it while he speaks, but only as a frame. Most of the time he tries to be as much himself as he can.

They ask questions, and he poses for photographs. He checks his phone and his *Twitter*, his *Facebook*, his emails all scream alerts at him as people congratulate him. Amit takes the phone.

'Clear your notifications,' he says. 'You won't have time to read them.' He pulls a schedule out.

'No,' Laurence says, 'nothing else today. I'm going home. Family time.'

'Bullshit,' Amit says, laughing.

'No,' Laurence tells him. He asks for Amit to get him a car and he loosens his tie. He texts Deanna: *I'm coming home.*

The house looks exactly as Laurence has been picturing it: the same ramshackle wooden walls; the same dock that stretches off out and over the water; the same view behind it, the mountain and the houses in the distant opposite, and the sun above them. The driver takes them along the dirt track that runs down the hill towards the shoreline and Laurence watches the house get closer, as if it is becoming more real, and it reveals itself to him in broken windows and splintered wood. He feels the peace washing over him, a sense that this is meant to be – at least for now. Barely ten minutes from their other house, yet it feels like a different place entirely. He winds the window down and

45

smells the air, listens to the sound of the tires on the gravel.

Laurence watches as the driver takes the car back up the hill, leaving him alone outside for a second. There's just him. He can't hear his family, not at that moment; and then he goes up to the front door, which is opened wide, and inside. He hears them upstairs, singing some song that he vaguely recognizes from the radio. Deanna is mostly humming the melody, but the kids know every word. He doesn't shout to let them know that he's here, not yet.

He walks through the downstairs, which is open-plan, a living area with 1950s wood-framed sofas around a fireplace, then the kitchen behind and the table for four, the units that are the same wood as everything else. The man who owned this place must have been a carpenter, he thinks; maybe he did this all himself, and built the house with his own two hands. There are gun racks on the walls, empty slots of what was once there; and a hook with a dust outline shape of what was clearly a mounted animal head. Laurence stands by the window at the end of the house, looking out over the water.

'How did it go?' Deanna asks him. She's at the foot of the stairs. He didn't hear her come down.

'Good,' he says. 'It went well.'

'I love you,' she says, and he smiles.

'It's so peaceful here,' he tells her. 'This is amazing.' He's transfixed, staring at some far-off point in the distance. There's a thin layer of mist stopping him from seeing what's actually over the other side of the lake, only the thin shapes of what have to be houses and trees, but that isn't stopping him. 'I wasn't joking when I said that I had always dreamed of this,' he tells her.

'I know.' She stands next to him while the twins run around behind her. 'Thank god you're here. There's no running water.'

'I'll turn it on,' he says. He doesn't stop staring out at the lake.

The cellar door off the kitchen opens onto stairs that go down into total darkness. There's a smell of more than damp: of absolute wetness, wet mud and wet stone. Laurence and Deanna both peer down into the black.

'Looks like it's flooded down there,' Laurence says.

'Could be from the lake.'

'Could be.' He pulls off his suit jacket and rolls up his sleeves.

'You should change,' she says.

'Didn't bring anything,' he replies. 'I can get this cleaned. It'll be fine.' He opens his toolbox and looks for the torch. It's not there, so he takes out his cellphone and turns the brightness up, holding that out in front of him as he takes the first few steps down. The stairs are wooden, a stained and polished pine, and they creak underneath his weight. He puts his free hand out to the wall to steady himself. 'I'll do this,' he says. 'You stay up there and call for help if I die.'

'Don't,' she says.

'It's fine. Joke.' She hears him smiling. He steps down again, a few more. In front of him he can see the floor now, the bottom of the steps, and there is water there. He can't tell how deep, because it's black with dirt and grime. 'Pass me a stick or something?'

'Wait,' she says, looking around. There's nothing. She runs past the kids, who are now playing with their phones on the sofas, sitting in little clouds of dust that puff around them every time that they move (like Pig-Pen, she thinks, from the *Peanuts* cartoons), and she goes outside to the trees that line the road. She finds a branch and takes it back to him, passing it down.

'About time,' he jokes. He holds it in front of him and steps down again, watching the stick go into the water until it stops. 'Ankle level,' he says. He sits on the steps and they creak horrifyingly, as if they're being pulled off the walls.

'We need these replaced,' Deanna says.

'They're fine. They need oiling or something, maybe a supporting strut.'

'You say that as if you know what it means.'

'It's a strut. It supports.' He pulls off his shoes and socks and folds the bottom of his suit trousers up to his knees. 'Or something.'

'You're not,' she says.

'What else am I going to do?' he asks. He steps

down into it and the water swirls around his feet. He gasps. 'Cold,' he says. 'Jesus, that is *cold*.'

'Can you see the water pipes?'

'Give me a second,' he shouts back. From where Deanna's standing at the top of the stairs she can't see him now, only the faint flashes of his phone's light as he swishes it around. 'Okay, got it,' he says. 'It's rusted to hell.'

'Can you turn it?'

'I don't know. I need a wrench or something.' She picks up the bag and takes the first few steps down, and they groan. He wades closer and she places it slightly further down the stairs, within his reach. He grabs at it, stepping up. His feet are filthy, she sees. 'I'll get on this,' he says. 'You tell me if it works?'

She stands at the sink and turns the taps on, and there's a dribble of brown sludge from them and a gurgling, but no water. She waits, as the clangs of him struggling with the pipe echoes through the stairwell. She thinks about Lane and how it's been a while since she last called to check in, so she dials the house; but there's no answer; she dials her daughter's cellphone, and there's still no reply. She leaves a message and then tries again, letting the phone ring and ring.

'Shit,' she says.

'Mom!' Sean shouts, hearing the word.

'I didn't mean it,' she mutters back. 'Laurence,' she calls, 'I can't get hold of Lane.'

'She'll be fine,' he shouts up to her.

'I told her to stay in the house.'

'So go and pick her up. Force her to come here, be with us. She can help me dredge the cellar out when I've got this working.' She hears the noises still coming, the strain in his voice as he fights against the decades-old plumbing of the house, trying to make it habitable. When they moved into their first apartment, there was a superintendent to fix anything that broke; when they bought their house in Staunton itself they had it gutted and renovated and made as modern as possible, switches and buttons put in, digital rather than analog to run their lives by. Working with the old is new to them.

'I'll take the kids,' she says. 'We won't be long.'

'Bring me a Coke?'

'Sure,' she says. She goes to the kids. 'Come on,' she tells them, 'we're going back to the house for a little while.'

'I want to stay here,' Sean says. He doesn't look up from his game, but Alyx does.

'You can't.'

'Mo-o-om,' he says. He hits the whine in his voice, a note that he and Alyx have perfected over the duration of their lives; some pitch that manages to work in the same way that Deanna's angry voice does. It's worse when it's in harmony.

'Fine,' she says. She shouts to Laurence. 'Sean's staying up here.'

'Can I swim now?' Sean asks.

'When your father's done,' she says. Alyx stands

up and coughs away dust, and she and Deanna leave. Sean sits and listens as the engine starts, then he watches them drive up the track until they're gone.

Laurence struggles. It's hot down in the cellar, or he is; he sweats, and he hears the patter of it dripping into the water around his feet. He tries again, because he's sure that there's some movement; an almost-infinitesimally small amount, but it's still movement. Eventually this will open up the sluices. He stands still, planting his feet in the murky water, and he really fights the thing. It doesn't move and he doesn't move. Total stillness.

The light has gone out on his phone, some sort of standby mode having kicked in, and he's in the dark now, but he doesn't stop. This is necessary. The house means something. Securing it, actually working on it, that's a way of making their future seem as if it's going to happen. His phone rings, Amit's name on the screen; the photo of his grinning face that was taken on their first meeting.

'Where are you?' Amit asks.

'At the lake house.' Laurence doesn't let go of the wrench; he's still forcing it, still trying to get the water to flow.

'You shouldn't have run off. There are people asking for you.'

'Tell them it's family time. Tell them this is the sort of candidate I'll be: a man who gives a shit about stuff like that still.'

'You done the questionnaire yet?'

'No. Not even close.'

'Larry.'

'Amit.'

'You need to, you know that.'

'I know,' Laurence says. He looks down, pulls the phone away from his ear. It's wet with sweat and, as he wipes the screen of the phone on his shirt, the light dances across the muddy water at his feet. There are ripples and he feels the water lapping at his ankle, the energy that it carries coming through and tickling the hairs on his legs. The sound of it echoes in the space. He wonders if this is an effect of his effort, maybe the pipes shuddering as they try to let their water out. It picks up, suddenly more violent, tiny waves coming from the far wall. 'I have to go,' he tells Amit, and he hangs up the phone, shining the light again. The waves bounce the light around. He walks towards the wall that the ripples seem to be coming from. He crouches and presses his hand against it, feeling around. There's a crack in the concrete; it's only slight and he can't tell if that's the cause of this, but it feels like it is. A crack like this, there has to be repercussions. He wonders where this has come from.

The house is empty and quiet apart from the reverberations of the water in the cellar as it eases, as the waves die down. He thinks about washing his feet, which are the color of soot now, so he walks upstairs and through the kitchen, to the outside. The back door is already wide open. He pads along the dock and catches himself looking across the water again. He's sure that he can see something in the distance, across the water, through the mist, a light, or the reflection of a light. He stares at it. It's almost hypnotic, for that second.

It's only so slight.

He sits and dangles his feet in the water, and they are wet, and he looks down at them to see if they're clean yet and there is Sean, suspended underneath, the crown of his head jutting from the surface. Laurence stares for a second as he tries to parse what he's just seen and then he hurls himself down from the dock and he pulls at his son's head and shoulders, trying to yank him up, but the boy doesn't move. Laurence heaves in air and then dives down, frantically pulling at his son's limbs, using his body almost as a ladder to get lower, and then he finally feels the weeds that are wrapped around Sean's foot and ankle, going between his toes and all around, and he wrenches but they won't tear. The weeds are like thick rubber.

So he feels lower, to the root, thinking that might be easiest. He finds it up against concrete at the bottom of the house, the foundations at the base of the dock. This is where the weeds have grown, boring into the concrete and cracking it. The wall here leads to the cellar. This is what caused the flooding; and what Laurence felt around his own legs, his son's frantic and desperate kicking before he stopped breathing.

Laurence pulls that part of the plant out somehow and thinks, in that second, of those moments where people find superhuman strength when in crisis, and Sean's body drifts upwards. It's free. He grabs it and he pushes his son's head above water, then climbs out onto the dock, pulling Sean with him. He tries to give him mouth-to-mouth as he knows to do it. He pushes on Sean's chest, worried about doing it with too much force. He doesn't want to hurt him. He turns his head and he breathes into his boy's lungs again.

'Please,' he says, 'oh God, please,' and he breathes again; and then so does Sean, coughing up water. He doesn't open his eyes, and his breathing is shallow and labored, heaves that sound somehow less than human. Laurence runs for his phone and dials 911. He shouts about where they are but the address is hard to find. He describes it to them and they say that they'll be minutes. Support him, they say. Keep him breathing. If he stops, breathe into him again. Keep repeating this.

He does. He hangs up and he waits for the ambulance and he watches his son's face so closely that he hopes Sean can feel his hot breath on his skin, willing him to stay alive.

It's only a minute before the Staunton Sheriff's department arrives. They come tearing down the track and the deputy gets out and rushes to the boy, taking over. Laurence backs away and watches it all as if from a dream.

Deanna storms through the house, shouting Lane's name. She goes to her room and throws the door open and her daughter is there, on her bed. There's a boy with her; he's not like Deanna imagined, being clean cut, wearing a bright rugby-style shirt; or, he was. Now, it's on the floor at the foot of the bed. Deanna doesn't even look at him; she stares instead into her eldest daughter's eyes.

'I've been calling you.'

'I was busy,' Lane says, but her voice is shaking and weak. She's ashamed, whether she'll admit it or not.

'Get dressed,' Deanna says, 'you're coming to the house with us.'

'No,' Lane replies, and Deanna is about to shout at her, and to shout at this boy, to tell him to get out of the room, when her own cellphone rings. It's Laurence. She turns away from Lane's room, hearing her daughter and the boy fumble for their clothes, and she answers. Dumbly, she listens to his slow, measured politician's voice as he tells her what happened, or some version of it as best he understands it; that Sean is alive and being treated. He tells her about how he found him, and how he didn't know. Deputy Robards came, and he held Sean's tongue back, because their son began choking on his own tongue, and Sean nearly bit through the finger. Apparently that's a good sign,

Laurence says. He has bite marks, almost through to the knuckle; that detail, offered up. She didn't need it but Laurence stresses: this is a good sign.

'How long was he under the water?' Deanna asks.

'Minutes,' Laurence tells her. 'Six or seven minutes, maybe eight. I don't know.' He tells her to come to the hospital. She says that she will.

Lane stands in front of her mother. She can see it in Deanna's face.

'I need you to watch Alyx,' Deanna says.

'What's happened?' Lane asks. No antagonism, no challenge. She knows from the look she's being given that this is serious.

'Your brother fell into the lake,' she says. 'He's alive.' That seems enough; a thing to latch onto for all of them, and then she goes to the car and gets in and starts the engine. She doesn't need anything else. She drives.

This is the first time that she's had to go to hospital for one of the kids. They were lucky with Lane: ten years older than the twins, and Deanna and Laurence were ten years younger when they had her, ten years more stupid; but still they got through with her having nothing more major than a scrape or two. Nothing broken, nothing lost, no emergency trips to the hospital. Maybe, she thinks, they got complacent.

She thinks about the eight minutes that Sean was underwater. She wonders if eight minutes is a long time to not take a breath.

She doesn't know the way to the hospital. She relies on the *ClearVista* app on her phone to tell her where to go. She listens to its voice and tries to let that be all that she can hear.

She parks in the short-stay – because, she thinks, that's all this can be, because she'll go in and they'll be sending Sean home with some medicine or an inhaler or something, and a lesson learned about what to do and what to not and when to listen to your parents, because that's the sort of injury that kids recover and learn from – and she rushes in, past the ambulance bay and into the ER reception. There's a queue at the window, so she waits, and she looks for her son. Maybe he'll be sitting out here waiting for her himself, because it's not at all serious. They have let him go already, this was a false alarm. Instead, there are people with bloody noses and hands wrapped in bags of frozen vegetables, and one woman whose skin is almost green, her eyes rolling back in her head, froth around her mouth. There's a television above them, tuned to the news. They're talking about Laurence, running a special later on, about his political career so far. She hopes that she isn't still waiting here to see it.

'Miss?' the woman at the desk says. Deanna doesn't hear her. She's somewhere else: imagining Sean in the water, imagining how he took his dive from the dock, and how he arced through the air; and why he didn't come up again. She can picture it, as if she is there. She doesn't know how. She is trying to imagine what was going through his mind. How lost he was, and how he needed her. Maybe he called her name through the water . . .

'Miss? Can you hear me?' Deanna turns. The woman behind the counter is impatient already.

'My son's here,' Deanna says. 'I don't know where he is. My husband brought him here in in an ambulance. He drowned.' Such finality in that phrase.

'Name?'

'His name? It's Sean. Sean Walker.' The woman types and stares at her screen. Deanna imagines the notes shared on these computers: even down to letting the front desk staff know how to treat the situations. *The patient is fine. The patient is in stable condition. The patient is dead.* Morgan – Deanna reads her name badge – doesn't say anything for a while. Instead she follows the notes on her screen, and then she sighs. It's almost imperceptible, but Deanna is watching for it. She's so focused now on this moment and nothing more. No point in dwelling on what happened before. This is all about what happens from this moment on.

'Okay,' Morgan eventually says, 'so you're going to come with me through here now.' She stands up from her desk and lifts the entry flap, and she puts her hand on Deanna's elbow to lead her through.

'Is Sean okay? Can I see him?' Deanna asks.

'Your husband is through here,' Morgan says, 'and the doctor will bring news as soon as she's got some.' They pass bays of beds where doctors fix the damaged and then reach the room. It doesn't have anything printed on the door: there's a darkened glass window in it and nothing more. There are three more of them adjacent, Deanna sees, but she can't see if they're vacant or not. The door creaks on the swing, and Laurence is there and he rushes to her. He's still damp, wet from having dredged Sean out of the water, but he's got his suit jacket back on. He shakes, a towel wrapped around him, and she holds him. It's not his fault, she tells herself. It's not. He sits down, and she does, and they don't talk.

The room is pale and bare. There are six chairs arranged as if for dinner, one at the head of the table, one at the foot, two on either side; and the table in the middle is low, cheap wood, covered in coffee stains. There's a green plastic box in the center filled with tissues. The box, Deanna notices, is glued to the table. There are no magazines, no television, no water cooler: this is like no waiting room Deanna has ever been in before. The chairs are covered in a fading red woolen fabric, but the arms have started to be unpicked, the strands pulled out and played with; worried. The carpet has, around the table, been worn into a path, like a running track. The ceiling tiles are yellowed with cigarette smoke. It's been decades since you were allowed to smoke in buildings like this, and nearly

59

twenty years since Deanna last had a cigarette; but now she looks at that and she misses it, because if ever there was an occasion it is now.

'I have to see if there's news,' Laurence says. 'I've spoken with Amit, asked him to come.'

'Okay,' Deanna says. He stands up and leaves, padding into the hallway – she watches him, sheet draped over his shoulders, looking for all the world like any other patient of this place – and she takes out her phone. She texts Lane – *No news xxx* – and then opens the *ClearVista* app. *Predict anything with our groundbreaking algorithm*, it reads. *The numbers don't lie.* She logs in and selects Sean's name from the drop-down list of her dependents, and then starts to type what she's looking for. *Predict how long you can survive*, she types, and it fills out the rest for her, guessing at her request. *Without breathing*, the second most requested search beginning with that phrase. She clicks the completed sentence. The little icon spins around (*While you are waiting, did you know that ClearVista can help you predict your chances of love with a new partner to a ninety-three percent accuracy?*) and then it gives her its answer.

We predict that Sean Walker can survive for 102 seconds without breathing, it says. She turns the Internet browser off and puts the phone back into her pocket. She fingers one of the tissues from the box, and she feels how thin it is, and somehow that's what sets her off.

★   ★   ★

Deanna looks out of the window. There's only one, and it looks out onto the gray concrete rear of the buildings. The fans from the air vents, the delivery area for medical supplies, a chain-link fence. There's nobody walking past, gawking in, which is a relief. The afternoon sun, briefly, shining through the window and onto her face. She's looking out when the door to the room opens and she sees the doctor's face reflected in the glass. She turns. The doctor takes her glasses off before saying anything, and she shakes Laurence's hand, and Deanna's, and Deanna thinks how warm her hands are. She keeps thinking about that warmth all the way through the explanation of what happened: that there were two sets of injuries to deal with: because when he stopped breathing it caused an embolism; and then his lungs were flooded as well, because before he stopped he tried desperately to breathe, taking water in where it should only have been air. The doctor is amazed that Laurence managed to get him breathing at the scene. She says something about Sean being artificially alive; or how he *was*. She doesn't say the words about what exactly happened after *was*, which makes it worse for Deanna, somehow. Everything sounds as if she is at altitude and her ears have popped, fading off into a fog of words that carry no meaning.

'I'm sorry,' the doctor says. That's all they need. Laurence holds Deanna, and he cries into her shoulder, and he falls to his knees and he screams but it comes out like he's gasping for air; but Deanna cannot soothe him. She is still picturing Sean stuck under the water, looking up at her, calling his father's name, desperately clawing at the surface of it, unable to break out; knowing what is coming as he drowns.

CHAPTER 3

The next year is the worst of their lives.

The funeral happens a week to the day after his death. Sean's skin was a shade of gray when they looked at it in the hospital. The make-up artist tells them he is one of the best and Laurence wonders what scale that's on: town, or state, or country, or even the world. He asks, bitterly, if there are competitions to decide such a thing: a parade of bodies lined up to be perfumed and preened? When they finally see Sean, his skin is the abnormal pink of a child's doll. They refuse an open casket, then, because this isn't their son any more. Laurence can't stand to look at him, or even at the casket as it lies on the table. They invite anybody who wants to come to the funeral, and pretty much the whole town does. They all bring trays of pies and pasta and salads, and they leave them piled up in the kitchen, shake Laurence's hand and kiss Deanna's cheek, say how sorry they are. Everybody in the town knows them; most remember Deanna from when she was a child. And they all knew Sean, and they all want to say goodbye to him. Everybody steps up to the closed box on the table and stands over it; they tell Sean whatever it is that they have to say. Alyx doesn't come, because Deanna doesn't know if that's right. Deanna explains it to her.

'Sean's gone to heaven,' she says, almost without thinking, and that starts a conversation that she then feels pitiably unable to deal with, but she tries. She buys a Bible for the express purpose of giving Alyx the story about how it works. She argues with Laurence that grief needs an outlet and that this might be a good one for Alyx. Laurence doesn't like it – he's practical about religion, pragmatic, as badly as that plays with the South; and now he's more stubborn. Any shot at belief that he maybe once had is devastated by the loss of their son – but, Deanna argues, that's beyond the point. The point is: Alyx needs it. She was a twin, and she is now missing the person she was closest to in the whole world. She'll never know that closeness again.

Once Sean is finally put into the ground, Deanna and Laurence take the girls to his grave, to do something that's small and private and just for them. They stand around the stone – the dates make Deanna feel sick to look at, so she avoids that – and they all tell stories about Sean and why they loved him. They have decided to bring some of his toys, to put them in the soil with their hands. Alyx buries one of her own toy ponies, the one that Sean always used to steal when he was younger; Lane chooses a dinosaur that he claimed he didn't like any more, but that he had absolute trouble letting go of as he grew older. They don't say why they're doing it, but they think that it might help. As they bury them, scooting the soil on top of them, pushing them under, Deanna feels a rip in herself: so much of her beloved son now relegated to the ground. She will miss the toys, because they would have reminded her of him. She thinks about coming back at night, when the rest of them are asleep, and pulling them from the soil; but she wonders where she would stop, or if she would just keep on digging.

They sit Alyx down and ask if she would like to talk to anybody about her brother, because they've heard too many stories about what happens if children are left to bottle up their emotions, how dangerous it can be. They hire a therapist, a specialist in childhood bereavement, and Lane is allowed to do whatever she wants for a while. Three weeks after her brother's death, Lane shaves her head almost down to nothing and she doesn't bat an eyelid when Laurence shouts – screams – at her about it.

'We had a deal!' he yells, and she doesn't respond or even acknowledge it. Deanna's listening and that evening they have a conversation about his career.

'What was that about?' she asks, when he gets off the phone then, because they haven't yet spoken politics yet. She had assumed. They're in bed and he's propped up like always, tablet on his lap. The *ClearVista* survey deadline has long expired; all of that stuff was forgotten in an attempt to find relative peace in the wake of Sean's death.

'The delegates called,' he says. 'They still want me to run.'

'This year?'

'I don't know,' he says. 'I haven't thought about it. I don't know.' She knows that this works in the party's favor; that their loss will be used, Sean an inadvertent sacrifice to the voting gods.

They have *The Daily Show* on as they lie in bed and they both laugh at the same joke and immediately feel guilty, as if they've forgotten too quickly about Sean. Then Jon Stewart starts talking about Homme's laughable efforts at beginning a campaign. He mentions Laurence dropping out and then he looks to the camera, full of actual sincerity, and sends out his best wishes to the Walker family. No jokes: just an appreciation of their tragedy. When they switch the set off, Deanna tries to sleep, but she imagines that she's drowning: she can see the sky above her, but the water is between her and it, a fluid mass of tropical blue that's destined to do nothing but end.

Amit, the man who would be Laurence's Chief of Staff, comes to the house with a plan. It's a year-long breakdown of their lives: of the things that they have to do and how they might set about moving everything forward. He doesn't mention Sean either, but the boy is there, floating in the

66

air above them. Everything that Amit says is tinged with the knowledge of how this might have been before and how it will be now. He has an argument that makes Deanna feel sick to hear: that this is a chance for Laurence to do something truly good, a chance to use his awful situation to his advantage. The words aren't Amit's: they come from the delegates, Deanna knows. They're desperate to harness this. The tragedy can mark every facet of the campaign, should Laurence choose to step up again: the charities that he will vouch for; the events that he will attend; every single time that he mentions the word *family* in a speech. Nobody will be able to forget what has happened. Deanna is about to start arguing: that Laurence shouldn't be running, that the family needs him, when Lane comes home. She walks into the kitchen in front of them and doesn't say a word. A month after her brother has died and she's tattooed herself again: this time across her right shoulder blade, a single word. It isn't announced, but it's flaunted, red and angry, on her thin skin, so much bigger than her past tattoos. Her parents freak out, shouting at her, and they get close to read it. She lets them, because this will happen sooner or later. It's her brother's name, clear as anything, in a slick, italicized script, framed on a bed of flowers and leaves, a vine stretching out and away from them. It leaves them breathless. Lane leaves the house again without saying a word.

In bed that night, Deanna asks Laurence how

they can be angry with her for it. She wishes it was something else: a swear word, or the name of one of the stupid bands again. That would make it easy to have something to rally against. This, though? It's grief, manifested as words and made indelible.

Alyx seems fine, but they know that she is not; not quite. She talks to the therapist and sometime Deanna goes along and watches through the false mirror in the room that they use. Alyx talks about anything but Sean: even when pushed, it's as if there's a gap there, where she doesn't know what's wrong and why she should be talking about him. The therapist sometimes leads her into those conversations, but it's always stilted, and Alyx is always unwilling to give anything up. One day they leave her alone in the office and Alyx doesn't know that she's being watched. The therapist and Deanna talk in the little room, Alyx playing behind them, past the mirror, and she talks to him. She says his name and she holds something out, a toy pony, and then she shakes her head. She agrees with the nothingness: it's not the right pony. In the little hidden room both women know what's happening.

'This is relatively common,' the therapist says, 'especially with twins. This isn't something to worry about.' She squeezes Deanna's arm, and Deanna thinks of the hospital receptionist leading her through to the pale room where they were told what had happened. The same squeeze that tells her that everything will be all right in the end, even if it isn't right now. She's not sure. They don't tell Alyx that they know and Deanna doesn't tell Laurence about it either. Instead she stands outside the twins' room – No, she reminds herself, it's only her daughter's room now, because Sean is under all of that soil, face up, maybe even trying to get out, somehow – and she listens for what might be happening behind the closed door. She imagines a conversation, or a play and she wonders if Alyx sees her brother as he was, or if he's something else, a vague and loose version of himself. She tries to fantasize Sean into being there herself while she listens, imagining him in front of her as she attempts to re-form him. Crouched on the floor, her eyes shut, she wonders if she can hear his voice herself if she tries. It would be so easy to go in and join Alyx in her fantasy.

Laurence is asked to do an interview on one of the bigger current affairs chat shows, as a pundit and nothing more. He's still a good talker, charismatic and personable, and he's more willing to say what needs to be said, to give sound-bites, than many others. He is, the TV producers think, good value for money. He has to buy a new suit as the others don't fit him any more. It's the same color as the one that he wore when he made his announcement. He gets the size smaller around the chest and waist, because he's lost weight. He hasn't been trying to, but it's happened. His middle-age puppy fat is almost completely gone.

If he sucks in his belly when he's dressing he can see his ribs.

They talk about schools and healthcare, the topics that he's there for, to actually try and pass judgment on some of the things going on across the country. And then the host rolls that into a conversation about Sean, blindsiding him. Laurence has no choice but to go with it. They talk about how the hospital tried to save him, and how hard they worked. They talk about universal healthcare and what it needs to work properly for the people. They talk about how it felt for him to lose his son, and Laurence cries, partly from the shock of being asked and partly because he simply cannot keep it in. There's something honest about this; everybody watching can see that.

He says, 'We have to move on. We have to go out and brave the rain. There is no other choice.'

Deanna doesn't watch the interview, but writes instead, her own form of catharsis, abandoning the book that she was working on (which suddenly feels like frippery), taking only fragments – themes, emotions, some passages describing events that only now she feels she can do justice to, with all that she has been through – and she starts to *create* instead. She's never written anything that she would term as fantasy before, but this is it: a mirror of our world that is underwater. It is the story of a woman and her son. The book has started to write itself and, fingers on the keyboard, she is powerless to stop it.

Lane does see her father's interview. She is in a mall, in a bar that she shouldn't be in, and it's on the TV. She is with her friends and they point out her father and they joke – but then they remember. He cries, and she sees it, and they all fall silent. This is serious, they know. After that, she goes back to the tattoo shop. More ink on her skin: to turn what she has, as crude a beginning as anything has ever had, into something more.

The blogs talk about Laurence's mental state of mind. They discuss the chance of him making a comeback, of him declaring. Maybe he's not ready for this; maybe he has been through too much. But they're split on Homme, and the younger elements of the party, those who want to move the party forward, are willing Laurence's return. Better a man in touch with his feelings than a man who can't see past the past, the blogs say. Laurence can mourn for now: the presidential election isn't for another eighteen months. They agree that he's the best man for the job. Somehow, his son's death is a driving force; it is, in some small way, almost a validation for his policies.

Laurence is called in front of the delegates and they ask him again. He says yes. It's announced that afternoon. Deanna and he don't speak, because he didn't talk to her first. His excuses – that he has done this for the family; that he is trying to be the man he knows that he can be – fall on deaf ears. He apologizes to her, but he doesn't back out.

The delegates remind him to complete the *ClearVista* questionnaire. Even since he first agreed to it, the process has advanced. More questions, more answers, more data kicked out at the end. The process can take months to get the results that they desire: the visualizations, the computer-generated videos. The report, *ClearVista* say, will tell you what sort of man you are and what sort of president you will be; it tells the world that they can trust you. Amit agrees: if there are any concerns about Laurence's well-being, his state of mind, his ability to run the country, the *ClearVista* algorithm will solve them. Laurence asks him how he's sure it will show he's the right man. Amit tells him that that's what the software does. It looks for best-case scenarios. It finds out who you are and it predicts what you will do. The other candidates are using it and their results will be out first, so this has got to be done. Be honest, Amit tells him.

Laurence fills in the form that night. He's regretful about so much of his life and he wants to lie, to electioneer, even here, to a faceless computer, but he doesn't. He tells the truth. It's cathartic, ticking the boxes that measure his sense of his own pain. He sends the results off.

ClearVista will, the email he gets in return informs him, *be in touch.*

Laurence and Deanna try with their marriage as much as they can. They go out for dinners in the town, but everybody knows them and they say hello and stop them from having to talk to each other. It lets them dance around the idea of speaking about anything that is actually important. They both know that they need to talk about Sean more than they do; Laurence has finally noticed Alyx talking to herself, and Lane going further off the rails. They all need a break. One night, he suggests a holiday.

'We should,' he says, and that's really it decided. He books a hotel in Rome. It's the furthest they've ever been, but nobody will know them there – Laurence doesn't want anything that will remind them of their son. They force Lane to come, but she's secretly pleased to be getting away. Her friends talk about the same things over and over and she's bored by them. She wants more, now. She wants a purpose. The first night they land late, after the longest flight of their lives, and they find a small restaurant in the city and eat the dishes that they recognize on the menu: pasta and pizza, the stuff they've eaten at home, but it tastes so much better. Even just being somewhere else makes it taste better. They're tired, but it's already good for them to be out of America; and they walk the streets, and see the sights at night. They pass a fountain, famous, in all of the guidebooks, and Deanna can't help but focus on the cherubs, spitting out water into the tiered pools. She tries to not let it get to her. She doesn't sleep, because she feels guilty that they're having this fun without him. She tells herself that she has to get over it, but she doesn't know how she will. The next morning, on the rooftop terrace, Lane comes out in her bikini and they see the extent of her tattoos, running up one side of her body a creeping vine and flowers budding from it. Each flower is an item, an icon. Each one has meaning, they think. Laurence stands up when he sees her, but Deanna snaps at him and tells him to leave it.

'What will it achieve?' she asks. That's what she worries about. She wants the family to be what they can be: as normal and whole as possible. She has lost her son already and now there are the four of them. She will do anything to preserve what she has and Laurence would likely say things to Lane that could irreparably harm their relationship. She begs him to calm down. He spends the afternoon looking at the tattoos through his sunglasses, quietly seething. In one of them, there is a toy dinosaur that Laurence recognizes as the one that Lane buried. He thinks, by the end of the day, as the sun is setting around them, that the print on her skin is, in some ways, even beautiful.

At the end of the week, Deanna realizes that Alyx hasn't been talking to herself. One night as she's tucking her into bed she asks about it, asks outright if her daughter has been seeing Sean since he died.

'Sometimes,' Alyx says.

'Not this week though?'

'He can't come on holiday,' Alyx says, and that

seems to be enough for Deanna. She holds Alyx for a while on the little girl's bed and they both fall asleep, because there's something about Alyx's smell that's calming. The next day they go walking and there's a moment where it seems as if Alyx has reverted, but she's singing to herself. And when they get home, after a week that they all needed, and that they are all desperately sad to say goodbye to, Deanna watches for it, but the Sean-fantasy isn't there. Alyx cries in the kitchen when she can't find him – or, at least, that's what Deanna supposes. They don't talk about it. Alyx is sick from school for a few days and she watches cartoons and eats Pop-Tarts and lies on the sofa where Sean used to lie. She takes up the whole space.

Birthdays come and go. Alyx's is quiet, and they think about Sean, because there's no other choice. They try, though. The therapist tells Deanna that it's important that they don't ignore it, but that this is Alyx's birthday. There are ways, she explains. So they have a cake, and a party, and they try to distract themselves. They don't know how else to do this. For Lane's birthday, they ask what she would like. She asks for money to extend her tattoo. Laurence gives it to her, on the condition that she talks to them about it as it goes. She agrees.

His campaign begins in earnest. Laurence goes out on the road, around the state, drumming up votes. He speaks at conferences. He does every-thing that's required. On the calendar, his name is blocked out on almost every single day. There's a gap, a week where there's nothing booked in, and none of them can avoid it because it's the anniversary of Sean's death. A week of nothing at all, even though there are major events he'll be missing. It's a countdown, they all know, as the weeks before it are ticked off. He flies home on the last day with something written in it and the very next day they all wake up early and drive to the graveyard.

There was a time that they visited it a lot, at the start, but Deanna had to stop herself. She worried that if she kept coming she would become too used to this place: to the faded glory of the more ancient headstones, the manicured grass, the wrought iron fencing that blocked some plots off from others. As if it wasn't all the same under the soil. So now it's once a month, or less. It's been so long since they were all here at the same time. Grass has grown all over the plot and they can't see where they buried the toys that day. Deanna puts flowers down, which is ridiculous, she thinks. He didn't like flowers and here I am, having spent nearly a hundred dollars on them. But she puts them down because they make her feel better. Around them, some plots don't have flowers at all, and she reads the headstones. Some of them were young; nearly as young as Sean was. She plucks some flowers from his arrangement and leaves them on the other graves and she says a little prayer to them as well. Alyx cries and Lane holds her close. The little girl buries her face in her sister's stomach.

In the car on the way home, Laurence says how quickly the year has gone. He says, 'I can't believe it's been a year.' The girls are silent. Deanna thinks, I don't know if it's been fast or slow. Everything has slipped into an expanse. Sean might as well have died a year ago, or yesterday, or tomorrow. It can never be undone.

She sits in the back, between her daughters, and she holds them close and kisses their heads: the soft child's hair on one side, the harsh brittle bristles on the other.

CHAPTER 4

Laurence brings all four of his favored news shows up in different corners of the screen and sits at the breakfast bar and eats his bacon and drinks the revolting milkshakes that Amit insists he has every morning. A blogger made a GIF from pictures of him that had been taken over the last thirteen months, showing his decreasing weight, a morphing slideshow sold as somewhere between comedy and tragedy; and that set the other blogs to speculating what it could mean. They touched on his personal traumas, of course, but also mentioned the S word: *sick*. They asked if there was maybe something wrong with Laurence that the public hadn't been told about, and that made Amit flip out. He called in the middle of the night after reading something that speculated with actual medical terms and told them – told Deanna, in no uncertain words – that it was something they had to change. They must never, ever use the S word and they weren't to let others use it either.

'As soon as people start asking about the health of any normal candidate, their campaign is essentially screwed,' he said. 'Somebody can go from weight-loss to cancer in two or three posts and all of a sudden they're out of the running. Laurence can take that even less than any of the others. Better a fat candidate than one who looks like he's the S word, Dee.'

So she began to cook pasta for dinners. She made rich sauces, with real cream, and she started baking breads with cheese running through the dough. Amit bought them an old Paula Deen cookbook as a partial joke, along with a packet of real butter, and he told them to deep-fry everything. She sets the cooker to fry the bacon rather than griddling it, and she takes it out when it's done and puts it into a thick-cut doorstep sandwich with full-sugar ketchup. It's not helping. His belts are new, and his trousers. He has to tuck his shirts in more; in the worst cases, Deanna pins them at the back to make them taut again across his new frame. When he undresses for bed, she sees his ribs, a ladder of loose skin. He's seen a doctor, quietly, to appease her – in case there was something wrong, the S word again, uttered privately – but he's medically fine. He's just thin. He's not eating enough, was the diagnosis. That and stress, but one is an easier fix than the other.

He's been away working for a fortnight, and only came back last night. Today, he's off again. This, he's warned them, is pretty much how it'll be for the next year of their lives. So breakfast with him feels rare, suddenly, as if it's a special occasion.

His face appears on Fox, top right corner of the screen, and he selects it and maximizes it. He jacks the volume up to hear a man talking to camera as if it's his friend, casual and smooth. His name is Bull Brady, the front wave of a new type of shock-pundit for the political channels as they attempt to make something dry considerably more popular. They're met a few times. He doesn't like Laurence, is the recollection.

'So, most predictions have Walker managing to climb another three points in his key demographics today,' the host says, 'which, of course, means very little at this stage. Three is nothing: three can be lost by spending time in the wrong place at the wrong time. So how does he hold? Get out.' The host stands and does a little walk-on-the-spot move. 'Get out, talk to people. He's had too much time off, and he lives in Podunk, Nowheresville; he needs to work more if he wants back in. He's got a big old chunk of the country, catching the more, shall we say, *cosmopolitan* parts of our great nation; but he hasn't got a chance in the red states. Not even close. Now, Homme might. He can win some of them, that's the word. So Walker plays well in New York. So he plays well in Boston.' (The host does the accent of these cities. That's his shtick.) 'So he plays well with core democrats. Big deal! If he can't play well with big oil, he could lose this before it's already begun. If they want to go Democrat, they'll go with Homme. Walker's going to Texas to try and see what he can do, but

80

I'll be damned if he's walking away from there with anything but a suntan.' He puts on a cowboy hat and climbs a mechanical bull in the corner of the studio, and he moos. Laurence mutes and minimizes it as Deanna walks in.

'Don't listen to him,' she says.

'I know. But people watch him. They like him.'

'People like spectacle.'

'He says I'm not doing enough of that.'

'Which is why you're up three points.'

'That's nothing. Three points is nothing. He said it himself.'

'Okay,' she says. She puts his plate in the dishwasher. 'Go and wake the girls and say goodbye, would you? They'll miss you.'

'They barely noticed that I was back.'

'Because you were only here for one night. They miss you. I don't know what else to say.'

'Lane?'

'Even Lane.' She kisses him. It's everything, these moments: they remember Sean with every single kiss and it doesn't stop them doing it. He calls for the girls from the hallway. School has just gone back. Alyx comes out and smiles at him in the doorway of her room.

'Hey, Pumpkin,' he says. 'I can take you, if you're quick getting dressed.'

'In the car?'

'In the car.' The car is a big black cross-country thing that his party has recently leased to drive him around, less conspicuous out here than the town cars, coming complete with low-paid driver and super-strict fuel budget. Laurence knows that budget doesn't extend to taking Alyx to school, but he doesn't care. 'Lane?' he calls, 'you up?'

'Yes,' she says.

'I'm off soon,' he tells her. 'Want to say goodbye?'

'Bye,' she shouts.

'Look at the college applications,' he says. She hasn't decided about what she's going to do next year yet and they're not pushing her too hard, in case it scares her off. They mentioned college once and she countered with a desire for a year to find herself. He and Deanna both hope that she likes what she finds. He rolls his eyes at Alyx who has reappeared, clutching her clothes. She starts to pull them on in the hallway.

'No shower?' he asks.

'Later,' she says, and she runs downstairs, past him and to the kitchen. 'Dad's taking me,' she tells Deanna. 'Can I have my breakfast to go?' She says it in a voice that she's heard on a TV show. Deanna pulls bread from the grille of the toaster and the spread out of the cupboard, and she puts it down in front of Alyx with a thick, rounded knife.

'You get the honor,' she says to her daughter, and then she leaves for the hallway and finds Laurence there, at the foot of the stairs. He's in the lemon tie, and she knows exactly when he was last wearing it. Exactly what day it was. She balks and stands back.

'What's up?' he asks.

'Nothing,' she says. If he can't remember it, she reasons, there's no point in saying it. The suit still hangs in the wardrobe. He hasn't worn it since Sean died. He's blamed it on the weight loss, but she knows that's not true. She's told herself that it was because of the connotations. The breast of it still has smears from her eyes on it, the dark tear-runs of her mascara like a print of her face. Deanna didn't see the point in cleaning it. She thought, instead, that they should just burn it, but they haven't. She doesn't know how they go about it without making it seem like ceremony, so it's inside a vacuum bag at the far end of the closet, beyond the part that you can see when the doors are opened. Out of sight, out of mind. But the tie is the first part of the puzzle to reappear, and he hasn't realized what it means that he's wearing it. Somehow it isn't water-stained. Somehow it doesn't need ironing.

He doesn't comment on it. Instead, he adjusts it in the mirror.

'I'll take Alyx,' he says. 'It'll be nice to spend some time with her.'

'Sure,' Deanna says. She focuses on his neck, his hands up and fiddling with the knot, and she wishes that he would realize what he's done.

As he hands his bags to driver, he notices that the side gate to their house is open. 'Shit,' he says. The trashcan lids are up. He goes to them and peers in. 'The bags are gone. Assholes.'

'Again?' she says from the porch.

'I know,' he says. He pulls the gate shut and looks at the cut-through lock that he put on after the last time that this happened, in the weeks following Sean's death. 'Can you buy a lock next time you're at *Henderson's*, something that'll keep it shut, something they can't cut through? Trent'll know what sort of thing. A chain or something.'

'Why do they do this?' Deanna asks, coming out to look at the fractured remains of the cheap lock. It's a rhetorical question. She looks at the pieces. Somebody came during the night and they were prepared. Laurence kicks the gate hard enough that it slams shut but swings right back open again, a clang of metal as the hinges meet and bounce against each other.

'Don't get stressed about it,' Deanna tells him. 'Please.'

'I didn't sign up for this part,' he says. She kisses him, and he breathes out, an exhalation that's part calm, part relief. 'Let's go,' he says to Alyx.

In the car, Alyx clambers. She presses the window button, making it descend and then rise again, watching the world be taken away by the slick blackness of the glass. When it's shut, the glass changes tone and shade, allowing just enough light in while still letting them see outside. She coos.

'This car is awesome,' she says.

'I know,' her father tells her. He puts the seat-back TV set on, flicking through the presets he's established. Alyx turns her attention to it and the people talking.

'Are you on here today?' she asks.

'No,' he says. 'Next week.' The only time Alyx watches him on TV is when he's in a one-to-one, because he always does a shout-out to her; always tells the family that he loves them. It's a recent thing. The cynics, and there are many, think it's working his personal situation to his benefit. Sometimes he wonders if he's been that cynical himself and just not realized. 'What have you got in school today?'

'We're reading *The Lion, the Witch and the Wardrobe*,' she says.

'That's it?'

'I don't know what else.' She undoes her seat belt and he sees past her, to the traffic on the streets, the busy morning intersections, the reckless drivers. It's the route chosen by the computer's algorithm, the most likely route to get them where they're going in the most efficient way possible. Traffic is mostly (but only marginally) better thanks to their *ClearVista* branded devices. But still, you can't account for other people and human error, Laurence thinks. Some things simply cannot be predicted.

'Sit down,' he says, and he reaches over and clips her in himself. 'Be more careful, okay?' She nods and he kisses her forehead. He looks behind and out of the window, to see if anybody's following them. He doesn't know why, but it doesn't hurt to be paranoid, he tells himself. This is what they want: the press, his enemies. They want him when he's dropped his guard.

Deanna's finished her new book. She's opened the file every day for the last week and read it all morning, right the way through until she picks up Alyx from school. It takes that full stretch of time: not because it's especially long, but because she focuses on it, gets as deep as she can. She's been editing it for weeks now, going over and over the words, searching for the truth in what she's written. It's important to find it because that informs the story, the characters. Every word is careful; every word has meaning. It's arduous; but, she reminds herself, it probably should be.

It's eleven when she finally hears Lane waking up. Doors slam – bedroom, bathroom, bedroom again – and then comes the sound of her boots on the stairs. Deanna shuts her laptop, so that her daughter doesn't see what she's been working on – as if she would care, Deanna thinks – but then Lane is gone without even coming into the kitchen. Another slam, this time from the front door. There's no shout of goodbye.

Deanna thinks about going after her, but it would be pointless. She would yell at her and Lane would ignore her; or she would chase her and Lane would bite her hand off. They're losing her, Deanna thinks. She's old enough to leave home but she has no job or indication of a desire to do anything with her life, and that's all that keeps Deanna hopeful: that Lane's own lack of ambition, of drive, will keep her here for a while. While she's at home, they can keep an eye on her; and it means that the house doesn't become even emptier. Because Lane makes noise. Alyx is quiet, appearing in doorways and padding around in her bare feet, but Lane is noisy, and she's difficult, and she fills the house with her presence.

Deanna returns to the manuscript and her emails. As well as the new book she has got an email in draft. It's been half written for the last few weeks, addressed to her agent. He stopped calling after Sean died, most likely because it suddenly became something that he would have to talk about but clearly wanted to avoid; and, Deanna reckons, he wrote her off. There was no chance of her finishing a book while she was still in mourning. And she felt the same, until she realized that the feeling of mourning was never going to go away. Then it became freeing, and that's when the words came. And it might be that he's not the best person to represent her now. Her previous books were flowing and grounded and real, but this new one is so sparse and fantastical he might be the wrong person to try and sell it for her. The email says all of this, but then it introduces the book to him anyway. *Into the Silent Water*, she's called it.

She describes the setting, the characters: a woman has forgotten who she is, but she wakes in a land that's flooded, a thick and grotesque scar marked across her forehead. Her mark means that she did not die accidentally: it means that she killed herself. In her hand there is a picture of a child, and all that she knows is that she is there to find him. But he is lost, and she wonders, as she goes, how intentional this all was; that maybe her own death was the first part of a quest that she cannot possibly hope to complete.

As she reads the synopsis, the novel, she thinks how thinly veiled it is, but that it doesn't matter to her. Not with this book. She wants to publish it under a pseudonym, if it's good enough to even be published in the first place. She can't tell; she's never been able to tell. She's sure that nobody will want to hide who she is, especially if Laurence gets further in the race. After that, everybody will want their blood; she just hopes that it's harder to take it if you don't know it's there, waiting to be tapped.

As they wait at the airport's check-in desk, Amit talks to Laurence about how this will be once he's secured the nomination.

'Then,' he says, 'they'll wheel out the plane to ferry you around. No waiting. Think about that. And then, you know, a couple of years down the road, Air Force One.'

'You're cursing it,' Laurence says.

'It's not a curse,' Amit says. 'You've seen the polls. Can't curse that.'

'I've seen three percentage points.'

'Exactly. Foundations.' In front of them an elderly couple bicker about the flight. They throw statistics at each other like curveballs. The airline hasn't had an accident in a while, the woman says; that means, statistically, they are now more likely to. She talks about safety protocols and how likely they are to have slipped, reading probability numbers from the *ClearVista* app on her phone. The man counters that, behind the scenes, the airline is likely to have picked their game up specifically because of the existence of *ClearVista*. They'll want to reassure their customers that they can be trusted. The woman asks why the likelihood of an accident – a percentage that's higher than the airline's nearest rivals – isn't higher, then. The man says that they haven't taken that into account yet. It hasn't propagated. Laurence listens while trying not to, and watches Amit tweeting about their day, about where they'll be and what they'll be doing.

The delegates picked him, not caring about his lack of experience. Statistics and predictions, that was the way that the business of politics was always going to be heading and Amit came from that background, having worked for *ClearVista* in their early days. He helped to write their algorithm, the algorithm that has now intruded on so much of the world in one way or another. Too much math, he said, when Laurence asked why he wanted out of such a big company. They were something close to friends now, sure, but business always comes first. Laurence can't imagine this relationship going further if he loses the race. Laurence knows how this works for Amit if they fail. He will bounce back, and he'll be here again in four years with another potential candidate. His numbers, based on his time with Laurence, will be better; his stock maybe even higher. Especially if he jumps ship before he's pushed. If he sees the way it's going, watches the tide.

The couple checks in, finally, and moves on, and then Laurence and Amit are second in the queue. The man in front of them holds his ticket up to the scanner and hands his ID to the girl behind the desk. He has no luggage, not even a carry-on, just a blue jacket, carried in his hand. It's expensive-looking but bundled up. He pockets his ID, and he looks at Laurence as he steps past them. He nods, and smiles. Amit notices.

'He knew who you were, see?'

'What?' Laurence is caught for a second, somewhere else.

'He recognized you. Foundations, then a ground swell of being recognized. That's as good as support, because he'll remember that. He sees your face on a ballot, he'll remember who he wants to vote for. You'll see.' Amit hands the assistant their IDs, and both men hold their phones out to scan their tickets. She asks them the usual questions and Amit answers for them. Laurence glances behind them.

'I don't like being recognized,' he says. 'They raided the trash this morning.'

'Who did?'

'Somebody in the night,' Laurence says. 'Didn't see who they were.'

'That's what some people will do. They're desperate for news.'

'News isn't in my fucking garbage cans, Amit.'

'Yeah it is. Larry, news is and always will be whatever somebody can get their hands on that somebody else will pay to read.' He hands Laurence back his ID card. 'Flight's twenty minutes late. Let's get a coffee.'

They walk through the terminal to a coffee shop and Laurence finds seats at a table while Amit goes to the counter. This is how it is, now, until there's a result one way or another: other people trying to bear the brunt of the stress for him, deferring whatever they're not sure he can take and treating him as if he's important. He doesn't push back. Amit's phone beeps as he comes back to the table. He grins.

'The prediction's done.'

'What?'

'The little tick boxes, Larry. Remember the tick boxes?' Laurence hates when he calls him that. He's the only person who does, an affectionate little tic. Larry and Dee, frivolous and light . . . 'The package is being put together, should be with us soon as anything.'

'This is ridiculous.'

'It is. But you've seen Homme's. You know that it's effective.'

Homme had his own prediction released to the public a couple of months ago, the product of spin and facts, but also deep-rooted in his public persona. Amit thought that it was managed – it had to be – but to the public it seemed to be honest. It was in some way a truth. The *ClearVista* algorithm took his information – his entire life, realistically, when you break it down – and fed out a picture of a candidate who wouldn't actually be a bad leader. Statistically, Homme was weak on so many issues, running with very few actual policies he seemed to care about but he was balanced, accessible, open to all. He would take red families in some places, that was his trick. Crossing party lines. Along with the hypothetical suppositions of what his stance would be on certain hot topics (which contradicted so much of the usual left stances, pandering to moneymen and the religious right), *ClearVista* created a short video. This was their most important gimmick: a new addition to the premium package, only possible with the most detailed survey and at a cost of hundreds of thousands of dollars; but, they promised, the trade-off was worth it. The video was useable, open source, free to be circulated however the recipient desired. Homme's was perfect for him. It was so on-message as to be almost laughable. There he was in a helmet and a flak jacket, surrounded by swirls of dust, running to a helicopter, waving at troops; shaking their hands as he passed them, mixed gender and color (and even, in their haircuts and rainbow pin-badges, crudely implied sexuality). It was very presidential, the press agreed. They joked, the first time that they saw the tech, about previous presidents, and what it would have shown of them: Marilyn Monroe; 'I am not a crook'; interns and cigars. A few days after the video was released – along with the full results of the tests, and the answers he gave to get the results, in the spirit of full disclosure and honesty – his numbers increased, stripping out votes from the other candidates. The video worked, even if it was only smoke and mirrors. 'Pointless to be nervous,' Amit says. 'It's done. Results come through later today, they've said.' They leave the Starbucks and head for the gate, scanning their ID cards as they pass through to the departure lounge.

They join the queue to board, and Laurence notices that the man who had been in front of them at the check-in desk is in front of them again now. He's wearing his blue jacket this time: the back is wrinkled from where he was gripping it. He turns and smiles.

'You're Laurence Walker, right?' the man asks. He holds out his hand, and Laurence looks at it: something wrong about this. It's the second time he's been here. He's stopped believing in coincidence. Amit notices and steps in, shaking it first.

'You're a supporter?' Amit is exuberant, as he always is.

'Yeah, I thought it was you. I'm a big fan,' the man says. 'We've been needing somebody like you

93

for a while now. We've been playing safe, I think. We need a shake-up, that's what I'm saying.'

'Yes,' Laurence says. 'I agree.' The man talks about the party and the future and Laurence nods his way through the conversation, relieved for some reason. Relieved, and yet still nervous.

The flight attendants run through the drills and show the exits; and they show the little movie about what to do in an emergency; and then the plane waits while the captain runs the airline's custom algorithm, to take into account the names of all the passengers, to generate a final figure that's meant to dictate their safety levels; and Amit fights the elbows of the man next to him, who reeks of cheap cologne and grips the seat's arms as they shuttle down the runway. He leans over, looking across the aisle at Laurence and the window, and he watches the ground seemingly get faster and faster, and then it tilts away from the plane as they head upwards, pulling away from the ground. His ears pop and he shuts his eyes and opens his jaw over and over in an approximation of a yawn. He's one of the first to his feet when the seatbelt sign goes dark, grabbing his laptop from the overhead locker.

'You want?' he asks Laurence. Laurence shakes his head and jacks his seat back a few degrees.

'I'll get some rest,' he says. 'Wake me when we land.' Amit sits down and logs into the Wi-Fi. He loads the calendar app and looks at the breakdown of the next few days, structured and tweaked to the minute in order to allow the maximum time with each of the potential investors, and at each photo opportunity. The little colored bars are packed tight, and he rearranges the ones that only involve the two of them – breakfasts, dinners – so that it maybe doesn't look too bad to Laurence's eyes. Artificial breathing room, Amit thinks: one of his finest tweaks to the system. And each of the appointments has information attached that both men have to memorize. They have to know who donated what previously, and why; what the thing was that swayed their wallets. They have to know how deep they can make them dig. One of Amit's junior staffers has prepared a full breakdown on every man for them, telling them who to discuss God (capital G) and religion with, and who is likely to want to talk about artillery instead of textbooks. There are lists of the names of their wives, husbands and children. One of them has lost a child, just as Laurence has; this is common ground. All of them will know everything about him; their own research just levels the playing field. Lies are pointless now, because information doesn't die like it used to. It all sits there on some server, waiting for somebody to discover it and mine it and crosscheck it and use it. Used to be in politics that you could tell a different story to two different moneymen and they'd both buy it. Now, Amit's rule is that you should stick to the truth, or what-ever version of it is most palatable. You only work with what you've got. Laurence's life is available to the world already. Everybody can read the words from the eulogy he delivered at Sean's funeral; that's nothing but material now.

His email pings. It's *ClearVista*. The whole thing is automated: no people sitting back and watching this, making it work. That was the tech that they were instigating when he finally left working for them. For whatever reason, that stuff always used to creep him out. The email is labeled *Your Laurence Walker Results*: there's something disquietingly possessive about it. Laurence opens the email.

Thank you for your contract with ClearVista, the world's foremost predictions and statistics company, it reads. *Your package [LW008] has been completed and the contract fulfilled. Please find the initial results attached. Further emails with package enhancements will follow. Thank you for using ClearVista.*

The numbers don't lie.

Attached to the email is a glossily produced PDF file, little more than a glorified spreadsheet holding a series of almost incomprehensible posits and answers. There are questions asked at the top, about Laurence's virtues and skills, things that are ambiguous but useful.

Is LAURENCE WALKER a good man: 96% chance of occurrence.

Does LAURENCE WALKER care about his country? 93% chance of occurrence.

Will LAURENCE WALKER remain faithful in his marriage? 93% chance of occurrence.

Is LAURENCE WALKER a good father? 82% chance of occurrence.

The list goes on and on. Amit scrolls down quickly, scanning the results for anything anomalous. It's all good; all stronger than Homme's. The percentages break Laurence down to predicted emotional responses – and the voting public is more likely to believe that than the words of a man standing on a stage. This will all help back up what they already know about him.

Can LAURENCE WALKER overcome grief? 07% chance of occurrence.

Will LAURENCE WALKER ever commit drug abuse? 28% chance of occurrence.

Will LAURENCE WALKER ever commit sexual abuse? 01% chance of occurrence.

They are all results that work. The *Grief* one might hurt them, but Amit has an answer for that: nobody ever recovers from the death of a child. It would be worse if it said that he would, he spins, because that would suggest a lack of heart, of basic human empathy. He hears the words from speeches in his head, taking the data and turning it into a portrait of a man who will do his best to honor the memory of his dead son, but who is driven and dedicated to running his country first and foremost. And, if they have to play dirty, there's the *sexual abuse* question. Homme had a 3.4% percent chance of committing sexual abuse, which his people spun as a number so small as to be insignificant. Laurence scored better. Amit doesn't ever want to have to use that – not in the way that some of the dirty political games in the past might have done – but he knows that some of the blogs will run with it themselves. That's the thing: it paints Homme in a worse light just by virtue of its existence. Nothing wrong with that.

Is LAURENCE WALKER likely to suffer from an emotional or mental breakdown? 51% chance of occurrence.

That's harder, Amit thinks. That's a tough one. It's on the wrong side of the fence, irritatingly; this will mean countermeasures, therapists and counselors on call to make sure that nothing goes wrong. It's fixable, that's the thing; an arbitrary number based on his situation. Who wouldn't suffer that risk? So they'll address that. A strong Vice President will be the key. Somebody that the country feels comfortable with if they were forced to step up, even though nobody will ever say that. Not Homme, no matter what happens.

He scrolls through the rest of the document, to the section headed *POLITICS*, and he runs through the likely outcomes of Laurence's voting habits. Who he will be likely to want as his political advisors, who he will want in key governmental roles, where he will side on certain issues. And, at this quick glance, the report syncs with the discussions that they've already had. Hundreds of answers booted out from thousands of questions, using Laurence's past voting habits, the past results of votes, all to predict a path forwards.

The report says that Laurence is liable to be fair to the oil companies, which is good – and slightly unexpected; Amit copies the line and pastes it into a new document, to use over the next few meetings. This is all ammunition. He keeps going, scrolling through page after page of the document, reading everything, trying to take it all in, and then he sees the final two questions, in their own boxed-out section at the very end of the file, printed larger, the answers to the very reasons that they got the survey done in the first place.

He doesn't parse them the first time. He reads them, over and over.

If LAURENCE WALKER runs for the role of DEMOCRATIC PARTY NOMINEE: 00% chance of success.

If LAURENCE WALKER runs for the role of PRESIDENT OF UNITED STATES: 00% chance of success.

'What the *fuck*?' Amit says. The man next to him tuts at the language, and Amit mutters an apology. He shuts the file and reopens it, but the results are the same. He pulls his phone from his pocket and turns it on.

'Hey,' the man next to him says, 'you can't do that!'

'It's fine,' Amit says.

'We're on a plane, asshole.'

Amit looks around and sees one of the cabin crew staring at them down the aisle, looking at what's going on. He can't have his phone confiscated, so he switches it off.

'Happy now?' he asks. The man rolls his eyes, smug at his win. Amit goes back to the laptop and opens the email. He hits reply and writes to them, as quickly as he can.

There's a problem with the results issued. See final two questions. Please address IMMEDIATELY, or we will be forced to take legal action. He hits the screen's keyboard so hard it stings the tips of his fingers.

'What's wrong?' Laurence asks. Amit looks across at his boss who is sleepy-eyed, rubbing his face.

'Nothing,' Amit says. He thinks about telling him – no lies, no secrets, that's how this works – but he knows that this will be corrected. When it is, this will be something to laugh about. He doesn't know, right now, how Laurence will react to it. 'Somebody is wrong on the Internet,' Amit says. He can hear the shakiness in his own voice, the lie coming through. Laurence smiles.

'There's always somebody wrong on the Internet,' he says. 'I'm going to try and get another half hour of shut-eye.'

'Do it.' Amit shuts the laptop. 'Me too.' Both men shut their eyes, but Amit clutches his phone in his hands. As soon as they land, as soon as they can get to the hotel, he'll be calling *ClearVista*; and he'll be getting angry, speaking to somebody directly, sorting this out.

He shuts his eyes and he sees the final results,

the numbers flashing behind his eyelids as if they're afterimages of the sun.

Deanna drives down to the stretch of shops that calls itself the town center. She could walk this easily – their house is at the end of a long stretch that calls itself Main Street, but it has no actual competition for that title, with almost all of the town's houses either sitting on it or just off it in neat little clusters – but she has a list of what needs doing, and one of the things involves getting the car checked out at the garage. And there's the shopping from *Henderson's*, for food and the new lock and simply walking around to clear her head. She likes living in this place, talking to the people, being a part of life here. They know Deanna, have done since she was a little girl. That sense of belonging is nice; the community feeling like a part of their lives. As they recovered – as they still recover – from Sean's death, the support of the town has been incredible. They have all wanted Laurence to pick himself up and, in his parlance, brave the rain. They're all going to vote for him, they say, whether they're Republican or Democrat, saying that they'll plant placards in their lawns and spread the word as much as they can. It's that sort of town.

The garage is at the far end of the street, past everything else. Deanna pulls in, driving onto the forecourt, and Ann runs out. She's a short woman, older than she looks, hair pulled back into a greasy net, and she perpetually leans, Deanna's noticed. On everything, resting her hands. She leans on the hood of the Walkers' SUV as Deanna gets out.

'Deanna,' she says, 'good to see you.' She adds a J to her pronunciation of the name that makes Deanna think of *I Dream Of Jeannie*; a classic sitcom vision of small-town America. 'She playing up?'

'Not quite,' Deanna says. 'There was a clunking coming from under the hood a few weeks back. Thought we should probably get it checked out.'

'I'd say you should for sure. You want me to do it right now?'

'Would you mind?' Deanna asks. 'I can go do the shopping then come back?' Everything is phrased as a question, not wanting to assume or put anybody out. Ann smiles and nods, and takes the keys from Deanna.

'Give me a half hour,' she says. Deanna thanks her and walks down the road towards *Henderson's*: past the diner, past the church, past the gun store (which does the most trade here of anything, given how close they are to one of the North-East's major hunting spots), past the liquor store. The owners and customers all stop and nod at her as she passes, all smiling. She goes into *Henderson's* and Trent and Martha, co-owners, married for fifty years, as they'll tell anybody whether they ask or not, and the closest thing to figureheads that the town has, come out and kiss her in greeting and tell her how happy they are to see her. They mean it, as well.

'Where's that husband of yours at today?' Trent asks.

'Texas,' Deanna says.

'Oil money?'

'Oil money.'

'That's politics now,' Martha says.

'That's *always* been politics,' Trent counters.

'As long as you're all safe and sound, that's all that matters,' Martha replies. She goes to the coffee machine in the corner – they had it installed a few years ago, to offer takeout when they started stocking varieties of different coffee beans as well – and makes Deanna a drink that she didn't even ask for. It's the way that they do things here; the way that they always have. They know what you want sometimes before you do, even.

'Not long now until he'll know, I suppose?'

'No,' Deanna says. 'Not long. A couple more months.'

'So maybe this'll all calm down after that.'

'Maybe. Probably not, the way that Laurence tells it.'

'Oh my word, we'll be so sad to see you leave,' Martha says. 'I mean, of course you'll come back for your vacations.'

Deanna thinks about the lake house, how that was the intention of owning it all along. Now, she doesn't know if she can even go there. It feels wrong to her; as if it's forever tainted. It will always be associated with Sean, with what happened. No getting past that, and the Hendersons realize that as well, if not too late. Trent and Martha shoot each other looks, not knowing whether to address the faux pas or not. It hangs in the air until Deanna breaks the tension. 'That's a long way away,' Deanna says, meaning in terms of votes and time both.

'I reckon this is a foregone conclusion,' Trent says. 'You can't call these things, but as much as you can, I'd say that it's a done deal.' He nods at the television in the corner, behind the counter. There's Laurence and the other potential nominees, the newscaster talking about their current vote split, the predicted results, and that 3% head start. 'Makes it easier when the television's saying he's the man, I reckon.'

'Maybe,' Deanna says.

'You got a list?' Martha asks. Deanna holds it up and Martha snatches it and forces it into Trent's hand. 'He'll do it. Nothing better to do. You can stay here and keep me company.'

'Oh, no,' Deanna says, but she knows how this goes. It's always the same.

Trent looks at the list. 'What do you need the chain for?' he asks.

'We had another intruder. They broke the old lock.'

'Again? Somebody's pushing their luck, you ask me. You know who it was?'

'Laurence thinks it's the press.'

Trent nods. 'I'll hate to see you leave Staunton, Deanna, you know that; but it'll be better for you. A house with a bit more security, keep you safe.'

'Maybe,' Deanna says. He nods and looks at the list, picks up a basket and goes off around the shop. There's a pain in his movements that Deanna hasn't noticed before, a slight favoring of one leg over the other.

'I feel terrible making him do this for me,' Deanna says to Martha.

'Oh, don't, Martha replies. 'He needs to work it or it'll fall off.' She smiles. They watch him go down the aisles, and they talk about the kids, and they talk about the town, the same conversations that they always have, just moved on in time, like updates to the same old information. When every item has been collected, Trent scans them at the till. The calorie counts and nutrition values tick up on the screen, *ClearVista* predicting the weight gain and exercise needed to counter the richer, fattier foods; and then he brings up the total before adjusting it. They always do a discount for Deanna.

By the time she gets back to the car it's been turned around, now facing the road. Ann comes out of the dark of the garage, holding something in her hand. It's shiny and golden, a stub of a thing. Deanna thinks that it could be a bullet for a second but then she gets closer and it's a screw. No: a bolt.

'Found this inside her,' Ann says. 'Must've come loose, but I'm damned if I can find from where.'

'From the engine?'

'It's not a car part, best I can tell. Maybe it got

kicked up there one day from the road. Happens, you'd be surprised.'

'Okay,' Deanna says. 'How much do I owe you?'

'I changed your oil, so just for that. Give me ten and we're even.' She leans again on the hood.

'You sure?'

'Ayuh.'

Deanna pulls a twenty out of her purse and hands it over.

'Consider the rest a tip.'

'Ha! Okay. We're giving tips, let me give one to you as well. You need to sell this soon, I reckon.' She puts her hand on the roof of the car. 'It's a few years old now, and you're losing money on it. All the new models, the tech's much better. That stuff ages a car more'n you'd imagine. You'll still get a good price for this right now. I ran it for you, if you want to have a look: software says this has got years left in it yet, but that the book value's gonna plummet.'

'I think we're okay,' Deanna says.

'Couple more years, it won't be worth a half of what it's worth now. Those algorithms aren't exactly kind to guzzlers like this.' She pronounces the word as if it's three: *aisle-go-rhythms*. 'They throw up much shorter lifecycles for them then you'll actually get.'

'I'll talk to Laurence about it,' Deanna says.

'Especially before you get to DC. Last thing you need is a guzzler. You do a trade-in today, I'll give you a heck of a deal. More'n it's likely worth, because I can sell this thing right on. Won't even knock any off for the nicks and dents you got in this thing. We take care of our own, you know.'

'Thanks, Ann,' Deanna says, 'but another day.' She gets in and starts the engine and backs out onto the road. Ann waves at her. She's not looking in her mirrors, and there's a thud; a crack. The car spins, the outside is a blur of lines and blocks of color, and then there's another crack, louder this time, and she looks through the window and she screams, because there's no other possible reaction. She sees a flash of black: another car, the front reared up into hers. This other car hit her, spinning the SUV, and then the front of hers hit it again. And now there's steam and smoke coming from the hood, filling her vision.

'The hell are you doing?' a voice yells from the street. There's a slam of a door and then hers opens. It's a man, his features so generic to be almost recognizable, but not quite. Well dressed, well kept. 'Get out. Jesus, get out of the car.'

'Oh God,' Deanna says. She unbuckles the safety belt and climbs down, into the street. She looks at the damage: both cars steaming from their hoods, both dented at the front, and hers at the back as well.

'Stupid bitch,' the man says, and then he finally looks at her face and his whole expression changes. He breaks eye contact almost as soon as he makes it, turns and walks to the rear doors of his car. Deanna watches him open them, grabbing papers from a bag; the car is a rental. There's equipment lying across the back seat: an expensive camera; a collection of lenses; one of those hand-held HD cameras; a distance microphone; sheets and sheets of paper. 'Give me your number. I'll let the insurance people fix this. Nobody's fault.' Again, he doesn't look at her. He writes his details down on a piece of paper as Ann runs over to Deanna.

'You all right?' she asks.

'Yes,' Deanna says. 'Shaken.'

'Well, of course you are.' She scowls at the man, even though there's no way of her knowing who is to blame here, not really, and he hands the paper to Deanna, again without looking at her. He looks at Ann, though.

'You reckon you can see if you can get me up and running? I have somewhere I have to be.'

'I'll do a diagnostic. Charge you for it, mind you.' He nods, and Ann retreats to her garage.

'I'm sorry,' Deanna says.

'Happens,' he replies. He doesn't look. He tries his best to hide his face from her. He's a journalist, she thinks. He's here to spy on her; or on Laurence. She finishes writing her own insurance details down and she holds the paper out; but not quite far enough. She wants him to take it. He glances at her.

'You live around here?' she asks.

'No.' He steps forward to take the information. She pulls it close to herself, out of his reach, and he looks at her, surprised. Looks right into her eyes.

'You're here to watch my family, is that right?'
He doesn't answer.

'You're disgusting,' she says, 'a parasite.'

He snatches the paper from her hand, and he goes back to his car. Deanna waits while Ann uses the diagnostic tool on the engine. She declares it safe, merely overheated. He gets into the driver's seat as soon as he can and starts the engine, and it chokes but then kicks in, and he pulls away, stopping only briefly as he makes his way back onto the road to wind down his window. He looks at Deanna.

'Every parasite needs a host,' he says. He drives off, and Ann comes and puts her hand on Deanna's arm to soothe her, like maybe she needs the calming down, the influence of somebody who isn't upset by this.

'You all right?' Ann asks.

'No,' Deanna says.

'Sure you don't want to talk about that trade-in now?' Ann leads Deanna inside, sits her down and fetches her a glass of water.

The light comes on for the passengers to fasten their seatbelts, waking Laurence up. He looks over at Amit.

'I feel like hell,' he says. Amit tries his best to smile, to hide whatever he's thinking from his boss. 'Sleeping on a plane always does this to me. Remind me to not do this.'

'Lots more flights in our future,' Amit says,

'you're going to need to get better at it.' The words feel rote in Amit's mouth; the sort of thing he *would* say, rather than actually carrying any meaning.

'You all right?'

'Same as you,' Amit lies. 'Weird flight.' The man next to him snorts, listening in to their conversation. That's a voter lost, Amit thinks; and that almost makes him laugh.

They stay silent for the descent, watching out of the windows at the ground coming towards them; at the desert, stretching off, the yellows and oranges and scatterings of green, as it all gives way to the concrete, to the hotels and office blocks and residential streets. They land, a bumpy landing, and at the back of the plane somebody gently screams and the rest of the passengers laugh, united in relief that *they* didn't, and then pull into the gate. The seatbelt sign goes off again and Laurence stands up.

'Okay,' he says, 'let's do this.' He switches on his phone. 'What's the first appointment?' His phone beeps, and he presses the screen. 'Email from *ClearVista*,' he says. 'Did you see this?'

'You shouldn't read that,' Amit says.

'What do you mean?' Laurence asks, but Amit doesn't reply. He stays seated and watches Laurence swipe through the document, squinting at the screen; and then, as the man next to Amit coughs and nudges him to stand so that they can leave the plane, Laurence's face falls. Amit knows the page that he's reading, but he doesn't know what to say to make it any better. 'What is this?' Laurence asks. He raises his voice, panic in his eyes. 'What does this mean, Amit?'

'Keep your voice down,' Amit says. 'Seriously, not here. It's a mistake. Look at the other results.'

'I'm looking at them!' Amit looks at Laurence's hand as it fumbles for the back of the seat in front of him, to steady himself.

'I'll call them and straighten this out. This is their mistake.'

'It's not a mistake. It's because of Sean,' Laurence says. His voice drops in volume, the words coming from between gritted teeth. 'This is because of Sean. They think that I can't handle the grief.'

'They?'

'They asked that question. Look, sixth page. About if I can handle grief.'

Amit reaches across the aisle. 'Laurence, listen. This is okay. This is nothing but a screw up. It's software.'

'They're fucking monsters,' Laurence says. 'What can I *do*? I lost my son. I lost him, and that's not my fucking fault.' There's panic in Laurence's eyes as they dart around. Amit leans across the aisle and grabs his shoulders, to calm him, even as the people behind them queue to leave the plane and he notices the man from when they were boarding, with the blue jacket. Five or six rows back, waiting to leave with everybody else. Amit watches as the man pulls his phone out and points the camera

111

at them, quickly taking a picture of this. Amit scans the rest of their section; he sees other people holding their own cameras out, above their heads, above the line of the headrests.

'You have to calm down,' Amit says. 'You calm down, and we get off the plane, and we sort this out. We can't do anything here and people are watching. We don't need this, Laurence. Okay?'

There's sudden clarity in Laurence's eyes; the politician is back.

'Okay,' he agrees.

Amit pulls their bags from the overhead lockers, passes Laurence his and ushers him to the aisle. They shuffle forward to the exit in silence and Amit prays that nobody else on flight 334 from Philadelphia International to Dallas/Fort Worth knows who Laurence is and that if they do they didn't see the ex-senator's minor break in composure.

Amit doesn't talk to Laurence all the way through baggage control. Instead, he leaves him standing by the carousel, staring at the black, slatted rubber that the plane's suitcases are being fed through; and he goes to find the man in the blue jacket. There's a photograph – or, worse, a video – of Laurence's panic, and Amit wants to control it before it becomes something.

He spots the man in the distance, no luggage, headed for the exit. Amit runs after him. He doesn't shout as he chases him – you don't put the sirens on a cruiser when you're pursuing a fugitive, he thinks – but when he catches up with him he grabs at the arm of his crumpled suit jacket, stopping him in his tracks.

'What were you doing?' he asks.

'Do I know you?' the man asks. His smile is over-exaggerated, a simpering grin of false ignorance.

'You were filming my boss, on the plane.'

'No,' the man says. He tries to leave, pulling away from Amit's grip. Amit tightens it.

'You were. You met him before we got on the plane. Don't play dumb with me.' Amit suspects that he probably works for one of the big gossipy websites, worst case; or, best case, he's just a random chancing his luck, thinking that he might have something worth selling. The footage won't show much more than Laurence being upset about his son. And who wants to be the asshole that mocks a man for that? Amit can spin this; he just doesn't want to have to, given the choice.

'Of course,' the man says. 'But I don't know what I've done wrong. Can I leave?' the man asks, looking down at Amit's hand, still clinging to his sleeve. Amit lets go. 'Thanks. Hey, good luck with your campaign, okay?'

'Prick,' Amit says, unable to tell if the man was being sincere or not, but assuming the worst. He watches him rush off, through the doors and past the cab stand – there'll be somebody waiting for him, Amit knows; there's always somebody waiting for people like that – and then turns and walks back to Laurence who is staring at the carousel, barely there. Amit can see his bag going round, completely missed. He grabs it, and Laurence's. 'Come on,' he tells his boss and leads him through the exit.

Outside, pulled up, is a town car, and Amit loads the trunk while Laurence gets inside. Amit climbs in after him and tells the driver that they're ready, and then he puts up the window between the front and back seats.

'You have to get yourself together,' he says, finally. 'This is a mistake. Accept that, and don't screw this.'

'What if it's already screwed?'

'I'll call and work out what's happened. They got it wrong, we can threaten all manner of shit. We don't live in a world where Homme gets a 60% possibility result and you get fuck all.' He checks his phone to see that he's got their contact details. 'But start to melt down, and we *are* screwed. That asshole from the queue with the jacket? All we need is somebody to see it like him. He maybe got a photo, so he's going to be pimping that the rest of today.' Outside, the landscape rushes: out of the gray buildup of the airport, and into the expanse, fields of rocks and golden dust that stretch off for as far as they can see. 'I have to do damage control. Maybe we say that you're ill – a migraine, that always works – that you're overworked. It's been a busy few weeks.'

'They'll know it's a lie.'

'It's all about how we sell it. We cancel today, maybe tomorrow, we book the meetings for another time.'

'We say I'm sick,' Laurence says.

'Don't *ever* use that word.' He opens his laptop and minimizes the report. Laurence sees a glimmer of the boxed-out section. Amit opens a document and writes URGENT at the top. 'I'll call *ClearVista* when we're at the hotel, sort this out. This means nothing, Laurence.'

Laurence watches Texas race by as Amit types. He thinks how flat it is; how the texture, the weight of the place, is all in the distance.

The hotel could be anywhere, which is the kind that Amit favors. Less confusion when moving from state to state: nothing distinct, nothing disorientating. If you always got to the same chain of hotels, the design and décor has real consistency, even down to the art on the walls of the bedrooms and the menu that they serve to the rooms. Then there are the reward schemes, allowing for complementary nights to build up. Amit fully intends to save them over the duration of his work for Laurence and then take an all-expenses holiday that won't cost him a dime. Between this and the air miles he'll be able to go anywhere in the world. Another reward scheme bonus: you rarely get put in one of the worst rooms, near an elevator or an ice machine or a laundry room. Chains like – and need – repeat business. The room that they've taken has two double beds, a shared bathroom, a large old-style plasma TV set hidden inside a wooden cupboard, a mini bar that looks not unlike a safe, a wall-mounted table with a stool in front of it. On the wall above the bed is a piece of abstract art that Amit's seen before, over and over. The hotel could be anywhere.

'Lie down and rest,' Amit says to Laurence, putting the bags at the foot of the bed. 'I'm going to cancel your meetings and then I'm calling about the report. Okay?'

'Fine,' Laurence says. He lies back on one of the mattresses, feeling it hard underneath him. He thinks that he should shower, but he doesn't. He sleeps instead, Amit's voice a thin murmur in the room with him, no louder than the stark, boxy air-conditioning unit that rattles against the wall beneath the window.

Amit waits on the phone for an answer. He knows how this goes: a certain number of rings, programmed to be just enough to make you feel that *ClearVista* is busy, but still eager for your custom. Then there is a voice, almost robotic in its hypnotic, soothing qualities. Behind it there is hold music, an ambient storm of guitars and synthesized drums.

'*ClearVista* thanks you for waiting,' the voice says.

Amit paces the room, looking at Laurence on the bed. His body is so lost in the clothes he's wearing and his chest and brow are sweaty; they'll need to put his suit in to be dry cleaned. Phone pressed to his ear, he goes into the wardrobe for the laundry bag and then looks on the desk for the form to fill in. He'll prepare it for Laurence, so that it can be done as soon as he wakes up.

There's a click on the line. '*ClearVista*,' the voice says, 'how can I help?' It's the same voice as the one that was asking him to hold: cold and slight and smooth. All of these systems are automated, designed to sound as real as possible. You know that they aren't when you call, but still. Amit was there when they were choosing how the system should work: a software robot that acts human, but not too much so. It had to be a representation of reality that never reached for the genuinely real. Testers liked to know that they were still speaking to robots, because it made them feel better about themselves, somehow. As soon as the voices crossed the uncanny valley, the testers got nervous. So *ClearVista* front-loaded them with intentional glitches. A glitch was a reminder of the caller's own humanity.

'Hi,' Amit says. 'I have an account number?'

'Thank you,' the voice says. Amit reels it off. 'I'm inputting that for you,' she replies.

'Do you have a password?' the voice asks.

'Oh-two-three-one-oh-oh-yankee-hotel-foxtrot,' Amit says.

'That's excellent,' she says, 'how can we help?' The pitch shifts on the last word, one of the intentional screw-ups.

'You sent some results through. A report,' Amit says, 'I had a report commissioned.'

'I can see that we have recently sent you a final results document,' she says.

'Yeah, you did. But I think there are problems with it,' he says. 'There are strange results that don't make sense.'

'I assure you that *ClearVista* makes every effort to ensure absolute accuracy in its products and reports.'

'Yeah, I don't doubt that. But I want to question the results. Can I speak with somebody about them?'

'Sir, the results you were given were created with the algorithm signed off in last February's agreement. They're relevant to within a—'

'I understand that,' he says. The voice cuts off when he interrupts it. 'I want to talk to somebody about them, okay? One of the decoders, or somebody.'

'Very well, sir. I'll flag the account,' she says. 'You will receive a telephone call from a specialist within the next seventy-two hours to discuss the results of the report with you,' she says. The line cuts dead. Amit thinks about calling back, explaining how much money they spent on the report, demanding to speak to somebody immediately. He doesn't. He slumps into a chair at the desk and looks at the still-sleeping Laurence, and starts writing emails and making calls to cancel or postpone their meetings.

Deanna parks the car – the new car, that she chose from the ones that Ann was able to get delivered to her straight away, brought over from one of the dealerships in the nearby towns. Ann was right, anyway: the old car was built for a family of five going on seven, large enough to have accommodated them all at any given point. Now, she knows, and she thinks of Sean as she counts the seats in the car, they only need something smaller. She wanted to go for something more efficient as well, because that felt like something she could do; and there was nothing fundamentally wrong with the old car – nothing, Ann told her, that couldn't be beaten out with some elbow grease or replaced from salvage – so she still got a good trade-in price. She paid for the rest on her credit card. Her car, she reasoned. Laurence will barely be around to drive it for the foreseeable future. He'll be off around the country, and Deanna will be here, still pretending that life is totally normal until the day that it suddenly isn't any more. So this is hers, now. It fits her. It's small and white – white! Laurence will go crazy, she thinks, although only because he always chooses black cars (which, he says, are easier to keep clean) – and when she ran the *ClearVista* algorithm on it, to check if it was the right car, it seemed to fit in perfectly with her lifestyle. She parks it and looks at it on their drive. She looks at their house, which will go on the market soon enough; as soon as Laurence knows more about his career, something that almost seems to be a done deal at the moment. And she thinks, This is all going to change, because it has no choice but to.

CHAPTER 5

When the article about what happened on their flight finally appears, it's not as bad as it could have been. It breaks on one of the smaller blogs, and the video is grainy and dark and it's hard to hear what's going on, taken from one of many cellphone cameras; there's nothing even vaguely professional about it. Amit can't be sure it was even from the blue-jacketed man. The video doesn't make the nationals, which is a relief. What does, albeit briefly, is Amit's statement about Laurence. He plays it up, writing that Laurence is taking a few days off the trail to spend time with his family, a bit of gentle R and R. Make it sound like he's a family man who works hard, nothing more. The statements repeat the phrases over and over, about how much Laurence has been on the road trying almost too hard to drill the point home. That's when a story suddenly clicks. Entirely too hard and it's lost, because people begin to pick holes. You can always tell when somebody's trying too hard to bullshit you. Amit's list of ways to run – and, in theory, win – a campaign, is huge. He began writing them when

121

he was at university and then reworked them when he was hired by *ClearVista* in their early days. It wasn't until the last election that people really began to notice his blog and his articles for the specialist press, when his predictions began jibing with – or trumping – the ones being made by the big boys, those companies who had invested billions over the years in their own software. His were a combination of math and guesswork, and they stood toe-to-toe.

Now, Amit reads the comments on the various blogs to serve as a distraction. Depending on who's reporting the story, they vary wildly. Some are sympathetic, insinuating the toll that personal tragedy takes, understanding how hard it is to win the nomination in these trying times; others are callous, calling him names – or, worse still, calling him weak. He looks at Laurence, lying on one of the room's beds: on top of the blanket that lies over the duvet, suit trousers still on, shirt a mess around his body. He is sunken into the mattress enough that he looks almost frail. It's a shock, Amit reminds himself. Getting that data, those results, that's not something that you expect – or want. And he knows that there wasn't a problem with the report itself. Laurence doesn't know it, but Amit logged in and proofed the answers before they were even submitted, making sure that there were no confessions slightly too askew to come back from. The survey was perfect. He thinks about the things that Laurence has said and done; those things that have caused issues with the public. But there are also the two major psychological factors that frequently come up, perhaps rightfully so – the twin traumas that he suffered in Afghanistan, and when Sean died.

Amit tells himself that the results of the report cannot be accurate, because there's nothing in Laurence's past that means they can be that cut and dried. The report works, he knows, by using every piece of information available about Laurence – hell, every piece of information about the election and anything related that it can find in the deepest, darkest corners of the Internet – in order to generate its results. There's a margin of error, but not much of one. So maybe there's something on the Internet that Amit hasn't seen, something that he hasn't taken into account?

There's a nightmare scenario, one that statistics and jargon and rules for debate cannot overcome: that there is information about Laurence that hasn't yet come to light. Information that maybe hasn't been confessed, but that is somewhere, a rumor turned into plausible truth. Maybe it's something that's been buried underneath the veneer, a moment from the past that's been dredged up by *ClearVista's* data mining algorithms. There's irony there, if that's the case: that's the part of the software that Amit was instrumental in helping to create.

He googles Laurence's name again, and he clicks on the last page – the lowest visits, the lowest hits.

He's done this enough, and had whole teams of investigators on it – dredging up all the madness that's going to be discovered when Laurence gets further down the line, when he's actually pitching his tent in the electoral nominee field, when people are trying to discredit him and point out the times he smoked pot, the women he slept with and never called, the DUI charges he once had as a teenager – but now Amit wants to look again, just in case there's anything new. He sorts it by date, to see the oldest mentions of Laurence, and then by popularity again. So many pages of hits, and nothing that, at a glance, he hasn't seen before.

He tries keywords. He types *Laurence Walker Should Not Be President Because* into the search engine. Something that the algorithm will have gone for: an easy target for negativity. The hits come thick and fast: talking about Laurence's time in the army, and what he went through, and how it might have left him too scarred, too unable to work well for a country that needs a strong military leader. That's the biggest reason. He did an interview on TV when he came home, only local news at the time, but his was a story worth telling. He was captured, he was tortured, he didn't betray his country, he survived. Got up and braved the rain. Politics was a natural place for him to go after that. Now, there are articles questioning whether he can be trusted, crazy über-right-wing mouthpieces who suspect that he was tainted during his time out there, brainwashed into being an enemy of America, using television shows and fiction to back up their theories.

Then there are those who question his mental fragility. They dwell on Sean's death. *How can any man who has been through the trauma that Laurence Walker has recover enough to lead our country?* one post asks. *How can he find the strength needed to make the hard decisions that need to be made?* It's a question that Amit has wondered himself, but in the great column of tick-boxes that he keeps in a spreadsheet on his computer, *War Hero* outweighs *Trauma Victim* every time.

Then there's the third group, the religious crazies; the ones who think that Laurence's own beliefs – or, they presume, lack thereof, because the question has never come up directly, and he has an Asian man as his campaign advisor – should preclude him from being anywhere near a role of governmental power. After that it's marginalized groups: those who simply dislike him; who call him volatile; those who think that he isn't actually human. Unstable words and judgments formed from nothing at all.

Amit's email pings as he's reading the articles. It's from *ClearVista* – a follow-up from the phone call, he assumes. He opens it, and he's wrong.

Thank you for choosing ClearVista, the email reads. *Please find attached your predicted video file. This is merely an approximation of an event, forged from the numbers provided by your survey, designed to give you a glimpse of a possible future based on the person that*

125

you are, and the path that you wish to explore. It's so pretentious, the language; driven by branding companies and copywriters rather than the people who established *ClearVista*. It's another business entirely than when he worked there. *Other formats (including H3D, HoloGas and TactBraille) available on request. Please click here for a list of terms and conditions, including fair-use policies for distribution of this video. Remember: the ClearVista watermark is not to be removed for broadcast purposes. We hope that you have found our service useful. The numbers don't lie.* There's a link attached, to a file stored on their servers. Amit clicks it, and the black box of the video loads. Amit swipes to start it playing.

It opens with a logo, swirling and central. Designed by committee, designed to tell you everything. It's cold and clean, meant to be lasting; and, around the font, a series of numbers swirl, some representation of the algorithm and what it can do for you. Then that passes, and the screen is a mess of false, animated static. Rows and rows of numbers and letters and symbols: representations of the algorithm for some reason. This is all window dressing, Amit knows. It's not the real thing – it is almost entirely meaningless, but the company is selling a product, and needs to dress it up as such. Images start to form through the false static, figures moving around, particles and digital atoms seeming to form into shapes. All of this is show-manship. He stopped working for *ClearVista* long before they moved onto the videos and the photographs, doctored visualizations that added perceived value, somehow swaying the general public towards believing the results of the reports. *ClearVista* is a company, not some grand project to enhance people's lives. That's one of the reasons he stopped working for them.

The video is dark, so he turns up the brightness on the screen, and then he sees shapes begin to form through the static. There's sound as well: a rush of something in the background, so overwhelming that if he concentrates enough it's all encompassing. This is a new addition: when Homme's video appeared, it was silent. (Amit joked at the time that as he grinned Homme could well be telling all the soldiers he was shaking the hands of that they were being sent to die, and the world would never know any better.) In the background, he sees more figures begin to form, their parts swirling, numbers and pixels and false dust coagulating into the shapes of what looks like four silhouettes: four, maybe only three. One of them is smaller than the others.

The video compiles the figure in the foreground first, juddering them into being: it's Laurence, in a gray suit and lemon-yellow tie. Obvious, really, that he would be here. It's unsettling, watching him form: the software takes photographs and videos from the Internet, recognizing faces, and it composites them into a new version of that face that it can use. So it looks like Laurence, because

127

it *is* him; just, in a place that he has never been, doing things that he hasn't yet done. Laurence's face flits through different sources – through expressions of joy, of cold sternness, of somber mourning – before settling on something that is so blank, it is like a face that Amit doesn't believe can exist. Even to look at it, it looks false it's so vacant. Amit wonders where it has come from. This facsimile of Laurence is looking at the camera, or what would be the camera. Amit wonders how they pick an angle for this; how any of it actually works. It's a guess, that's all, based on nothing. Some designer somewhere thought up a scenario based on data. That makes Amit balk. What if they've used the bad data? The results that were sent through already, that sent Laurence reeling? The point of this is gentle lies. He knows that, should Homme win – maybe even before – he will recreate the shot that was generated by his report, because it's a great promo; a solid opportunity for positive press. *Here is the man that you were promised when you cast your vote.* Given half a chance, Amit will have Laurence do the same.

The rest of them start drawing themselves in: the next is Deanna, and her face does the same as Laurence's did. It goes through her expressions – fewer than for Laurence, certainly, but there's enough to draw on for her. She's been in the public eye for a while: before he was as high-profile as he is, she was at book events, and there are publicity photos of her that her publisher draped

128

all over the Internet; her hair glossy, her smile knowingly only half-there. She is drawn in, her clothes approximated, based on what she's worn in other photographs, an outfit that Amit has seen her wearing before – and then it draws the person next to her. He imagines a head of state, or a soldier, but it's Lane. She forms quickly – fewer expressions still, thanks to a scarcity of photos. The software resorts to screen grabs of YouTube videos she's been tagged in: one of her singing while some boy plays an acoustic-guitar version of a hyped-up dance song; one of her leaping off a cliff-edge and into a lake a few years ago before she even had a single tattoo on her skin; one of her laughing hysterically at a party, collapsing to the floor while another girl attempts to drink beer through a funnel. She is standing next to her mother at the back of the room, with Laurence front and center; the image framed somehow, Laurence the focus. As, Amit thinks, he probably should be. Laurence's face changes again, as if the software cannot settle on an appropriate expression; then it goes back to the original. Cold and gone.

The fourth shape is still waiting to draw in, Amit notices; and then it crackles into images and light. The face first, and Amit is terrified, because it's Sean. It's the Walkers' son, somehow alive. Then it changes again to another – chubbier, slightly, the teeth slightly neater, less of a jawline – and the hair is drawn, the clothes, and Amit realizes that it's not Sean: it's Alyx. The face changes again to Sean's, and back, and back. Over and over. This is *ClearVista's* software, not clever enough to distinguish between very similar twins, even when they're of different sexes. Now, as it finishes its process, the figure is definably Alyx, but there are pieces of Sean in her. She doesn't quite have her own eyes. Portions of her face move sluggishly and alter until they settle. Amit looks at the bar at the bottom of the video, willing it to move on faster.

As the fragments stop swirling, Amit thinks of dust after a terrible storm: when the wind dies down and the air settles, the dust hanging in it, visible through rays of light for days. The tableau has been established; now, time for the money shot. Amit wants this to be an embrace: the four of them turn and hold each other. This is proof of Laurence's being over the traumas that he has endured, despite having lost an election, here he is, the consummate family man. Even if he doesn't win, there's family. He is a good man, that's the takeaway from this.

But that doesn't happen. On the screen, the Walker family judders into life, automatons at some ancient fairground, lurching and stuttering into place. The Laurence in the video stays perfectly still; only his family reacts. All three of their faces distort and contort into looks of trauma, of panic. Expressions that there's no frame of reference for, so the software bends and manipulates what it's got, turning smiles upside down, forcing false tears from previously happy eyes. Alyx looks sad; the other two look terrified. There is abject fear on their faces, or some approximation of it. Laurence doesn't move, or change, for the rest of the video. His expression is as a monolith. Then there finally comes a sound from the speakers, the soundtrack to this piece: quiet sobbing, the voices female and small.

Amit feels his heart race. He feels sick, in his throat, rising to his mouth. He looks at the representation of Laurence, willing it to change, to show something resembling justification. The face remains blank; no expression picked by the software, not remorse or sadness or actually even anything at all.

Amit opens the original email again and reads their terms and conditions, as if that will change anything. But there is nothing, only a clause that says that users are entitled to their rights and that he needs to speak to them about any issues with the report or video; so he shuts the laptop and packs it into his satchel. He needs to wait for *ClearVista* to call him; and he needs to watch it again. He wants to understand exactly what it is; he wants to know where it came from.

He looks at the email again. It's been sent to Laurence as well; of course it has. Both of their names were on the account. He'll wake up and see the video, and Amit does not want that to happen, not until this is fixed. So he backtracks, creeping into the room quietly, fetching Laurence's laptop from the bag, and then he sits on the floor of the bathroom – in case Laurence should suddenly wake up and ask what he's doing – and he opens the email app and deletes the one from *ClearVista*, making sure to empty the trash when he's done. This can be controlled from here on out. He puts the laptop back in Laurence's bag and leaves the room again, into the corridor of this spartan Texan hotel. He tries to call *ClearVista* again, in an attempt to rush the customer service specialist, and the automated voice answers.

'We have received your request for a callback,' it says, before he can say a word, 'and will be in contact with you imminently. Please have patience with us.' The line goes dead and Amit tries once more, getting the same message. He doesn't have a clue what he's meant to do next. He thinks about people in films, when they're this frustrated: they cry, or they punch walls. Or they go and get drunk.

He heads to the elevators and presses the button for the first level. Above it is a small label: *The Cowpoke*, it reads, *Bar & Restaurant*.

'That'll do,' he says.

Amit orders a beer and some buffalo wings, and he sits at a high bar-side table by himself. He puts his tablet on the table in front of him, and his phone, and he taps on one while scrolling on the other, loading up blogs and searching *Twitter*. He tries to distract himself. He tells himself that everything from *ClearVista* has to be wrong, that there's no way there's validation in this. Laurence's results do not speak of the man that he knows, that he's been working with these past months. He may be fragile – more fragile than the public realizes; maybe even more than Deanna realizes – but that man in the video isn't Laurence. He tries to put the image from his mind, but it's pervasive. He sees his boss's face, cold and free of all expression, looking away from his loved ones. He knows that it's the software, and he knows that it's an accident. No, he tells himself, not an accident: a fucking disaster. He drinks his beer and then another; and he eats the wings and wipes his hands on the wet, lemon-scented napkin, and then orders another beer.

The rumble of his phone on the table makes him jump. It's this girl he's almost been seeing, a student at Georgetown who came to a seminar that he gave. She's so much younger than he is, and she asks how he is, and what's wrong, because he sounds like he's not really there, and he says that he's not. He explains that Laurence has a migraine, maintaining the lie because he doesn't know who in the bar might be listening. She tells him to be careful. She asks if they can go out when he gets back, and he says that he doesn't know. He tells her that he doesn't know if he'll have the time to get into anything serious; at least, not for a few years, if all goes to plan. He isn't trying to be an asshole, he tells her; he's just being honest.

133

'I'm being realistic,' he says. Even as the words come out, he thinks that he's pushing his luck, both with her and his promises for Laurence's campaign. She hangs up on him, angry. She tells him not to bother calling her. He orders another beer, and he checks his phone to see if he's missed a call from *ClearVista*; if the reception is good here. He goes to the *ClearVista* website, and clicks the button to start the process of a new application, thinking that it might give him a different phone number he can call, to actually speak with somebody. They always want new custom; maybe he can circumvent the system that way.

The *ClearVista* logo in the middle of the screen swirls, the screen dissolving into a publicity video, an extended talk-through of the services that they offer. It shows a man and a woman talking about having a baby; an older woman contemplating applying for a job; a committee having a meeting, discussing the plausibility of some vague policy. The video asks if the viewer has ever considered any of these things. Perhaps they have been afraid of failure? Or wondered if they can do – if they can be – better? *ClearVista* can help, the video offers. It explains about the algorithm: that it began development in 2015, created by a team of technology experts who had, between them, worked for some of the world's most powerful politicians and Fortune 500 companies. They had all banded together to research the future of predictability and what they found wasn't infallible, but close. Technology now allows for the statistics to speak for themselves; for your percentages of success to be broken down into exacting detail. We can, the video says, answer any and all of your questions to within a percentage probability margin – and, at higher payment tiers, even visually predict the outcomes of a given situation, using state of the art audiovisual technologies. They show representations of those same people having achieved their goals: the happy family around a crib; the woman sitting behind a desk at her new job; the committee smiling at a product launch. *Remove the chaos from your decision-making, and start to predict your future now. ClearVista: the numbers don't lie.* But there's no number to call: just a form to fill in on their website, and the promise of a swift callback.

The website loads a series of FAQs. Amit has read these so many times before – both when he was working for them way back when and they were developing the questions that they would need to ask, the data that they would need to obtain; and then again, when Laurence was told to begin this process, and he tore the information provided apart to see if anything had changed – but he goes through them once more now. It can't hurt, he reasons.

What happens if your result isn't satisfactory? one question asks.

This is a fallible science, the answer reads. *Sometimes, things will be askew. We try our best to achieve results that are as accurate as possible, but occasionally things will slip through the cracks. If you have any queries, simply contact us, and we'll run that part of the algorithm again. Maybe you'll get the answer you were hoping for this time?* They list the contact number that he's been calling, the only way of getting in touch with them. There's no email and no emergency number. Why would there be? Amit thinks. Nothing to do with *ClearVista* is an emergency. This is a mistake. Mistakes can be rectified, and this can all be reset, as if it never even happened. Nothing about this is life or death. But he's exhausted. They both are. Best case, it will be another nine years before they get to have a proper holiday and some time off, time away from politics and worrying about one thing or another. This can be good training, maybe: a trial by fire.

Amit orders another beer. He shuts his eyes and drinks from the bottle, cradling his phone in his hand, waiting for it to ring.

Laurence dreams.

He is on the bed, in this hotel, and there is a knock at the door. He answers it, moving from bed to door in one smooth, swift motion. It's Sean. There's nothing disquieting about seeing his son here. Instead, it is completely expected; this is where Sean lives now. The boy runs off towards the elevators at the end of the hallway and Laurence chases after him. Sean reaches the elevator and runs in, and the doors ping to a close in front of Laurence's face, shutting him outside. He pumps the button, furious and frantic, but nothing happens. The LED above the doors that shows the current floor is blank and it stays that way. Laurence turns to run back to his room, but the corridor stretches on and on into infinity, as if he is running on the spot and somebody else is moving the walls. He turns back and the elevator doors open: not to the metal box that's expected, but onto a dock, the ramshackle wooden strut that is attached to the house that they own, at the lake. This is the house where Sean died. He is there, at the end of the dock, which seems so implausibly far away from Laurence. Sean clumsily dives from the end: up, into the air, and then down. There is no splash of water when he impacts, at least not that can be seen. Laurence runs down the dock, the jetty, trying to reach him; because if he can, maybe this – all of this – doesn't need to happen. But he's too late. He's always too late.

Laurence wakes up. The dream happens, or a variation of it, over and over. Some aspects of it are always the same. Usually he'll be in their house and he'll be running and Sean will be gone down the stairs, suddenly disappeared out of the front door, and it will be locked from the inside. Sometimes Laurence is at the lake cabin the entire time, which he remembers so vividly in the dream but can, for some reason, barely remember when he's awake; and his son will be on the dock and Laurence will see him through a murky window; he will shout but won't be heard. And sometimes Laurence is at war, crawling through the dust, injured and clinging on; but Sean is still there, and so is the lake house. Those things are the constants, and they never leave.

He reaches over to the complimentary bottle of water on the nightstand and opens it, almost completely draining it, feeling it run down his throat. His mouth is dry from the air-conditioning unit; it's all he can taste. The water is acidic, almost, cheap and filtered rather than from a spring. He has, over the past god-knows-how-many months of hotel visiting, become a connoisseur of local bottled waters. He looks at the clock. It's just gone ten here. It'll be eight back at home. He's fucked up his sleeping patterns completely, he knows. Typical.

And then, in a rush, he remembers the results from the report. It hits him with a headache. *00% chance of success.* Cut and dried, a definite No. Not even a hint of a chance. He wonders what would make anybody vote for him after that, if even his family will see him as a viable contender now. Amit said that it was a mistake, and he has to believe that. He does believe one thing:

that he is a good man. He's always tried to be a good man. He is fractured, he knows, and he is suffering, but it's been getting easier to be him. Every day, Sean gets further away. He thinks of chasing after him: his dreams as blunt metaphor.

He stands up and goes to the bathroom, uses the toilet, then he rubs his face and looks in the mirror and splashes water over his skin. He thinks about the plane. He doesn't know what came over him: there have always been the rules about what he shows in public and he's never broken them before. He's always composed. Even at Sean's funeral he didn't break: he held his reserve, the stoic, immoveable father, keeping his grief at bay when his family needed him to.

He thinks that he should call and let Amit know that he's awake and that he's feeling better. He wants to do the meetings this week: even if Amit thinks it's better to call off a day for recovery, maybe the rest of them can be salvaged. He will forge onwards, only needing a moment to catch his breath before he is back at maximum, back at one hundred percent. As soon as the results from *ClearVista* are sorted out, this will become much easier, Laurence thinks. That's when this all works as it should, all of the pieces in their right place.

He picks up his phone to call Amit, and there's an inundation of messages waiting. There are notifications about emails, about tweets, and a message from Deanna, worried about him. He presses the button to return her call.

Deanna hears the phone ringing, but she's with Alyx, their hands deep in cookie dough. Alyx loves baking, says that it is what she wants to do when she's older. She's got a plan, apparently, and she draws pictures of cakes and biscuits and muffins and the ingredients around them, and her in a baker's hat. So when they get the chance, this is what they do together. Deanna finds it relaxing: everything today, since the accident, has been about calming herself down. The call goes to the answering machine as she's washing the dough from her hands and she tells Alyx to keep kneading it. It's Laurence.

'Hello?' he says into the machine. 'Are you there?'

'Yes,' Deanna says, before she picks it up. 'I'm coming, hang on!' She grabs the handset and says his name, and he's silent for a second. She thinks that she has missed him and is about to hang up when he finally speaks back.

'I'm sorry, I was asleep,' he says.

'I was so worried,' she says. Alyx looks over, wondering what she was worried about. She's at that age of understanding the conversations of others; of listening in and attempting to decode them. 'I saw the blog and Amit's statement. You've got a migraine?' It's posed as a question, because she knows that he's never had one before.

It sparks further worries, a procession of increasingly terrible ailments that such a powerful headache could mean.

'Yeah, I felt odd. I'm just so tired.' She hears the lie in his voice. 'Amit says that I need a break. Some time off, to recover.'

'Has something happened?' He doesn't answer, which means it has. Still, she knows: he doesn't like to talk on the phone about anything that could be incriminating 'When will you be home?' she asks.

'Still a few days,' he says. 'We're powering through.'

'Okay,' she says. 'Just be safe.' She thinks about telling him about her accident and the car, but there's no point. He's not feeling well and it'll only make him worry. 'I love you,' she tells him instead.

'I love you,' he replies. 'Kiss the girls for me.'

'Alyx is here. Want to tell her?'

'Yes,' he says. Deanna holds the phone up to her daughter's ear. She can't hear what Laurence says, but Alyx laughs.

'We're making cookies,' she says. Deanna imagines Laurence asking her to save one for him; predictable, but what she wants from him. 'I will,' she says. 'Bye, Daddy.'

When Deanna goes back to the phone, it's quiet, the line dead. She thinks about calling him back but decides to let him be. She worries about him, but only briefly; he sounds tired and the story on the blogs suggested an *imminent breakdown*. That's the words that they used. Talking to him now, she knows it's not that bad; but still, she can't help but worry.

Amit sits and goes through the results in the PDF, line by line, reading every single one. He makes notes of anything anomalous, anything that might be a red flag, anything that he cannot explain. Laurence was honest about everything: that he still missed Sean and that he always would; that Sean's death caused stress to his marriage; that he hated being in the army, that the things he was subjected to there scarred him more than he ever thought he would be scarred; that capital punishment is a crime, that torture is something he could never put another human being through. He ticked the boxes saying that his stress levels were at seventy percent, even though that seemed high to Amit (and Amit adjusted them down a few percentage points of his own volition, knowing that Laurence likely wouldn't remember what number he arbitrarily plucked from the sky); and he ticked the boxes saying that he felt that he was only fifteen percent likely to crumble under the pressure of running the country, even though Amit argued – again – that such a number was maybe too high. Laurence thought that it was better to be honest. Amit flags them all now: anything that could have pushed him underneath a fiftieth percentile. They're all about mental health, about fortitude, about

142

chances of self-destruction, but there's nothing as extreme as the final two answers might suggest. Amit cannot see where they have come from: a prediction from a year, two years down the line, and a prediction with no grounding that he can fathom.

After a while he's distracted by the news on the television, the most right wing of the right wing shows. It mentions Laurence's episode on the plane, albeit briefly – and then, in a move that Amit thinks is almost sarcastic, prays that he gets better soon, and back into the race – and before Amit knows it there's a woman at his table, another beer in front of him, some imported British cider in front of her. He's ordered more wings, and he listens to her talking about herself, both as drunk as each other; and he thinks how nearly erotic this actually is, this woman sucking the thick orange sauce from her fingers when she's done with a piece of the chicken, stopping before she sucks the bones. Her name is Clara and she's a local, Texas born and raised. She's worked for the past few years in telemarketing and is here now for a conference, but she isn't happy. She wants something more fulfilling: a purpose, of sorts, but she doesn't know what. Amit doesn't listen as she talks, because he's distracted, and thinking about the video and Laurence's campaign and also Clara's body, and she doesn't notice that he's tuned out. He's good at the eye-contact-while-not-actually-being-there thing: something he picked up over the past few years in politics. He checks his phone while she's talking, but there's nothing from Laurence. He hasn't called Amit, or texted or tweeted. Either he's asleep still – not impossible – or he needs some space. Either way, Amit decides to leave him until the morning.

'Are you listening to me?' Clara asks him.

'Yes,' he says. 'You have my absolute attention.' He fixes eye contact. 'I'm sorry,' he says, 'but I was just dealing with something for my boss.'

'Who's your boss?' she asks.

'I can't say,' he tells her. 'But he's important. He's a pretty big deal.'

Clara has her own room in the hotel, which is useful. She asks him to come with her and he does. They walk through the hotel, stumbling, as she tries to find her way. He stands in the hallway, waiting for her to dig her key out of her bag, and then she can't find it. She tells him that she'll be back, that she has to go to the front desk for another, and she rushes off. Amit sits on the floor by her door and shuts his eyes. He hears the ping of the elevators and he opens them. There, at one end of the corridor, in the distance, he sees a man. He's sure that he's looking at Amit, that he knows him, recognizes him. And then the man turns away from Amit, and in his hand is the blue jacket. It's *him*.

Amit stands, because it seems like too much of

a coincidence. He wonders if he's here to find Laurence, been tipped off about where they're staying. But why? Laurence isn't a big deal, not yet: he's only a few steps above being a nobody. Amit runs down the corridor but there's nobody there when he gets to the junction; and then the elevator pings again and he hears Clara's voice beckoning him back. He tells himself to forget about the man. He's nothing. Coincidences happen all the time.

When he gets into Clara's room he does what's expected of him – this being some sort of mutually agreed pact, signed by lips and hands and other parts of their bodies – but he's slightly too gone to properly be in the moment and he can taste the buffalo wings (*Frank's Hot Sauce*) on her lips and it distracts him. She falls asleep when they're done and he follows, sprawled on her crisp white hotel sheets, the same thread count as every other hotel in this chain.

His phone beeps. Amit wakes up, pushing himself to standing, and he finds his pants on the floor and goes to the pockets for the handset.

Please find attached your predicted video file, the first line of the email reads. They've resent the original email; a glitch, maybe, or a result of his repeated calling. He doesn't want to look at it again and ignores it. He can hear the sound of the maids stacking their trolleys in the storeroom next door, the whispered gaggle of their voices, their accents coming through the walls and underneath the door. This is one of the cheapest rooms, the ones that they comp with conference tickets, when you can't go complaining about the quality. He sits up and looks for a drink, but there are no bottles of water on the bedside tables. He goes to the minibar and finds it empty, another sign that the room was given away free, purged of anything that might cause accidental charges to be made. He tiptoes to the bathroom and drinks from the tap and then goes back into the room, thinking he'll get dressed and take a cab to find a coffee place or something. Maybe just go and wait for breakfast to be served. It's a quarter of five, so it won't be long. He pulls his trousers on, and his shirt, and then checks for his phone. He finds it in his shoes and he picks them up and carries them with him as he opens the door and sneaks out. The door softly shuts itself behind him and he sees the first of the maids pushing her cart down the corridor, starting on the unoccupied rooms, getting them ready for the day.

He sits on a sofa down the corridor and pulls his shoes on while he checks his phone. The video is still up in the browser app. With the maid gone into the room, the hotel seems to fall silent. There's just Amit and the video. The elevators are silent and there's no distant murmur of televisions or the rumble of dragged suitcases. He opens the email and presses play, watches it one more time.

He wonders if anybody at *ClearVista* saw this before they sent it out; what dream they hoped it would realize when it landed in Laurence's hands.

Laurence. The email. Amit goes to it and looks to see who it was sent to – and there's Laurence's email address right next to his. He stands and rushes to the elevator, hammers the button for their floor; the elevator seems to take forever. It stops two floors down, to let some British tourists on – early morning, a family of four woken by jetlag and forced to get on with their day – and then carries on its descent. When he's out he goes to the room and he breathes deeply outside, then he opens the door quietly, hoping to repeat the trick from last night and delete the email before Laurence even has a sniff of its existence, but the lights are on in the room: Laurence is awake. There's a moment – brief, unexpected, terrifying – where he expects to see Laurence's body strung from the ceiling, not swinging but perfectly still, the face bloated and purple, too gone to be saved.

But Laurence is lying on the bed, propped up by pillows. He's got his laptop open, the sound of slight crying coming from the tinny speakers. He looks up at Amit and he turns the screen, frozen on the terrified and distorted faces of his family.

'What the hell is this?' he asks, his voice small and quiet. 'I don't understand.'

'I don't know,' Amit says. Laurence shuts his eyes for a second, holding them tightly closed, and then reaches out. He swipes the air over the keyboard and the video begins to play again.

CHAPTER 6

The original plan is that Lane will look after Alyx while Deanna collects Laurence from the airport, but Deanna changes her mind as she's almost out of the door. She asks them both to come with her.

'No,' Lane says. 'I've got stuff to do.'

'We'll get food,' her mother says. 'We'll go and get some dinner and then you can do whatever it is that's so urgent when we get home.' She looks at Alyx. 'Go get in the car, honey,' she says, opening it with the fob, and then she turns her attention to Lane. 'I don't ask much of you,' she says. 'Please, just do this for me.' And she stands to one side so that Lane can get past, because it's not even really a request. Amit has texted her, telling her that Laurence needs to relax. *Stress at a maximum*, he wrote. All of his appearances have been cancelled. *Might be a mistake*, he had written, *because we flew all the way out here, but I think he should come back. He needs some time.* Deanna agreed. *Nothing to worry about.*

In the car, which smells so new and clean, she tunes the radio to Alyx's choice, some pop station

149

full of songs that sound like every possible type of music all at once. Deanna likes it, though, because the songs are all so slight as to be immediately catchy. They fade rather than being overwhelming and she catches herself singing along with tunes that she's only now hearing for the first time. Or, it could be that she's heard them before and they're just forgotten. She keeps looking at her youngest daughter in the rearview mirror: watching her bouncing in her seat, mouthing the words wrong, occasionally becoming distracted and forgetting about the lyrics entirely. It's a stark contract to Lane, who stares outside the entire time, only pausing to look down at her phone to furiously tap on the screen. She doesn't even look while she's writing some of the texts or tweets or whatever they are. She also mouths the words, sometimes, which makes Deanna smile. Lane would deny it, of course, but that doesn't mean it isn't happening.

The drive to the airport at this time of day is okay, the traffic just starting to quieten down, and they manage to find a space in one of the short-stay car parks. Laurence's flight is on time and they wait at the barrier to greet him. Alyx writes his name on an unfolded napkin taken from the closest coffee shop and she and Deanna whoop and cheer when they see him. Amit's stayed behind in Texas to smooth things over, to go and meet the investors himself and keep them sweet. Laurence smiles when he spots them, but it's false.

Deanna sees through it straightaway: he's a ghost. If the kids notice, they don't show it. They follow him to the end of the barrier. He holds Alyx first – Deanna notices his arm wrapped around her, his hand gripping her shirt with an almost claw-like grip – and then Deanna and Lane.

'You never come to collect me,' he says. 'They would have sent a car.'

'We're just pleased to have you home,' Deanna tells him. She looks into his eyes, and they're vacant and spare. 'We missed you,' she says. She kisses him, and he kisses her back, and she thinks how dry it is.

'What is this?' Laurence asks as Deanna tells him to close his eyes as they walk through the garage.

'Just, go on,' she says, 'keep them shut.'

'I don't want to,' he tells her. 'What is this?' She sighs and holds up the fob, and beeps the lights on the new car. 'I don't understand,' he says.

'I got a deal on the SUV. I traded it in with Ann for this. We didn't need it any more and we'd been talking about getting rid of it.' She doesn't mention the accident. 'I wanted to do something,' she says, 'and it was about time.'

'Oh,' he says. She thought that he would care; that it would get some sort of a reaction from him. Instead he opens the passenger door and rests both hands on the roof. 'Do you mind if I don't drive?' he asks.

'Of course not,' she says. They climb in.

'Where do you want to eat?' she asks him, as they leave the parking lot. He's staring forward, but not at the road. She knows that he's watching Alyx in the mirror, just as she did.

'Wherever you like,' he says. There's something wrong about him, Deanna thinks, beyond anything that Amit's messages set her up for.

'How hungry are you?' she asks.

'I don't know.' His voice is still and monotone.

'What about T.G.I. Friday's or something?'

'Sure,' he says. He watches everything, through the windscreen and the mirrors. Glimpses flashing by catch his attention: a poster with his face on, stuck to the window of a shop; a billboard advertising *ClearVista*; and, in the rearview mirror as they leave the airport compound, a man in a blue jacket. He stays quiet. He is, he thinks, imagining these things. He's seeing faces in clouds.

He doesn't say anything all through dinner, so Deanna doesn't really either. Instead they let Alyx jabber at them. They share a platter of mozzarella dippers and chicken wings and potato skins, all of them drinking Cokes apart from Laurence, who orders a single beer that he doesn't sip from even once. In the back seat, on the drive home, the girls sing, both of them. Deanna holds her husband's hand, resting it in his lap, and thinks – though it cannot be true – that he's too cold, as if his whole body has been frozen by something and cannot thaw itself.

★ ★ ★

At home, Laurence goes to the bedroom while Deanna puts Alyx to bed. When she's done and returns to him, thinking that they might talk, he's already in bed. His eyes are shut, but still she says his name as she climbs under the duvet next to him; he doesn't even attempt to respond and she doesn't know if he's lying to her or not.

During the night he wakes her. He rolls over and puts his hands on her shoulders and shakes her awake. She opens her eyes to see his face, his eyes red and bleary. She doesn't know if it's from tears or lack of sleep. She reaches for his face; not to comfort him, but to feel his cheeks, to see if they're wet.

'What's wrong?' she asks him.

'Are you sure about the person that I am?' he asks. The words sound wrong and slow, but there they are. It's not something he's ever asked before, or that she's ever contemplated. Ever since they met, he has been who he is. He is unchangeable, a man of constancy.

'Look at what you've done – at everything you have achieved,' Deanna tells him. He lets go and turns away from her.

'I've wondered,' he says, speaking into the darkness on the far side of the room, and then he goes silent. She questions if he was even awake, or if this was some sort of lucid dream. She sits up slightly, listening as he goes back to sleep, or falls into a deeper sleep. His whole body seems to shake with his inhalations. He snores, which he never usually does, unless he's stressed or ill. (She remembers to not even think the S word, Amit's rules intruding into her subconscious.) Eventually she gets out of bed and goes downstairs. She sits in the darkness of the kitchen at her laptop and opens the photo application, and she clicks to sort it by faces. She looks at the pictures of them as a family: the five of them, then becoming four. How abrupt it seems, and how their faces are never as happy after the change. She remembers how difficult it was, taking that first family photograph without Sean in it. They were in Italy, and a woman at a restaurant offered. They said yes, without thinking, and then stood around, parents at the back, children at the front; and, behind them, in the distance, a lake, an expanse of water stretching off into the distance. She wishes that she couldn't see that lake, but there it is.

There was such a gap in that photograph, as if it had been taken and then sliced out, and all that can be seen through it is the water. Deanna thinks of water – of lakes and seas and rivers – as universal now. They are all to blame, a single entity of destruction.

In the photograph, Laurence looks lost. He is trying the hardest, but Deanna can see it in his eyes: that he is failing.

She scrolls back to the earliest picture that they have of Sean, when he was only hours old, his skin a shade lighter and more wrinkled than she can remember it being, and from this point she cycles through his timeline, watching how his face changed over time, as he grew. The features coming through; his eyes, almost changing color as he got older; his hair becoming thicker. Onesies to T-shirts to school uniforms. And then the last photo, taken only a fortnight before he died. She looks at that boy, and she knows that he's the boy from the book that she's been writing, but she thinks that that's okay. She opens the book document then, and she goes to the start. The page after the title doesn't have anything on it, no dedication, yet, but the space left for one. She types, *For Sean*. She thinks that she should type something else, but she doesn't know what. Just dedicating it to him doesn't seem like it's enough; anything more seems crass, somehow. She tries phrases and words but none of them work. Only, *For Sean*.

She picks up her phone from the breakfast bar and finds Amit's telephone number. It's just gone five; she tells herself that she'll leave it another hour before calling him and asking him about Laurence. She wonders what he knows, what he's not telling her. She turns the phone over and over in her hands. She puts the TV on and it's the same old channels: all the political pundits, all the speculation. She watches them, and she feels as if she's heard everything that they're saying before: as if it's just the same old tune, over and over. She zones out, watching it, snapping back when she hears Laurence's name. It's nothing, just a run down of the past few weeks. It's nothing.

It's five forty-five. She presses the button to call Amit.

He answers after long enough that she's almost sure he won't. 'Dee. Everything all right?' he asks, as if he's been awake for hours, but a crack in his voice gives him away.

'No,' Deanna says. 'What happened out there? Why have you really sent him home?' She breathes: she thinks that she has to, before she can say the words. 'What's wrong with him?'

'Haven't you seen the blogs? He's stressed, is all.'

'I've seen them. There's something else. You wouldn't send him home because he had a migraine. You were there,' Deanna says. 'You're meant to be taking care of him. Don't screw with me, Amit.' He is silent for a second. There's a murmur in the background, another voice. He isn't alone. Deanna doesn't care.

'All right. I'll call you back in five minutes,' he says.

'Make sure you do,' she tells him. He hangs up, and she keeps the phone in her hands.

Amit's second night in a row sleeping with Clara, and this time he was far less drunk. This time it wasn't something he can excuse to himself quite as easily. He likes her, he thinks. Not so much that he would get into anything serious, but he likes her, and he doesn't want to lead her on. He dresses, no charade. This won't happen again, he tells himself. He puts the light on, apologizing to Clara, who pulls the sheet over her face to shield herself. It's too early.

'I have to go,' he says.

'Oh,' she replies. She sits up in bed. She hasn't taken her make-up off from last night, and it's smeared, as if she's in some classic rock band from decades back. 'So.'

'And I have to go back home later today, so . . .'

'No, I get it,' she says. 'You come out here again, you've got my number?'

'Of course,' he says, and then he pauses. There's more to say to her. There are precautions, in this day and age. 'Listen: don't tweet about me, or whatever. My boss. You know?'

'It's fine. You weren't impressive enough for me to tell the world anything.' She isn't quite smiling when she makes the joke, and it's disarming. He rolls with it. He never knows the protocol for this situation: whether you should hug – or, even, kiss – when saying goodbye. He errs on the side of caution and raises one hand in a static wave from the doorway as he leaves.

In the hallway he ties his shoelaces and then he calls Deanna back as he's walking to the elevator. She answers straightaway, before he even hears it ring.

'Okay,' he says. 'So, you need to not freak out.'

'What happened?'

157

'You remember *ClearVista*? That report that we did, to get the prediction about what would happen in the election?' How could she forget, she thinks: it's what Laurence sat in front of for weeks after Sean died. When he thought that nobody else was looking, he was there, fingers hovering as if he was just waiting to carry on; but he never ticked a box on the file, not until Amit told him he had to. He just liked having the questions up there in front of him. 'We had the results through, and there was something wrong with them.'

'He was affected by Sean, Amit.' Even as she says it, not knowing the actual problem, she feels like that's the default excuse; not just for Laurence, but for them all.

'It's not that. Some of the results are completely wrong. Like, they make no sense. And there's a video.'

'What?'

'They make a video, some CG thing. We told you, I'm sure. I don't know. It's fucked up, either way. I'm trying to call them, but Larry . . . He didn't take it well, not one bit.'

'I'll bet,' she says. 'So what are you doing about it?'

'I'm waiting for them to call back.' He pauses. 'Look, Dee, I'll get this fixed. I'll get the results, the right results, and we can get him back on the horse.'

'Are you sure there was something wrong with

them?' she asks. She sounds nervous; as if she should have the faith in him in the first place.

'I'm sure.' He thinks about the video: about the nothing in Laurence's eyes; about the fear in Deanna's. 'Look, don't tell him I told you. Let him tell you. I'm sure he will eventually. Might not be until this is over, but he will.' Another pause. 'You know how it's been for him. You know how it's been, and you're pretty much the only one who can know. He's worked too hard and he didn't take the time he should have, maybe. After Sean.'

'I know,' she says, 'I told him to take more.'

'Wasn't more to take, that's the problem. I should go,' Amit tells her. 'I've got a meeting this morning with one of the guys Laurence was here to meet. Some of them wouldn't cancel this late. I'm smoothing things over. He can take a week off. Two, if he needs it. Take him to speak to somebody. You guys have a therapist.' It's not a question.

'Okay,' she repeats, and then, 'Do you think he's all right?'

'No question. He's stressed. He's been through a lot.'

'We all have,' Deanna says.

He hangs up the call and goes to the restaurant to eat something. He stops in front of the mirrored walls as he walks and pushes down his hair, wets his hand with spit to manage a cow-lick, and he tucks his shirt in and smells his armpits, to check.

When he sits down at a table, a waiter gives him a menu and he orders a coffee. He opens the results of the survey again. He wants to be prepared when *ClearVista* finally calls him back. He watches his handset and he wills it to ring again.

'Come with me,' Deanna asks. She wants to get him out of the house, to take him anywhere that he can't simply fixate on what's happened. If he won't share, she reasons, she can push him; not to tell her, not to get worse, but to claw himself back to normal.

'I'm tired,' he tells her.

'I need your help,' she replies. 'It's only *Henderson's*. That's the only place we have to go.' She knows that Trent and Martha will raise Laurence's spirits as well, or they'll try to. He doesn't reply. 'Get dressed,' she says.

When he finally appears downstairs a few minutes later he's resigned to this. He stands by the front door and stares out at the street.

'Might do me good,' he says.

'It really might.'

'Can we walk?'

'If you help me carry the bags back,' she replies. He nods and opens the door and he walks down the drive. He smells the air, Deanna notices; holding it in for too long before he breathes out. She pulls her shoes onto her feet and slams the door behind her. 'Let's go then,' she says. She takes his hand and leads him down the pavement.

He's always a step behind her, slightly out of sync. It's as if his feet are lazy, not quite willing to make that effort that they should be.

They reach the junction with the path down to their lake house. They haven't spoken about what to do with it, not seriously. It's there as a totem now. They'll sell it eventually, when it suits them, but Deanna knows she can't go back there now. Whatever happens to Laurence, if he makes it to the highest office or not, she will never spend another night in that house. She doesn't believe she could sleep there, simply for knowing what happened just outside the windows, off the dock, in the water.

She catches Laurence staring at it as they pass. He stops, briefly, and he looks down the path. Through the trees, in the distance, they can see the shimmer of the water.

'Come on,' she says, and she pulls him forward. They pass people who greet them, townsfolk who smile and wish them well. Nobody stops to talk properly – Deanna knows that Laurence's body language doesn't suggest a man who wants small talk – but everybody knows them. At *Henderson's*, Trent is already standing outside. He's stretching, and he laughs as they come closer.

'Well, there's a face like thunder,' he says. 'News says you're not feeling your finest.' He holds out his hand to Laurence, who takes it. Deanna watches Trent shake hands with her husband; the energy isn't mutual.

'That's true,' Laurence says.

'You need to be back in bed,' Trent says.

'Yes.' Laurence nods.

'We'll get you some comfort food,' Deanna says. 'Martha inside?'

'Sure is.' Trent opens the door for them. Laurence follows Deanna inside. It's cold, the fridges pumping out wafts of gassy iced air. The shop is full of customers, people from all over the area. So much of the stock comes from local farmers, and it's not cheap, but it sells. Deanna takes a basket and starts filling it, saying hello to the few people that she recognizes. All of the things that Laurence likes go into the basket, whether he notices or not. She thinks about cooking for him, making him the meals that have always cheered him in the past. She doesn't know if it will work, but this is what they do for each other. It's what they've always done.

Deanna goes to Martha and greets her with a hug, and they talk in a slight hush about Laurence's health; how he'll be fine, he just needs some rest. They work him so hard already.

'Imagine what it'll be like when he's President,' Martha says. She smiles, and Deanna touches the wooden surface of the counter.

'Don't curse it,' she says. She turns to look for Laurence, to urge him to say hello to Martha. He's standing a way back, near the wines, staring up at the television screen in the corner of the shop. 'Laurence?' she calls, but he doesn't react. 'What's

162

wrong?' She steps back towards him, leaving her shopping with Martha, who starts to put it through the register. Laurence doesn't move. Deanna says his name, and touches him, and he stands stock-still, staring at the screen. He doesn't flinch. 'What's wrong with you?' she asks, and she glances at the screen. There's a photograph of him up on it, taken by a member of the press on the day that Sean died. He's in the suit he was wearing, the lemon-yellow tie that Deanna loved on him. He looks ill, gaunt and drawn. The newsreader seems to be talking about Laurence being off the trail for a short while – nothing serious, just a lead-in to another discussion about the state of the candidates, the likely successor to the throne – but this is the photograph that they have used: nothing Presidential, not one of the official promotional shots. It's cold, to see him like that. And now, in the shop, Laurence seems to be mimicking who he was that day. His expression is the same. He is just as lost, in his eyes. She says his name again, and she holds him, and he collapses. He turns into jelly in her arms, slumping down to his knees, and he sobs.

Martha rushes over, through the other shoppers who are staring at them, and she acts like a shield.

'Get him up and to the back,' she says. They both try to lift him, but he's a dead weight, even as thin as he's been getting. Deanna hears the shoppers talking, saying his name, asking what's wrong with him. She thinks about begging them

163

to leave, to give him space and air. Then there's a flash, a photograph being taken. She looks around to see who took it, but there's no sign.

'Please,' she says to them, as if they'll know what it is she's asking. Trent appears at the rear of the crowd.

'Everybody out,' he says. 'Nothing to see here. Five minutes, you can all come back in. Baskets on the floor, we won't touch them.' The crowd listens to him, and they disperse. When they're gone, he switches off the TV set and then he squats next to Deanna and Laurence. He hooks his arms under Laurence's and pulls him to his feet. Martha fetches water and Laurence sips it. Deanna watches his eyes and they come back, something in them changing.

'I'm sorry,' Laurence says, his voice barely even a whisper.

'It's fine,' Trent says. 'But I'd say you're worse off than you're letting on.' He looks at Deanna. 'You want to get yourself better, I'd warrant.'

'Yes,' Deanna says, answering for him. Laurence doesn't say anything else; he sips at the water, and he blinks furiously, as if there is something in his eyes.

Deanna calls their therapist's office. The receptionist answers and asks her to wait, and she does. Their hold music is a slowed-down piano dirge of *Moon River* and Deanna sings along under her breath, hearing her voice echo slightly in the

164

receiver. She always wonders with this stuff if it's a trick: if that song is carefully considered to calm down clients, so that they are more amenable. That's one of the parts of therapy as a business, she thinks. It's all smoke and mirrors. When the receptionist comes back onto the line she gives Deanna an emergency appointment, which is twice the cost of a regularly scheduled one. They haven't seen Dr Diaz in months, a failing of Laurence's schedule. He complained about the time it took, and how hard it was to actually schedule in time with Diaz and he stopped attending the meetings as soon as they actually needed them.

She brings Laurence a sandwich as he sits on the sofa.

'I'm not hungry,' he says. 'I'm sorry. I'm just not.'

'You should try,' she says. He nods and sits up, and she puts the tray on his lap. He eats the whole thing in only four or five mouthfuls. 'You can tell me what happened in Texas,' Deanna says to him. 'And in the shop.'

'It was nothing,' he says. 'Really. I will be fine.'

'I've booked us in to see Dr Diaz in an hour. I thought it would be good.' He doesn't argue. He nods, slowly, as if it makes sense to him as well.

Diaz's waiting room is an oasis: a feature wall turned into a waterfall, green-tinted water that smells like a theme park running down orange-veneer wood paneling into a trough filled with curious hand-carved stones of slightly off geometric shapes. It's an intentionally artificial replica of something more intrinsically real. Deanna has always focused on the metaphor of it: that such a thing should be here, while people try to find a plateau of normality through such false means. The other walls are the same wooden panels, making this feel like a sauna – another likeness that, Deanna is sure, isn't accidental – and the furniture is either highly functional or nearly decadent, nowhere between the two. There are never other clients waiting, which, again, Deanna is sure is part of the therapy. You sit and talk to each other, or you're silent. Either way, it's a prelude to taking part in the session itself.

Their initial visits with Dr Diaz were preventative. Amit's research told them that the things most likely to destroy a candidate's potential were familial collapse or crisis. This was before Sean died and he told them to think about making sure they kept the lines of communication open. Maybe, he told them, therapy would be a good start. They laughed, because they had always been perfectly happy. They argued, but they saw theirs as healthy arguments, because what couple didn't argue? They aired their grievances, got them out in the open. From there, you move on. Still, they listened to him. He was insistent.

Now, they sit next to each other on a sofa that's so low to the ground and so curved they're almost lying down. The receptionist brings them both a small glass containing some variant of green tea and then goes to her desk which is in another room entirely. There's no choice of drink: it's always tea, and it's always pungent, and it's always intended to be calming. The first few times they hated it, then after a while it just became something that they drank when they came here. They grew to like the taste. (Laurence looked it up: if you try something five times, he read, you can persuade your body to like it. Don't reject it, embrace it, and your body changes its mind. Like, he reasoned, Stockholm Syndrome, but with herbal tea.) Laurence drinks his straight down, as hot as it is, and the receptionist brings him another immediately. She must be watching them, Deanna thinks. There must be a hidden camera in here.

'Won't be long now,' she says. Another part of the process: the waiting. This way, you feel relief when you finally get into the room. Such a wait – never too long to make you angry, never too short to not become troublesome – engenders the desire to talk. Appointments are an hour, but you're paying for ninety minutes of therapy, when you factor everything in. Then the door opens – it's hidden, almost, in one of the walls, defined only by where the lines in the wood panels are – and Dr Diaz beckons them in, shaking their hands as they pass her, smiling at them over her glasses.

'It's been a while,' she says.

'Yes,' Deanna replies. They take their usual seats: two utterly functional chairs in her wooden-chalet office. Laurence looks around at the décor and he's reminded of the video, for some reason. Something so false that feels so very real. 'I felt it important that we came now. Laurence has been . . . It's been a hard few days.' He looks up when he hears his name, suddenly in the moment. It's a reaction that he can't help.

'Laurence? Do you want to tell me what happened?' Diaz asks, looking at Deanna still, but directing the question to Laurence.

'I had a lapse,' Laurence says, abruptly and truthfully. It comes out of nowhere, surprising Deanna. She hadn't really expected him to speak much. 'A fugue, almost. I passed out.'

'Did anything happen to spark that?'

'I panicked. I had a panic attack, I think.'

'It felt the same as the ones you've had before? Brought about by the same thoughts?' They've spoken about Laurence's time at war in the past, who he was then, and what happened to him when he was in the army.

'Yes. Not the same thoughts, but the same feeling.' He looks at Deanna. 'I blacked out a bit and I had trouble breathing. So, maybe some of the same thoughts, yes. But not the rest of it, that was different. I wasn't there.'

'Okay. So do you maybe think this is because of how hard you're working?' Diaz asks. 'I've seen you on the Internet. You're very good with your audience, at putting your case across. You're very convincing.'

'I have to be,' he says.

'Amit – his advisor – he sent him home. He's given him a break from the schedule,' Deanna says. She nods at Diaz, confirming her question.

'So you're tired,' Diaz says to Laurence. She has a smile that works, tells them to trust her.

'I am.' He looks it, in that moment. So tired, more than Deanna's ever seen him before.

'Do you think about Sean a lot?' Diaz asks.

'Yes,' he says. 'Every moment.'

'Which is natural.'

He nods his head. 'I know. I can't shake him.'

'Nor should you. So you had a blip. What do you think caused it?'

'Probably the stress,' he says.

'More than that,' Deanna says. He's lying, she knows. They agreed, when they started coming to see Diaz, that they wouldn't lie in these sessions. They were useless if they did; they only worked with honesty on the table. Now, Deanna wants to be a part of the conversation. She wants to say what she knows, and talk about the *ClearVista* report. He still hasn't told her, and she desperately wants him to. Lying like this, she knows, is simply bottling it up.

'It wasn't,' he says. 'This is just all too much for me, maybe. I need a rest.'

'Please, Laurence,' she says. He looks at her. He stares at her, and she meets it, and he can tell.

169

'Amit told you,' he says. 'Amit fucking told you, didn't he.' Deanna doesn't reply. Dr Diaz sits back and lets them do this. This is what she's best at: starting something and then letting it play out. 'What do you know?'

'He told me about *ClearVista*,' she says, 'and what they said.' Laurence looks at the door. Everything said in the room is private and confidential, but that doesn't make him feel better about it. These are secrets; these are potentially ruinous to him.

'I don't want to do this,' he says.

'We have to,' Deanna tells him.

'Maybe this is important to Deanna, Laurence?' Diaz asks.

'No,' he says. 'It was a mistake, and nobody's business. I am not like that.' He stands up and walks to the door, pressing it so that it swings wide. He rushes through the waterfall-room and out into the parking lot which is surrounded by single-storey pale-brick buildings, nail salons and sandwich shops and coffee shops. Suddenly America as it is all over, these little oases of commercialism. It feels safer here, somehow. He puts his hands on his thighs and bends forward, feeling as if he is going to be sick, as if all of his fears have manifested themselves inside him and now they're forcing their way out. He shudders, and as he does so he feels a hand on his shoulder. It's Deanna, her touch warm, even through his sweater.

'Come on,' she says. He's reticent but complies, walking slowly – shuffling, almost – but letting her take his hand. She leads him back inside, past the waterfall – she hears the sound and thinks how familiar it is to her, that rustle of water, the noise that it makes when droplets of it collide with each other, like a tide drawing back from a shoreline – and to the chair in Diaz's office. Diaz asks him to explain about the report, if he wants to. Deanna begins to do it for him, but Diaz indicates that she should be quiet. This is Laurence's information to share. He holds his breath inside him. He thinks that, if he doesn't, there's a chance he won't be able to find it again, each breath, each inhalation suddenly so precious. He stays silent, and they wait for him.

When the hour is up, Diaz asks them to make another appointment. She tells Laurence that it will be helpful.

'There's no downside,' she says. He nods. He tells Deanna that he'll drive, but he sits behind the wheel and puts his hands at ten and two and doesn't start the engine. He stares forward across the car park at the bookstore and the giant discount store that are across the road.

'Let me take over,' Deanna says. He nods and silently gets out of the car. They swap seats – she holds him as they cross at the front of the hood, just for a second, and he lets her – and then she starts the engine.

'I don't want to go home yet,' he tells her, as

they're pulling out of the lot. 'I need to have some peace for a second.'

She knows where to take him.

They get out at the front of cemetery. They never come at this time: the middle of the day, mid-week. A different sort of people comes here at this time of day. They're older, in general. They're single, older men and women coming to visit their loved ones, ambling between the rows of head-stones as if they're aisles at a supermarket. They're almost browsing, they walk so slowly, their heads reading the names of other people's dead relatives as they pass.

Sean's lot is in a far corner. They paid more for the privacy. There were different tiered packages and they spoke about it almost endlessly in the days after they first met with the undertaker and the lot manager; a way of taking their minds off what had happened and trying to do the best by their son. The conversations where they discussed the money made them feel worse, because they were doing this for themselves, not Sean. The privacy was so that they couldn't be seen when they cried over the stone that marked him. They imagined that their mourning would be eternal, that they would never recover from how broken they felt in those first few terrible weeks. The plot that they finally chose is near some trees, behind a wall. It was in the second highest tier. There are five others here in this nook, but they're always alone when they come to visit. It's like a subliminal schedule created by the mutual experience of the families. The other headstones are all for children as well, all between the ages of four and sixteen. Deanna and Laurence have never spoken about that, but Deanna's thought it: that the parents of those children must have felt the same way as they did. That losing a child is one of the few incontrovertible shared emotional truths.

Now, they don't cry as they once did. They don't change the flowers. Deanna looks for the shape of the toys through the soil, as she always does. They're eternal, or nearly, and that's how he will be. Sean will never get old now and the toys will always be appropriate for him. He'll never grow out of them. Laurence stands at the foot of their son's plot and looks at the headstone. He reads it every time they come here. They always wonder if maybe they couldn't have said more with it. Deanna reads it now and thinks of the dedication in her book. The same resonance – and yet, somehow, there aren't words enough.

She holds Laurence's hand. 'It's okay,' she says.

'I know,' he tells her. 'I mean, it's not.' She pulls him close. She thinks of the cover art of his favorite album, a Bob Dylan record from the 1960s. They have the sleeve framed in their kitchen: the singer and his girlfriend, huddled together in each other's presence, walking along a street. So close that you can feel the love between them, and there's no mystery of what it means.

'I love you,' she says. He's silent. 'Amit said that there was a video.' She doesn't know if this is the right time to bring this up. She doesn't know that there will ever be a right time. He nods, and he kisses her.

'I only want to protect you all, you know. It's all that I've ever wanted.' He says it while he looks at the grave, as if he can see through it, right down, past the topsoil, the toys, into the thin wood of the coffin itself. The fact that he admitted it to her has to be enough, for now. She kisses her hand and rests it briefly on the headstone, and she whispers to her son that she loves him.

'Do you want to go?' she asks. Laurence shakes his head.

'Let's stay here for a while,' he says. They sit down on the ground, leaning back against the wall, and they stare out. Across the way, behind the cemetery, there's a hill, and behind the hill the sun begins to descend, and then its light comes around them, golden orange. It frames them as they look at all the stones.

'I can't believe how long it's been,' Deanna says as it becomes dark.

She opens the front door. There are no lights downstairs. Some light comes down from upstairs, and from the moon, through the windows – the girls didn't darken the glass – but the house is otherwise dark.

'I feel a little better,' Laurence says. 'I'm sorry

174

to have given you a scare.' He stretches as he takes off his coat and Deanna flicks all the lights on. 'I'm so tired,' he says. He walks to the kitchen, which is chaos: the unwashed bowls of some dinner or other that might have been attempted – a dessert, Deanna sees, sugar and flour both out of the cupboards, their dust on the surfaces – and then a pizza box on the table, the slices half-eaten, the topping peeled from them. 'Pigs,' Laurence says. He smiles, half-there but honest, and he takes one of the untouched slices and bites from it. 'Where are they?'

'Bed, I guess,' Deanna says. 'It's quiet. I'll go check.' She leans in and kisses him on the lips. Their faces fit together the way that they have for years and years now, knowing instinctively how to find each other. That never changes.

Upstairs, there's a light left on in the bathroom that the girls share. Deanna looks in, and there's hair in the sink, Lane's clippers plugged in at the wall still. Deanna pulls them out and puts them in a plastic tray on the side with her other accouterments. She scoops handfuls of the damp hair out, balling it up and throwing it into the small trashcan under the sink.

'Gross,' she says. 'Lane,' slightly raising her voice, hoping that her daughter hears her, knowing that she won't be asleep, 'this is gross.' She puts the light out and walks into Alyx's room. Her youngest is already in bed, the covers pulled up tight around her head. Deanna backs out, pulling the door to.

She knocks on Lane's door, and her daughter answers.

'What?' she asks. Deanna tries the handle, but it's locked.

'Listen,' she says, close to the wood so that she'll be heard, 'you left the house in a hell of a state. Your hair will clog the drains, I've told you.' She thinks, as she says it: that Lane's been keeping her hair short now for months, but the hair that she pulled out of the sink was much longer. It must have grown more than she realized.

'I'm sorry,' Lane says. There's something in her voice: an actual contrition. She's not apologizing for the mess. Deanna rushes to Alyx's room and throws back the duvet, and her daughter is still awake: lying there, terrified, her hair taken back so close to her head that it's almost non-existent. Deanna wants to think it's a joke, a wig, a trick that's being played on her, but she sees the uneven lengths, the section where they worked out that they had gone too far and obviously turned chicken – a mullet, almost, a longer rat-tail of hair at the back – and Alyx starts to cry. Deanna doesn't know what to say: she just stands there and looks at her daughter, now writhing on the sheets.

She looks like Sean, she keeps thinking. She looks like Sean.

The crying escalates, and Deanna bends down and holds her, and tells her that it'll be okay. Alyx tries to form words, but they're distorted by her tears and the huffs of air that she drags in. She starts to hyperventilate; she's done this a few times before, especially in the wake of Sean's death. Heaving breaths that she can't quite fully form.

'Okay,' Deanna says. She goes to her daughter and sits on the bed and she cradles her. 'Okay, calm down.' She leans back, towards the door, so that she'll be heard. 'Lane,' she says, 'get in here.' She hears the click of Lane's door lock, and the creak.

'Alyx asked me to do it,' Lane says, before she's even in the room.

'She's eight years old! She doesn't know what she wants!'

'I thought it might look cute,' Lane says. She's swaying, and she smells of something.

'You're drunk,' she says. 'What the hell did you think you were doing, drinking when you were looking after her?' Lane half-smirks and tries to hide it. 'For god's sake, Lane!'

'I asked her to do it,' Alyx says. 'I wanted to look like Lane does.' She says it with such innocence, with almost a sense of protecting her sister. It wasn't malicious – neither of them thought. Lane should have known better, but she didn't. That's an argument for another time, Deanna thinks.

'I'm sorry,' Alyx says. She sobs harder, into her mother's shoulder. Deanna wraps herself around her daughter, almost entirely cradling her.

'What's going on up there?' Laurence asks. His voice comes up through the stairwell and they all turn.

177

'Daddy?' Alyx asks.

'Hey Pumpkin,' he says. He seems to almost skip up the stairs, taking them so lightly, and then he's in the hallway. Fragments of the old Laurence; where the day they've had has, in some way, been cathartic for him.

'Please don't freak out,' Lane says.

'At what?' Deanna leans back and he sees Alyx as he enters the room. Her face is lost and confused and sad, bleary-eyed, tears streaming down her face. He sees her, with her hair so short, and she looks so much like her dead brother. She is a reminder. He rushes into the room and stands over her, and touches Alyx's head. He puts his hand to it, gently, to turn it and see the damage, and he looks at Lane as he feels the thin, soft stubble.

'What did you do?' he asks. His voice is quiet, though not calm. It quivers. He feels the vibrations of his anger, through his chest and arms. He sees his hand shaking. 'What did you do, Lane?' he screams, sudden and vicious. He spits with each word, and Lane falls to her sister's bed in shock.

'Laurence,' Deanna says, trying to calm him. She lets go of Alyx and stands up, moving to the end of the bed, almost blocking her daughters from him. He's usually a calm man: his angry moments are quiet and tempered, and always borne of frustration, not fury. He clenches his fists, his arms at his sides.

'What did you do?' he roars. He turns away from

them, trying to control his breathing, to calm himself down. He sees himself, standing there on one side of the room, Deanna and Lane and Alyx on the other, terrified of his rage. This is not the same as the video, he knows – a coincidence, nothing more, because they are not as scared of him now as they are in that, not even close; and he is not blank, but incandescent with rage – but otherwise this is the same: the layout of them, the three of them separated from him as he stands alone. He feels his throat close and his eyes well up; he cannot breathe. He puts his hand out, to find the doorframe so that he can steady himself.

'I know it's bad,' Deanna says, 'but we can fix it, I'm sure.' She steps towards him and touches Alyx's head with one hand, reaches out the other to touch him, to calm him down. He flinches away from her. 'It'll be okay, Laurence.'

He doesn't say it, because he can't; but he thinks that nothing will ever be okay again.

CHAPTER 7

He lies on the bed and sobs. Deanna asks him what's wrong but he won't tell her. He brushes her off, and she touches him, and he acts as if her fingers are burning him. Her touch: it's a reminder of something else, somehow.

Eventually he stands up and he goes to the girls and wakes them and holds them. He tells them that he loves them and he says that he's sorry. He doesn't know what made him do it, he says. Afterwards he doesn't go back to bed. He looks at his laptop in the kitchen and he hides the screen every time Deanna walks near him. She makes him a drink – decaf coffee with whisky in it, a ratio of one shot to three, designed to calm him right down while he thinks he's being kept awake – and as he drinks it he paces. He doesn't talk. Instead, he bites at his nails. They're meant to be manicured for the sake of handshakes and signings and television close-ups, but they've been destroyed by stress. He hasn't bitten his nails in years and he has started at the flesh around them as well. Deanna sees how red they are, where a couple have started to bleed.

At one point he stands at the window and looks

out onto their garden. She sees his reflection in the dark of the glass, and his eyes are closed. She wonders what he's thinking.

'So where is he?' the Texan asks. Amit has a breakdown of this man's actual worth, right down to the cent. He knows the boards that he sits on, the people he employs, the properties that are in his name. The chances of major investment in Laurence's campaign at this point are small, but the promise of it in the future is what they're really after. If he decides that Laurence is the man to run the party – and, therefore, the country – his money will buy support and votes from the rest of the party. It's a simple process: you get the big guns behind a candidate and the smaller ones will all turn their sights in procession.

'Laurence really had to go back to see his family,' Amit says. 'He's been travelling a lot.' It's universal: everybody's been there. No need to go into further details, keep the lie clean. 'He wanted to come, you know that.'

'So you keep saying.' The rings on the investor's fingers are too tight, the fat of his hands bulging over the gold. 'You know, I like Laurence, I really do. He's a good man.'

'He is.'

'No bullshit with him, either. That is, so I thought. Maybe it was just no bullshit until now?' He smiles, full and broad. 'Tell me, son, are you bullshitting me?'

'No,' Amit says. He knows that something's wrong but that there's a story that has to be stuck to. The Texan pushes his phone across the table, the screen bright with a webpage. It's one of the political gossip blogs, and there's a photo taken in a supermarket in Staunton, grainy and out of focus, but clearly Laurence. He's on the floor, being attended to. Amit hasn't seen that yet, it must have just gone up, and he's blindsided.

'Here's what I think happened,' the Texan says.

'I haven't seen that,' Amit interrupts.

'Here's what I think happened,' the large man repeats. 'Laurence is pretty fragile. He'll get better, sure, but he's had one hell of a shitty year. He's having trouble coping with the stress of this all, and it's getting too much for him. Am I right?'

'It's been hard on him, of course, but he's overcome the adversity—'

'Don't play that card with me, son. I said already, no bullshit. All that crap flies with the newspapers and the TV assholes, but not with me. He's falling apart, right?'

'He's tired,' Amit says. 'He's fine, I swear to God that he's fine. But he needed a break. He needed to be with his family for a week or two.' The investor doesn't say anything. He's got a smile that begs Amit to keep talking, even though inside he knows he should shut up. 'I told him to take time off, to get his head together. It's a long trail now, between this and then if he gets the nomination; then there's the path to the White House, and then, you know, four years of whatever, then four more years, because this is a long haul. It's a marathon not a sprint, that's what we're always saying.' He breathes and checks himself. 'He'll be fine, though.'

'And now I believe you. That wasn't so hard, was it?'

'Yes,' Amit says. 'It's also true that he wanted to meet you and that he wanted to talk his plans through with you himself. He didn't want this to be a closed door.'

'And it isn't. It's open, still. But he needs to come out here sometime soon, fit as a fiddle. Shake some hands and kiss some babies. Talk about abortion with some people here, let them understand he isn't trying to support the birth of the antichrist.' He plays with the signet ring on his wedding finger; unlike all of the others, it's loose, ready to be taken off. 'He needs to be here and only here for a good while, you get what I'm saying?' He starts tapping the table again, his fingers making little tick-tick noises on the wood.

'I know what you're saying,' Amit tells him. 'And he will be.'

'Then I suspect that we're done here for today.' The investor stands up and shakes Amit's hand, his grip intense; the meeting is done. 'I'll see you real soon, when you come back with Laurence. You call my girl and have her set it up for as soon as he's able. Don't leave it too long, though. I've been getting pestered by Homme for quite some time now, and I'm going to have to pick a side I think could actually win this time.'

He leaves Amit alone in the boardroom. There's a window behind the desk that looks out onto the floodlit football stadium that the man owns. These are the best seats, Amit thinks: it's like looking down from the camera's view, even though there's nothing down there to see. He takes out his phone and checks for missed calls, but there's nothing. Forty-eight hours, they said. That means they'll have to call by tomorrow morning at the latest. He texts Laurence, telling him that the meeting went well, that he'll be in touch in the morning with news from *ClearVista*.

He looks out at the grass. It's patchy, used and trodden up. Even from as high as he is he can see where the turf needs attending under the glare of the lights.

It's the middle of the night when Deanna finally goes back to sleep. She asks Laurence to come upstairs with her, tells him that he needs his sleep, but he refuses. He says that he isn't tired. She gets into their bed by herself and she lies on her back and doesn't sleep. Instead, she thinks about when he first entered politics: a well-liked, well-respected lawyer, courted by the party to throw his hat into the ring as a State Senator. They met with one of the previous nominees, who, in the 1980s, had been predicted as a future president. He never was, of course, and he existed only as a footnote, a moment in history where white men with money suggested something that never actually paid off. Laurence and Deanna met with the once-nominee at a party in the early days: him and his wife, both now well into their retirement. They sat in a quiet room with a plate of canapés that they had commandeered from a wandering waiter, and they spoke about their families, their hopes for the future. The once-nominee asked Laurence what he hoped to achieve over the span of his career.

'Not the role, but the goal,' the older man said. Laurence told them – the Presidency – and they nodded, and they smiled. 'It won't happen,' the older man told him. 'Won't happen, you have to remember that, or you'll go crazy trying. But the very best of luck to you.' They all drank to it as if they were sharing a joke. Now, Deanna wonders.

She listens to the house, the bedroom door left open. She can hear Laurence downstairs, back at the laptop; the occasional tapping of his fingers on the keyboard. She thinks that it almost sounds like rain if she closes her eyes and imagines water running down windows and gutters and roof tiles.

Alyx shakes her, and Deanna wakes up and sees her face. It takes her second to remember that it's not Sean. She sees him there for that second, as she does when she's dreaming. They look so similar now. Alyx climbs into bed with her mother and they hold each other, and Deanna runs her hand over her daughter's head. The feel of the short hair, almost stubble in places, longer in others – this is all too familiar. Deana kisses her head, right on the top. She thinks about when they were babies; that you aren't meant to put pressure on that part. How soft it is, and how you can see it rise and fall with as their blood pulses around their bodies, if you look carefully.

'Stay here,' Deanna says after a while, 'I'm going to get some coffee.' She slides out of bed and Alyx cuddles down into the mattress. Her father is in bed next to her. He didn't wake Deanna when he came upstairs, but he hasn't been next to her for long, she reckons. She decides to let them both sleep again.

She turns the coffee machine on and opens the French windows, so that she can feel the coldness of the outside world on her skin, through the T-shirt that she slept in. Her phone beeps. It's a text from Amit.

How is he? I haven't heard from him.

I don't know, Deanna replies. *He's very upset. I feel so useless.*

Don't. So little you can do. Support him.

That's not what I signed up for.

But it's what you've got to do.

He won't tell me what was in the report or the video. He won't talk about them.

Amit's reply takes longer to come. He is writing it, Deanna can see that much, but he doesn't send it for over a minute. When it finally does, it's short. *He will*, it says. *When this is fixed. Give him time.*

Deanna waits to see if there's another text, but nothing comes.

Amit paces the room, clutching his phone in his hand. He keeps thinking that it has started ringing: some residual vibration running through it and into his hand. It hasn't, and it doesn't. He orders breakfast – the reception in his hotel room is good, and he doesn't want to lose that, to risk stepping into the elevator and somehow missing that tiny window where *ClearVista* would try to make contact with him – and he eats his croissants while he stares at the handset. He checks the time he first called them and begins a countdown. The contract with them – he's checked – assures a callback within seventy-two hours. He dares them to break that rule.

His phone finally rings just after eleven. Ten minutes shy of the deadline. It's not a number that he recognizes – it doesn't say *ClearVista* on the handset's screen – and it's a chain of numbers that doesn't look like a phone number to him. There's no discernable area code; a phone number that comes from nowhere, just like the video. He answers, and the automated voice asks him to wait while his call is connected. There's no hold music this time, and no sign that anything is happening for a minute or so. He checks his cellphone to see that the call is still connected. Then the line clicks and there's suddenly ambient noise: the hubbub of an office, of a call center.

'Hello?' he asks.

'You're through to *ClearVista*,' the woman's voice says, 'and speaking to Amy. How can I help you today?'

'Hi Amy,' Amit says. 'I called the other day because we had some results through from our survey.'

'Account three-five-seven-oh-six-one-nine?'

'That's the one.'

'Can you confirm the pass for me?' He recites the code again. 'I can see your account right here. I've got the account up on my screen. What seems to be the issue?'

'The results that came through. They don't seem as if they can be accurate, not for the survey that we submitted.'

'We make every effort to ensure accuracy, but of course some data can fall through the cracks. Did you read the section in the contracts about fallibility?' There's something off, he thinks. The voice sounds too clean, too crisp. Most people would assume that means composure, but he knows different. When he left *ClearVista* – when he quit – they were talking about whether they could use the algorithm to predict the reasons that people would call them, to head off customer service enquiries before they because an issue. Listening to her now, and her pretense that she is real, Amit thinks that they might have been successful. But the background noise; it's all designed to add comfort to the listener. The earlier

188

voice is meant to sound fake: this one is intended to deceive. He plays along. There's still, he thinks, a good chance he's wrong. Maybe he's just paranoid.

'I've gone through the contracts over and over,' Amit says, 'but this seems like more than that. It seems like the results were wrong. I've seen other results and they seem different.'

'Okay, sir. Well, *ClearVista* updates its results based on current market trends and Internet results, so often the results can seem inaccurate until you've taken into account all of our sources.'

'Can you open the file? Just have a look at what—'

'Sir,' Amy interrupts, 'we're not allowed to look at any clients' files. That information is strictly personal.'

'Right, but I'm giving you permission,' Amit says.

'I just can't do it,' Amy says. 'It's a hard and fast rule for all employees here.'

'Are you even real?' Amit asks. There's a pause, where she doesn't reply. He doesn't suppose she can. If she lies to him, that's an issue in itself; some bullshit Asimovian *law of robotics* or some-thing. There were always people in the office, in the early days, going on about that; saying that if you automate something, if it starts to nudge into AI territory, there are other considerations. Now, though, he doesn't have time for this. 'Look, I've got a problem with this, and you're telling me that

189

there *can't* be a problem, but you can't look at the file to check?'

'Sir.'

'Watch the video. Watch the video. There's a video that makes no sense.'

'The video is distorted?'

Amit sighs. 'Yes. Fine. It's distorted.'

'Would you like us to make a new video for you? I can action that immediately.' There's the sound of typing in the background. 'Is there anything else we can do for you today?'

'Can I speak to somebody who *has* read the report? A supervisor or something?'

'I'm afraid nobody at *ClearVista* has access to the reports. Confidentiality dictates that we don't.'

'Can I get somebody to read it? So that I can talk to them then?'

'Confidentiality dictates—'

'For God's sake,' Amit says, interrupting her. 'Fine. Whatever. Can you run the whole report again?'

'Based on the results of the initial test? Of course. We'll send that through before close of day.'

'And the video.'

'And the video, of course. Thank you for using *ClearVista*.' The line goes dead and Amit is left in the hotel room. He doesn't know what he wants from this place. He goes online and books a flight home, and he gets a cab straight to the airport and he waits there even though his flight isn't for hours yet; and he walks around and through the

190

identical magazine and perfume shops that seem to repeat themselves over and over through every terminal at every airport, and browses vending machines which sell headphones that cost more than he would ever spend on them.

Deanna cuts the rest of Alyx's hair back to nearly zero, the straggling threads and parts that Lane did a bad job on; and she uses the scissors first, then Lane's clippers. Deanna tells her daughter to stay quiet, because she's been protesting. She's decided that she likes it: the ramshackle nature of it, the straggly threads of hair that her school would go insane over; and, Deanna thinks, the fact that it reminds her of her brother, even if she doesn't realize it. Deanna tries to make the best of this, working her daughter's hair to as neat a state as she can manage. Alyx sits on a chair in the kitchen, newspaper surrounding her on the floor, and Deanna cuts it all down to the same level using Lane's clippers: a grade two, all over. When they're done, Deanna puts talc on her head, because she doesn't want Alyx to get any sort of rash. She smells like she did when she was a baby.

Laurence spends the day doing nothing around the house, walking from room to room, following the rest of his family and being where they are as much as possible. He doesn't speak: more, he watches them, wanting to just stay close. The only times he interjects are when either of his daughters volunteer that they want to do something. Lane, he fights with, and she storms out, refusing to be grounded because of what she did; and refusing to kowtow to Laurence's rules. With Alyx, he controls it more, not telling Deanna why, but instructing Alyx that she shouldn't spend long in the garden by herself, not with reporters (or whoever) likely to break in; and when she asks if she can go to her friend's house at the weekend, he tells her that she can't.

'It's better if we spend some time together,' he says. She stamps her feet, but only a little. They order Chinese takeout for dinner, and they let her pick the dishes. They let her pick the movie to watch afterwards as well (and she chooses from the Disney shelf, which was almost inevitable), and they all sit on the sofa and let her stay up well past her bedtime. Laurence doesn't say anything, or watch the movie. He's there but his eyes are elsewhere, glazed and looking through the TV and the wall and the house, off into something else.

Deanna listens to Laurence saying goodnight to Alyx after that, putting her into bed. He offers to read to her. He hasn't done it in years, and she tells him that she's okay; she can read to herself. She likes the sound of her own voice in her head. His voice cracks as he wishes her goodnight. He comes downstairs then and he takes the glass of wine that Deanna pours for him but then doesn't sip from it, and he doesn't watch the television or talk to her. Instead he keeps his eyes mostly shut while Deanna tries not to watch him.

'I need a bath,' he says after a while. 'I need to think.'

He goes upstairs. Deanna is alone.

Amit's apartment is both too warm and too small. He forgot to take the trash out before he left, which was a mistake, because it's stewed in his absence: a reek of stale doughy goods, pizzas and submarine sandwiches that he only ever ate half of because of his near constant state of perpetual rush. He puts his phone onto charge – it's a cell reception black hole in here, buried in the middle of hundreds of apartments as he is – and then checks his messages on his land line. There's only one, from his father, practically begging him to call when he gets the chance, but he knows that he doesn't have the time for his family right now, that he's very busy with work: the usual guilt-trip stuff. As he listens to his father's tinny voice snaking around his apartment, he opens the windows to try and let some clean air in and some of the stale out.

He checks the fridge, and there's the usual stale milk and hardened yellow cheese. He doesn't even know why he keeps paying rent on this place: might as well get rid of it and stay in hotels on the few nights he isn't actually on the road. But, he thinks, maybe this is wise; not to put all of his cards into the campaign. What if Laurence is a time bomb? He dismisses the thought. He's the candidate. He's always been the candidate. There's a torn-out editorial article stuck to his fridge door, from one of the last print newspapers' politics sections. It's dated the week before Sean died. *This is going to be Laurence Walker's race to lose*, it says. And they're talking about the presidency, not even the nomination, predicting where they were going to be two, nearly three years after that point. It mentions Amit – *Princeton wunderkind Amit Suri* – as a key part of Laurence's success. *They're a team.* Amit wonders what they would make of the *ClearVista* video. No: he wonders what they would make of Laurence's reaction to it. Because he was afraid, Amit knows, that maybe, somehow, it could be true.

He opens the video on his computer and streams it to the TV. It's a new set, bought to celebrate getting Laurence back on the road: state of the art, the nicest set within his budget. The salesman assured him that HoloGas – 3D images, right in the middle of your living room – was the next big thing. Amit has barely used it, and he's never bothered to replace the gas canister that actually makes it work. It'll have to be glorious old-school, flat-as-life-isn't, instead. He sits on the sofa and watches the images on the TV, larger than he's seen them before. Still, the video is the same. He doesn't know what he expected. He flicks the channels to something else, the normality of television where they're not talking about politics. A fashion show, a cookery show, a cartoon. He tries to switch himself off as much as possible and just take this for what it is. He sleeps a little, shutting his eyes and then opening them when an hour has passed. This is, he tells himself, no way to live.

He stands and stretches, and then sits in front of his computer and opens his emails. A few days' worth of the unimportant stuff, the stuff that he can probably just abandon and forget about if he really wants, but that he should probably answer. *Can Laurence do this?* and *We were wondering if Laurence . . .* He marks some as important and forwards a few to his assistant (who works out of her old office at the moment, where she's a law clerk), and deletes the most banal. *Laurence Walker might be interested in the plight of the road-wolves*: delete. He checks his email again, refreshing it, because *ClearVista* haven't sent the new results or video through yet. They'll be in no rush, he reasons. It's probably all automated anyway. He stands up, steps away from the computer, and then the familiar ping of an incoming email sounds. A watched pot never boils, he thinks.

Please find attached your ClearVista report, reads the subject line. *We have run these a second time, for optimization.* Amit opens it and flicks straight to the end of the file, praying that this time the final numbers are different, but they aren't. He hoped for error – either human or in the numbers, he doesn't care which – but the results are exactly the same. It's disappointing but obvious. He hopes that the video will be different, but he knows that it won't. So, he reasons, there's a problem somewhere else down the line. There's a glitch somewhere that they can't see. It's fine: they just don't release the fact that they ever even had a report made. Spin that: Homme needed to prove that he's honest; Laurence Walker doesn't need to convince anybody of such an obvious truth.

But then there's the issue of the delegates. *They* won't go for not releasing the video; and, if they do, it will only be after some heady persuasion. He doesn't want them to see the video or the report; it might scare them. Maybe some of the people he worked with back at *ClearVista* could help? It was years ago, and there was a mass exodus not that long after he left, but a few people saw it through. They'll know much more than him about how this works; might even have some contacts still there who can dig in for him. Back when they all started working there, they spent the first year examining other people's algorithms and systems; looking at them in an almost terrifying level of detail, trying to work out how they did what they did. Their first job was to reverse-engineer previous systems and algorithms, to see what they did. As a team, they turned them into useable data and picked holes in them; looked for ways to improve them, to turn the system in on itself, use it to predict something else. They fine-tuned it by adding in extra information, worked out exactly how to start pinpointing this stuff, how to make it less fallible. They were all good at deciphering the results and understanding the hows and whys, but Thomas Hershel was the best.

Hershel – he went by his surname, an affectation that everybody understood, somehow, from the minute that they met him – was the closest thing that they had to a savant in their research group. He was a natural mathematician. He scammed an online casino when he was in high school, breaking systems that were meant to be infallible; but he was brilliant, avoiding a prison sentence on a technicality. After that, he went to university on a grant that precluded him from gambling, so naturally he spent his days smoking pot and doing coke and farming money from MMO subsystems. He was part of the cabal that broke *Bitcoin* way back, was the rumor, rendering the entire currency useless overnight. *ClearVista* poached him during his final year, throwing money at him – money, and the opportunity to make his name in the field that he understood better than almost anybody else. But it was a job that was weirdly below him. If he had given half a shit, Amit knew, Hershel could have changed the world. As it was, he was headhunted by every statistics company in the world, finance companies, futurists and banks. He didn't bother turning up for interviews or open days, but everybody still wanted him. *ClearVista* gave him power and told him he could keep his own hours. That was enough for him. He was there when Amit quit, but then – rumor was – left a couple of years later, when the algorithm was done.

Like everybody else when there was little more work to be done, he cashed out.

Amit searches his name in his emails. He doesn't have a telephone number for Hershel, but he's got other details. *Facebook*, *Twitter*. No sooner has Amit sent his DM, making contact, than Hershel has replied. Always in front of a computer of some sort.

Amit long time no hear u good

I'm fine, Amit writes. *I have something I need to talk to you about. Totally off the record, black ops stuff. You interested?*

Sure okay you want to get together 4 lunch nxt wk

Amit replies. *I was thinking sooner. Where are you living?*

Georgetown

Seriously? That's only twenty minutes away.

srsly

Can I come over now?

Bring pizza u got a deal

The message is followed by a map pin. The house is just behind the main stretch of shops. Expensive houses. Amit flicks to street view; it's private, nothing to be seen past thick black metal gates. He changes his suit for a tracksuit and a faded T-shirt of a band he hasn't listened to in years, and he pops his ear buds in, pulls his trainers on, and goes out into the night.

It's been a while since he's been in this part of the city, not since he visited a girlfriend who lived here back in his college days. She couldn't have afforded the rent now. Hershel's street is barely recognizable from how it was a decade ago; they've gated the ends, two large wrought-iron sealed egresses leading in, a security hut at one side. The houses here have been knocked through, it looks like, and what was once thirty or so on this stretch is now – going by the colors and doorways and paths – only ten, five on each side. It's started to rain and Amit is soaked through, the pizza box clutched up to his chest. He goes to the small hut and knocks on the door, sheltering under the small canopy above the doorway. It swings open, the handle pulled by a security officer who has stayed sitting at his desk. In front of him, a bank of miniature screens shows the security cameras that obviously line this place.

'Nobody told me they're waiting for a delivery,' the man says.

'No,' Amit tells him. 'I'm here to see Hershel. Thomas Hershel.'

'Mr Hershel?' He rolls his eyes slightly, as if this is a common occurrence. 'I'll call it through.' Amit waits there, the rain beating his back. The pizza box feels slightly damp in his hands, but warm still. 'Mr Hershel? I've got a guest for you,' the security guard says, and then waits before leaning back to Amit. 'He says to send you through. Second on the left.' He presses a button on the desk and the gates creak into life. They're only barely apart before Amit's squeezed through the gap and is running to the porch of the house. He gets to the door – finally, underneath an overhang, dry for a second – and looks for a doorbell, but there's nothing. He knocks, and he waits; and when it opens, he barely recognizes the Hershel that's standing there.

'It's been a long time,' Hershel says. He's changed. His teeth have been done, fixed and straightened. And hair plugs, Amit thinks, because before he was receding from both the front and the middle, and now there's a full head, scraped back into a ponytail that's held with a thick, yellow elastic band. He's put on weight and he's wearing a dressing gown and Croc sandals. Amit holds out his hand to shake Hershel's, and then notices that his right hand isn't all there: two fingers gone from it, from the outside. It's been smoothed over, an excellent plastic surgery job, but it's jarring. Hershel looks down and notices. 'Jesus Christ! Where did they go?' he shouts, and then he laughs, a dry roll that turns into a wheezed cough. He stands aside and waves the hand with a flourish. 'Welcome to Casa del Hershel.'

The décor is gaudy: marble floors and faux-antique furniture, and paintings – or prints, Amit can't be sure – of art, shapes and colors and canvases built up from noise. Money has been spent. Hershel pads through the house, showing it off, talking Amit through. Giving him a tour that he didn't offer and that Amit didn't ask for.

'Two dining rooms,' he says, 'formal and informal. Whatever the sitch.'

'Where do you want this pizza?' Amit asks. Hershel spins on his heel, remembering the food.

'Oh dude! Yes! I'm starving. You still smoke?' Amit shakes his head. 'I still smoke, which, you know. At our age, right? Come through here, come through. We'll whatever.' He walks through an arched doorway and into a living room that seems to stretch the width of the house. A fish tank lines one wall, a television the other, a HoloGas unit that's hooked up to a videogame console. A boy and a girl, looking as if they're barely out of college, swipe at the air with their hands held out like rackets, playing against digital versions of famous tennis players. There are five others here, Amit counts, all around the same age. Beautiful and tanned, like the models that work outside those pitch-dark clothes shops that line the malls. All of them seem to be wearing the same cut-off shorts and slackened vests. Amit wonders where Hershel met them: they don't have the air of being his friends, that's immediately apparent. He likely found them in some bar, told them what was at his place – drugs, games, money – and they flocked. There are bottles on the sideboards, empty, and a thick, heavy bag of powder by the fish tank, on a table all of its own. Amit puts the pizza on a table behind the tennis players and Hershel opens the box, pulling a slice out with his good hand, eating while he talks. 'This is Amit,' he says to the younger people sitting around the room, 'I used to work with him. He's a good guy.' They all turn and wave. 'You've been well – I've seen you, on the TV. Doing good work with that guy, seems like.'

'Vote Laurence Walker,' Amit says, in his best electioneering voice.

'Yeah, I don't vote,' Hershel says. 'You know how it is. All this,' he says, and he swoops his arm around the room, as if that provides an excuse. 'But you . . .' He wags his finger. 'Not like you can escape it.'

'Not really,' Amit says.

'So what can I do you for, Amit? I'm guessing this isn't a social visit.'

'*ClearVista*,' Amit says. 'You still got contacts there?'

'What do you want with them?' he asks. He shakes his head. 'They're locked tight.' He sits on one of the sofas, immediately slumping down on the soft leather. He looks over at the tennis players and smiles at one of the girls. 'You know how I lost these?' he asks Amit, holding up his hand, the soft section where there should be two fingers at the end that are simply not there any more.

'Didn't like to ask.'

'I got it because I was a fucking idiot. I left a trail. Vegas, you believe that? This is some middle-ages level shit, doing this sort of thing. Like Joe Pesci in a movie, they took my fucking fingers. Since then, I have kept my nose clean.' He grins;

a golden tooth just off-center, next to perfectly gleaming porcelains that look like they cost a fortune. 'Metaphorically, of course.' One of the girls comes over and sits next to him, draping herself over almost a half of his body, and she kisses him, something in her mouth that she passes across, pushing it with her tongue onto his. 'This is Cindy. Cindy, Amit and I worked together, once. Long time ago.'

'It wasn't that long.'

'It's a fraction of a life, Amit. It's been, what, six years? That's a tenth, a twelfth of the whole. It's a huge amount of time. I thought maybe you were coming to me to ask for money.'

'No,' Amit says, 'but if you're offering it, I have a campaign to manage.' He smiles as well. This isn't the Hershel he remembers. He's older than these kids in here by a decade at least, and he looks older still. He looks tired, playing at being a child himself.

'What do you need with *ClearVista*?'

'Circle of trust?'

'Sure,' Hershel says, sitting forward. Whatever he took from Cindy hasn't set in yet, but it will. Amit thinks about how good Hershel's mind was with this stuff, how he could decode things that the rest of them barely had a shot at.

'It's my client.' He assumes that Cindy won't have a clue who that is. 'We got a report commissioned from *ClearVista* about his chances of success in the elections.'

'Didn't say what you wanted?'

'No. But, I mean—'

'And that happens. It's the algorithm. There'll be something there. He likes abortion, right? It'll be that.'

'He doesn't *like* abortion. Nobody *likes* abortion. He's—'

'Whatever. You can't change the numbers. Like they say, the numbers don't lie.' He approximates the cold female robot voice of the video.

'It's not just that. It's the video that was sent through.' Hershel perks up, sitting forward, brushing Cindy off.

'You went premium? Excellent. What did it show?'

'It was awful.' Amit lowers his voice. 'It was his family crying. And Larry – Lawrence – was . . . I mean, I don't know.'

'Must have come from something.'

'They're in mourning still. Maybe that.'

'Maybe.' Hershel sits back and runs his tongue over his teeth. 'Show it to me.'

'What?'

'The video. Show it to me.' He snatches Amit's phone and holds to sync it with the television. 'It on here?' he asks, and before Amit can answer he's opened the video app and pressed play on the only file that Amit's got saved. The models all groan as their game is interrupted, but they don't make too much fuss, shuffling over instead to another of the sofas, where they spark up and dig in to the pizza.

Amit watches the scene being drawn in in 3D. It's an approximation rather than true 3D, but the system does what it can: Laurence and his family; the crying, louder than he's heard it before, over this far-too expensive sound system. He's seen this too many times, he thinks; he knows the beats of it, the count of the sobs, the exact way that their faces look. It's too familiar.

'Well, now,' Hershel says, leaning forward, and then standing up to get close to the projection, 'this really is quite fucked up.' Everybody in the room is watching it; nobody's smiling any more.

Hershel slaps his own face, then brings up Laurence's results on his screen and stares at them. He mumbles under his breath; he fights off the effect of whatever the pill was, waves his half-whole hand at the screen to control it, scrolling through the results. He makes notes in another app and murmurs. Amit sits behind him, drinking flat Coke from a whisky tumbler – the only clean glass he could find; for all the money here, everything is dirty and in need of attention. He watches Hershel work.

'Have you got the original questions?'

'Laurence does.'

'Get me those. I can't see why the results did what they did. The algorithm shouldn't have done this.'

'You see the problem?'

'I mean, it's too tight a margin, but there's

nothing here that'll totally cut him out. This isn't how the algorithm behaves.'

'Maybe the algorithm doesn't work?'

Hershel doesn't even hesitate. 'The algorithm's as close to perfect as these things get. The data miner adapts, but that's all automated, and then that feeds into the algorithm. Hasn't been touched by a human being in nearly two years now, and it hasn't needed to be.'

'So you are still in contact?'

Hershel hesitates. 'If they need me,' he says. 'But they haven't. Like I say, *ClearVista* is basically self-sufficient. Runs itself, man.' He turns around. 'But sure, I'll look at this. It's a challenge, right? No guarantees. You give me all the data, and I'll see what I can find out.'

'That's all I wanted.'

Hershel flicks through the file again, but his eyes have gone glassy, and his head lolls. 'This is good,' he says.

'Not good.'

'Maybe not. But, you know. Interesting.' He smiles at Amit, and that smile falls into a laugh. 'It's so great to see you, man!'

'Yeah, you too,' Amit says. Hershel's done for the night, he knows. 'Great to see you,' he repeats; but as he walks past the reflective surfaces of the mansion on the way to the front door, and back out into the rain, he wonders if he's telling the truth.

★　★　★

Deanna doesn't sleep. She lies next to Laurence and listens to his breathing and she feels the ebb of his chest as he does. His face is a scowl, his hands tightly clenched, the duvet balled up into tight fists. He woke up in the night to an email. She caught a glimpse of the sense – some email address *@ClearVista* – and realized that they must be sending the report through again. He didn't tell her, though: he only opened it, read it and then put it away. He went back to sleep, or shut his eyes and pretended to. Now, she watches him sleep, and then gets up, the same way she always does when she doesn't want to wake him. She makes it downstairs without waking the house. She sits at the table and she swipes at the tablet that's on the surface in front of her. There's an email from her agent, about her novel, sent to her in the middle of the night. She opens it and reads it.

He's just finished reading *Into the Silent Water*, he writes. She looks at the time the email was sent: nearly half past two in the morning. He says that he couldn't stop; that's the sort of a book it is. He loves it. He says it's odd, but *powerful*, and *emotional*, and *resonant*. His words are carefully chosen, trying to avoid saying exactly what he means; trying to not upset her with anything. He's focused on the work, as if she wasn't even a part of it, and as if her life hasn't fed into what she was writing. He asks her to call him in the morning to chat about it, because he thinks it's important. He writes,

There's a story here, and he means the book, but he means her personal story as well. Something that they both know will help to sell this to publishers and readers. If that's something she wants, he says that he can sell it. She wonders if it was meant for that, really; or if sending it to him was just catharsis. She thinks about other people reading it – sitting down as she is now, only they're going into her world, a world that she created, for better or for worse – and she isn't sure that she can cope with that.

She goes back upstairs, thinking that she might get dressed, maybe go for a run. Laurence is stepping out of the shower as she opens the bedroom door and he picks up the remote control for the air-conditioning unit and flicks it.

'It's freezing in here,' he says. He stretches and dries himself, and Deanna watches him. She wonders if he knows how thin he actually is, or if he thinks it's just a blip; if he notices at all. He stretches his arms upwards as he sprays his anti-perspirant and it billows clouds around his body, making him appear even whiter, even paler. As he bends to dry his legs and feet she sees the top of his head, the hair thinning at the back; and she sees his shoulder blades, jutting so much further back than they ever used to. They almost remind her of shark fins. 'I think we should all spend the day together,' he says. 'Get out and do something as a family.' He pulls on jeans and a T-shirt, and Deanna struggles to remember when she last saw

208

him looking so casual. His clothes are far too big for him. He hasn't replenished the day-to-day parts of his wardrobe since well before Sean died. The T-shirt he's wearing is the same as he's wearing in the family picture they keep on the refrigerator; only it's faded by time and hangs on him like a sack now. He tucks it in at the back, pushing it down below the belt in order to make it taut at the front. 'We should go to the mall or something. Treat the girls.'

Deanna sits on the edge of the bed and watches him as he looks in the mirror, as he teases his hair with his fingers. 'What was the video of, Laurence?' she asks.

'I don't want to talk about it,' he says.

'You're not being fair to me,' she replies.

'Yes,' he tells her. 'I am. I am being so fair, you have no idea.' He pauses, seemingly to catch his breath. 'So do you want to come?'

'Today?'

'I just want normality back,' he says. 'I just want my life back. Do you want to come?'

'You go with the girls,' Deanna says. 'I have to work on the book.' She hasn't told him that she has finished a draft; or that it's readable, finally; or that her agent has read it. He talks about this as being *his* life; she's keeping secrets. She wonders when this happened to them, exactly, if this is new, or if this is the way that they've always been.

'All right.' He goes downstairs without her. She hears him speaking to the girls from the hallway, telling them that they're all going out. She's not even surprised when Lane says that she'll go with her father and little sister, knowing that she'll return with bags of clothes that she couldn't afford without Laurence's credit card and him feeling guilty enough to buy her things.

Deanna takes her time getting dressed, only going to the kitchen as they're all ready to head out. She kisses them and tells Alyx to stay safe, tells Laurence to take care of them. As they're leaving, she grabs Lane's arm and pulls her back.

'Anything happens, you watch your sister,' she says.

'What?' Lane asks.

'Just make sure your sister is safe. Don't leave her side. Okay? Call me.' She kisses Lane on the cheek and holds her for a second before letting her go out to the car. She looks around at the other cars parked on their street as they drive off, trying to see if there's anybody sitting in them and watching the house. It's to be expected, that they'll be watched. People will be back for their trash and they'll keep trying. She searches for the glint of a camera lens. She wonders when it became like this: when it wasn't just movie stars that weren't safe from having their privacy invaded. At the moment, technically, Laurence is a nobody. Before Sean died he had been a clean politician as well, one of the few who could truly say that. (And she prayed that this was true every time a fresh scandal appeared in the newspapers: that

210

there were no secrets between them that would tear her life apart more than it already had been.) But still, they hounded him. She wonders what it must have been like in the last century: when there were still secrets and lies in the business and politicians could get away with them. Wiretaps were once a rarity, but over the past few years the press has been full of stories about the ways conversations have been manipulated and hacked and recorded. Lying now feels routine. When Amit became involved he instructed them all to delete text messages and answering machine messages as soon as they had read them. He told them to simply make it a part of their lives. *Don't keep anything* – another of his rules. He gave them worst-case scenarios and they scared Deanna enough to listen to him. Now, she doesn't keep records of anything.

She looks inside the recycling bins and sees paper, thrown away like it's nothing. The remains of envelopes, of circular letters from their bank. She takes out all the paper and carries it inside and then pulls the shredder from the cupboard and plugs it in. She feeds everything in – there are no bills, because they've moved totally digital with those, but anything that suggests even the slightest glimpse into the way that they conduct their lives. She wants to make this harder for anybody who might be desperate enough to rifle through this stuff. She mixes up the paper, stuffing it into different bags, making sure that this takes whoever steals their trash as long as possible to realize that they're looking at old charity donation statements and circulars from Alyx's school rather than anything actually important.

When she's finished she sits at the table and looks at her book on the screen and the email from her agent. She reads the start of her novel again and she thinks that it's okay. She doesn't hate it. It's what she needed to write. She looks at the email once more. *This is not what I was expecting,* her agent wrote. She picks up the phone and finds his number. She dials it, and it rings. His voice: they haven't spoken in months. She cancels the call and reads the start of the book again and again. They say that the first chapter is the most important and so she reads it aloud, speaking every word to see if any of them are wrong. But they're not. They work.

Laurence asked her once, the first day that they went to the lake house, if she minded him beginning this journey. They had only owned the house a few days, and they went out there to spend the night, the whole family, sleeping in sleeping bags on filthy floors. Laurence was gearing up to announce, and his future career, their future lives, felt – suddenly – very real.

'Just tell me,' he said, 'and I won't do this. I'll do something else with my life; consulting, or I'll stay a senator, or I'll go back into law.' She told him that she wanted him to be happy. She said that he could make life better for many, many people. That's what he wanted. In his eyes, she could see how happy he was. And she loves his eyes most, because he shared them with his children: all three of them taking that part of him, as if they were his strongest, most defined thing that he passed along. Sean had those eyes, and now they're all she sees in all three of them, that reminder.

Laurence and the girls eat cinnamon rolls as soon as they get into the mall, sitting on a bench with their backs to the fountain. When they're finished, his daughters want to drag him in different directions. Lane drops her pretenses for a second, her hood pulled up over her head, hiding her lack of hair. Laurence thinks that she looks younger again. Remove the piercings and the tattoo that peeks out of the top of her manufacturer-distressed vest and she could almost be a kid again, he thinks. Laurence decides that they're going to Lane's shops first, taking Alyx's hand and joke-dragging her along behind him. Lane picks a clothes shop that he's never been into. The walls are covered in wire mesh, as if they're security fences, and a sweet perfume smell comes from hidden vents. T-shirts hang from the mesh, along every single wall. She pulls down a couple – emblazoned with the names of bands that Laurence knows from the posters on her bedroom walls, *WMBLDN* and *Lost Boise OH* and *Semi-Coma* – and she asks Laurence to hold them for her. He obliges. She pulls out

213

trousers, thin, glossy black jeans that look more like leather than denim, and she hands these off to her father as well. He watches while Alyx potters around the shop, picking up small items from tables. His phone buzzes in his pocket. He picks it out and he sees another email from *ClearVista*.

We are sorry for the confusion, the email reads. *Please find your video link attached*. Laurence feels his heart in his body, in every part of himself. He thinks, This could be my redemption. This is when it's all fixed – if not the result of an election, then at least as a vision of my future. He is lying to himself in his desperation and he knows that, but he stands there in the darkness of the shop and presses play on the video regardless.

This one begins in the same way: the vague figures being drawn in through the darkness. No set around them: just the four of them in a space. He watches the figures become themselves. He watches their faces twitch and change, and alter. He watches them contort into their terrified facial expressions. There's a difference, this time, in their poses. This time, his wife and daughters are huddled together, clutching at each other, a cluster. He is fixated on them. There's something wrong about the angles, as if he isn't meant to see them this way. They look towards the Laurence in the video, even more terrified than before. It's distressing to see them like this, he thinks. And in their eyes there's a reflection of something; a slight glimmer of light. This is how exact the technology is; how perfect they have managed to make it. But these eyes are theirs, taken from photographs or videos, he reminds himself. They only look real. He looks at the version of him that's there, and he sees the biggest difference in the scene. In his hand is the dark metal of a handgun. Laurence recognizes the make and model. In the video, the digital version of Laurence flexes his finger around the trigger. He doesn't turn to look his family in their faces; he looks straight at the camera instead. He is still free of all expressions, as if the algorithm couldn't find the right look to fit to his face. What does a broken man look like when threatening his family? When they are terrified of him? What sort of expression would that man wear? The video cuts to black and there is a noise: static, like water, almost; followed by a harsh snap over the speakers like a distortion.

Laurence drops his phone. He feels his stomach churn, his head pound. He rushes to a counter, goes behind it, grabbing the small trashcan there. He tastes the vomit behind his teeth and then spits. He holds himself together, but only barely. Alyx and Lane rush over, concerned for him. Alyx reaches for his phone, on the floor, and he realizes that there's every chance the video will be repeating itself, and that she will see it. She glances down and he lurches for it, snatching it away.

'No,' he says. 'That's mine.' He puts it into his pocket. He sees the shop staff looking at him. Other customers have their phones out, and he imagines more videos appearing on the Internet, and what the bloggers will write. *Sick, Sick, Sick*: Amit's dreaded S word, invoked over and over. 'We have to go,' he says. He ushers his daughters out of the shop, despite their protests, and towards the elevators. He wipes his mouth. He can't control his own breathing and they get into the elevator and Lane asks if he's all right, but he doesn't answer. They ride to their floor and get out and walk to the car, and he leans on the hood and tries to get himself under control, but he can't. 'Get in the front,' he tells Lane. 'Are you okay to drive?'

'Sure,' she says. He opens the doors and lets the girls get inside, and he stands next to it for a second while they both watch him through the windscreen. He breathes. He puts his hand into his pocket to feel his phone handset there, and it vibrates again. He doesn't want to see whom it is – Deanna, Amit, *ClearVista* again – so he pulls it out and throws it hard against the floor. It clatters and skids off, down one of the ramps, shattered into pieces. He can't leave it, he knows: the hard drive can still be accessed. He picks up the fragments, a few pieces of plastic and glass, the guts hanging out. He snaps the chip and then throws the shell away. As he walks back up the ramp he sees a man in the distance, standing and watching him; and there, the glint of a camera lens. He tries to make out who it is, but his head is swimming and his vision is fuzzy; there's a smear of blue to his clothes. He can't quite see, so he starts walking closer. The blue is a jacket; and while he can't see the man's face, he knows that he's seen him before.

'Stop,' Laurence shouts. He walks up the ramp and then runs across the parking lot. His feet smack the concrete of the floor and they echo. His head begins to clear. He sees more of what is happening. He sees the blue-jacketed man turn and run away from him, and he hears his daughters shout his name, but he doesn't stop. The man has gone up the ramp, to the next level, and Laurence follows. He steps out to see row after row of cars in the darkness, a parking-lot scene from a movie. He listens, but there's only the rumble of his car on the level below and his own breathing. Suddenly a car flicks on its headlights, a small black vehicle that's almost nondescript, and it tears out of a space and towards him. He can't be sure, but it looks as though it's aiming for him, so he hurls himself to one side, to the floor, and the car goes past. He can't see inside, can't see if it's the man, but he knows. He *knows*.

Laurence picks himself up and rushes down the ramp, back to his daughters. He can hear himself breathing; he can hear the sound of his own blood inside his body.

'Let's go,' he says as he gets to the car. Alyx is scared silent, but Lane asks what happened, why he ran off. 'We just have to fucking go!' he shouts, and he pounds the dash with one open palm. 'Please,' he begs. Lane puts the car in drive and

217

pulls out, and he watches the outside because he wants to see if the car is anywhere. Maybe it's waiting for him.

But it isn't. The rest of the parking lot is nothing but empty cars and they all look the same to him: all darkened windows, nobody sitting in them, nothing at all to see. 'I'm sorry,' he says to his daughters, as they pull out into the sunlight. He puts the window down because he still feels sick, but the air outside is so warm it doesn't really help.

Amit's phone buzzes the arrival of an email, waking him up. His hair is still damp from last night's rain, that's his first thought, and he didn't brush his teeth when he got in. He can still taste the pizza and the familiar fuzz on his gums. He rushes to the bathroom, desperate to piss, and hears his phone buzz again as a reminder, and again. It's incessant.

'All right!' he shouts. He finishes in the bathroom and goes to the phone, picking it up and silencing the alert. 'Fucking idiot thing,' he says to it. He sees the notification: the new video from *ClearVista*. He presses play and waits a second while it streams to him; and then he watches Laurence and the gun and his terrified, huddled family. He doesn't know what it is, or how this has happened, but it's worse. It's gotten worse, and there's no way that can be.

He tries to call Laurence, to see if he's seen this

yet – and praying that he hasn't, because maybe he can still manage this – but the phone goes straight to the answering service; so he calls Hershel instead, who answers without a hello, acting as if their conversation hasn't stopped.

'Amit,' he says, 'long time no see.'

'I just had another email,' Amit replies.

'What?'

'I got *ClearVista* to make another version of the video. To run the data again, in case there was a mistake.'

'You have to send it to me.' Hershel sounds annoyed; as if this challenge has been stolen away from him in its prime.

'On it as we speak.' He pings it over, and then he waits while Hershel watches it: listening to Hershel's reaction as the sound – the sobbing that runs through the background, and the crack at the end, loud and jarring – fills the room and the phone call; and then Hershel comes back on the line.

'Holy shit,' Hershel says. 'Holy shit.'

'You have to help me,' Amit says.

'Doing my best,' Hershel replies. Amit hangs up and tries Laurence again, but there's no answer; so he calls the Walkers' home line, but again there's nothing. He thinks about driving up there, because he's worried. He imagines a worst case, what could have happened. He tries not to think about it.

'You left them alone, Laurence. Lane said you smashed your phone, then chased after this man?'

219

Deanna says. She has shut the bedroom door, keeping the pair of them blocked off from the rest of the house. He fidgets on the bed, looking at the wardrobe, the window, the door: all the points of exit. 'Show me the video,' she says. He lies to her and tells her again that it's nothing. She shakes her head and walks out, down the stairs. He chases her, begging her to stop. He's in tears. She tells him that she has to watch it, or they can't move past this. There's just no way past it if they aren't in this together.

He shows it to her on her tablet. He explains that the first video was different. She doesn't speak, so he talks more, filling the air between them, because he feels that he has to say something. Her face is rigid after she watches it and he can't gauge how she feels. She doesn't touch him, or look at him. He shows her the results from the report, and he talks to her about those – how they cannot be correct, they simply can't, and how he answered the questions truthfully, and how there's never been anything like this in his life before. She still doesn't talk. She watches the video again. This time she zooms in on it to get a better look at her own face, at the faces of her daughters.

'It isn't real,' he tells her, over and over.

'I know,' she finally says. 'Of course it isn't.'

'Because it can't be.' He sits next to her, and he tries to take her hand. She flinches, shifting away from him, but doesn't stand up. 'I don't know what to say. Only, this isn't my fault,' he insists.

'Maybe it is,' she replies. It's cruel to say that when he wants reassurance, but she means it, and not just this video: that his distractions, his desires for his career . . . maybe she can go back in time and pin Sean's death on them, somehow, because maybe he was distracted when Sean died, thinking about anything other than his family; and now this, the fact that he's one of the highest-profile politicians in the country right now, and the fact that he advocates things that maybe aren't popular, and how that is always going to lead to reactionaries and people trying to drive their concerns home. She tells him that he's not here, she says that much, and he says that it's for all of their futures. He asks her why she suddenly doesn't understand that, because she used to. She used to absolutely get that.

She says, 'You brought this into our home, Laurence. It's your fault, that's how I see it.' She wants to call the police, she says. She wants to get to the bottom of it. He says that they can't, because of what it will do. Doesn't she understand? Their privacy is the most important thing and this will be all over the Internet. It's not a threat, it's a mistake. It's something that barely even exists. They have to keep together and keep themselves to themselves. This family is all that they've got left. This is an argument. A rarity: it's one with no possible resolution, shouting for the sake of breathing in the air and then getting it exhumed.

In Alyx's bedroom, Lane sits with her on the bed. She plays her songs, telling her why she should listen to them, and failing to persuade her younger sister. They put on videos on the computer, watching cats jumping into boxes and people dancing to stupid songs, and they both cackle with laughter, laughing loudly because neither of them really wants to hear the argument happening downstairs.

Amit sits alone in his apartment. He watches the new video again. He rubs his face in his hands. He tries to sleep, but it's hard: because he sees their faces and the gun and he wonders what it actually means. He wonders if the video might somehow be right.

CHAPTER 8

Laurence turns the living room into an office, of sorts. He sets his laptop up on the coffee table and puts his telephone next to it, and then a pad of A4 paper, the top sheet torn off. He writes *Agenda* on the first ruled line, and then makes bullet-pointed notes beneath, one by one. He hasn't Googled himself in a few days, so that's the first thing on the list. He has to see whatever is being said about him and he has to take control of this situation, he's told himself. He has a career to think about, and a family.

Alyx is sitting next to him on the sofa playing a game, where she has to build a castle and try to survive an assault from cartoonish animal enemies. She presses the screen to construct ramparts and battlements and hire soldiers. Laurence watches this over her shoulder and wonders if he shouldn't hire some security for the family, to keep them all protected. Maybe it's ridiculous, this early in his campaign, but there's likely a fund for it, an amount in the senatorial coffers to put into that. He thinks about the man in the jacket, and how the video must have been altered or tampered with, because that's something that resembles logic; and he thinks that maybe those things are reason enough. He has enemies. He'll have to sell it to the delegates well enough that they'll authorize the spend, and sell it without mentioning the video – so far it's only three of them who know, him and Deanna and Amit, and none of them will tell another living soul. The threat of the press seems like the most viable excuse. He can be vague about what the threats are; the delegates will certainly understand that, in this media climate.

Lane comes into the kitchen. She's in a T-shirt and shorts and she yawns and stretches and waves good morning to Alyx, who waves back.

'What are you doing today?' Laurence asks.

'I'm going out,' Lane says.

'You should stay around here with us. I've called Alyx in sick and we're having a sofa day, aren't we, Pumpkin.' He pokes Alyx in her belly and she giggles and flops to one side.

'I'm getting inked again.'

'More?'

She nods. 'Here.' She lifts her T-shirt at the side, showing him the plant. It's stretched around towards her back, and there's the trace outline, in black, not yet painted in, of a flower on her shoulder blade; only it's not a flower he knows, instead being made of a sharp geometric pattern, almost as if it were created with a gyroscope, all looped, intersecting lines. 'I designed it,' she says, 'to remind me of now. I drew it, and I thought it would look good.' She's defensive, because she's used to answering questions about this stuff. She's got her guard up in advance of being told that it's bad, or embarrassing, or that she'll regret it later in her life.

'It's nice,' he tells her. He thinks that he's telling the truth, even: it's a good design, and complicated, but executed well. 'You should do more of that, you know.'

'The ink?'

'No! Maybe not that. I meant the art. Did you draw it?'

'On the computer.'

'It's good.'

'Okay,' she says. 'Thanks.' She pours herself a drink and goes to leave the kitchen.

'Listen, you have to be careful, okay?' He looks at her as she stands in the doorway, and he tries to imagine her in ten, fifteen, twenty years time. He wonders if she'll ever look like her mother; settle down, grow her hair, get past this phase – which, he tells himself, is surely all it is.

'I am.'

'No, I'm telling you. You have to be. This is all getting serious.' She looks at him blankly. 'This is all getting serious. There are nut-jobs out there, Laney.'

'I know. I'm fine. I'll be with William.' Laurence hasn't met William, but he's seen pictures. He's huge. Were he not with Lane's crowd, he'd be on some football team somewhere, getting every football college scholarship scout in the US drooling. But as it is, he's got a shaved head and thick-rimmed glasses, plays bass in a band, and has the words *Straight Edge* printed across his thorax. Recent changes, by all accounts, in order to impress Lane.

'Okay.' He doesn't say: I'd give anything to keep you safe. He lets her go upstairs and get dressed, and when she reappears, barely wearing any more clothing than she slept in, he's lost all track of time and he's just been standing there, thinking about when she was a little kid. They've had her for seventeen years now. She's essentially indelible. Some days – and it's rare that this happens, but – some days he forgets about Sean for a few hours, and then the memory is back, that he was once there; like a word on the tip of the tongue, waiting to be uttered. But Lane . . . She is their tattoo.

Deanna's feet hit the pavements hard. She sticks to the residential roads, which all look similar. The rain started as soon as she left the house, violent and pounding, so she spends most of the time looking down, avoiding both puddles and cars pulling out of driveways. The rain makes it hard to hear, it's so heavy, and the cars are getting quieter, hybrids pulling backwards with a creepy silence. She runs to clear her head, to put every-thing out of her mind.

She runs through puddles on purpose, splashing the water out, seeing how hard her sneakers can collide with the surface of the water. She wants to tell Laurence that this needs to be over. She doesn't know what the video is – it makes her head hurt to even think of it, almost, because it makes so little sense to her – but she knows that they wouldn't have been sent it were it not for who her husband is now. He's not the man that she married. That man worked long days and the occasional weekend, but he was present. So, he can leave the race now with no shame at all. He can, she thinks with something approaching guilt, blame it on Sean. He can say that their son's passing is hanging over them; a dark spot that they cannot erase.

She crosses an intersection and watches the kids going to school, walking along hand in hand or in gaggles of three or more, or waiting for the bus that comes along to take them off. She turns the corner, back onto the main road; and there's the church, Staunton's sole house of prayer. The doors are open. She takes this as a sign.

The church is an anomaly in the town: it's Catholic, one of the first buildings built here, and preserved because of it. Eschewing the modern facelifts that many buildings are getting, unwilling to succumb to technology, it instead relies on a single new beam of wood to act as a joist where the ceiling is slightly bowed. The pews are the originals, cracking and chipped and even prone to rotting in the humid summers, but still here. It's not like the church is rich, but the town gives where it can. After Sean's funeral, which was held in one of the larger churches outside town – they discussed it, and decided that it was better that Sean wasn't buried on their doorstep, crammed into the small lot that the church owned (and part of the reason would be the draw of his body on their doorstep, so close that they could never forget it, that they would be able to see him whenever they wanted) – they gave money to help. Their priest, Father Caulk, performed the rites for them, at their request, because he knew Sean. Deanna has always loved this church, ever since she came here as a kid. The community barely uses it, and she sort of likes that. It's peaceful; and while she might not be religious, or not as much as her mother would have had her be, she likes the peace of it, and the smell. It's usually quiet enough; only ever busy on Sundays, and even then it's still not exactly crammed.

Deanna picks a pew and sits down, and she looks at the altar and the crucifix that hangs behind it, and the gold-paint that's fading from the pillars. She shuts her eyes and says a prayer that she remembers, that's wound so tightly into her subconscious that it spills out without her even thinking. She's not sure that she believes in this God, not specifically; but she has faith in something. It's a faith that has been tested the last couple of years – she has wondered, as everybody who suffers loss wonders, what sort of God would have taken Sean, who was young and innocent

228

and a good boy – but there's *something* there. Because she needs to believe that there's something after this. Sean has to be somewhere else.

Father Caulk comes out of the side room and sees her, and he raises his hand in a wave. He doesn't want to interrupt – not everybody who comes here wants to talk – but Deanna waves back, and she starts speaking immediately, almost as if she's apologizing for being in here. For being caught.

'I didn't mean to disturb you,' she says.

'You didn't. Take your time,' he says.

'Okay,' she replies. 'Thanks.'

'Do you want to talk?' He stands at the end of the pew. Deanna stares past him at the confessional box. She wonders if she has anything to confess. He follows her gaze. 'You want me to open them up?'

'No,' she says. 'But thank you.'

'How are your parents?' he asks.

'Fine,' Deanna says. 'Dad is fine. Mom's bored.'

'More or less than when they still lived here?' He grins. 'You wish them the best from me.'

'I will.' He puts his hand on her arm and squeezes it, the universal sign of condolence, and then he opens the door to the confessional, to the side that he is meant to sit in. She sees a bottle of water in there, in case he's there for the long haul.

'I was opening it up anyway.' That's a lie and Deanna knows it, but he steps inside and pulls the door shut, and there's a little light above the other door that comes one. Green, beckoning her towards it. She's still sweaty from the run and she needs a shower; but she sidles along the pew and opens the door and climbs in, taking a seat on the small wooden stool. In front of her, grated metal, hiding them from each other, as if he won't know who she is. Neither of them speaks for the longest time, and then he clears his throat.

'Do you know what you're meant to say?' he asks. 'Can you remember?'

'No,' she says.

'Bless me Father, for I have sinned. It's been . . . Then you say how long it's been since you last confessed.'

'Bless me Father, for I have sinned,' she repeats. 'I haven't been to confession since I got pregnant for the first time. Seventeen years.'

'That's a lot to cover in one session,' he says and she laughs. 'Let's start with what's on your mind today.'

'I've kept secrets,' she says, 'from my husband. I've been writing a book about our son; about me, as well. Laurence isn't in it, because . . . I don't know.'

'That's not such a bad secret,' Caulk says.

'No, I suppose not.' She can't see him through the mesh, only the shape of a person, dark and mysterious. It's easier this way, she thinks.

'Will you tell him about it?'

'Yes,' she says, 'eventually. I think I want to publish it.'

'That's good, isn't it?'

'I think so.'

'There's a "but" there.'

'Laurence is having trouble. This is between us, isn't it?'

'Of course, everything here is. But I don't even know who you are to tell anybody if it wasn't,' he says. She hears the smile on his face.

'He's been suffering. He's been sick.' Such a relief, to use the S word; and here, out of her lips, it sounds appropriate. As if she's been searching for the right word for so long, and it's been there, trapped below tongues the entire time. 'He's been getting thinner, and he's been sleeping badly.' He is unraveling, she thinks.

'What do you think's caused it?'

'He's under so much pressure. He shouldn't be doing what he's doing. And now this video's appeared, and it's not fair. It's not him.'

'A video?'

She sighs. This is private, and yet this is also catharsis. 'A mock-up, a thing about whether he can be president: and the video is scary. It's not a man that I know. It's not my Laurence. It's like when somebody sees something you just have never seen in another person? It's like it's lifted a veil, so that I can see it as well. It's forced me to look at him, really look at him.'

'And what do you see when you do?'

'I see a darkness,' she says.

★ ★ ★

The gate at the side of their house is open, she notices, and she goes to shut it, slowing to a walk as she approaches; thinking that she might stretch out right here, before she goes inside. She wants to avoid Laurence for a little while longer. Whether he knows about it or not, she feels guilty for talking about him. But as she gets close to the gate she sees the trashcans with their lids off, the bags gone from inside them again, and the chain that was holding the gate shut missing. The first time that they were broken into – that's how Laurence sees it, that's what he has always called it, that much of an intrusion – she thought that it was only hobos, going around taking the bags and pillaging them for whatever they could find. It was Amit who told them the truth, and told them how bad this was likely going to get. He presented them with horror stories, because his logic was to sell this as a worst-case scenario, and then let the reality hopefully be better. Start at the bottom, and then the only way is up. Now, they've gone through a heavy-duty chain, and they did it literally on their doorstep.

She picks up the trashcan lids and puts them back on. There are black marks on the metal, she sees. Scuff marks, they look like. She looks on the wall, and they're there as well: and on the window-sill, on the fence. They go up to the first floor, the placement of feet as they climbed the outside of their house. She puts her feet where the marks are, trying to get up and see what the intruder would have seen. It's tricky – whoever it was must have been taller than her, so she has to stretch to get her legs into the same positions as they held – but then with one leg on the fence and one on the window below, precariously jammed on the latch, she can see into her own bedroom. To her left she can see into Alyx's bedroom as well; or she would be able to, if her curtains were opened. The angle would be terrible, but that's barely the point. She sees something. There's a nail up here, jutting from the brickwork. A piece of the house's brickwork juts, a small sharp point of paint by her arm. There is something attached to it, perhaps caught on this when the intruder was up here: a tangle of blue thread. She pulls it off then she climbs down and drags the bin to the back of the garden, goes back and pulls the gate shut, picking up another broken lock from the floor, this time looking as if it's been burned through; and she goes into the house. Laurence and Alyx are both on the sofa still, neither having moved in the entire time she was gone.

'Somebody was here,' Deanna says. She bends down and looks her daughter straight in the face. 'Upstairs,' she says. 'Go get dressed, and keep your curtains shut, okay?' Deanna dims the windows throughout the downstairs, partially blocking out the light, making them unable to be seen through. There's nobody looking in; their garden is walled, too high to climb over without help, and beyond that there is just the field and then the woods and then the lake. There's no vantage point to spy on them, but again, that isn't the point. 'I was outside, in the alley. They used the trashcans to climb up. They were at the *windows*, Laurence. I found this, as well.' She holds out her palm, the blue thread in it.

'What?' He knows this color. He imagines the man in the blue jacket there, peering in at them.

'I'm calling the police,' she says. 'We can't have this.'

'Don't mention the video,' he says. He feels sick: if that got out, a cop with loose lips, he'd be ruined. Back when, somebody leaked the news about Sean before Amit had put out a press release. Laurence always imagined it was one of the staffers from the sheriff's department.

'Don't be so fucking selfish,' she replies. She picks up the handset and dials 911.

Amit arrives before the sheriff's department does, and he talks to Deanna and Laurence out at the front of the house. Alyx stays upstairs, playing her game, totally unwilling to be distracted. Laurence tells Amit that they'll talk about the other stuff later; Amit nods. He's not worried about who is in the right in this situation. Laurence will see sense, he knows, because he's always been that way inclined. He's always been able to see the wood for the trees; that's why he's perfect for politics. The long game, and the hard choices: navigating those is a skill that Laurence holds tight to himself. They show Amit what happened and he tells them to calm down. He manages the situation, because that's his job.

'Just remember to stay calm,' he says. 'This goes better the more reasonable you are about it all.'

'This is our house,' Deanna tells him.

'And this is my job. I'm here to protect you guys. You play it calm, collected and it makes it seem more as if there's a real threat. Then you're not just being hysterical and blowing this out of proportion.' He looks at Laurence as he says it. The doorbell rings, and Deanna goes to answer it. As soon as she's gone Amit turns to Laurence. 'Did you see the second video?' he asks. 'You haven't answered your phone.'

'Yes,' Laurence replies. He looks at the floor. He is trying not to picture the scene – the gun, his family cowering – as the police officers walk in. Laurence recognizes them: they're like everybody else here, have lived here their entire lives. He smiles, his big, false, would-be presidential smile, and he shakes the hands of Officers Robards and Templeton. They were there when Sean died. It was Robards who tried to save their son: who gave him mouth to mouth; who held his body and kept it warm until the ambulance arrived; who was a pallbearer at Sean's funeral. Laurence knows both of their parents as well. Not to have dinner with, but to stop and talk to in the streets, and to ask how they're doing, to make small talk with, to canvas for votes from. Both men are almost implausibly young, Laurence thinks. They both have moustaches, as if to make them look older and more authoritative, even though neither of them seems at ease with the room. Deanna introduces Amit. Templeton asks Laurence how the campaign is going.

'It's fine,' Laurence says. 'It's good.' It's a lie, Laurence knows, but his voice doesn't show it.

'I've seen you on the interviews,' Robards says, 'and you've been coming across real well, I'd say. My parents are voting for you, that's what they tell me.'

'What about you?' Laurence asks.

'Oh, I've never voted yet,' he says. 'Barely know what's best for myself, let alone the best of the country. But if I do,' he adds, 'it'll be for you, Mr Walker.' They sit and accept the coffee that Deanna offers them. 'Mrs Walker tells us you've had an intruder?'

'Yes,' Laurence replies. 'Somebody's been breaking into our trash, cutting the lock on the gate. Spying through the windows.'

'Can we take a look?'

'We'll show you,' Deanna says, and they follow her and Laurence, carrying their drinks with them. Amit waits in the kitchen. He looks at the fridge: at the photograph stuck there of the five of them; at the hand-drawn notes and pictures, signed by all three kids from various stages of their lives; at the calendar on the embedded screen, which has a color-code for each member of the household, including Sean still, the sea-green color reflecting what are now the only two important days of the year for him (his birthday, the day that he died). He pulls down the photograph. Laurence looks so calm in it. This was the man that was going to win the election, unite the party, do good for the country – or, at least, as much good as he was able to get through congress. Amit looks out of the window at him now. He is standing behind the police and Deanna, watching what they're doing. He's barely present, his face sagging, a gray-yellow color. Amit wonders if *ClearVista*'s algorithm can somehow decipher the images it dredges from the Internet for the video as well. Maybe it's looked at him now – a picture of him recently, compared to how he used to look – and decided that he can never lead the party, let alone the country. It has seen how sallow he is.

That doesn't explain the videos though. Nothing explains them. The back door clicks, and Deanna walks in with the police officers, and they walk through. Laurence follows at the back of the pack. He shuts the door and stares outside for a moment, as if he's watching for something.

'It's straightforward, now,' Robards says. 'We stick this house on the rotation, so a car'll come by every hour or so, drive past, keep an eye out for anything out of the ordinary. You guys call this number,' he says, handing Deanna a business card, a security firm's details, 'and get a new gate fitted. Get something with barb at the top. Get yourself an alarm as well, one that links right to the station. I know, this is Staunton, not New York City. But you probably can't be too careful, that's what I reckon.'

'There's something else,' Laurence says. He offers the thread to the officers, extending his arm out, turning his palm upwards. 'I have seen a man in a blue jacket a few times. He's following me, I think. Maybe a reporter, something like that.' He's chasing me, he thinks. There's a conspiracy.

'And you found this outside?' Robards asks.

'I did,' Deanna says.

'Could you describe this man?'

'I don't think so,' Laurence says.

'I've seen him,' Amit says. 'White man, mid-forties, bit of stubble, greyish hair.'

'Anything else?'

'Afraid not,' Amit says. 'He just looks like a normal man.'

'That spring anything else in you, Mr Walker?'

'Just the jacket,' Laurence says. He can see it, clear as anything; but everything else about the man is as if through a fog. Robards nods.

'Okay. So, best we can do is put the blue jacket on the alert and hope somebody sees him. We spot him, we get him into the station, sit down and have a conversation with him. It's likely nothing.'

'So that's it?' Deanna asks.

'Best we can offer. And it's more than we'd offer most folks, because you're higher profile, Mr

Walker.' He smiles; they share something, in Sean. 'And, you know, because we like you guys. Anything else happens, you just call us.'

'Okay,' he says. 'Thank you.' He reaches out his hand to the officers and they shake it, one by one. Deanna watches it happen, as if in slow motion: his thin, alien arm up and down, his smile drawn back, the lines around his mouth belying his weight loss. They leave, escorted out. Deanna shouts at them to pass her love onto their mothers. This is what happens when you live in a small town; they know you. And they know Laurence; or, at least, the Laurence that he used to be.

The three of them sit on the sofas and Deanna asks Amit about the video and the report. She wants to know everything.

'It must have come from somewhere,' she says.

'Yes,' Amit tells her. 'I've got people on it. Look, it's an algorithm. That's the point. It's all automated, ones and zeroes in a system that boots out this stuff at the other end. The video, it's bullshit. If it had shown Laurence winning the election, it still would have been bullshit. This is an algorithm and some quick-fix CG generation software. Nothing more, not really.'

'An algorithm?'

'It's what I worked on when I was there, before all of this. It's a series of equations that tries to predict the outcome of a given situation when you feed it variables. But it's more than that.

Everybody's got one of those. Ours – *ClearVista*'s – was built with these other software plugins. It data mines, for accuracy. They were trying to actually perfect this. You feed it answers to questions and it builds up a profile of you, and then it tries to reinforce or contradict that. It goes through everything it can: web pages, news reports, videos, photos, *Facebook*, *Twitter*, whatever it can find. It builds up a perfect picture—'

'It's not perfect,' Laurence interrupts.

'No, it's not. It's meant to know who you are, and then make the results based on that. Close to perfect. Laurence asked the algorithm if he could be President; it tried to give us the best answer it could. Complicated thing, because it's not just him. With something that big, it's other voters, voter behavior, existing policies, other candidates. So much goes into it.'

'And the video?' Deanna asks.

'That's just a cherry. It's a bit of promotional crap, meant to be a glimpse at your future. It's nothing,' he says.

'So they got it wrong?'

'Or somebody interfered,' Laurence says. He leans in, as if there might be people listening. 'Have we thought about that?'

'It's unlikely. The company isn't going to be bought. This is probably just an error. It's a fucking terrible one, and we'll sue the living shit out of them, but it's only ever going to be an error.'

'What if it's not?'

'Then . . .' Amit shakes his head. 'Then I don't know.'

Amit sits in his car and calls Hershel's number. It's answered straight away, but it's not Hershel's voice. It's a female voice, a lazy Californian drawl, her greeting upon answering almost noncommittal.

'Can I speak to Hershel?' Amit asks.

'I'll ask him,' she says. There's murmuring, and then she comes back. 'Who is it shall I say is calling?' She asks it in a faux-receptionist voice that erupts into giggles.

'It's Amit Suri,' he says. She says the name, and then there's a click and Hershel shouts. It's on speaker.

'Hey,' he says. 'My man, I've got nothing for you.' Amit imagines him lying in bed with that girl, smoking, eating cold pizza, whatever. He doesn't owe Amit anything; it's not like he's being paid for this.

'It's fine,' Amit says, knowing that it isn't. 'Let me know if you get anything.'

'Okay, sure. Oh! One thing.'

'Yes?'

'The sound in the video. That crack at the end. You hear that?'

'Yes.'

'I'm getting somebody to try and work out exactly what it is. I've got some people on it.' Amit balks. Hershel's asked a friend to do this, or maybe hired somebody. The circle that knows about this video has opened.

'As long as they're people you trust,' Amit says. He hangs up. He presses the button to call *ClearVista*, because he wants them to run this one more time. He wants to see what changes and why. They say that somebody will be calling him back shortly, the same message as before. The cycle, all over again.

When nobody is looking, Deanna watches the video over and over. She feels as if she is drilling it into her head. She thinks that this is unfair. All she did was marry somebody with ambition, and it was an ambition that he didn't even know he had when they met. And then children, and a future. He dreamt of something: of trying to contribute to making this better, all of this. That's all he wanted.

She doesn't sleep. She wonders what happens after the clip that they have seen. She tells herself to forget that thought, because it's not real. But still, why end there? Why not show what happens next?

There's been a vote on inner-city education in troubled areas, one of Laurence's key areas, and Amit tries to keep track of the mentions of him across the blogs. They all seem to be discussing the importance of structure and implementing systems that could help. The current government are putting money into keeping the kids in schools and upping security; Laurence wants to syphon the money into making sure that the schools understand issues that help them to support the kids at home better, to raise general educational awareness – subtle differences, but a huge divergence for where the money should be going. There's a bill proposed, one that Amit knows is nothing more than a Hail Mary: an attempt to get something passed within the final year that will benefit them if they carry on, and if not screw up the first term of the Democratic run as they try to undo it. Laurence's policies and ideas are all invoked as potential solutions. *Potential candidate; likely candidate; wunderkind; would-be party savior.* The Fox News website has a video about him, almost all of the footage taken from a long time ago. He looks so healthy compared to now, and that's something they need back if they're going to win this. His hair was so strong, and his skin good, and he looked All-American. This is something to get the heartland behind them. They like the ideal, and Laurence can be that, quite easily. Amit makes notes to hire a nutritionist, or at least get a consultation; and to get Laurence some suits that don't hang off him, maybe get some photos taken of him in jogging gear, doing exercise, that sort of thing. That's a way of controlling the weight loss. And he writes *Doctor* on his phone as well, because he wants him checked out. The vote is fast approaching. Assuming that Laurence makes it as the candidate, he'll have all sorts of medical checks. They need to be prepared for every eventuality. And, Amit thinks, looking at recent pictures of Laurence, they are anything but.

CHAPTER 9

Jessie Ng is working late, because they've put her on the post-cycle Breaking News team. These are the stories that come in after America is asleep, when very little ever happens. She's been told that, if there's an explosion somewhere else – a list of countries on a giant whiteboard, the names listed in order of crisis state – she's to call certain numbers, get other people involved. Everything else, those who are working the graveyard shift are to handle. Tidy up the stories; get them ready to go on the air in a package; let the senior editor see them, okay them, put them out.

Her team orders in some pizza, because there's a place that stays open all night on their block. It's not good pizza, but that hardly seems the point. The point is: cheese and bread and meat and Coke (and, for some, coke) to keep them going, and the team – six of them, not counting the interns and the tech guys who are forced to be here with them – get together in the boardroom and take ten minutes and don't talk about the news. Other topics that are embargoed: better food; their beds; the drinks, fun, arguments or sex that they could be having. So they talk about music or TV shows or movies or books and they treat it like a ten-minute respite from the rest of the night. They work a ten-hour shift. Most of them smoke still, because it's a burst of something when you need it, standing out in the night air, shivering to wake yourself up. It's a cycle that they know all too well, because this is the shift that you are forced to work if you want to stand any chance of being promoted. Most of these six, Jessie included, have been here for well over a year now. There's little sign of promotion until it suddenly happens – that's how they keep you hungry and working – so they're all hanging on. It's what you do.

Tonight, Jessie finishes her two slices of pepperoni pizza (which is so greasy that there's an exact shadow of the slices in yellow butter on the cardboard of the box) and then stands by the plants out the front of the building and has a cigarette. She doesn't use the smoking terrace with the rest of them. She tried electrics, but it wasn't the same, so switched to low-carcinogens instead. She likes the pause it gives her: a chance to get away from everybody else. Her ex-boyfriend told her that she could get that same pause just by standing outside and *not* smoking, but he didn't get it. It's not the same. She watches the steam from the manholes and the street down the way, where cop cars are waiting around the bottom end of Times Square, four of them up on the sidewalk. The cops are standing next to them with coffees, waiting to be called. That's what happens at this time of night, she thinks. Everybody is waiting for something to happen. It rained earlier, and the streets are still glazed in that way they get, reflecting the lights of the signs and billboards. She thinks how much better this always looks in postcards and photographs. She finishes the cigarette and flicks the butt into one of the grilles at the side of the street. She's gotten good with her aim, now: first time, every time.

Back at her desk, she has two new emails. The first is from one of her colleagues, gently flirting with her. They've had this back and forth for a while now, each nudging the other into making a move that is, apparently, never going to actually happen. It began with them hoping to find out if the other was a nice person, then digging to see if they were into each other, and now it's the dance. They circle, neither of them willing to make the move. They see each other around the office, at the printers or whatever, and the talk becomes stilted, and they can stand next to each other by the coffee machine and barely say a word, emailing as soon as they get back to their desks and acting like the clumsy near-conversation about coffee pods (or whatever) had never actually happened. Jessie's nearly bored with it. The flirting is rote now.

The other email comes from a gibberish name, a series of numbers and letters. She's seen them before, because they're how people like to send confidential information: sign up for some disposable email account, designed to be untraceable. All the rage when you're breaking non-disclose agreements. Most sources run it through a proxy as well, to mask their IP address. It's information that's often barely useable, but people don't even contemplate that there might need to be a chain of evidence, or a verifiable source at the other end of a leak. There's no accountability if the sender pretends that they don't exist, simply because nothing can be proven. Jessie knows things that she believes to be true – sometimes celebrity scuttle and tittle-tattle, but sometimes bigger information, about governments and multinational corporations – that have never made it to print or screen, simply because there wasn't anybody willing to go on record. She knows things that would ruin lives and make careers. Still. She opens this new email and reads it, expecting the same.

Please find attached the result of a ClearVista FutureVision report.

Nothing more, nothing less; no name, no source. Jessie's frustrated, because that means this could be nothing. It could be a hoax, whatever it is. She clicks to download the video and goes for another cigarette. It's stopped raining, at least; and the sun is starting to come up somewhere in the vague distance, which means the city has started to wake up. The cops that were waiting for something have all moved on, and there's this brief period of quiet before the real storm begins and the city does as it does every single day.

The file has opened itself by the time she returns, and she sits down and presses play. She watches the characters be drawn in. She recognizes Laurence Walker, but his face is different than she's ever seen it, his eyes almost glitching, his face frozen; and his wife and daughters are with him, terrified of him, she's sure, and there's a gun in the Senator's hand. She watches it again before she calls her boss, waking her up. She sounds angry, but Jessie doesn't care. This isn't the sort of news you wait on. Jessie plays it over and over while she waits for her to come in, and she gets a crowd around her desk, and starts charging staffers with amassing information for the story that's going to run alongside this video. They need a background package on Walker, every bit of video that they can find on him, anything that they can claw together. Do they know anybody who would make a good talking head on this, anybody that they can get to the studio on short notice? Jessie takes charge.

When her boss arrives she takes her to a conference room alone and she plays it to her on the big screen. Her boss sits forward in her chair for the whole thirty seconds or whatever it is, and she doesn't show a single emotion. When it's done, she plays it again.

'We need to clear this with legal,' she says.

'We can't just run it?'

'We can. We ran Homme's. This is fair game. But I want us airtight. You've got the story in hand?'

'Yes,' Jessie says.

'Okay. Get some of the ad team on the job of selling space. Let them know what we've got; show them, but *only* them. Tell them to not tell the buyers too much, but we can inflate this, I'm sure. Get audio working on this as well, see if they can't clean up the noise in the background. Otherwise we go out muted. Don't want people to think that this is broken.' She presses play again. They can't stop watching it. 'You just got sent this out of the blue?'

'Yes,' Jessie says.

'That's what happens when you build contacts; build a reputation,' she says. 'You get to this stage and people want to share secrets with you. Good work.' She leaves Jessie in the boardroom, the video playing on the screen. The girls look so terrified, Jessie thinks. She hopes that they're okay, and that they're safe, because their lives are about to change.

Amit wakes with the sunlight on his face. He didn't close the curtains last night, and it's still far too early to be awake. He gets out of bed and shuts them and he thinks about going back to sleep for a while. It's going to be a long day – a long week, month, year – and he knows it. He strips, having slept the first stretch in his suit, and gets into bed, and his phone rings as he lies down. It's Hershel's number.

'Dude,' Hershel says, 'you have to hear this.'

'What?' Amit yawns. He's done with the panic over this. Suddenly, in the fug of wanting to sleep, the video seems almost mundane to him.

'That click at the end? And the water noise, that static noise? You know those?' He doesn't wait for an answer. 'So the guys I know, who work at Sound City, they did some work on this for me. You know Sound City?'

'Sure,' Amit says, not knowing what Sound City is, and barely caring. He wants Hershel to get to the point.

'They ripped the audio, did some editing to it. Tweaked it. Anyway, listen to this.' The phone rustles as Thom holds it close to speakers, and then presses play. There's the familiar rush of water, only then he starts to make out noise. It's not water: it's people. It's the shouting of a crowd, and then the click in the audio, that final sound, is suddenly clear. It's a bang; a gunshot.

Jessie goes to the coffee machine and gets herself a triple espresso, biting back the taste as she pours it down her throat. She takes a headache pill and she starts to write the lead-in. An email pings in from her boss, telling her they're live in five, asking if she's heard back from the sound guys yet. She calls them and they tell her what they've found. They boosted the mid-range or something that she doesn't give a damn about. They can hear noises but the only one that's clear is the sound of a gunshot at the very end of the video.

'Maybe we should give the Walkers a chance to know we're going to broadcast this?' she asks. 'Give him a chance to response first?'

'No time.' Her boss tells her that it's airing; that she's got to get the brief ready. She types quickly and tries not to be distracted by the video, and she's still typing as she hears the newsreader start to read her words, and they flash a *Breaking* banner over the screen, and they tell viewers of a nervous disposition that they may want to avert their eyes, but knowing full well that they won't.

Amit is standing in the queue for the coffee shop when his phone starts going in his pocket. It beeps and rings, every type of alert going off at once. Tweets and emails and Facebook, even though he hasn't used it in forever, and then text messages and calls, all in the moment it takes for him to order and apologize to the barista. The other customers look at him as if he's a menace and he ducks outside to one of the tables. He pulls the phone from his jacket and reads the notifications, but they're coming in as fast as he can read them, pushing the rest off the screen. He gets glimpses: *Laurence; Senator Walker; all over the TV; check the blogs; have you seen this?; did this just happen?; did you know about this?* He runs back to his apartment, switches on the set in the corner of the room, grabs his laptop, and he's inundated. He switches through the news channels, and then he sees it: the video he's done nothing but think about for days now; that should never have leaked, that was never going to be made public.

He picks up the phone and calls Laurence, but it goes straight to his voicemail. He tries the house and Deanna, but it's the same. He flicks the channels in a cycle, one right through to one again. Every newsreader is the same: each saying that the footage prediction is a representation of what could happen. They're showing Homme's footage as well, to give it context, and then they're insinuating things that they cannot say. They discuss the audio and what the sound – unmistakably a gunshot, played loud, slowed down, clear as day – might mean within the context of the rest of the video. Media teams on the ground have verified – cue shaky hand-held footage through the front windows of the Walker house – that the Walker family are currently at home. They have been asked for comment but, so far, have declined.

Amit splits his screen into all the major news outlets, and he opens his feeds in his phone's browser, and all the information is the same: the same headlines, or variations on the same theme. Every single one of them is talking about Laurence Walker – and all in the worst possible way.

PART II

CHAPTER 10

Deanna pulls the batteries from the back of the phone handset and unplugs it from the wall, then goes around the house doing the same to all of the others. She bundles up the handsets, wrapping the wires around them, and takes a fabric tote bag from the cupboard under the stairs to put them all in. She already has the cellphones on the side, their numbers disconnected. New numbers will be sent to them, so the handsets have to wait until then. It's amazing, she thinks, how willing some of their friends have been to give them up, to sell them out to people who only want to cause them pain. She puts the bag into one of the kitchen cupboards, tucked behind pots and pans. The room is dark, because she has dimmed the windows as much as possible, and pulled every other blind or curtain in the house and they're trying to keep the lights off. Another of Amit's tips, coming out when they're in desperate need of council; don't let them see anything you're doing and they might get bored. If they see lights going on and off, they'll count that as activity. He cites Nixon and the hordes following him post-Watergate; and Clinton, after his own scandal. Deanna pleaded that this was very different – that nobody in her family had done anything wrong – but he shrugged.

'That's not how they'll see it,' he told her.

So now, with the rest of the house asleep, Deanna works. She sees this as something akin to a cleansing; she wants to cut back anything that might give the outside world a way into their shell. Lane was on *Tumblr* the night before, posting up song lyrics that pointedly referred to their situation, and her posts were re-blogged hundreds of times within minutes, shared and thrown around as if they carried a meaning far beyond that which they did. Those lyrics ended up on the news as *the poetic musings of Walker's daughter*. Every political journalist and blogger is watching them, desperate for any new nugget of information. Amit told them that their phones were likely hacked, which was the last straw for Deanna.

'You'll hear a click,' he said, 'on the home line. A subtle ticking when you start speaking. Or, on your cellphones, it's messages. They'll listen in, get into your mailbox. Safest bet is to switch off your answering machines and shut the phones down.' So Deanna's done everything that she can. She's kept her computer running (having run her anti-virus to check for Trojans or whatever else people might have been using to spy on them), but the other computers and tablets have gone into the bag. Alyx used to tweet high-scores from the games that she was playing; even those would be guzzled up now. She can imagine it. *In this time of crisis, the Walker family has got the time to be playing games.*

She peeks out of the hole in the middle of the front door, a fish-eye lens view of the vans parked outside, trying to cram themselves into the spaces between driveways. They're pulled in at curious angles to allow access to their doors, half-parked on the sidewalk. Some of the crews are standing around talking, waiting for one of the Walkers to stick their head outside and offer to give an interview. Deanna imagines it; they will ask what she thinks of this all, and she will say, Well, we're stars. She'll beg for a reality TV show. She'll do her best fuck-off smile.

But still, they want answers. That's what the news says: that there must be something to this. They have experts on their shows, statisticians: nobody from *ClearVista*, admittedly, but others in the field. The guy who first predicted that Obama would be president a couple of terms back, he's the gold standard, and he's paraded on every show, telling every single host the same story about how this could have happened. He talks about the glorification of the science, but that the facts – the raw data – they cannot be cheated. *ClearVista*'s algorithm is accurate, he says. It's as close to a digital truth as we're liable to get.

Deanna has one cellphone still going, a disposable one that Amit brought around for them late yesterday. He had to fight through the reporters and cameras to get into the house, and when he did they ripped his suit, tearing a pocket from it in the crush. Laurence told him that he was to stay in their house; of course he was to stay with them. No arguments. Deanna didn't want him there, because he represented something to her. He was the beginning of a downward slope. Still, he gave them a phone that nobody had the number to, what he called a burner, designed to be thrown away when it was done with. Deanna calls Alyx's school and she explains who she is. The woman at the other end is silent.

'Alyx won't be in today,' Deanna says.

'Is everything okay?' the receptionist asks. Her tone is immediately one of shock, of slight panic. It's almost conspiratorial. *Tell me if you're in trouble and I'll help you.*

'It's fine,' Deanna says. 'Honestly, it's fine.' Whatever happens, both women know this to be a lie: one because she can see the TV crews outside her house when she looks; the other because she's watching it on her own television. Deanna goes back to the fish-eye spyhole and peers through again, and she sees the reporters amassing, somebody having done a coffee run. They stand around in small groups and talk, nodding their heads in agreement over something. They aren't leaving any time soon.

She turns on the television, muting it. Subtitles spring up along the bottom of the screen. She doesn't want Alyx to hear anything bad, anything that might scare her, so she tries to keep that stuff locked down. Last night, one of the more overtly right-wing shows said that perhaps they should be being harder on Laurence. Perhaps there's something we don't know; something in his past.

'*ClearVista* does this. Like they say, the numbers don't lie. Maybe they know something that we don't, and Laurence Walker . . . Maybe he's not the man that Americans thought he was.' It was throwaway, a cursory glance of a phrase that was left hanging as soon as it was said, none of the other hosts responding, but Deanna felt something inside her: wanting to defend him, but not knowing if she could.

On one of the channels they are still showing snippets of the video. Most of them are not, because they have had complaints; about the imagery, which isn't graphic, but is so suggestive. It's almost salacious, therefore, for the ones who are still showing it. The ones who have stuck to their guns seem almost obsessed. It's become a mission for them, to get to the bottom of it.

She hears Alyx pad down the stairs and then come into the kitchen, rubbing at her eyes.

'You hungry, Pumpkin?' Deanna asks. Alyx nods, still in her pyjamas. She yawns and climbs onto her stool, and then looks up at the TV screen. Deanna flicks it over.

'Was that us?' the little girl asks.

'No,' Deanna says. 'Just somebody who looks

like us.' She puts Pop-Tarts into the toaster and pours a glass of juice. 'Drink your drink,' she says.

When Laurence finally comes downstairs, he's dressed in a shirt and trousers. The shirt is hanging off him – she doesn't know how it's possible, that he could look this much thinner only a few days after she last saw him in clothes like this, that they could look even more like rags draped over a coat-hanger frame – but he's done his best. He's shaved his face, tidied himself up and combed his hair. Amit is with him, standing behind him on the stairs as he calls to Deanna. She leaves Alyx watching cartoons and takes the remote with her so that she can't switch over and catch anything of what's going on.

'I'm going to talk to them,' her husband says. 'We've spoken about this,' he looks at Amit, 'and we think it's a good idea.'

'No,' Amit says, '*you* think it's a good idea.'

Laurence takes Deanna's hand. 'It can't hurt.'

'Of course it can,' she says.

'I can't be done,' Laurence tells her.

'Why not? Why can't you be done?' She laughs to herself, at how ridiculous this all is, the thing that he's put first, ever since Sean died. 'Just do what you want, Laurence. You save this, if it's that important to you.' She goes to the kitchen and tells Alyx to go upstairs and wake her sister. 'I need to watch something on the television,' she says. She switches to Channel 5, to the live news

262

feed, as she hears the roar of the reporters outside the front of the house, and they cut to their live feed. She turns the volume back on, so quiet that she can barely hear it, so she stands right up close to the set. She wants to know what he can possibly say to make this better now.

'We go now to Sandra Leppets, outside the Walker residence.' Deanna watches this woman appear on her screen, blonde hair and a tan that's far beyond natural. Behind her, Deanna sees their front door opening, and then he's there, and he clears his throat. Nothing about this is prepared; this is simply a man who would have been king, wearing a five hundred dollar white shirt that doesn't fit any more. He has polished himself as best he can, but he still looks ruined, Deanna thinks. For a second, she forgives him for everything; for a second, she feels sorry for him.

'I won't keep you long,' Laurence says to the assembled cameras. He's got an easy charisma when he talks politics, one that's far subtler when he's in family mode. When he's working, he almost makes it seem effortless. Deanna thinks that holding in how he's feeling now is wrong. Now, maybe, he should be focused on being more human, less politician. 'You've all seen the video of something that hasn't happened, and is not going to happen. It cannot and will not be true. This is mechanical error; it's the result of a computer going wrong. We've all had that, and we all know what a pain in the ass it can be. Imagine what this feels like. There's no trying to turn it off and on again.' He goes for a laugh, and doesn't get one. 'I can't explain it, because I'm not a man who knows about technology.' Earthy, homely language. 'I'm just like you.' He's electioneering, Deanna thinks. Refusing to accept that he's out of the race; instead, he's still clinging on, or clawing back. 'Ever since I lost my son,' he says, and that makes Deanna feel sick. Using that, here and now.

She shuts off the television and opens the back door to the house. Standing in the garden, she can feel the cold of the morning on her face, and she breathes in as deeply as she can. She doesn't want to hate him for this. That would be the worst thing that could happen.

Lane finally gets up and showers and dresses and she comes downstairs and tells her parents – sitting with Amit in the living room, watching her father on the television from earlier in the day – that she's going out.

'You can't,' Deanna says. 'You really should stay here today, Laney.'

'I'm meeting my friends,' Lane says. 'I won't be late.' She doesn't wait for the conversation to go any further; she turns and opens the front door, and she's out. She knows that Deanna won't follow her out to the cameras, because she won't want to make a scene in front of them, so they're almost a barrier of protection; a way of her getting exactly what she wants. The reporters all stand up as she comes out, clearly not expecting action again so fast, and they try to ask her questions. They ask her about her father. They ask why this happened; if he's done anything untoward; given any indication that he's not the man that he says he is; if he's ever hurt any of them before. One of them asks if he's ever tried to abuse her, the question hard and direct, come from nowhere. She doesn't see who asked it.

'Screw you,' she says, and she gives them the finger, some young punk gesture that makes her feel almost empowered. She starts to run down the street, and she carries on until she gets to the bus stop. While she catches her breath and waits for it to come she watches the end of the road to see if the reporters and cameras have followed her. But there's nothing, only a couple of cars on the street, some rubberneckers gawping at her – not because they recognize her, but because of how she looks. The bus comes, right on schedule, and she swipes her card and sits at the back, and she watches the television screens embedded into the plastic lining of the walls, the pundits talking about her family. They show the *ClearVista* video again, here in public. Everybody on the bus has seen it already, but what's another view? Some women a few rows ahead of Lane talk about how terrible it is, and how they totally misjudged Laurence Walker. He seemed – past tense – like such a nice man. Now, evidently, he's not. This is all, to them, a foregone conclusion.

When the bus arrives at the mall, Lane pushes her way off, through the people dawdling and taking their time. She doesn't want to be recognized, and she pulls the hood of her sweatshirt over her head. She goes in through the big doors, and she smells the fountains and the bakeries that sit near the entrance, and she looks to see if there's anybody she knows so that she can avoid them. Her friends all called her before her mother had their numbers wiped out, but she cancelled every single call. Even William tried to phone: William, whom she's been having sex with, not because she even really likes him but because it's something to do; who wasn't even popular until he began following her around like that old cartoon skunk, smitten and besotted and buying her conventional romantic bullshit like flowers that she doesn't want and chocolates that she doesn't eat; who didn't even know what the fuck to do with himself in bed, until she taught him. She doesn't want anybody to ask her if she's okay. So instead she goes upstairs, to where the tattoo place is, and she walks in and sits opposite Carmela, the receptionist, and they talk for a while. Carmela doesn't know who she is in the context of the wider world; she's just Lane, who comes in here for her ink. Carmella doesn't strike Lane as the news-watching type.

'Is he busy?' Lane asks.

'Only for another five minutes. What are you thinking?'

'Another bud.'

266

'I'll put you down for an hour.' She looks over at the door as the person before Lane – a heavy-set man in a jacket with Iron Man painted onto the back, his forearm bandaged – comes out. Behind him stands Reif. He's got his needle in his hand, and he sticks his tongue out at Lane and wriggles it in lieu of actually saying hello. He's had his tongue split, one of the many body mods he's taken on over the years, and he's trained himself to make each half of the tongue move of its own accord. Lane and he had a thing for a couple of weeks, after she began getting work done on the vine. She hated kissing him with it; the things he would do, rolling his tongues around hers, searching her teeth, like tentacles digging around inside her mouth. He talked to her about the other things he could do with it, if she would only let him. After that, she broke it off with him, told him that she had a boyfriend. Now, it's a working relation-ship. She's a model and muse (and occasional artist), and he's doing his finest work on her skin.

'Strip off and sit yourself down,' he says. She pulls off her top and bra, crossing her arms across her chest, and she lies on his chair, face down.

'Next bud,' she says.

'I've been waiting for this. Where are you thinking?'

'Take it round, up between the shoulder blades.'

'Okay. Know what you want on it yet?' She usually brings him a sketch, a drawing, and he translates it. It's all co-operative.

'No. Just do the base.' Her tattoo is to remember everything that happens in her life: the day-to-day, the events, indelibly rendered on her skin. She wonders when she will be filled up, when she will feel that there is no more skin – no more life – to paint onto herself. This one will remember this time. She doesn't know what it will be.

'Got an image in mind, even?'

'Not yet,' she says. 'Words, probably. We'll do it another time.'

'Sure thing.' He preps the needle and straddles her, sitting on her ass. He's so light; thinner than her even, she thinks. 'You're a work of art, you know. You're pretty much my masterpiece.'

'I know,' she says. He tells her to brace herself, but she doesn't even really feel the needle any more. It's a scratching on her skin, an itch that she can never reach herself.

She's sore when she's done, resisting the urge to go at the newly bandaged skin. This is when it hurts most; when she's out of there and she wants it to just be ready for the world. The design itself has gotten more complicated, both as Reif's work has improved and as she has stopped balking as much at the pain of the procedure. The early leaves and stems are primitive, she thinks, as she looks at herself in the mirrored walls of the studio, the latter ones more delicate. Reif has said that he can go over the earlier ones again, adding texture in the blacks, the lines that run around and through the whole thing, but she's refused. She likes that it's crude. The point was always to capture times and places and events. It was about memories. She imagines that, by the end – she pictures the buds across her back, her chest, down her legs, with the final bud, whatever that may be, on the back of her head, pushing its way into her skull from her neck – by the end this will all be beautiful, and the final stems will be so well drawn that the progression will make even more sense. Something about it will become as whole as she is; or as she will one day become.

She dresses and kisses Reif on the cheek, to say goodbye.

'You're really amazing,' he says. 'A work of bloody art.' She kisses him again, to thank him. He's unflinching in his devotion to her. She waves to Carmela, who is talking to another client, and she walks through the mall, shrugging off the ache on her back. She goes to a store and tries on a leather jacket, and she loves it – the hang of it on her body, the way it's short enough to let her skin show through – and so she buys it. She doesn't even think. She's been saving money for years, every cent she's ever earned or scrimped. It's three hundred dollars, but some things, she reasons, are worth it. She goes to a small telephone store and buys a disposable SIM card and a cheap handset, and she syncs her contacts from the cloud and then dials William, who asks her how she is, and tells her how worried he's been about her. She hears his mother's voice in the background, asking about her as well. There's always a first time to show any sign of giving a shit about somebody, Lane thinks. William's mother asks if she wants to go and stay there for a while. She hangs up before William can tell her that he loves her, or something stupid like that. She doesn't want this to play out this way.

She wanders the food court and buys a plate of sushi from one of the vendors, but it's warm and she can't face the tuna, because it's gone nearly full-brown; and then she makes her way to an electronics shop, thinking about buying herself a new camera, because that's part of her future, she thinks. It's something that she's always wanted to do. Her father told her to do something artistic and she thinks that this could be her option. She's good at drawing, but better at memories, at recording them. Maybe, when all of this ends, when life returns to being back how it was, she can think about it. She remembers what it used to be like, when Sean was alive. The two seem so linked in her mind: her father as being present, and her brother still being a part of their lives. She knows that it's not why he pushed away, but she wishes that the two hadn't happened at the same time. She wants him back, and everything else that they had.

It's like magic, the timing: she ends up in the television section of the store, and her family is on every set, broadcast in beautiful HD, beamed across all the sets in some fractured unity. There they all are, in some cases as large as day. Lane looks down at the far end of the shop and there, in the non-screen section, the video is filling the walls. The smell from the HoloGas projectors hits her and a 3D projection of her father steps out of those walls, brought forward, becoming manifest. Behind him, she sees herself, and her father's eye glitches.

'Can I help you?' a voice asks. She turns quickly, to stop having to look. It's a shop assistant, only a couple of years older than Lane. His face lights up, the gleam of seeing a celebrity. 'Oh shit, it's you!' he says. 'From the video. Oh my God!' Lane turns and runs, sprints, through the shop. She pulls out the new cellphone and dials her mother's number, but that's dead, and her father's. She can't remember the number for the disposable phone her mother bought, so she keeps going to the bus stop, but there isn't one waiting and she doesn't want to stand here, she needs to keep moving. She gets into a cab and tells the driver an address around the corner from where she lives and the whole drive she tries to not make eye contact with him, even though he keeps glancing into the mirror, sizing her up. His car stinks of cigarette smoke and decaying plastic, and he sings under his breath to the songs on the radio, rock songs that Lane doesn't know, but that just sound so very old to her.

By the time she gets to the house, the news crews are talking, drinking coffees again, waiting for something, anything, to happen. Most of them are tucked into the backs of the vans, the doors swung wide, relishing the chance to sit and not pay attention to the house. They've gotten slack so quickly. She stays on the other side of the road, walking slowly, hidden behind cars so as not to be noticed. She's at the front door and inside before they've even managed to get their cameras out.

'You're home,' Deanna says. Her father and Amit are nowhere to be seen; just her mother and sister, watching telenovelas with the subtitles on.

'Did they ask you anything?' Deanna asks, standing and walking over to her eldest daughter.

'I ran past them,' Lane says. She grabs her mother's arm and drags her out of the room, into the hall, and she pulls the door shut between them. She whispers, 'We can't keep this from her forever.'

'We can try,' Deanna says. 'This will blow over.'

'You really think?' Lane asks. Deanna nods. She holds her daughter, pulling her in and wrapping her arms around her. Lane winces at the pain on her new tattoo, but doesn't give herself away. They breathe each other in; old, familiar smells that will never change, no matter what body spray or perfume they might use.

'We'll find out way back to normal,' Deanna says. She thinks, while they stand there and slightly sway in each other's embrace, that she doesn't remember what normal is any more: because normal was before politics; before they lost Sean;

before any of this became a part of their lives that they simply didn't have a chance of escaping from.

'I hope it's soon,' Lane says. She's sobbing into her mother's shoulder. Deanna doesn't know if she means the situation, or everything else.

'Me too,' she says.

Amit reads *Twitter* while Laurence watches the news channels pick apart his statement. He looks gaunt on the screen, yes, but there's a fire in his belly, or at least the imitation of one. The television show hosts talk about it in terms that they understand, the raised eyes of somebody controlling spin on their own terms, trying to get to grips with what has happened while still being unable to avoid irrefutable facts. Here, they have a video. They all have it, and they all show it, and they all talk about Laurence's chances as a viable candidate after this.

'If he overcomes this situation,' one of them says, 'maybe in another four, maybe eight years, he could run. Maybe, if he manages to prove that *ClearVista* screwed the pooch, gets the visual out of the public's mind, and he can step up, use this somehow, run on issues relating to it; something to do with privacy and . . .' He can't finish the thought, because it just sounds so unconvincing.

'He hasn't got a chance,' another says, in reply. 'There is not a chance in hell of this man ever becoming our President. You try picturing Laurence Walker as he was before this video came out. You try it. Not going to happen, even if he spends the rest of his life saving puppies from fires and curing, I don't know, curing cancer. It is simply never going to happen.'

He flicks to another channel. Bull Brady's show is on. He's at his desk, ten-gallon hat on his head, and there's a picture of three men – Laurence and the other two candidates – hanging from a wire that runs above him.

'It's now a two-horse race, Homme and Maitland. And that pretty much means it's a one-horse race, right? Homme's going to be the next Democratic nominee, staunch left be damned, so get your voting buttons printed, your leaflets, your websites prepared. Because Laurence Walker? He's out of this.' He takes a Zippo lighter from his pocket and he flicks it with one hand, the skill of a lifelong cigar smoker, and he holds it up to the printed photograph of Laurence. It catches immediately, obviously pre-treated, and the flames rush up and over Laurence's face. It flakes away and Bull laughs as people run in with fire extinguishers. 'Yeah, you put that out,' he says. 'That is *done*.' He laughs. Amit reaches over and switches off the set.

'I don't know what to say,' he tells Laurence.

'No, you don't.' Laurence keeps his eyes on where the screen was: focused on the wall now, intently staring. 'You're fired,' he says.

'Laurence!'

'This leaked because of you.'

'I didn't do anything—'

'Just go.' He doesn't look at him, not once. Amit stands up.

'Okay,' he says, 'your call. I'm still talking to *ClearVista*, to find out what happened. I want to know. I take it you do as well.' Laurence doesn't reply. 'You're a good man, Laurence. I've seen it. I know it.' He leaves the room and heads downstairs. Deanna looks over at him.

'You're leaving?' she asks.

'He fired me. Says it's my fault.'

'Oh.' She doesn't ask if it is. Everything is, and nothing. If this all blows over, Deanna thinks, Amit should be commended; he'll have dragged Laurence out of politics, which – she now realizes – is something she's wanted for the longest time.

'Listen, Dee, I wasn't planning on going anywhere until this was done. This is going to get worse before it gets better. They're not going to let this lie. They haven't broken him yet, but they will, because there's a reason for them to do it.' He reaches out to her, taking her arm. She lets him. 'You've got my number, my email. Get in touch if this gets worse. I don't know what I can do, but I'll do whatever I can.'

'Okay,' she says. He opens the door. The news teams are ready this time, and there are cameras flashes and shouts for his attention – as if he could miss them – and their calls are what suddenly alerts him to their otherwise subtle presence. The door slams behind him as he steps into the throng. As Deanna turns, she sees Laurence standing halfway up the stairs. 'Are you all right?' she asks.

'I'm fine,' he says. 'I'm absolutely fine.' He stretches, and she thinks of a mantis, rising up to strike. 'We've got to brave the rain, right?' He comes towards her and squeezes her arm, the same arm that Amit just held, and he walks into the living room and starts talking to Alyx. His feet seem to drag across the floor as he walks. She doesn't know where he's gone; only that he's not here any more.

Amit drives back to DC. He puts gobby nineties punk music on the stereo, the stuff that he listened to when he was a kid, and he spits the lyrics along with the songs, relishing every swear word and 'oi' screamed from the speakers. He hammers the steering wheel with his hands to the drumbeats, trying to pick himself up. Laurence's career might be done, but his isn't. Amit has got another career ahead of him, another candidate entirely. All he needs to do is lay the blame firmly at Laurence's door, claim that he was unstable, that he was difficult, insinuate there were *secrets* in that family that nobody talked about with half-truths and vague lies, and he's fine. If he makes suggestions that this was out of his control, buries the past fully, he'll get another candidate. But still, he thinks, there's more to this. He pictures Laurence with the gun, an image that came from nothing.

He doesn't turn off for his apartment. Instead he stays on roads that lead him up through the tourist areas, up past hotels and boutique shops and towards Georgetown. He parks in a shopping-center car park, watching to see if he's followed in. Laurence was sure that there were people watching them before; if he was wrong, there certainly will be now. The delegates will have made sure of that. Amit has enough missed calls from them, begging for him to call them. They say that they just want to talk strategy, but these are conversations that only really end one way.

He walks to Hershel's gated street. Hershel was the only other person who knew about the video, who had access to it. He hasn't heard from him since it leaked, no emails or tweets or texts asking him if he's all right, nothing asking if he should stop working on it. It's possible that he doesn't watch the news, so maybe he's missed what has happened; but it's equally possible that there's another reason. Somebody had to have leaked the video.

Amit goes to the security gate. It's the same officer as before, and he seems to recognize him.

'You're here for . . .' he says, leaving it hanging, as if it's on the tip of his tongue.

'Hershel. Thom Hershel.'

'Yeah, yeah. Of course. I remember you now.' He picks up the small telephone on the desk and presses a button, and the phone rings and rings. He frowns. 'No answer,' he says to Amit. 'Maybe you should try calling his phone or something.'

'I can't just get in myself? I knock on the door, he'll wake up. He must be asleep or something.'

'Not going to happen,' the guard says. His eyes twitch past Amit at the door. 'Shut that on your way out.'

Amit stands in the street. He wonders if Hershel is avoiding him on purpose; if this is his guilt at leaking the video manifesting itself in avoidance. A car turns off the main road, and Amit sees the driver for a second, an elderly lady, string of jewels lying across her neck. The gates open, creaking, and Amit runs. He doesn't know why, exactly, other than he needs to look Hershel in the eyes and ask him what he did, and why he let the video out into the world.

He runs to Hershel's house, to his front door, and he hammers his palms on it. It's reinforced, barely making a sound under his hands. A shout comes from the security guard, now in pursuit. Amit tries the handle and it turns, the door opening. All the lights are on, but the house is quiet. Everything reflects off everything else: all the marble, the lights and the mirrors and the glass that covers the paintings hanging from the walls. He runs through, shouting Hershel's name, and there's nobody here; so he runs up the stairs. The security guard is in the house as well, shouting wordless cries to get Amit to stop. Amit tries the doors on the upper level: empty bedrooms, the beds made up. Then, finally, he finds Hershel. From the light in the hallway, Amit can see two other people, a woman and a man, sprawled out on top of the covers next to Hershel.

They stir at the light; Hershel turns over, away from it.

'Wake the fuck up!' Amit says. The security guard appears, grabbing Amit's shoulder.

'I am so sorry, Mr Hershel,' he says.

'It's fine,' Hershel says. He sits up and rubs his face, and he looks at Amit. 'It's fine. Let him be, whatever.' He shuffles to the edge of the bed and covers his groin, hiding his penis behind his hands. 'Didn't expect this,' he says. The guard lets Amit go and walks off, huffing and heaving as he goes downstairs. Hershel stands up and finds a pair of boxer shorts on the floor and pulls them on; and then a T-shirt, emblazoned with a logo from some sci-fi television show that hasn't been on the air in decades. 'I saw what happened,' he says. He walks out of the bedroom, pulling the door shut, letting his companions sleep still. He wipes his face. 'Big night.'

'Did you leak it?' Amit asks.

'What?'

'You had the video. Did you leak it?'

'Why the fuck would I do that?'

'Maybe somebody paid you for it.'

'And you think I need the money?' Amit follows Hershel down the marble staircase. On the far wall is a painting of some man on a horse; a lord or a baron or something. It's not nice, doesn't even demonstrate much skill that Amit can see, but it's evidently worth something. That says a lot.

'Maybe one of the people who was here.'

'They've got better things to do. Besides, you think they know who the fuck you even are?'

'They might know who Laurence is.'

'They don't.' He says it sternly. 'Look, I've got some stuff for you.'

'What do you mean?'

'When did you leave *ClearVista*?' In the living room Hershel boots a PC, a thick black box that's in a drawer, bringing up the OS on the HoloGas. He swipes to maneuver the desktop, loading up software that Amit recognizes the name of. *TNG, The Numbers Game*, the software that they created at *ClearVista* to test the algorithm.

'You took builds when you left?'

'I took everything,' Hershel says. He grins. 'Where was it at when you quit?'

'It was running, just about. Start of 2014.'

'Jesus. You weren't there when they got the miner up and running, then.'

'No.'

'Okay, so that's when the algorithm started to work. We were able to gather enough variable information to start to actually decipher things. We went back through history, testing the algo-rithm – which was still growing, I should stress, we weren't even close to a final equation – but we tested it with the miner, seeing what it could help to do. It enhanced everything. We called every single election result we could get any data for. Everywhere. UK election in '15 was the big one. We called that two months before it actually happened, got it down to a percentile. Not even joking. After that, every major world election we refined the algorithm; every sporting event, every fricking Oscar winner. We did nothing but push that thing to be able to sift and work data. But here's the thing: we didn't know exactly how it worked.'

'What do you mean?'

'Look, it's numbers. And there's a part between feeding in the info from the data miner and running the algorithm with that data that just . . . worked. I mean, look, we knew what we were doing for most of it. But then, it's not like you can watch the cogs.' He brings up a keyboard. 'Pick something. A sports event, something like that.'

'Football.'

'Right. The Superbowl, okay? So we take the Giants, and we ask their chances of winning. Simple. Pick these values . . .' He drags in data, websites and newspapers. He types quickly, beating out formulae in the air. 'Okay. So, we run this – and this isn't the full thing, because obviously that's cloud-powered over at *ClearVista*. Far, far more processing power than this. This is, like, a muted version of it, but the point should stand.' He points at the desktop in the air, walks up to it. 'I press go, and it does the data mining first. It goes through the Internet and it finds out everything it can. Past results of the teams involved, past results of the players taking part, injury form, personal details. Does their defense hold up when they're, I don't know, playing against the 49ers? I don't have the answers, but the Internet does, so now the algorithm will. And it brings that information in.' They wait; there's a beep. 'That's done. I only used the first twenty pages of Google results, but still. That's raw data. Now, I click this, and I apply the algorithm to it.' He presses a button on the desktop. Another beep; an icon bounces in the dock, and a PDF document fills the screen. 'And we've got an answer. That's all happened, and we can't see it. Can't check it. We trust it, because it works. But there's no way of looking under the hood and seeing exactly *what* it did with the information. It just works.' He scrolls through the document: the Giants, no chance of winning the Superbowl. That's likely going to be the Chiefs. Maybe the Ravens. It's almost a foregone conclusion.

'It's not an accident. You all knew what you were doing when you programmed it.'

'Yeah, we did. But sometimes, with math . . . I don't know, sometimes things just *work*. Some of the guys said it was like doing math in the dark. Like, you can't see it, and you can't tell it's happening. It was like magic. And that's the problem now.' He tosses out the new document and opens Laurence's results. 'I can see this stuff, and I can see the results of the data mining. There's nothing throwing up red flags. It's all normal stuff, far as I can see. But it's what I can't see that's caused this. There's something twisted in the machine.'

'So it's wrong?'

'No. No! It's right. But I'm going to try and pick this thing apart, maybe find out why and how. It's going to take time.'

'How long?'

'Took us years to put the algorithm together. No idea what it's going to be like going the other way. But I'm on it. No idea what else I can tell you, man. I'm on it.' He minimizes the desktop. 'Now, if you'll excuse me, I'm going to go back to bed.' He walks off through the house, the sound of his plastic sandals clapping against the marble. Amit lets himself out and walks back to his car. The gates open as he approaches, and he stands outside the guard's hut, wondering if he should knock and apologize. He does, but there's no answer. He wonders if the guard is asleep as well.

Deanna goes to bed early, because she wants to keep the lights in the house off; and she orders the girls to do the same. She doesn't ask what Laurence is doing. She leaves him downstairs alone, and when the house is quiet he puts his coat on and leaves through the kitchen's French windows. In the garden he moves some of the lawn furniture, a table and a chair, to the inter-secting wall at the end, which leads onto the woodlands that run behind their house. He reasons that nobody's going to be watching the back at this time of night, so he pulls himself up and over. He'll have to return through the front, sure, but that's not the part he's worried about. This is more important to him; getting out of the house and feeling something like freedom again. He pulls his hood out of the back of the coat, up and over his hair, and he trudges through the long grass towards the edge of the field. He sees the paths here that lead down towards the woods, and the lake, and the cabin. In the distance, lit by the moon, he can see glimpses of the lake through the trees, the reflective black of the water – and then a flash of Sean underwater. He can feel the water in the basement lapping at his shins, the water licking at him as his son tries to not drown. He walks on.

The grass is wet with the night and it soaks his shoes, but he doesn't care. He breathes the air and turns from the path, towards the street. He can see the lights of the town, the handful of restaurants and bars that keep this place powered during the evenings. People going about their business, doing as they want to do. Freedom, as a commodity, cannot be underestimated, he thinks. Actually, it's a right. It is a basic human right.

He climbs the fence that runs alongside the road and sets foot on the tarmac, cracked and dug up and in need of repair. The road stretches off, the night sky reflected on it. It glistens from the earlier rain. He walks down further, past the houses of people he knows and who know him. He has friends here. They have shared beers; they have promised to vote for him, given the chance. Had promised, he reminds himself. Past tense. Seems like everything is in the past tense, now.

He sees *Peaforks,* the town's best restaurant. He smells crab, their specialty, on the air. But it's busy, and it's bright, and through the window he sees people that he knows, grinning, eating meals together. *The Four Fathers,* Staunton's only bar, is opposite, the inside darker, and the lot nearly empty; so he chooses that instead, running up the steps. The soaked-through hardwood is damp and muffled. There's very little noise from inside, only a few voices, and the crack of the pool table. As he opens the door, he hears rock music, stuff that they listened to when he was at college; the distant chunk of power-chords and strained vocals. There are four people here: they all turn to look at him.

'Hi,' he says. They don't break their stares; and they don't greet him, or ask how he is. 'Sorry about the journalists. I've been, uh, stuck in the house. I needed a break.' He feels as if he should make an excuse. They'll be wondering why he isn't at home. They'll be wondering all sorts of things. 'They won't leave us alone. I had to get out, you know?' None of the four say anything. Amy Scarsdale, the daughter of the old man who owns the place, is behind the bar. Laurence nods at her. 'I'll have one, if you're pouring.' She doesn't move to. She looks at Trent Henderson instead, who is sitting in front of her, nursing one himself. He has both hands around the glass – it's freshly poured and already half-gone, Laurence can tell, from the prints in the condensation on it – and he looks at her and nods.

Who is he to give her permission? Laurence thinks. Who the hell is Trent Henderson? He's a grocer. He doesn't run this town. She pulls the beer and sets it down, and Laurence walks over and lays a five on the counter for her. 'Keep the rest,' he says. He stands at the far end of the bar and sips from it. It tastes amazing, he thinks. It's better than anything. He doesn't know how long it's been since he's had one, not freshly poured like this, but this tastes better than any he can remember. He drinks again, a bigger gulp this time, and looks over at Trent Henderson again, who hasn't stopped staring at him.

'What are you doing here, Laurence?' Trent asks. He doesn't break eye contact; he doesn't take his hands from his glass, either. Behind him, Andrew Chase and some boy that Laurence doesn't recognize – barely eighteen, let alone old enough to be drinking beer – stop playing pool. They stay hunched over the table, their cues in their hands. Trent brings his head to his glass, almost, raising it only slightly from the bar, and he drinks. 'Don't you have other matters to attend to?'

'Trent, I needed to breathe,' Laurence says. 'You've seen the news.' He lets that hang, as if that's all the excuse he needs. They'll understand, he thinks. I'm a wronged man. Trent doesn't reply, so Laurence speaks again. 'They're outside the house. They're ruining our lives.'

286

'We've all seen the news,' Trent says. 'Saw that video of you, as well.'

'And that video is a lie, is what that is. A mistake. I've got people looking into it.' He thinks about Amit; how maybe he was rash in firing him. 'It's horseshit, frankly. It'll all get sorted out.'

'Good,' Trent says, 'because you understand how it looks to us. People like us, we see that . . . we call it how we see it, and we're frightful protective of Deanna. She's been here her whole life; we know her. She's a part of us. You understand that, Laurence.'

'But you know that I'm not that man,' Laurence says. 'You were at our wedding, Trent. You know me.'

'I'm not sure that I do, Laurence. The measure of a man comes in his deeds, not his words. And I've heard your words, but until now, hadn't really seen your deeds.'

'You *still* haven't. The video isn't real. It isn't my deeds.' Laurence realizes that he's gritting his teeth; that he's raised his voice. The boys at the pool table stand upright, cues in hand. 'Listen. That stuff, I don't understand it. I ticked boxes, and I ticked one wrong. You understand that it isn't real, video like that.'

'Sure seems like that's not how the television is treating it.'

'No. I know. I mean, they're fucking—' Trent seems to squint at Laurence's swearing. As if that's a crime in itself, another affront. 'They're after *anything*. They've turned this into a story when there's nothing there. All I want is to protect my family. You have to see that.'

'I don't have to do anything,' Trent says. 'And as long as your wife and daughters stay safe, that won't change.' He takes his hands from the glass. The beer is all gone and another takes its place. 'I think you should probably just leave now, Laurence.'

'I'm only trying to have a quiet drink,' Laurence says. He lifts his own glass to his mouth and takes a gulp. He feels his arm shake, the glass chatter against his teeth slightly. 'Please. I just needed a break.'

'As it seems we all do, Laurence. I suggest you take yours away from this establishment. In fact, I suggest you take yours away from Staunton. You say you want to protect your family? Why not remove yourself from the equation entirely?' And then Trent reaches into his pocket. He doesn't pull anything out, and there's no click of a safety catch, but Laurence knows what he's got in there. He's seen him at weekends, down at the range. During hunting season he's seen him heading out to the forests by the lake with his shotgun and his rifle and his deerstalker, the ties knotted underneath his chin as if he's still a kid. Laurence stands up and puts the beer glass down on the counter.

'Whatever you say,' he says. He turns and walks out, into the cold of the air, and there are people on the streets, having just left *Peaforks*. He knows

288

them all; some better than others, but they're all at least acquaintances, all people he would have stopped and talked with before. He would have asked about their kids and told them about his. They might have asked about Sean, or asked how he was, and they would have cocked their heads when they asked, the knowing gesture of gentle unheralded sympathy; and he would have nodded that it was getting better. He misses that. He misses that connection. They look at him and they stop talking, and they start to walk off, away from him; or some of them stay standing where they are, waiting for him to leave. He knows them all, every single one of them by name. He knows where they live. His children have played with theirs; he has eaten with them, gotten drunk with them, fired off fireworks with them.

'You have to understand,' he says, in the street, into the air between them, but he doesn't know what he's going to follow it up with. They don't have to understand anything; they don't have to listen to him, or talk to him. They don't have to empathize. They have seen what they needed to see.

Laurence turns and walks off, back down towards his house. He can't go back the way he came, because there's no way back over the wall from this side; no lawn furniture for him to stand on and climb over with. He has to take the road. He looks back and the people of Staunton are still standing there, watching him leave. He focuses again on his house, in the distance, the small stretch of clapboard houses with their front yards and expansive driveways.

'Asshole,' he hears, through the air. He knows the voice but can't put a finger on it. There's no laughter; it's slightly pitiful, how somber the shout is. It's almost token, made to fill the void between them. Laurence keeps going, past houses and cars, and he sees the hubbub of reporters and journalists ahead, so he crosses the road, trying to stay inconspicuous for as long as possible. He gets closer and sees them on the pavement, eating takeaway from boxes of food. *Peaforks*, the boxes have printed on their side, and he can see it from here: the reporters enjoying the crab he once loved, lifting the soft-shell legs to their mouths, drinking beer from cans. They have swapped shifts: a new woman is there, doing her hair, checking her face in a mirror. And there, a new man: tall, with a white shirt. Laurence can't see his face. He puts a jacket on and it's blue and crumpled and he talks and jokes with some of the other people sitting around. He doesn't know if it's the same man, but this is too coincidental. How many blue jackets can there be like that?

Laurence stays a few houses away, listening to their voices. He becomes aware of his fear; of the feeling of it inside his body. It feels as if he's drunk: like when he was in *Henderson's*; like when he was in the army; the heave of a desperation for air, or for something that he doesn't have inside him. He feels his blood in his temples, pulsing so terribly that it almost hurts for it to be there; and he staggers into one of the hedges that marks the garden of his neighbor's house. He coughs and sputters, and he clutches at his chest. He hears a door opening behind him, and a woman's voice asking him if he's all right.

'It's Walker,' she says. There's a gasp as he hits the floor, a second's wait before they come towards him; giving him time to die, he thinks, if that's what is happening.

'Are you filming?' another voice asks. He looks upwards, but all that he can see is the moon and the stars; and then light from the cameras. A flash of that blue jacket, as if he knew. *He knew.* Somebody asks if he's all right and he tries to move, but he can't get himself up any further than he already is. He wants to crawl away from them, to get back inside, but instead he rolls backwards, hitting his head on the soil next to the bush, and he says Deanna's name, but he's not sure that the news crews are listening to him. They ask him questions – some about how he is, but some about the video, and about his prospects, and about who he is, what measure of man – and he tries to shout his wife's name, but if he manages it he can't hear it over their voices, as they crowd him and don't give him the air he desperately craves.

CHAPTER 11

Laurence opens his eyes to stark white walls; to the table next to the bed, which has a clipboard resting across it; to the chair in the corner of the room. He sees its worn fabric arms; it's varnished, orange wooden frame; and Sean, sitting in it. His son, propped up, asleep in the chair. Laurence leans up to speak to him. It's been so long since he saw him, since he last held him. He thinks that this could be the answer to all of his problems; that being able to hold Sean might somehow change this all. If Sean is alive, then none of the last however-long-it's-been is real. If Sean is alive, he can hold the family together, and his future. He reaches out to him and says his name, and Sean opens his eyes as Deanna takes Laurence's hand, blocking his view of the chair.

'Wait,' Laurence says, and he moves his head. Alyx is on the chair, her hair cut short, just as her brother's was. He mistook her, that's all. It is such an easy mistake. He feels something slip away, then: the possibility that all of this might have been somehow imagined. The room reminds him of Sean. That's when he was last here, at the hospital.

He wonders if it could even be the same room where he held his son's body. Fate would make that happen. Fate does everything behind his back, sneaking around, stabbing and cajoling.

'Am I okay?' he asks.

'You scared us, that's all,' Deanna says; and he pictures the video again, the terror in their eyes. Of course I did, he thinks.

The doctor tells him to avoid anything that will cause undue stress. She buries her eyes behind her glasses, trying to not make eye contact. He asks her if he can have something to help him sleep.

'I have trouble,' Laurence explains. 'I don't know if I will be able.'

'I can write you a script for some antihistamines,' she says, 'but I think we should be avoid anything stronger for now.' He feels himself tremble; something inside him, shaking him. It feels like invisible hands. 'Mr Walker, if you're having trouble I would suggest therapy. There's obviously some serious stuff happening with you right now. All I can think is that you should talk to somebody. I can recommend some names.'

'We have someone,' he says.

'Then make appointments. Rest.' She puts the clipboard in the slot at the bottom of his bed. Laurence watches her leave. In the hallway, she squeezes Deanna's arm. She gives her a piece of paper as well, and writes something onto it. Laurence doesn't need to ask what it is: it'll be a private number, offering help if Deanna ever needs it. None of them know Laurence, not really, but they're all assuming what he might be capable of. He lies in the bed and wonders if he could be.

Deanna drives them all back home, and the new car is almost unreasonably silent. Alyx plays with her toys; Lane thinks about the design on her back and the sore ache of the last addition. She'll get it filled next week; she just needs to know how to commemorate this time in their lives. For better or worse, this is important. This is a milestone.

Deanna doesn't slow down as she comes towards the news crews. They've grown in number since Laurence was rushed off to the hospital, those few stations that had held out finally getting people along to follow this new branch of the story. They don't see it going away. Laurence hasn't formally stepped out of the running yet and they all know there's been no answer about the video. Either there will be answers eventually, or everything will come to a head. So they've massed, camping out on the side of the road. There's a gap barely wide enough for their car to fit through in between their vans. Deanna doesn't stop. She doesn't beep her horn; those of them standing in their driveway are forced to dive out of the way as she pulls up and onto the ramp. They start filming them, shouting questions. Deanna leans back and looks at Alyx.

'Hands over your ears, and don't listen to what

I'm going to say to these people,' she says. She looks at Lane. 'You get your sister inside, then come and help me with your father.'

'I'm fine,' he says, but he knows that he's weak. If they rushed him, he'd be on the ground. He would be back where he began.

'Let me help you,' Deanna says, and then she opens the car door. 'Back the fuck off,' she yells. She swears so that they can't use this on air. 'Come on,' she says to the kids. 'Let's go.' They all get out of the car, Laurence trying to move as fast as he can. She helps him, supports him, and they make it to the porch. The crowd shouts at him, ignoring Deanna and the kids: asking him about his health; if he's ever threatened his family; if he told the truth about what happened to Sean. That last one makes Laurence and Deanna stop. It's not obvious who asked it, in the throng. The question isn't repeated. Lane opens the door and they bundle themselves inside, straight down the hallway and into the living room. The kids stop in the doorway.

'Mom,' Lane says. Deanna pushes past. The living room has been ransacked. The sofas are on their backs, the fabric torn and debased and the cushions pulled apart; the drawers opened and their contents pulled out and tipped onto the floor; the kitchen cupboards hanging wide, plates and glasses smashed, and food pulled out, and there is a bag of flour smeared over the counter, red wine poured on top of it, the smashed glass of the bottle on the side of the chaos; the photo albums from the shelves pulled down and pictures taken from behind the plastic sleeves, yanked out and the plastic left ripped; the fridge door open, as if there might have been secrets inside that; the calendar screen in the fridge door smashed; the photograph of them all missing, the magnet that held it up on the ground; the drawings that had been made, Sean's drawings that they had kept and would never ever have thrown away, torn up and screwed up or missing; the back doors swinging wide open; and in the garden, the doors to the shed thrown wide, the gardening tools and gloves and bags of seeds left strewn on the lawn; Deanna's laptop torn into two, the screen and the keyboard next to each other, taunting each other. Deanna takes out the cellphone she has been using and dials the police, and she waits and then explains what's been going on. The operator asks her if they've touched anything.

'No,' Deanna says.

'Be careful to not. Maybe go and stand outside, if you can. We'll send some officers round straight away.' Deanna hangs up.

'Don't touch anything,' she says to her family. 'Stay here. I'll be back.' She runs upstairs, to see the rest of the house. They have been everywhere, whoever it was. Every part of their home defiled. The house is ruined. She sits on their bed, which has been knifed at, the duvet torn apart, the mattress dug into, feathers and foam everywhere, and she sobs. I have to have this second, she thinks. I have to give myself that. She looks over, at the wardrobe, where the doors are opened, pulled wide and her clothes, his clothes, bundled on the floor, his suits all destroyed, cut up and torn apart. She sees a Converse shoebox tucked at the back of the wardrobe on Laurence's side. He hasn't worn those trainers in years. She hasn't even noticed that. Keepsakes, she reasons. She leans down and picks it up and opens it, and she finds photographs of the two of them from years ago, occasions that she barely remembers. There are pictures of his parents as well, which she has never seen; and underneath them, a stubby bolt-black pistol. She drops the box onto the shredded bedding at her feet and the weight of the gun makes it thud.

'Are you all right?' Lane calls up to her.

'Stay down there,' Deanna says. 'I'm fine. Stay there.' She can't be sure, not completely positive, but she's seen the gun before. She's seen it in his hand in that video. She leans down and picks it up, and she holds it. She has never held one before. It's lighter than she imagined. She thought that it would be weighed down, the power of it somehow imbuing it with heft. She holds it as if she were aiming it, pointing it at the wall. But there's nothing to target.

There's a knock on the door downstairs, heavy fists. She jumps, and she stands up. That will be the police. She has to put this somewhere. She opens her bedside table and moves her hairdryer and straighteners aside and slides it in underneath them, a drawer now full of ambiguous metallic black technology.

Robards and Templeton step into the room and ask the rest of them to stay behind them. They look around, peering into the cupboards. 'We saw on the news that you passed out,' Robards says to Laurence. 'You went to hospital. How long was the house unattended?'

'We were out all night,' 'Deanna says. 'We all went.' Robards nods. He mutters to Templeton, sending him out to the reporters to ask them if they saw anything.

'Rest of the house the same, you say?'

'Yes,' Deanna says.

'I mean, you know that there's a very good chance we'll never know who did this.' He pokes his tongue into the space below his bottom lip, making it jut, and he shakes his head. 'You think they were looking for anything?'

'There's nothing to look for.'

'No, I guess there's not.'

Deanna looks at Laurence, who is sitting on a seat in the corner, head bowed. 'We didn't want this.'

'Of course you didn't.' She tries to make eye contact, but he's focused on Laurence and he doesn't lift his eyes away. He watches Laurence's hands move, as he rubs them on his thighs. His palms are sweaty and they leave dark tracks on the gray fabric. Robards walks closer to him, and he glances at the rest of the room as if he's looking for something, but really – and it's obvious, because he's young and relatively new at this and not really at all subtle – he wants to get closer to Laurence. He wants to examine him.

'Listen,' Robards says, 'there are lots of folk in town who have questions.' Laurence looks up. 'You understand why, of course. People who trusted you, Mr Walker.'

'I haven't done anything,' Laurence says.

'I know, I know.' He smiles. 'Just want to make sure you're all feeling all right, that's all. You know how it is.' Templeton comes back and stands in the doorway, leaning back, his arms folded, hands tucked into his armpits.

'Nobody saw nothing,' he says.

'Which means, chances are they came in through the back. Somebody must've known to do that. You got any access at the back of the house?'

'There's a wall to the fields and the woods,' Deanna says, 'but there's no way over it.'

'That right?' He walks to the garden and out, and he keeps walking down towards the wall. Deanna follows, and Templeton. She sees the table up against the wall. 'Well, this is likely how they got over when they left,' he says. He stands on it and then on his tiptoes, and he peers over. 'Must make jumping the wall easy, having this here. Nothing the other side, mind you. Likely more than one of them, helped each other over.' He

299

walks back to the house and raises his voice in order to talk to Laurence. 'You shouldn't leave anything like this lying around. Could have trapped them here, or forced them out the front.'

Laurence stands up. 'The man in the jacket,' he says. He comes through to the garden, swift sharp movements that belie his previous state. 'There was a man outside, in a blue jacket. I've seen him before; at the airport, back when . . . before. And then again, when I was at the mall. He was here.'

'The blue jacket man again?' Robards and Templeton look at each other and smile, a shared, somehow weary joke.

'Yes. We gave you the thread, when you came before. That was him; he was back here.' Robards and Templeton look at each other.

'We'll ask outside if they know who you're talking about,' Robards says.

'They were with him,' Laurence says. 'He must have been watching me.'

'You sound awful paranoid,' Robards says.

'No, look outside. Against the wall. I put the table there, against the wall. I used it. He must have known that.'

'You put that there? You should be more careful,' Robards says. His response is calm but antagonistic; there's something there, Deanna thinks. Some insinuation. Laurence sees it as well.

'Was it you? Were you here?' he asks

'Don't make accusations, now, Mr Walker. We have better things to do than come and raid your house.' He gets closer to Laurence. Deanna can see this unraveling, suddenly. It turns from something natural to something dangerous. 'We're simply trying to keep the people of Staunton safe.'

'So why aren't you taking this more seriously? There was somebody here—'

'We're dealing with your situation in the manner that—'

'You're ignoring the fact that we are being hounded! There have been other people here, people going through our trash. I have been followed. I have been followed, and my family has been followed, and we've had an intruder in our house. Our goddamned house!' He raises his voice to a shout. Deanna puts her hand on his arm, to calm him, but he snaps it off; another jerk of his limbs. He gasps in air and his voice roars. 'We are being threatened. My family is being threatened. Can't you see that?'

'The only person we've seen threatening your family is you, Mr Laurence.' Robards steps closer, to within contact distance. 'Or have you not been watching the news?' Laurence steps forward, eye-to-eye.

'Don't,' Deanna says, but she doesn't touch him again. She's not seen him like this before.

'When your son died, you were there. But it seemed awful coincidental that you didn't hear him. Maybe we should have looked into what happened to your son more?' Robards says, and Laurence lunges, throwing his body on top of him, and then both fall to the floor. Templeton is ready and grabs at Laurence before he can do any damage. He yanks back Laurence's arm and pulls him backwards, snapping handcuffs onto his wrists. Robards pushes himself to standing and wipes his mouth with the back of his hand.

'Please don't do this,' Deanna says to Robards.

'This is all for your own sake, Mrs Walker. He's dangerous.'

'No,' she says.

'We're going to let him cool off in a cell. Won't do him any harm.' Robards grabs the bar between the cuffs and wrenches Laurence to his feet. He's crying, Deanna sees.

'Why are you doing this?' she asks.

'Laurence Walker,' Robards says, walking Laurence forward, through the living room and kitchen and into the hall, 'you have the right to remain silent when questioned.' He carries on the speech through semi-gritted teeth and opens the front door. Most of the camera crews are ready, and the ones that aren't jump to attention. He holds Laurence in the doorway while they prepare themselves, and they start shouting questions, but some of them are too slack-jawed to bother; and then Robards marches Laurence forward, Templeton following behind, and the camera crews and reporters swallow them entirely, engulfing them. It takes them five minutes to get Laurence into the squad car. Every single one of the reporters gets their shot, and their question ignored.

Deanna watches from the front door, and then, as the car pulls away, the reporters turn their attention to her, asking her what happened.

'Did he threaten you? Was he violent?' one of them asks. She slams the door and stands against it. At the top of the stairs, her daughters stare.

Emails come all afternoon, and notes are pushed through the door when knocks are ignored. People from the town, desperate to offer their commiserations and help. It's like when Sean died: offers of help; food being made to help Deanna through this time; words of understanding and congenial affection, and of pushing her away from Laurence, as if she has finally seen what they have all recently realized.

We've always liked you, Deanna. Words written by people who barely know her or her family. *Anything you need, we'll be there. Just say the word. This is a hard time, but it's for the best.* Deanna puts a ban on televisions. Deanna tells Alyx she can't watch it at all, not even the Spanish-language soaps. She doesn't want to run the risk of the channel being changed.

The three of them try to put the house back to something resembling normality. They clear away the trash and sort anything that they can into drawers. Lane sews up holes in the sofa cushions, just a patch job, but something to hold them together for as long as possible. They make it into a game for Alyx; cleaning up, something fun to do. They sing songs, but Deanna's heart isn't in it. She telephones her parents. They ask how she is. They beg her to go and stay with them. Her father takes the phone and asks her what happened.

He says, 'I'm not going to do anything about it, because it's your business; but so help me God, Laurence better not have lain a hand on you or the girls.'

'Of course he didn't,' Deanna says. She thinks about that moment where she tried to comfort him, then, but it's fleeting. It's a glance at the past, and wrong to judge him on that. Instead, with the telephone cradled between her shoulder and chin, she sits on the bed and turns the gun around and around in her hands. She balances the weight of it on her palm while her mother tells her that they will make up the bedrooms, just in case. They only live in Canada, her father reminds her; she could leave now and be there by midnight. 'I have to be here for Laurence,' Deanna replies. Besides, she thinks, you can't have another of your children running home with their tails between their legs. She talks to her sister, neutered and rehabbed so much that she barely sounds even real, and when she asks her to come home in this passive, small voice that doesn't emote the same way it used to, Deanna lets her hand hang down, the gun in it; and then she pulls it up, trying to get a feel for the weight of it. Everybody says that the kick is more than you expect; that it hurts if you aren't expecting it. She opens the barrel, to see if it's loaded; and she cocks the hammer at the back, and feels it click.

'I have to stay here for Laurence,' she says to her sister. 'When we've got this sorted out we'll all come to stay.'

'I don't know that he'll be welcome,' her sister says. 'Not after what he did.'

'He hasn't done anything,' Deanna tells her. 'That was a *prediction*.' She stops at that word. That's exactly what it was, she thinks. But of when? And does it have to come true? She holds the gun in her hand, and wonders what this is evidence of.

She says goodbye, promising them all that she'll be safe, that she knows how to handle herself, and that Laurence would never do anything to hurt her; and she dials Amit as soon as she's done. She lets it ring, but he doesn't answer. She leaves a message, begging him to call her back.

Amit emails the news channel that broke the story about Laurence, asking them who intercepted the story. He writes that he works for the Walker campaign, and he dangles the vague lure of an interview. They give him Jessie Ng's address within seconds.

I worked with Laurence Walker. We should probably talk, his email to her reads. He puts his phone number at the bottom and then waits, holding the handset. Everything feels like waiting to him.

He sifts through Hershel's notes. One is a list of details from the video. *Gun. Water (?). Gray suit, lemon tie, white shirt*; all details cross-referenced. Laurence had a gun license, and there's a photo of the make and model – the same as in the video. This is what the data miner did: picked up on this and made it a part of the prediction. The last subject has photographs of Laurence in the suit, taken the day that Sean died. *Coincidence?*, Hershel has written next to it. Hershel has manually attempted the equations that the algorithm made, knocking off approximate numbers; looking for causes and reasons to bring the percentile down. Repeatedly underlined are matters of public record: the fact that Laurence was tortured when he was in the war; the public's perception of him as a man not unlikely to have a breakdown; the death of Sean. All are mitigating factors. But he can't drive it as low as the algorithm did. There's something missing still.

Amit's phone rings, a number that he doesn't know. He lets it go to messages, even though it could be Jessie Ng – he's been fielding calls from the delegates all day, pulling support and attempting their own forms of damage control. He switches on the television and eats his sandwich, cold meatballs in cold tomato sauce, and he sees a news report about Laurence being led out of his house in cuffs. The narrative has changed. It's no longer about the prediction of what he could do, or how terribly he has lost this race; now it's about what he might have done that got him arrested. It's about how far he has fallen.

Deanna leaves a message on his machine, saying that she needs his help. She asks him to call her back. In the background of the television footage, she's standing in the doorway, watching her husband being taken off in the squad car.

Ten minutes later he's driving to Staunton. He stops at a Wal-Mart and buys her a new computer, putting it on the Walker Campaign credit card – he know this will be cancelled soon enough, so he takes advantage, and he buys some food as well, bags of sweets and fresh pizzas. When he arrives at the Walkers' house he parks where he can and fights through the journalists. Deanna only answers the door when he shouts through the letterbox. In the hallway, he holds her for a second.

'It's okay,' he says.

Laurence sits in his cell and doesn't move. He hangs his head, staring at a spot on the floor, a scuff on the concrete that's so shiny as to almost look silver. He feels sick and hungry, and he shivers because he doesn't have a jacket; his shirt sticks to his skin with now-cold sweat. He's alone in here, the only occasional company being when one of the officers comes down to look at him. There are six working here, and two assistants, and they all come for a look at him, acting as if they have another interest downstairs – going into the evidence locker – but they all stare. Robards comes and stands in the corner by the stairs and doesn't take his eyes off Laurence. Night comes and they bring him a meal. It's a tray that's been heated in a microwave, sodden omelet with warm salad and a juice box. Robards passes it through the hatch and watches while Laurence doesn't touch it.

'You should eat that,' he says. 'You're looking thin.'

Later, they switch the lights off and leave Laurence in the dark, and he curls up on the bed and tries to sleep. He shuts his eyes but sees Sean there, in the cell with him, sitting on the floor, knees pulled up to his chin. He doesn't say anything to his father. Instead, he keeps his eyes down as well, as if he is looking at the same mark on the floor as Laurence was. Laurence doesn't speak to him, because there are cameras here filming him, and he knows that Sean isn't really here. He is dead, which means he cannot be here. But still, it looks so much like him.

CHAPTER 12

Robards is the one who signs Laurence out. He stands at the front desk and fills out the forms and Laurence signs them. Amit pays bail – again, using that credit card that now won't be needed for plane tickets and campaign banners, and that, miraculously, is still working. He takes Laurence out to the car and puts his hand on Laurence's back to keep pushing him forward, to nudge him into moving as quickly as possible. The press is here, having split their forces. They swarm. Laurence doesn't say a word, but Amit can feel the muscles and bones in his back draw tight, feels the shoulder blades pull close. The journalists take photos and video as Amit starts the car; carrying on, he drives towards them slowly, forcing them to scatter. He only speaks when they are on the main road, back towards the house.

'They treat you all right?' Amit asks.

'Yes,' Laurence says. As they pass the garage, *Henderson's*, *Peaforks*, the townsfolk glance at the car. They know who's in it. 'Why are you here?'

'Dee called me. She thought you might need my

help.' Laurence stares straight ahead. As soon as they stop he opens the door and walks out. No protection, no attempt to guard himself. He pushes through the journalists to get to his front door, Amit running in behind him, and beats on the door. He doesn't have his keys.

'Let me in,' he shouts. 'Deanna, please.' Amit brings out the keys and opens the door himself. Laurence's face falls. 'She isn't here.'

'Come in,' Amit says, 'and I'll explain.' Laurence pushes past and stands at the foot of the stairs. He breathes, clinging to the downstairs bannister. 'She's at a hotel, with the kids. I told them they should go.' Laurence looks at him with dead eyes. 'I told them it was better to get away from this circus. We can try and fix this, or deflect it. Turn this down. That's what you need, Laurence; not to turn this into more of a show.'

'This can't be fixed,' Laurence says.

'Some things can be. You can't run again, that's done; but you don't need to be a villain. I've emailed some TV stations to try and get an interview. There's a path, Laurence. We do damage control, and we get this to die down. We do a news show, and then we try for one of the chat shows. *Ellen*, maybe. Give her an exclusive. You tell your side of the story; how *ClearVista* did this to you, how they ruined your life. They took advantage of you when you were at your weakest. We sue them. Doesn't matter if we have any chance of winning. They'll settle. We get you and your family back together as part of a photo-op. We show you as a man who is back in control. Ruined, but coming back.'

'I'm not ruined,' Laurence says.

'Sure, not yet,' Amit tells him. 'But they're trying. So we can't let them.' They walk to the living room and Laurence pours himself a drink. There's a solitary bottle of Scotch in there, the only thing that wasn't smashed when the house was raided. He pours some into a glass and tops it off with water. There's so much Scotch the water is barely worth anything. 'You know who did this?' Amit asks, indicating the remnants of the mess in the room.

'They did,' Laurence says. 'They all did.'

'Who?'

'The people who are trying to destroy my fucking life,' Laurence tells him.

Laurence explains his theory; that one of the other candidates – Homme, most likely, because he's been number two for a while, and it's always safest to look to your most direct competition – has somehow enacted this. He focuses on the man with the jacket from their flight. He says, 'This all started that day. We were flying to Texas and everything began to fall apart.'

'He was a nobody,' Amit says.

'Maybe he wasn't. I've seen him over and over.'

'But he didn't know that the report would say what it did.'

'What if he *did* know?' Laurence asks. He talks Amit through his worries: that somebody was going through his trash; that he was being watched, spied on, and there was blue thread, the only evidence of their intruder; that the *ClearVista* results might somehow have been tampered with. He sounds paranoid, Amit thinks, but perhaps he has reason to be. There's something there, a nugget of logic in what Laurence is saying. This cannot all be a series of accidents and coincidences.

'But we can't prove it,' Amit says.

'No,' Laurence says. 'We can't.' He finishes his drink, swallowing half the contents of the glass in one go. He grimaces away from the glass for a second; and briefly it's the old Laurence back again. It's almost a comic gesture, how harsh he finds the alcohol. 'But maybe it just ends, now that I'm out of this. They want me out of the race; they don't want me destroyed.'

'So that's why we do damage control,' Amit says. 'That's why we try and fix this.' He holds out his hand to shake Laurence's. This is how they first began working together. There was no contract, no documents of employment. There was just a handshake that signified intent and trust.

'Why are you doing this?' Laurence asks. 'Why did you come back?'

'We're in this together,' Amit tells him. There are other reasons that he doesn't say: that turning this around saves some of Amit's face, if he's known to be behind rescuing the PR nightmare;

that he wants to know what happened, because he thought that he backed the right horse; that he wants to keep an eye on Laurence, because he's worried about what could happen if he doesn't.

Laurence's handshake is so weak. It's not the handshake of a man who wants to win over the country, not any more. But, Amit thinks, now it doesn't need to be.

Amit spends the night on the inflatable mattress in the living room. He can't sleep, so he tidies; cleaning the floor where he can, moving things back to how they should be. He attempts to put the family's photo albums back into order. He doesn't know how this works, but he can gauge it to some extent: how old they are, and then also how many of them are in each picture. It's strange, to see the actual photographs. He only has a single printed-out picture in his apartment: one of his mother and father, from when they were young. Everything else is on his various devices or stored in the cloud. There's nothing tangible. He wonders if they've always had these pictures printed out, or if this is something that they did after Sean died. He looks at who Laurence used to be. Realistically, he realizes, he probably should have thought, when Sean died, that this was all too much too soon. He should have told Laurence to wait another four years. Get over this. Be with his family.

His phone pings with an email. It's from Jessie Ng.

I've been advised to pass your email onto my superiors and the legal department. It goes on, covering herself and the station. They're assuming the worst.

Don't freak out, he emails back. *It's not that sort of thing. I'm trying to find out who sent you the video.* He sends it and waits. She replies straight away:

I don't know, she writes. *No name or anything.*

They didn't charge for it? Amit asks.

Not a cent. Sorry I can't help, she writes. He thinks that she would never reveal her sources, anyway. That was a long shot at best.

Maybe you can do me a favor, he writes. *Laurence Walker is looking at doing an interview somewhere to address what's happened. An appearance.*

To clear his name? she writes.

Nothing to clear, Amit replies. *This is to just get his point across. To try and get rid of some of the wolves.* He imagines her furiously getting this okayed. She's not big enough to control this by herself. He holds the phone and watches it for the reply.

When can you come in? she asks. *Can you come tomorrow?*

Today? he clarifies.

Sure, sorry, she says. *Night shift. You know how it is.*

I know how it is, he replies. He Googles her: the work she's done, her picture, her CV. On the TV, everybody is still talking about Laurence's arrest. There's nothing else for the cycle to move onto.

He feels guilty as he prays for earthquakes and hurricanes; anything that will help to shift the cycle on.

Deanna doesn't sleep because of the noise from down the hall. There is sobbing coming from another room, and she wouldn't ordinarily notice it were it not so familiar. It's faint, almost blending in with the machinery of the motel. This is the area's least likely hotel for her to be staying in, a roadside place outside the town's main stretch that only tends to serve truckers and dirty weekenders. They don't know her, at least not by name: the woman behind the counter didn't coo or offer sympathies when Deanna and her daughters came in, which was a relief. She gave them a room with a double and a single and a minibar and a television, each extra nudging the cost up by a dollar or two. They ate takeaway McDonalds, and Deanna put dimes into the box at the side of the bed to make it shake and vibrate as Alyx and Lane lay on top of it and giggled. Deanna tried to laugh with them, and Alyx asked why they weren't at home, and Deanna said that their father needed a little space. She said that he was tired, that he couldn't sleep with them all there, running around, making the noise that they were making. They replaced the bed's sheets with ones that Deanna brought with her, and they sprayed air freshener and talked all night, telling each other stories.
The girls slept on the double and Deanna took

the single, pressed up against the wall. Now, in the middle of the night, she can hear the sobbing. It's keeping her awake. It gets everywhere, the sound resonating; it seeps into the walls and the floors, all around them. Deanna remembers when she used to wake herself up with her own tears. She would be in a dream, with Sean, after he died, and then she would hear the sound; and it would shake her, just enough to lose Sean and be awake again. Her face would be wet; she had never known you could cry in your sleep. Whoever this is now, she can hear them all too loud in the room. She wants to tell them that it will all be okay, but that's a lie.

She focuses on the girls' breathing to distract her. Whenever one of them pauses – when their breath isn't uniform and constant, like a motor turning over – she contemplates the notion that something has happened, for a second. She hasn't stopped worrying about them ever since Sean died, and she never will.

Before she finally sleeps, as she sees the sky through the curtains begin to turn from black to orange, she thinks about Laurence; and about how maybe it's better that they aren't with him, until he's fixed. She thinks about the video of him and the gun, and she reaches into her bag, kept next to her at the side of the bed, and feels the cold metal of it against her palm.

Amit cooks breakfast in the kitchen. The bread is stale, but he finds jams and spreads in the cupboards, and he works out how to use the coffee pods in this machine (which is about ten models more complicated than the basic one that he keeps in his apartment). He puts it onto a tray and carries it upstairs to the main bedroom. Laurence hasn't tidied or tried to put the room back into any sort of order: the bed is askew and away from the wall; the wall strewn with clothes and discarded shoes and jewelry; Laurence asleep still, and dressed from yesterday, face down on the bed. He's looking away from Amit, and there's a second – only brief – where Amit wonders if he won't be able to wake him up. That would be how this ends: with Laurence doing something that doesn't make sense. There is no hole, Amit thinks, that cannot be dug out of. There can't be.

He shakes Laurence's leg. 'Wake up,' he says. 'Big day.'

'What?' Laurence asks. He doesn't move.

'I've had a request for you to do some TV. They want to do an interview, let you clear this up.' He puts the tray down. 'This could be really good, Laurence. You do this, you can get this all behind you. That's what you want, right?'

'Right,' Laurence says. He doesn't sound as if he means it but Amit doesn't give him a choice.

'Eat something, drink coffee, take a shower. Shave yourself. Put on a suit. We need to get out of here in an hour.' He steps into the bathroom and turns on the shower for Laurence. He leaves the room and stands in the hallway and takes out his phone.

We're definitely coming, he writes to Jessie, *two hours, maybe a little more. Be with you by lunchtime.*

We'll schedule you for the lunchtime slot, she replies. Amit puts the phone back in his pocket, then changes his mind. He opens his *Twitter* app. *Laurence Walker on Channel 9 at 1. Answering questions about ClearVista video and future plans. Pls RT.* He watches as the retweets soar, as people talk about this. Even the non-political gossip bloggers get involved. The story changes, suddenly, as people start talking about Laurence in a slightly new way; that he's facing up to his demons, whatever they may be.

Laurence lets the water wash over him. He rubs himself and washes his hair, but this is all rote. When he's done he dries himself on the first towel he finds – they have been pulled out of the cupboard, and he doesn't know which is clean and which is not, though he supposes that it doesn't matter now – and he looks at his clothes on the floor. They're all filthy; they've been trampled and creased and there's no time to do anything with them. He opens the wardrobe, where a few trousers still hang, a shirt, a sweater. And there, at the far end, tucked in the corner, is a dark gray suit. It takes him a second to recognize it; and when he last wore it. It meant something, that he hid it away. He takes it out and pulls the plastic wrap from it. It has been kept like an artefact; and he sees marks on the lapel, dark smears of mascara. He goes to the bathroom and wets tissue and scrubs at the make-up. He uses a wet nailbrush on it and it starts to shift.

He puts on a white shirt and digs the lemon-yellow tie out from the rubble around his feet, because he knows that it looks nice with this suit. It has always looked nice with the suit. Gray and yellow, the darkness and the light; and he wants to feel that he is projecting something. An air of joy. Isn't that what Deanna said it reminded her of? That it was joyous?

Most of the journalists abandoned the front of the house as soon as the news about Laurence's inter-view broke, which makes it easier to get off the driveway. Amit drives, and Laurence puts the window down and looks out of it, feeling the rush of the wind on his face. He tries to concentrate on what he's going to have to say when he's on the air. He's going to talk about the nature of the prediction; about *ClearVista*, and the information that he gave them; and he's going to subtly suggest that there's more to this than meets the eye, that maybe there are other people involved. But Amit has said he is not to go so far as to actually say that – one of his rules is, Never sound like a conspiracy theorist, and he's going to talk about how strong his family is, and how he's taking time away from politics in order to reconnect. He needs to go back and be a husband and father again. All he can do is blame technology and focus on humanity. Nature will out.

They stop at a service station. Laurence picks up a cap from the back seat of the car and puts it on and follows Amit into the shop. He feels like a character in a movie, becoming inconspicuous because they're wearing just this one item that hides their face slightly; and he browses the magazines and newspapers for his name. He works his way through, from the serious prints to the trash. They call him *disgraced*, or *ex-politician*, or (in the case of the *Weekly World News*) *the Antichrist*. He stands and reads them while Amit pays for the gas. The man at the counter tries to see his face, because he's got the hat on. A hat means suspicion. You wear a hat when you're going to rob a place.

The rest of the drive is uneventful. The roads move between gray and beige and back again, and then they build up as they enter the city. They drive past buildings that Laurence recognizes, because he's done this drive hundreds of times before, but he doesn't know what a single one of them is. As you come into the city and you pass the car dealerships and the vacant lots and the billboards on the sides of buildings that look derelict and the streets that seem to sprawl off with nothing on them and the people standing outside their cars in the middle of the daytime, everything becomes New York City. It's distinct.

They fight traffic, and park in a sub-level car park underneath a gallery that has nobody in it, and doesn't even look open. Amit pays, using the credit card again. They'll worry about paying this off when this is all over, he reasons. There's a way of do this, he's sure, but he doesn't know what this is. The fundraising money will all be done, now, not another cent coming through, but the account that had some in isn't bled dry yet. Amit supposes some of the donors will want their money back. They might even sue, though they wouldn't have a case; they bought into Laurence, better or worse. They paid for the man that he was. He's still the same man. He has always been this man.

When they get onto the street, Amit helps Laurence with his tie and jacket, straightening him, making him look slightly more in control. He tells Laurence to smooth his hair down, and he adjusts the lapels. He sees the make-up stain and rubs at it with his thumb.

'There's a mark,' he says. Laurence ignores him. As they walk up towards Times Square, people recognize Laurence, glancing at his face, whispering to each other. One person shouts at them, a simple, 'Hey!' that doesn't mean anything.

'Ignore them,' Amit says. Laurence keeps his head down.

At the TV studios, Amit rings the buzzer and speaks into the grilled microphone. 'We have an appointment with Jessie Ng,' he says. There's a pause, and then the door beeps and swings open. In the lobby, they wait. The floor is marble and polished steel, and the walls are mirrors. Laurence cannot look at them, because they go on and on, back into the whatever, reflections ricocheting off each other until they are further and further away; at least, until he is.

'Can I use your phone?' he asks. Amit passes it.

'You're calling Deanna?'

'Yes,' Laurence says.

'Okay,' Amit says. He feels like this is the first step. It's rehab, an intervention. This is when everything starts coming back to normal. This is when Laurence begins to climb that ladder.

Laurence paces, close to one mirrored wall, and he dials the number. She answers. 'It's me,' he says.

'Are you okay?' she asks. She sounds relieved.

'I don't really know,' he tells her. 'I am trying.' He paces, and he tries to not look up, at the mirrors.

Everything about this has been ripped away from Jessie. As soon as she told them that she had the interview locked, it wasn't hers any more. In-studio interviews rely on experience, she was told. You cannot make notes or prepare questions for this. So, instead, Jessie is to take him upstairs, make sure that he's comfortable, keep him out of the studio until it's time for him to be on the air, make sure that he heads straight to the couch. The studio is out of bounds for anybody not working there – the print journalists from upstairs banned from the floor because this is a real, old school exclusive.

Jessie's boss says to her that this is the culmination of their coverage; of having the reputation that they have as a station. It's all about the long game, she says.

Now, Jessie stays at her desk and watches the hosts and crews getting themselves ready, because this is suddenly a big deal. There are emails beeping on consoles all around her, last-minute things being scrawled onto pieces of paper and physically rushed over to the prompt guys – paper and feet are faster than technology in circumstances like this – and there are tech guys in the studio setting up something that she cannot see, establishing something in the studio for this. This hardly seems the time to break what they already know. They have emails come in from *ClearVista* – the standard email that avoids disclosing any information, that defers any responsibility, that gives a blanket statement about the company – though some of the team are trying to find somebody who worked on the algorithm to come in and talk to them; but nobody's answering their phones. It's chaos. It's always chaos before something like this.

Her computer alerts her that her guests have arrived and she takes the lift down, pulling her cardigan on as it descends. The lobby is so cold. They keep it this temperature because it gets the guests jittery. She sees them standing by the doorway, faces down, avoiding looking into the mirrors; Amit, dressed well, smiling his best aide's smile and rushing to shake her hand.

'Good to meet,' he says.

'You, too. And you must be Senator Walker,' she says. She moves towards Laurence as he ends his telephone call and he holds out his hand to hers.

'Laurence,' he says.

'Laurence.' His hand, Jessie notices, is all bone. She can feel his knuckles against hers, between her fingers, and his skin seems to slip a little, as if it's loose. As if it has give. 'Come with me, I'll get you all settled in.' She steps into the lift and scans her card, and the doors shut them inside. She smells aftershave, sharp and citrusy. Laurence doesn't look at her. He looks past her, she thinks. She smiles at him, and he notices and returns it, but there's nothing inside it. She wishes, in that instant, that she could take this all back and cancel the deal, send him downstairs. This isn't going to go as planned, she knows, but the doors open silently on her floor, and her boss sees the three of them and paces over.

'Mr Walker,' she says. 'We won't keep you waiting long. Have a coffee, get settled. We'll send somebody to do your make-up, get you ready.' She smiles. 'This is going to be great,' she says.

The room that they are sent to wait in has an old-style coffee percolator on the sideboard. Jessie offers them cups. Laurence shakes his head, but then takes it anyway, and he sips at it. It's so bitter; he hasn't a cup of coffee like this in years, he thinks. He can't remember the last time. It doesn't

324

taste like what he's used to now, milky and fully roasted and fair trade and from pods that seem lovingly prepared, and just *better*. This is the coffee that he once fell in love with. He sits on a sofa that barely qualifies being called that, being undulating tubes of foam, red and firm, seemingly made to perch on rather than relax; and he watches the rest of the studio through the glass wall of the room. They're working and trying not to look back at him. He's that much of a sideshow, now; they all try to not look at him, but they can't help it. There's hostility in the air, and he knows it. What has to happen now is that he clears his name. There is no other choice.

'Okay,' Jessie says, 'so I'm going to take you onto the couch during the headline breakdown and weather, just before one. You know Bury?' Laurence nods. Bury is their lead; has been in the game for decades now, unswerving. He wasn't the biggest fan of Laurence before all of this, favoring Homme as the candidate, and it's clear that he'll go for the jugular. In some ways, Amit thinks, that's what Laurence needs. 'He's doing the interview. Patricia'll be sitting in as well. You know Patricia?'

'Yes,' Laurence says. He knows them all. They're acting as if he's not been here before, as if he's a stranger to this world. *Do you understand politics? Do you even know why you're here?* He looks at Jessie – again, maybe, not at her but through her – and he says, 'I've probably even met you before. I've been here.'

'I don't think so,' she says. 'Look, I'll be back. Anything you need, just ask.' Amit and Laurence watch her take her seat at her desk. She has windows open on her computer screen of them: pictures of Laurence, of Amit, and the *ClearVista* video of Laurence. She turns the screen slightly, but Amit can still see as Jessie watches the video. When it's finished she glances back at Laurence as if she's trying to work out where these two representations of the man who would have been President fit into each other: one, a twisted amalgam, a collection of falsehoods that he gave at photo calls and headshots; and the other a thin vulture of what he used to be, broken and gnarled and peeling away from himself.

A woman comes into the room. She's wearing a clichéd power suit, electric blue and shoulder pads. She's got a small box with her, as if she's an electrician, but she opens it and inside there are brushes and powders.

'I'm going to prep you,' she says. Laurence leans back and she goes to work, dusting his face – it makes Amit think of an archeologist, trying to find what is hidden below all of this, something of value and worth – and then putting something on his lips, a thick, rich raspberry color. She combs his hair and she puts a wax on it; and she makes him look, Amit thinks, like a doll. He looks almost like the man from the video again; or, a version of him. They're even in the same clothes, Amit realizes.

'You need to take the tie off,' he says to Laurence. He reaches for it.

'No,' Laurence snaps. 'Deanna gave me this. It's special.'

And then Jessie comes back. 'It's time,' she says. Laurence stands up and sighs, and he checks what he looks like in the reflection of the glass wall, and then he follows her through to the studio proper. The people stop what they're doing for a second – a pause in frantic typing, in note taking, in mouse clicking – and they watch him head onto the studio floor proper. Amit goes as well, and Bury is waiting. The anchor stands up and adjusts his shirt and jacket over his belly.

'Laurence, good to see you,' he says. They shake hands. 'It's been a while. Sorry that it had to be under these circumstances. We're going to get to the bottom of this today, okay?'

'Okay,' Laurence says. Amit looks at his face; he's buying into this. This is his redemption. 'Thank you.'

'What we're going to do is this: a little bit of an intro, and then we're going to talk about your career, and we're going to talk about what's happened, okay? We'll do that bit, myself and Patricia – you know Patricia?' He shuffles aside to reveal her, sitting on the sofa. She offers her hand and a smile that is dragged across her teeth rather than drawn. 'Myself and Patricia do that, then we bring you on. Now, listen: we're going to have to watch the video, okay? Because that's a part of this. And then the floor's yours. You tell us what's gone on here. We haven't had time for the researchers, that sort of thing, so the onus is on you, here. You can carry it?' He keeps smoothing his clothes with his hand, Amit notices, as if he is pushing them down. It's not that there's a problem with his belly; it's a tell, like a liar at a poker table.

'No, I'll be fine. I've done this a million times,' Laurence says. He stands taller. He adjusts himself. He cricks his neck. Under the lights, it's clearer that he's wearing make-up to hide something – his skin looks whiter, and he looks less ill. Amit still doesn't want to think of the S word.

'Maybe not a million, but enough, am I right?' Bury asks. He holds out his hand to shake Laurence's again. 'Can't thank you enough for being here,' Laurence. 'This is going to be good for you, I think. Give you a chance to get everything out in the open.'

It's a trap, Amit thinks. This is all a trap. But then the cameras begin to count down and the floor manager tells everybody to take their seats, and Laurence is already on the sofa, and it's too late.

'Good afternoon. You're joining myself and Patricia Buchanan for a very special edition of our show. We're going to be speaking with Laurence Walker, who has been in the news a lot recently for his very high profile retreat from the world of politics. Mr Walker was, until a week or so ago, in contention for the race to be the next Democratic Party nominee. He has a solid political background, he was well liked, was respected on both sides of the divide. And then everything came crashing down when a video from the tech-gen company *ClearVista* appeared to show Mr Walker threatening his family with a weapon. Now, the video hadn't as yet happened – the nature of the technology is that they show events that are, according to their promotional materials, only likely to occur – but this story has proven to be a fascinating one for America, and for what it means for the future of our political system. We're joined by Mr Walker now, and we're going to get his side of the story.'

'Thanks for having me, Bury, Patricia.'

'Our pleasure. Let's kick things off with this video. So you took out a report from *ClearVista*, that's right?'

'Yes. Mostly a PR thing.'

'And that also fed out a video, right?'

'They make them. They have software. It's all behind the scenes, done by a computer. Total guesswork.'

'And what you saw took you by surprise?'

'Utterly,' Laurence says. He conducts himself as he always has; no media training, but you would never know it. So controlled, and so in control. 'When I first watched it, I knew that it couldn't be real. I knew that it couldn't be an accurate representation of who I was, who I am; or of who

329

I am going to be. I have focused upon the concepts of family in my work, and—'

'Now, you say you knew it couldn't be *real*.'

'Yes.'

'That's a curious choice of words, there. Because it *is* real; the video, I mean. It's as real as you or I.' Bury smiles.

'Right, but the video hasn't happened. It isn't a truth, perhaps. That's a better word.' Laurence looks around the studio. Only a brief glance, but he sees that there's a crowd watching them. Not just the usual people, but all the reporters, all the tech staff. They want something from him; like rubberneckers passing by the scene of an accident.

'Okay. So the software takes from everything that it can find on the Internet, correct?'

'Yes.'

'And it also uses your answers to some questions for this report.'

'A thousand questions.'

'One thousand! That's accuracy.'

'Depends on what the questions are.'

'*ClearVista* say, on their promotional materials, that this is the *product of the sum of human knowledge*. They say, *The numbers don't lie*. I know, I know, it's all promotional jargon, but that's their thing. They claim to know you better than you know yourself.'

'But they can't. They can't, it's as simple as that.'

'Maybe not. Let me ask you: do you own a gun, Mr Walker?'

'A gun?'

'A gun.'

'Yes.' Laurence nods.

'What sort?'

'It's a Glock. I don't know the model.'

'So that's why there's a gun in the video, I'd guess. Because the Internet knows that you own a weapon, a handgun. So that's where it got that from.'

'Yes.'

'Is it the same gun?'

'I don't—'

'It is, I can tell you. We've looked it up. And it knew to only include the four of you, of course. You and your wife and your daughters.'

'Yes.' Amit sees Laurence sweating, the creep of a dark patch across his forehead and shirt. It's the lights, and the questions. This is unfair, and going badly. 'I lost my son,' Laurence says. It feels desperate, then; it feels used.

'And it knew that. So why doesn't it know everything about you?'

'I don't—'

'In the report, it said that you were likely to have a mental breakdown, did it not?' Laurence doesn't answer. 'How do you think a breakdown is likely to manifest, Mr Walker?'

'I don't know—'

'Have you ever been tortured, Mr Walker? Kept in a room, threatened at gunpoint? Have you ever been physically terrified?'

'Yes,' Laurence says, panic in his voice, sweat on his face, 'but I can't—'

'So, now, I think we should probably watch this video again,' Bury says. He stands up and moves across, to the far side of the studio. 'We've got some new technology to try out, just for this. We thought that this would be interesting.' He flattens his clothes with the palm of one sweaty hand. Whatever he's been hiding, Amit knows, is about to come out.

'What's happening?' Amit asks. He's shushed by the floor manager, so he retreats back to where Jessie is standing. 'What's happening?'

'I don't know,' she says. She looks at them all, suddenly switching something on. There's a hum and a whine, and a puff of liquid, like an aerosol, into the air, and a smell of cleaning fluids. It's a HoloGas projector.

They watch the picture click into being in the round of the studio. Static on top of static, and then it's in front of them, a 3D representation of the video, life-size and vividly clear. The colors are muted but the picture is exactly as it was online. It's Laurence and his family – and he is there with his gun.

'What the hell,' Laurence says. He stands up, shaking, and walks towards himself; the same suit that he is wearing now, and the same face. He looks at the dead eyes of the figure holding the gun and he reaches out and through it. It dissipates. He – the real Laurence, the one who is moving in and around this scene – lurches forward, unsteady on his feet. Amit moves to run across and get him, to pull him off the floor and take him out of there, but the floor manager blocks him, and two men with the muscles of ex-army security guards hold him back. Jessie rushes back further, to see the feed. She wants to see how this looks on the air. Laurence steps through and looks at the amalgam Alyx's face.

'We should play this,' Bury says. And it starts. Laurence staggers back, but the video plays; those few seconds of him holding the gun, and his family terrified and cowering. In the distance, the sound of something, water, a river, a crowd. A crackle. A gunshot, as the video ends, and the figures disappear into clouds of vapor on the air.

Laurence, now, breathes; his chest rises and falls. He is in the suit, but nobody could have known that, and the tie. He looks the same. The visual of this is ruinous. They couldn't have known that this would happen. A suit, that's all it was. A suit. He falls to his knees and he retches. Bury stands back, making out that he's shocked. This was never the intended reaction, his face suggests for the cameras. The men holding back Amit let go and he runs to Laurence and helps him to his feet.

'You fucking liars!' Laurence screams at Bury. 'Why would you do this to me? What the fuck have I ever done to you?' There is bile trailing his raspberry-pink mouth, his chin; his eyes are dark and soaking. The make-up runs down his face. It's on camera, now.

Here he is, the broken man.

Amit grabs at him and pulls him towards the elevator, and the cameras track them across the studio floor. Amit presses to open the doors and they step inside, but there are no buttons to send them downstairs, only the panel for the key-cards. He looks at Jessie, and he pleads with her. She runs over and steps in and scans it. Laurence is crumpled against the wall, gasping for breath.

'I didn't know,' Jessie says, 'I swear I didn't know.'

'Okay,' Amit tells her. He looks at Laurence.

'Is he okay?' Jessie asks.

'No,' Amit says, 'he's sick.' She steps backwards. The doors close.

Laurence slumps to his knees. Amit takes out his phone and calls Deanna.

'Don't let the kids see the television,' he says to her.

'What happened?' she asks.

'I'll tell you later. Don't let them see it. Stay inside.' He puts a hand on Laurence's back. 'Okay,' he says, 'we'll get you home.' The doors opens onto the lobby, and Laurence sits in the lift and sobs. Amit steps out and looks at him: suddenly so small, shrunken away. The doors begin to close, so he puts his hand out to stop them. 'Come on,' he says, 'we have to leave.' Laurence crawls forward. 'Don't be this,' Amit says. 'Come on, Laurence. You're going to be all right.' Laurence is sobbing, unable to catch his breath. He slides forward. He lies flat on the ground. 'Laurence?' Amit asks, and then he dials 911, and he asks for an ambulance as fast as possible. He thinks that it's a heart attack, because Laurence is coughing, and there's froth at his lips. He lies on the floor, and he chokes.

'I have to protect them,' Laurence says. 'Don't you get that?' He spits the words out, and they sound wrong, as if his voice is not his own; and then he sobs, and gasps in air.

The EMTs load Laurence onto the gurney. He is awake and conscious. He sees Amit, worrying and he sees Jessie, watching from the side, film crews capturing this for whatever part of the cycle they'll use it. He knows how broken he must look.

He watches the streets as they lift the bed, putting it onto the ambulance truck, and he sees something: a blue jacket, in the distance. The man from before, on a telephone, talking to somebody. Laurence shouts, because he knows. He *knows*. He shouts, and he tries to stand, and the EMTs hold him down. One of them injects him with something, and the world is lost to a haze.

Amit paces. They won't let him into the family waiting rooms, so he waits in the admissions area, and he paces. He goes outside for air, and he buys a cigarette from a woman smoking out there, giving her a dollar for it. He thinks about how good it tastes to him; how there's always that part of him that feels incomplete since he quit. It's a relief, and it starts to rain, and he waits.

His phone rings. It's Hershel.

'I saw the news,' he says. He sounds quiet and sad, a different tone to every other time. Amit wonders if he's just projecting.

'I'm at the hospital.'

'How are you?'

'Me? Fine.'

'Okay. Look, I've got something for you. Don't ask me how, but I've got a booted-out video.' Amit's heart leaps. A true video? Something that erases what's been before? 'It's from running the software again.' He drops his voice, as if he can be heard; or, as if he doesn't want to run the risk of anybody else hearing. 'It's bad, Amit. Just warning you. You might not want to show Laurence.'

'What—'

'I have to go away on business for a while. Only a week or two, to the west coast; I'll be in touch.'

'I need your—'

'I'm sorry I can't help more,' Hershel says. 'I hope this all ends well for you, man.' The line goes dead, and then Amit's phone beeps. It's an email, with a link to a video. Amit clicks it, walking away from the other smokers outside the hospital doors, to find a place that's quiet; and he turns the volume up, in case.

★　★　★

The video begins with the logo, and the static of numbers; and then Laurence drawn in first. It's a complete Laurence, the one that was just on the television. As if the algorithm realized that suddenly the version it was looking for, that it was trying to create, actually finally existed in millions of new screen grabs and videos.

CHAPTER 13

Deanna leaves the hotel. Amit's told her that everything is all right; that her husband is going to be absolutely fine. He has been given fluids and he's going to be checked out soon as anything; free to go. He tells her that there have been many, many doctors look at him; second, third, fourth opinions, and there's no chance that they missed anything. They've run tests on his heart and apparently there's an arrhythmia. It can happen. It can't be explained. He can take tablets. They wanted to know if it was an existing heart condition, but Laurence said that it wasn't. He asked what caused it, already knowing the answer.

'So many things; stress, mostly, your general health level. You'll be susceptible to it, should you fall into certain categories. Did you father have heart troubles?'

'It's what killed him,' Laurence said.

'Well, that's one thing. And you've had a stress.' He was a nice doctor, Amit told Deanna; didn't seem to be judging or making assumptions. Maybe he didn't watch the television, she thought.

338

She walks to the roadside bar outside the motel's forecourt and she orders a beer, asks them if they'd mind turning their set on. She's the only customer paying attention: there's a man clutching a bottle to himself, avoiding eye contact; a girl cleaning the floors; another girl sitting in a booth reading a book, something well-thumbed, with a cracked spine.

'Any channel?' the bartender asks.

'Fox,' she tells him. He shakes his head and puts it on. They're playing the interview over and over, it seems. There is nothing else happening in the world; only a man having a very public breakdown. The cameras tail him to the elevator, and she watches as he slumps into it.

'Sometimes, people have to answer for who they are,' the host says. 'Sometimes that's just the way it goes.' It's almost a closed book: Laurence is like a war criminal to them, guilty with no chance of being proven innocent.

'His poor wife,' the female co-anchor says as they try to focus the cameras on Laurence's face, on Amit as he urges the door to shut and let them escape the studio. 'And those poor girls.' They show it again, another reporter talking about it as if it had happened somewhere else; repeating the information in a seemingly endless loop. They have made their own news.

They note that he's in the same outfit as on the video. It's the same yellow tie. Deanna remembers everything about why she bought that tie for him:

that whole shopping trip being one of positivity, of wrangling the twins out of stores and actually connecting with Lane on some mother-daughter level that she felt was missing, and seeing one of her books in a *Barnes & Noble* and thinking that she wasn't done, not yet.

She calls her agent. She remembers his telephone number, because she's had him since the days that she had to actually dial it on occasion, and those numbers remain locked tight in some box that she can't erase from her memory.

'This is Macleod,' he says.

'It's Deanna,' she says. 'Walker.'

'Deanna. Jesus! I didn't expect . . .' He fumbles something. She hears a rustle in the background. 'I didn't think I'd hear from you. We were just watching the news.'

'Oh,' she says. There's no answer to that, she thinks; no reasonable response.

'Are you all right?'

'No,' she says. 'Laurence is in hospital.'

'Jesus. Right. But I mean, are you *all right*?' He asks it with the same complicit voice that everybody seems to be using around her. Your husband is a maniac, the voices say, so what aren't you telling us? Are you in danger? Do we need to save you?

'I'm fine. The video is a lie.'

'I mean, of course it is. Of *course* it is.'

'You know him.'

'I do. I did.' He pauses, his breath making the

line momentarily dead as it waits for him to speak. 'But, you know that if you need me, Deanna. If you need anything at all . . .'

'You said that you can sell the book,' she tells him.

'Oh, good God yes. Certainly. I probably shouldn't say that. I mean, it's very different.' She can read him. They've known each other too long. He means she won't make much from it. 'But it's so very good, exceptional, even. A book for prizes.'

'Not under my name – I don't want a sideshow made of this.'

'Are you sure?' he asks. 'I mean, of course, if that's what you want. Understandable.' She knows that he's disappointed: her work would likely sell for triple what it will otherwise if it had her name attached. Or, more realistically, Laurence's name. Deanna Walker, wife of the disgraced. 'Do you have a name you want to use?'

'No,' she tells him. 'Jane Smith. Anything.'

'Jane Smith.'

'I don't care. Pick something. Send it out. See what happens. Don't say it's from me. I just want it out there, I think. I want to know.'

'I understand,' he repeats. 'I'll start drafting a letter, make a few calls. I have some editors in mind.'

'Let me know,' she says.

'I meant what I said, Deanna,' he tells her. 'As long as you're safe.'

'Why wouldn't I be safe?' she asks. She hangs

341

up the phone and looks at the screen, suspended over the bottles and the beer taps. Laurence is looking at himself, large on the screen; a 3D hologram of who he is, of the scene that scares him so much. He seems to swat at himself, almost, a feeble punch of self-disgust and terror. It's almost slapstick; his terror, torn from a 1970s horror movie. A slow-zoom close-up of a face that's too scared of what might be true to even begin to cope.

She puts money on the counter and thanks the bartender, and she leaves the bar. The street is empty apart from the rush of cars. She follows them, back towards the motel.

Amit sits at the end of Laurence's bed while his boss sleeps. Funny to think of him using that term. There's no financial commitment now, and no money coming in any time in the future. Although maybe Amit can sell his story when this is all over. The doctors gave Laurence something to sleep – Amit joked, asking if he could have some, and they didn't laugh – and then left them both there. Amit reads the chart and see the medicine that they've prescribed to him; all sedatives, all to calm him down. He emails a few people, just testing the waters, reigniting contacts that have gone cold. He needs to sort out a job. He knows that they won't pan out: he's tainted now, and appearing on television with Laurence won't have done him any favors, but he has to start somewhere.

He looks at his inbox and selects everything that he hasn't filed away as important, and deletes it all. So many of them are from the delegates. The tone is uniformly one of disgust. They had hoped that this could be sorted out, that a resolution could be found, but Laurence's actions have changed the narrative. His actions have changed their plans.

He thinks that Laurence could disappear, move somewhere quiet, take himself out of the public eye entirely. Maybe he can write a book. He'd get a good advance, a good sell-through. Somebody will want it; scandal always sells. And there can be no meltdowns when it's written down and printed. There's nothing to control there.

His phone beeps, a text from Jessie. *I am so sorry, I didn't have a clue,* she says. *Seriously, not even a hint.*

It's fine, Amit replies. *Wasn't your fault.*

I thought about quitting, she writes.

Don't, Amit says. *No point.*

I am so sorry, she repeats. He doesn't reply to that, and then another one comes in. *If I can help, please let me know.*

Thanks, he writes. *Got any jobs going?* He puts a smiley face in there. He leaves it, putting his phone back, and he feels good about it. Like, maybe they can move past this now. There's a second where that lasts and then he takes his phone out again. He writes another message to Jessie. *Actually, here you go: what can you find out for me about ClearVista?*

343

Why? she asks.

I want to ask them about the video. You must have people. Moles. Diggers. Whatever you call them. Can't you get me somebody I can speak to?

I'll see what I can do, she writes. *No promises.*

No promises, he agrees. He calls Deanna again, to give her another update. She whispers, because the kids – she calls them that, and it's amazing how young Lane has suddenly become in her eyes – are asleep. Amit tells her he'll call back in the morning, when Laurence is awake.

'Don't,' Deanna says. 'Maybe give it a day or two.'

She lies in bed and thinks about what the video showed. She thinks about Sean, and how she can't forgive Laurence. They haven't spoken about it, not ever. Or, not since; but that time, the week around his death, feels as if it never even happened, really. Because they know who is to blame, really. They know how this works. Laurence was preoccupied, and Sean died. Really, when you say it like that it's remarkably simple. She mourned, and the girls mourned. Alyx couldn't let him go, and Lane tattoos her body in tribute to him, and Deanna wrote her novel. What did *he* do? He went back to work. They were all selfish in their own way, but nothing from his selfishness could be shown or shared, nothing could be learned from it by the rest of them.

She sits upright and opens the curtains at the foot

of her single bed. In the moonlight, the room is blues and whites. The colors make the room seem colder. She puts the bag on the table and takes the gun out. The best thing to do with it would be to throw it away. Take it to a police station or one of those anonymous gun drop stations. If it doesn't exist then it cannot be used.

But then, she thinks, if she has it, she has it. It will protect them, if it needs to. She wonders if she could bring herself to use it. She puts the gun back into the bag and goes to her daughters, and she sits on the side of the bed and holds Alyx while she sleeps, for a second; then she goes to Lane's side and looks at her, and touches her shoulder. Even through the darkness she can see the angry red of the fresh tattoo on her skin, an unfinished bud. She touches it, gently, running her finger along the outside of it.

'I love you,' she tells her daughters. She stands up and walks to the door, and she opens it and steps out onto the platform that runs along the top level of the motel. She is dressed in only a T-shirt and shorts, and she thinks how easy it would be to leave with them. To take her pseudonym, whatever it might be, and own it. Run with it. She looks out over the road, which is now totally still; and the woods in front of them, stretching off. There are lights in them, dots of something that could be civilization on the other side. She imagines something else: a reflection of the moon, or water, or some animal, a firefly making its own path. All along the run the rooms are silent, even the one where she has previously heard the sobbing. She wonders what made it stop.

Back in the room, Deanna lies back in the only chair. She shuts her eyes, and she dreams, but the dream is so real and tangible that it might as well be what just happened, her in the room and holding her family tight and then feeling the night air on her skin and *knowing* that this can get better, if she only lets it.

Amit wakes up and Laurence is gone. The bed is empty. His clothes are gone as well, and his watch, his wallet. Everything that might have suggested that he was ever even here. Amit stands up and rushes to the desk, to the nurse on duty.

'Laurence Walker?' he asks. The nurse consults a chart.

'Says he's in 3C.'

'He's not,' Amit replies. 'He's gone. He didn't discharge himself?'

'Not on the records.' The nurse shrugs. Amit takes his phone out and dials Deanna again, the last number he called. The only number that he's really called, the last few days.

'Dee,' he says, 'have you heard from him?'

'No,' she replies. 'What's happened?'

'Nothing,' he tells her. 'I've been asleep.' Lie with the truth; his own rule. 'I wondered if he had called you.' He doesn't want to tell her that her husband is missing yet. No sense in worrying her, or the kids. Missing could mean anything. It could mean that he went to the bathroom; or he went for coffee and he's going to appear again, and he'll have a new face for this new day.

'I don't think he even has this number,' she says. Amit goes back to the room and grabs his satchel. He rifles through it; the car keys are gone. He runs to the elevator and hits the button. He rubs his face, days' worth of stubble covering his chin; his mouth tastes of being asleep. The doors close and the ride down takes forever. He knows, before he's even near the bay that they used, that the car will be gone. He thinks about reporting it stolen, calling the police and telling them who did it. But that will end Laurence, he knows. That would be it. Everything feels so fractured around him, and he doesn't know how to pull it together. He wonders how Laurence feels. He calls Hertz, because he's got a loyalty card, and he asks them where their nearest branch is. They give him a location, only a mile down the road, sending him a pinpoint for his GPS, and he starts to walk.

The car that the *ClearVista* software predicts for him to want to use is identical to the one that he drove before, the same make and model, the exact same color. It's a large car that's everywhere and almost invisible, and he can get this car anywhere and drive it and it will always feel the same. His favored hotel chain, his car, his coffee . . . Everything is done because it's easy and familiar.

Nothing needs adapting to, because the adaptation has already occurred somewhere way back in the past. Amit searches *Twitter* while he navigates the parking lot to get out, looking for Laurence's name. If somebody out there in the world has seen him, maybe they tweeted something about it, he figures; but there's nothing. Only bullshit. New bullshit, admittedly, but it's the same as the old. Name calling and slurring and slander. So he drives back towards Staunton, away from New York. This was always going to be his life, he figures: New York to Syracuse to Washington DC, a triangle of freeways and interstates. His phone pings an alert. Laurence has been found. He has made an appearance.

He's back at the house.

Amit pushes the car harder. He tells himself that he should just stop caring, that he should pull over or turn around. He should drive home and let it lie. But he can't. That's not who he is.

The chaos can be seen all along the street. Amit's stolen car is slammed into two news vans that had been shoved up nose to nose, blocking the driveway. Now, they are almost fused together, their body-work entwined, the glass from their windshields spilled between them and all over. The trunk door of Amit's car is hanging open. He sees that his stuff is still in there, the cops on the scene – he recognizes them from the day that they came to examine the broken gate – both examining the pieces of paper Amit had left there, his notes, business cards, phone numbers, pamphlets. The cops are bagging things, siphoning them off, as if they're evidence. They don't know how little any of it means now.

Somebody's injured, that much is clear; there's an ambulance waiting in the street, and two paramedics examining people, checking their eyes, clicking their fingers around their heads and expecting them to react. One of them, a cameraman, has a bandage round his head and is cradling his arm. A woman, an on-air personality – Amit is loathe to think of her as a journalist, because she's one of the worst, one of the most desperate and cynical – is cradling a swollen ankle. The house's front door is open and cordoned off. Amit parks down the street, as close as he can, and one of the cops – the less memorable of the two – half-jogs over towards him.

'No closer,' he says, as Amit gets out of the car. He squints in recognition, but he can't place from where.

'That's my car,' Amit says.

'Which one?'

'What do you mean, which one? The big black thing smashed into those vans. That's mine.'

'Oh,' the cop says. 'Was it stolen?'

'Yes,' Amit says. 'No. I work for Laurence. For Senator Walker.' The cop smirks. 'Is he all right?'

'He stole your car? That makes sense.' He clicks his earpiece with his finger, and Amit goes to speak again, to answer him. 'Wait,' the cop says, raising a single finger in the air; and Amit listens as he reports that the vehicle's owner has arrived on scene, that Walker did indeed steal the vehicle: yet another thing that they should add to the list. He turns back to Amit when he's done. 'You were saying?'

'Where's Laurence now?'

'Maybe you can tell us,' the cop says. 'Where do you think he would go?'

'I don't know.' Amit wants to find him as much as they do.

'What about the rest of the family? Do you know where they are?'

'No idea,' Amit lies. He knows which hotel they're in. There are only a couple of options, really, so it won't take them long to track them down, but Amit's got a head start on them, however brief. He wants to find Laurence first, get a story sorted. Get him back to a hospital, let the narrative play out from there. It's all about controlling the narrative. That's all it's ever been about. That's politics; *this* is politics. 'Was Laurence looking for them?'

'No idea. Came through here like a fucking maniac. Smashed into those cars. Nearly killed the nice lady from NBC, you believe that?' He looks over at the chaos, and then back at Amit. He runs his tongue around his mouth. 'What you make of it? You work for him. You think he's gone totally loco?'

'I think he's having a breakdown.'

'Yeah, sure. He was in the war. You hear stories, you know. And there's a rumor, about his kid? The one who died? Bruises, that sort of thing.'

'That's bullshit.'

'Like I say, you hear stories.' He looks back, and then clarifies, 'Being a cop.'

Amit looks at the cop's badge, on his shirt for his name. 'Listen, Officer Templeton, can I go to my car? I just want to see if anything's missing. Anything that could be useful to finding Laurence.'

Templeton nods. 'Yeah, sure. Don't take anything from it, though. And tell Officer Robards over there if you find anything? He'll have some sheets for you to sign, about your vehicle. Before we can release it.'

'Of course,' Amit says. He plays ball. He walks towards the wreck of his car, but there's nothing that he wants from it. He moves instead past the van, out of the gaze of Robards, who is interviewing on the other side; and out of sight of Templeton. The gate at the side is still open, the door hanging wide. Amit rushes down the path at the side of the house and into the garden. The patio doors are unlocked, and he gets inside the house, into the kitchen. He doesn't know what he's looking for. Something. A clue as to what Laurence came here for. He goes through the kitchen quietly and then upstairs, into the kids' rooms. Amit helped Deanna and the kids pack, and he saw the house when they went to the hotel. He saw what they took and how

351

they left this. Nothing is disturbed. In the master bedroom, there is nothing gone: but the wardrobe has been pulled apart again, and there's a shoebox on the bed, the lid off. There are photographs strewn – Amit picks some up, and they are of Laurence and Deanna when they were younger, private photos of them smoking and drinking, having fun, kissing, on holidays in swimwear; photographs that you wouldn't want the press to get their hands on – and the rest of the box is empty. Whatever he was after, it was in here.

And then Amit sees the bullet: a sad, single bullet, lying on the floor at his feet. He picks it up and turns it around in his fingers, examining it. There was a gun, he realizes. *That's* what Laurence came back here for.

They are broadcasting from outside the house already. The newscaster, injured ankle strapped up, is standing outside the house, holding a microphone – the boom operator is still being checked by the paramedics, because his side hurts him, though they aren't sure how bad it is just yet – and telling the country what happened. Amit listens, unsure of what's true or not; what's been expanded upon, bent and manipulated.

Laurence Walker is wanted for questioning. He has broken bail. He came here and injured her colleagues, showing scant regard for human life. There was a fury in his eyes: a rage. He was a series of similes: a bull; a bomb; a tornado. He is to be considered dangerous.

He goes back downstairs and out of the garden doors and into the garden, and then the street, back to his car, and he sits there and calls Deanna. The phone rings and rings and he drives away, towards the hotel where she's been staying. He drives fast.

Deanna and the kids leave the hotel in search of food. Explaining to Alyx why they are staying there is tough, especially given that they're going back to where their house will be in walking distance. They could go back there to eat, or to get more clothes – or to avoid the shower in the motel, which is old and yellowing and the water comes out almost gray. But that's not the plan. They'll have another night in the hotel, maybe two. After that, she doesn't know. Maybe she can talk with Laurence. Maybe he can persuade her that he is okay; that he just needs to get away from this. Maybe he can persuade her that he is stable. They could call this a day, this part of their lives, and pack up and move. She could go back to work – she was a hell of a copywriter when she first left college and she could pick it up again, she's sure – and if he can't get a job for a while, that's fine. He can take the time off that he surely needs. They could find a little town somewhere just like this where they might not judge Laurence for something that he hasn't done, Colorado or Utah or somewhere else. Over time, all things blow over, she tells herself. She

353

knows one thing; they have to talk about Sean, and she needs to say all of the things that she never said. She needs to hear that he understands what he did. She bargains with herself. They could go to another country; buy a house in the sun; learn a language. Nobody would know them, there; they would only come back once a year, to visit Sean, to do the ritual with the toys, and to mourn him. She thinks about the practicalities of that solitary visit.

She parks and lets the kids out. A woman that she knows from the church – she works there, handing pamphlets out – sees her and stops.

'We were all so worried,' she says, and she reaches for Deanna's arm. That stupid gesture, Deanna thinks, as if it means anything. It's so token; so placid.

'Thank you,' Deanna says, 'but there's really no need.'

'We haven't seen you in days. Weeks! We were saying, we should go and see if you were okay. But with the news crews there, we thought . . . Well, you know.'

'I know. It's fine. Thank you for the thought.' She tries to walk into the diner, the girls in her wake. She stretches her arm out behind her, keeping them guarded.

'What about your husband? I saw that he was arrested.' The woman drops her tone, saying it without judgment; or, with the judgment as silent as she can manage. 'Is he with you now?'

'No,' Deanna says. 'Just me and the girls.' The woman's face beams at her.

'Oh, well! I'm sure this will all be better soon.' She reaches out and puts her hand on Deanna's arm again. 'You enjoy yourselves while you can,' she says, and she lets go and walks off, glancing back as she heads away from them. Deanna brushes her arm where she had been touched, as if the woman's grip is still there, like an imprint.

'Let's eat,' she says to the girls, still shielding them slightly as she steps forward. She opens the door and the diner tires to pretend that it hasn't noticed who she is. A booth is free and Deanna takes the girls there. They find seats and June comes over to them. She's known them for years now, since they first moved here.

'My God!' she says. She puts menus on the table in front of them. 'I was so worried, when I saw the news.'

'What part of it?' Deanna asks.

'Well, what with . . . well, the *arrest*.' She says the word with a scandalized hush. 'And the video, before! Must have scared you half to death!'

'The video isn't real, June,' Deanna says.

'There's not real and then there's not *real*,' June replies. 'Real as anything, seeing it on a screen like that.' She smiles at the girls and then crouches next to Deanna and drops her voice to a whisper. 'We were talking, all of us. It's hard to lose a little one, and sometimes people don't deal with it. Sometimes, something goes wrong. You get what

I'm saying? Well, and all we want here is to make sure that you and the girls are fine, that's it.' A perky smile. 'Nothing more, but you have to think on yourself.'

'Laurence is fine,' Deanna says. She hears her voice; how unsure she sounds to herself, even. 'Please, June. He's been under such pressure, and the video was an accident. The company who makes it, they screwed up.' June flinches at the tone. 'I'm sorry, June, but that happens, you know it does. And the press . . . You know what they're like. They're taking advantage. Laurence is sick, June. He's sick, and they're preying on him. On us.'

June nods. 'Well, I'm sure . . . I'm sure that's all that it is. But listen to me; if you need anything, you know where to come. I was talking to the Hendersons and, as I say, all we want is you all to be safe and sound. We're open all hours, here. Even if the door is shut, you bang on it, and we'll come help you out.' She stands up and smiles at the girls, makes a little wave at Alyx. 'What can I get you all?'

They order. Around them, the other patrons of the diner try to not stare, but all glance, turning their heads while they take bites of their pastries or eat their huevos rancheros. Deanna tries to meet as many of their eyes as she can, to hold their gaze.

It's only when June brings their own food out – and puts her hand on Deanna's arm and squeezes

356

it in way of comfort, and Deanna thinks, Another person does that it's going to leave a mark – that she realizes that she used the S word. She said that Laurence was sick, and that's because he is. Maybe now is the time to accept it; to embrace it. Call a spade a spade.

As they're standing up to leave, Alyx running to the bathroom, Lane asks if they can go to the mall. Deanna asks why.

'I want to finish this off,' she says. She turns herself slightly, to indicate the tattoo. 'I've got the rose needs doing.'

'What are you having put on it?' Deanna asks.

'Our names,' Lane says. 'The four of us.' Sean is already there, on her neck, Deanna knows. This is a tribute. 'It's not done. There's more. But I want to remember the four of us like we were.' She doesn't say it, but Deanna knows what she's getting at. This will never be the same again. Even if this ends well, none of this will ever be the same.

'Okay,' Deanna says. 'I'll pay.' They leave, and everybody still eating watches them. June rushes after them and stands in the doorway as they get into Deanna's car.

'You remember what I said,' she shouts. 'Any time, day or night. You need to protect yourself.' She waves.

Deanna slams the car door and starts the engine.

'What did she mean?' Alyx asks.

'Nothing,' Deanna says. 'Let's go. What's on the

radio?' She flicks through the stations until she finds one that Alyx likes, signified by immediate and loud singing along. They forget, for a second; or they act as if they have.

When they park, Deanna has a missed call from her agent. He's left a message on her machine. There's been an offer for the book already; a good offer, he says. He wants to tell her more in person. She should call him. He tells her that he hopes she's all right, that everything hits at once, the good and the bad. He asks her to call him, and she thinks that she will, but another day. There's no rush, not right now.

The mall is heaving. Deanna has lost track of what day it is. Lane goes immediately to the tattoo parlour, and she signs in and gets a slot. They have an hour and a half to kill, and then after that the wait while Lane has it done. Four names on a flower. Lane brings a sampler of fonts out of the tattoo parlour and they get a coffee – Deanna's third of the day, and it makes her jittery, feeling the caffeine in her teeth and her fingertips – and they talk them over. Sean's name is written in something complicated and conjoined, the letters almost gothic in design, running into each other; the blacks bleeding, leaving the name spelled out in the white spaces between. They go through and choose one for this new design; it's subtle and classic, like the font from the cover of an old book.

Lane circles it, and then they walk around shops. They go to clothes shops and Lane persuades Deanna to try an outfit on. This feels as if they are incognito and she pulls on jeans that she would never have worn before today, and a top that she thinks is too young for her but that Lane assures her she can get away with; and she looks at herself in the mirror of the changing rooms and pulls back her hair from her face. She imagines a different look, maybe dyeing it, getting it cut.

'You look so good,' the girl in the changing rooms says. She brings the new Deanna a pair of ankle boots and Deanna tries them on; they're perfect. She stands there for ten, fifteen minutes, until Alyx tells her that she's bored and starts playing up, and then she takes the clothes off, pays for them, and goes straight back into the changing rooms and puts them on again, tearing off the tags as she puts each piece of the outfit together. When she's done she puts her old clothes into the bag and walks out, and they all go upstairs, the girls laughing conspiratorially, shocked at their mother's behavior. Even after Laurence's actions the past few weeks, the slightest change in their mother amuses them. Lane goes into the tattoo place, and Deanna tells her that she'll be back in an hour.

Across the way there's a row of hairdresser boutiques, and Deanna picks the nicest looking one and goes in. They have a free slot, and Alyx sits next to her, rocking on the chair. They offer to wash her hair as well, to keep her involved, and she grins the whole time. Deanna tells them to do whatever. She says, 'I'm not fussed about it any more,' and the stylist takes some off and pulls it back and gives her what is almost a fringe. Deanna takes her phone out, taking a photograph of herself. She's got missed calls from Amit. She didn't hear it ring, or feel it vibrate. She tries to call him back, but there's no answer.

When Lane is done, she comes out and peels off the dressing to show them the tattoo. It's lovely; the letters of each word spilling over, as with Sean's name, but they're piled up on top of each other. Alyx at the top, Laurence at the bottom, the weight of each word scaling to the size of it. The petals of the bud lick Laurence's name, red tickling against the black of the lettering.

On the way back to the car, they pass the technology shop. The windows are full of television screens. Lane tries to rush them past, because she knows – as if what happened before was a warning, a prelude to the real reveal – but she can't, not in time. Every screen in the front window of the shop shows Laurence's face, a furious rage on it. His whole being is hunched and howling. He drives a car, screaming as it smacks into news vans; as a woman is hit by it, sent reeling; as people on the other side of the vans scatter, some hit by debris, some hit by each other. It's lucky that there were so many cameras there to capture it all. They get it from every single angle. The cars smash, and the crunch is recorded. Deanna gets closer to the screens and he gets out of the car and he's dazed. He puts his hand out to steady himself, and then a cameraman comes towards him. On the televisions now, they show this first-person, as if you are there; as if Laurence is in front of you, and you're the one who is trying to stop him. Deanna watches it and feels dizzy. The urge to fall, to give in, rises inside her. He is so sick. *Sick, sick, sick.* He is gray and yellow and he is so, so thin; he is a wraith. He reaches for the camera and pulls it from the man, and he bares his teeth and spits garbled words that make him seem alien, as if he doesn't even understand this language. Here is first contact. Laurence pulls the camera close to him and then swings it out in front of him, as a weapon. It collides with the head of the cameraman, who just isn't expecting it. Nobody expects it. Around this, the reporters try to record themselves. They treat this as if it's a warzone and they are crouched behind barricades, under enemy fire. They're afraid of him, because they *know*. They have seen him with a gun, threatening his own family; threatening even his youngest daughter. Everybody is afraid, because everybody has seen what Laurence is capable of. He is a man to be feared. He is a man you should stay away from. He is not a good man.

They scramble on the floor as he comes to them, and he stands in the middle of the fray and he gasps and catches his breath. His shoulders rock up and down in his suit; the colors of ash and

361

lemon yellow, and the tie's color bleeds onto the near-white of his shirt. It makes his skin worse, echoes of jaundice creeping in. Laurence turns from the cameras and pulls something from his pocket. The crews recoil, but it's only his keys; a bundle of them, everything that he needs to access all of his life; his car, his house, his offices. He goes into the house and shuts the door behind him. The camera crews and reporters relax. They report what has happened, and it can be seen for itself. What they say is pretty much irrefutable. He was like a man possessed. He was not the man that she knows.

And then, on the screens, here he comes again, the front door yanked open as he strides. He stops and hurls his keys at the mess of vans and car that he caused in the road, but he doesn't scream or make any noise this time. Instead, he walks. He turns and he goes, walking off, and then running, as he gets further down the road. The cameras follow him until the road bends, and then they cannot see him. The journalists call the police. They leave it until last, because maybe this was their last. If the cops came, they would have to stop. Maybe, letting Laurence be here and then not, that's their story. It's better if there's a chase at the end. Everything is better with a chase at the end, somebody in a creative writing course once told her. Everything is better when it ends with a bang.

Deanna looks at her children. Alyx's face buried

in Lane's hair, the older sister having picked up the younger, mothering her. On the screens now they are showing the video that started this; the little *ClearVista* stamp on the bottom right, as if that gives it some degree of authenticity. The shop's staff stands in the doorway watching Deanna. They know who she is, because everybody does.

And here's her face, on the television; a close up of the video, where she looks terrified, or what is meant to be terrified. She wonders if that is how she looks now, right at this moment.

'Okay,' she says, when they are all back in the car. 'We're going to see Nana and Pop-pop, okay?' The kids don't say anything. Alyx is befuddled, but Lane understands what's going on. She knows that Laurence is having problems. He's crashing. 'We get to the hotel and we pack our bags and we can be there by midnight. Okay?' She turns, because she wants their permission. She wants them to be complicit in this. She doesn't want to talk to Laurence, not yet. He needs help, she knows; and all she can think about is the video, as if it knew. Maybe there's something in it, she thinks. Maybe there's something true there. The girls eventually nod.

She drives, and they don't have the radio on, and there's silence. There's only the rush of the outside against the car itself; the slight whistle of the wind at the window. She puts hers down a crack just to have more. The wind outside suddenly ups and starts whipping around more, and it gets into her ears in the front of the car, like it's beating them, the rush of whatever is outside – trees and bushes and houses – changing the thrum of the wind into a steady beat, beat.

In the car park of the motel, she parks near the exit, reversing in (the fastest route out), and she tells the girls to go up and get their bags packed, and she stands outside the car and watches them go into the room, and then she calls Amit on the phone. He answers on the second ring.

'Jesus Christ, Dee,' he says.

'I saw the news,' she says.

'I don't know what happened to him. I don't know. I'm so sorry.'

'Where is he now?'

'Not got a clue. I went to the house after he was there. Got inside.' He drops his voice, as if he has to whisper; because he doesn't want anybody to hear. 'Listen, Dee, did you know he owned a gun?'

'Yes,' she says. She thinks about it, currently in her bag. 'Why?'

'It's what he was at the house for, I think. It was in a shoebox, in the bedroom?'

'Right. A white shoebox.'

'Well, it wasn't there any more. I found a bullet. But he must have taken the gun.' He sighs. 'I thought he would come for you, then. I don't know why, because he knows what the video showed. I

364

don't know where he is now, but if the press sees him with that, they'll—'

Deanna drops the phone to her side. It clatters to the floor, and it breaks. Cheap; meant to be replaceable. There are two hotels in Staunton. They were such *idiots*. She looks up at the room that they've been staying in, and the door is still wide open. The girls would have closed it behind them. They would have come to look for her after this long a wait. They would. She runs up the stairs. The room is silent. She shouldn't go in, she thinks. She should call the police. But she hears Alyx's hard, shocked breathing, and she can't wait out there one second more.

There is Laurence, reunited with his gun. Standing at the far wall, back pressed up to it. He is crying. The girls are crying too, sitting on the double bed next to each other. He doesn't seem to see Deanna for a second. He doesn't look up as she stands in the doorway. She doesn't want to startle him. She wonders if she can get the girls out of there. Beckon them towards her and, if they're quiet, maybe they can make their way out. What's that game? Murder in the dark? Where you are quiet, and the killer cannot find you in the pitch-blackness?

But then he speaks. 'I'm sorry,' he says to her. 'Because I had to come here and see you all.'

'How did you find us?' she asks.

'I went to the front desk. I asked them.' He

holds out a photograph, the one from their fridge. It has been crumpled and folded. His thumb is on Sean's face, and as he holds it out, Deanna watches his thumb moving against it, worrying the paper. There goes their son, being rubbed away. 'They said that you were in here. They gave me a key.' Deanna wonders if the person at the desk recognized Laurence, if they called the police. She prays that they are on their way.

'I think you need help, Laurence,' she says. She holds out her hands, palms up. This was something Diaz told them, in therapy; palms exposed, and you have nothing to hide. It tricks the subconscious. It's a mark of trust. 'I want you back. We can move past this.'

'No,' he says. 'I don't think that we can. I'm Laurence Walker. Everybody says who I am. You know it, Deanna. You've seen them. The world knows who I am. What sort of man I am.'

'No,' she tells him.

'Have you seen the news?' He looks at the girls. 'So I think I should protect you. I should take you away from here, and then I can protect you.'

'You think you're protecting us?' she asks. Laurence touches Alyx on her head. It doesn't matter that he is her father; she is already afraid of him. She flinches, and he persists.

'It's okay,' he tells her. He turns back to Deanna. 'What if I change what it showed?' He switches on the television, and there he is, assaulting the cameramen again, his trail of havoc. But then he changes the channel, and it's Homme and *his ClearVista* video. But Deanna watches it and sees that it's different. The soldiers aren't generic faces; his smile is no longer a rictus grin made by composite images.

This is real.

He is stepping down from a helicopter and running to shake the hands of soldiers, who all smile and greet him. They have their guns at their backs and their boots polished. He turns to the camera and smiles, a brief, half second of glory. This is a shared understanding; he's telling the audience that they asked for this, and lo, it has become true. The prophecy is realized. Back in the studio, they talk about how accurate the software from *ClearVista* was, and they mention Laurence again. They talk about this as something that is going to come true. Laurence and the Walker family, they have a destiny.

'But he staged that,' Deanna says. 'He staged that, to make it what the video showed.'

'Yes,' Laurence says. 'But maybe the video wasn't me threatening you, Deanna. Maybe I am protecting you, because you are scared of something else entirely. You are scared of them or of what could happen. But not of me.' He smiles at her. It doesn't work on his face; his new face, so gaunt and drawn, that the smile almost looks as if it's been designed.

He takes them to the car that Deanna bought, and he opens the doors for them, and he takes the keys from Deanna's hand. She stops to tie her shoelaces, which aren't actually untied and she picks up the fractured shell of her phone from the tarmac and puts it into her pocket. He doesn't see. It's something, she thinks.

He drives. His knuckles are white on the wheel and his fingers flex as they go. Constantly, like the hands of a pianist, they move left to right, little runs of movement, kinetic energy transferred from one finger to another. On the back seat, the girls are terrified; Lane staring at the back of her father's head, her sister quietly crying. She knows to not push this, Deanna thinks, but she cannot help herself. The sobbing is like a noise from far away. Deanna thinks about the girl who was crying in the hotel. Girl, woman, she doesn't know; crying through the walls. She wonders what was wrong with her.

They drive across the freeway, not turning off, and then back towards the house. She sees the stretch of shops: the diner, and June inside it; the garage, her old car in the forecourt, the body-work now patched up; the grocers, Trent serving customers, sweeping the floors; the church, and the priest inside, listening to confession, doling out punishments to be self-administered; and the bar at this end, the regulars already drinking, that same old nineties rock music on the jukebox; and then the road down towards their house, the resi-dential housing, this place that they have loved for so long; this place that they have called home.

'We're going to the house?' she asks, but Laurence doesn't answer. He indicates and turns the car off, down the dirt track that runs to the woods. This car doesn't have the suspension for this. They all shake. Deanna feels the car in her teeth, making them chatter. 'The cabin,' she says, realizing it. 'We're going to the cabin.'

'Only for a few days,' he says. 'It's clean. I've been down here, earlier. It's clean enough.'

Deanna doesn't say anything. Not about what's down here, or why they haven't been. She knows. They all know; it's been implied the whole of this year, even if they haven't spoken about it. Because it's stupid to not come here because of what happened. They drive down the path, and then it snakes through the field and into the woods itself. It all falls dark, the tree canopy overhead blocking the sun; and it only stops when it reaches the lake. There it is, in front of them, a mass of water that just goes on and on, and their cabin, perched on the edge of it. They haven't been here in over a year. The land will take it back, they were told when they bought the place, and it has happened. Grass as high as the windows alongside the car, which almost runs up to the waterline. Here is where, when it happened, the reporters stood; in this grass, on these fields, with the woods around them, and the lake, and the house framed behind them: an old, wooden building that's now haunted.

The water is still. Laurence drives them up the path. The car shudders again on the gravel.

'We're nearly there,' he says.

★   ★   ★

He steps out and smells the air, as if this is a holiday. Even where they live, getting this far away from the roads you can suddenly taste how clean it is in comparison. The air comes off the lake and brings the wetness with it, and that makes its way into your throat.

Laurence opens the doors for the rest of them. 'We won't be here long,' he says, 'just until everything dies down. It's quieter here.' He looks happy, Deanna thinks, and he sounds it; there's a break in his voice, a slight quiver as he looks around. 'I can feel it, already. Healing, being away from that mess.' He reaches for Alyx, for her head, to ruffle her hair. 'Isn't it, Pumpkin?' he asks. She flinches and backs away. 'Okay,' he says. He breathes, as if he has to catch himself. Deanna sees it. It's restraint. He's holding himself back.

He takes out the bags from the boot and he puts one hand in his suit pocket – to check for the gun, Deanna thinks – and then he locks the car. 'I probably don't even need to do that,' he says, 'because it's not like there are people here who'll steal it. Remember we said that? We said that we wanted somewhere that we could leave the doors open.' He looks at Lane. 'We used to live in the city, when we left college. This was back before you were born. It makes such a difference.' He turns and walks up to the house, and he stops. He doesn't turn back. 'We have to move on. We have to.'

'I think that you're sick, Laurence,' Deanna says.

'I think that maybe you need help. We should go and see Doctor Diaz.' She doesn't know if Diaz will help, but she's somewhere else entirely; somewhere that isn't here, somewhere they will be with other people, and where she can make a concerted effort to get him real help.

'I'm not,' he says. 'I am judged. It's all so different now.' He roots around underneath flowerpots for the key to the door. 'They all think that they know. They all think that I cannot control myself.'

'That isn't it,' Deanna says. She doesn't know how to talk her way out of this. She steps towards him. 'Laurence, please . . . The girls are scared. You have to see that.'

'All I am going to do is protect you,' he says. 'It doesn't have to play out the way that they say. I can change the narrative, Deanna.' He turns, and he pulls the gun from his pocket, and he holds it up. He points it at Alyx. 'This means nothing. This means absolutely nothing at all,' he says. He puts the gun back and Alyx collapses into tears. He rushes to her and kneels in front of her. 'No, Pumpkin, no! This was to prove a point. You don't need to be scared of me, honey.' He wraps his arms around her and she doesn't resist. She gives herself over to it. All she wants, Deanna thinks, is to believe this.

He ushers them up the steps and he unlocks the door. The lock is stiff and clogged, and when it finally turns and he brings the key out, he has to clean it off. They haven't come up here since Sean died, because why would they? It is a place of nothing but memories. Or, rather, a single memory. It is a memory of her son, and the water, and his final moments. The whole house is tainted; there is nothing here that she wants to see.

Laurence pushes the door wide.

CHAPTER 14

Every time Amit tries to call Deanna's phone it goes straight to the answering machine. There's no pause or hesitation, which means it's not even trying to connect. Her phone is off or the battery is dead. When he gets to the hotel he runs to the room that they were staying in and he bangs on the door, but he can't get an answer. He tries to look through the front window but the curtain has been drawn across. The woman from the front desk comes out and stares at him.

'I help you?' she asks.

'The people who are staying here. Have you seen them?'

'None of your business.'

'Look. I need to know if they're here, or where they went.'

'Are you family?' she asks. 'You don't look like family.' She goes back to her office, but Amit sees her creak the blinds down and continue staring at him. He tries to call again, but there's no answer. He sits in his car and watches the sun go down, and he watches people come in and out of the hotel – trucks with couples in them; men on their own; women on their own; no other families, not a single situation that doesn't look as if it's transitory – and he walks to the vending machines and buys a sandwich that feels as if it's made from sponge and tastes even worse; and then he tries to call Deanna again. But again, there's nothing.

His phone buzzes. It's Jessie.

I don't have anything yet, she writes. *Are you okay?*

Yes, he says. *Everything's fine.* White lies until the truth makes itself apparent. He leans back, jacks the chair as flat as he can make it, and he shuts his eyes. He opens them every time a car comes into the lot and he watches the people get out and stumble or dance their way to the rooms. At one point he thinks he hears crying, on the wind, but when he gets out of the car to look it's gone and the place is silent again.

Jessie starts the night shift by messaging Amit, and then she writes her stories straight away, reeling them off. She can touch-type – that's the benefit of a private education, her father once told her, those basic skills that most other graduates will lack, and in this day and age it's about differentiating yourself (he used *ClearVista*'s algorithms to show her her chances of employability if she listened to him versus if she chose not to) – and she goes into autopilot to do this. She's waiting on emails from various people about *ClearVista*, still. She went through the archives to find the names of those most likely to have been hired or poached. She starts with the founders, emailing them and asking them if they know anybody still working there. Chancing her luck, telling them that it's for a documentary. Most tell her that they didn't work there. A couple say that they left as soon as the algorithm was complete. She follows those up, asking how it works. One doesn't reply. The other sends a mocking answer, spotted with truth; they worked in bubbles, on aspects. None of them ever worked there long enough to see the algorithm in its final state. The computers – plural, a series of networked systems daisy-chained together, like nothing you've ever seen outside of NASA or MIT – they did the assembly. The different parts dealt with different aspects. Jessie's contact tells her that he was on the data-mining side. His part of the equation sifted through personal records: property tax, hospital records, insurance, equities, licenses. It worked out what you owned and where you owned it and what stake you had in it, and it applied that information as a factor to the algorithm as a whole. They paid him off and he's had no contact since. Nearly everybody he worked with left when he did. He gives her some names; one of them is Thomas Hershel. She tries to call him, and she gets his machine. Nothing else.

She looks at the *ClearVista* premises on *Google StreetView*. A steel and glass lump of Silicon Valley, on a road as long as any she's ever seen, lined with similar steel and glass lumps. She writes the address down for Amit, and she tries to call the offices. She says who she is and who she works for and the automated woman tells her that some-body will call her back. But nobody calls, and the phone won't let her into the system again. She checks her email, pressing F5 to refresh over and over.

She tells her boss that she might have a story. She rattles off what she knows, that it seems as if nobody actually works for them any more, because she can't find a single name of a current employee, and everything on the phone lines is automated. And Laurence Walker's video, where did that come from? Her boss stops her, raising her hand.

'Listen,' she says, 'this is a dead end. It's a dead end, and it can't be a story.'

'Why?' Jessie asks. She looks at the screens. They're showing the Homme footage again. The commentary includes the words *evidence* and *proof*. It's treated as fact, and she can see the slippery slope, even if the others can't.

'He's going to be the nominee, and then he's going to be our next president. Nothing can upset that apple cart now. So they're a tech company. Bunch of nerds in a room somewhere too scared to answer a telephone. It's not a story, Jessie.'

'Laurence Walker's life has been ruined.'

'As the video said it would be. Maybe that's the story, when all of this is over. You want to write about truth, maybe start there.'

Back at her desk, Jessie realizes how she thinks

this is going to end. They are all just waiting for the money shot, where Walker recreates his own *ClearVista* video.

She presses F5, but there's still nothing.

All night she searches for information on a single name: Thomas Hershel. The men and women who set up the company, they're all gone. They cashed in their money, giving it to a private investor. None of them want anything to do with her, or the company, or interviews. One of them emails her at nearly four in the morning and tells her that he's signed an NDA. Just that and nothing else. I can't talk, that sort of message says. I've been gagged.

So she digs into property records and she roots around in work permits. It's all signed off to people who no longer work there. *ClearVista* is a ghost town. She thinks about the software that they use, then; that maybe that's a good way in. Software has licenses, and somebody's going to have to pay for them. Somebody's going to have to put his or her name down somewhere. She looks through those records, everything open, nothing hidden to her and her contacts even at this time of night.

And more and more it comes back to the same name. She speaks with a cleaning company, hired to go and wipe the windows of the glass-covered building *ClearVista* operates out of, and they tell her their contact name: Thomas Hershel. Thomas Hershel, who signed for a *Windows Cyan* license earlier this year. Thomas Hershel, who is listed as the driver of the only company car now leased to *ClearVista*. She tries to call him again, but there's no answer still; and it's not even going to the machine any more. She calls Amit instead.

'I know him,' Amit tells her. 'I know him. I have been talking to him.'

'He's only on the records the last year or so. The shareholders all sold up in January.'

'So he bought them?'

'Or he took over. But he signed the *Microsoft* license, and then he signed an *Adobe* license three weeks later. Both were for *ClearVista*. At the very least, he's working for them.'

'He told me he'd left.'

'Which means he had something to hide.'

'He's been looking at the algorithm for me. Reverse engineering it.' He pauses. 'He had the software.'

'Seriously?'

'Can you email me everything you've got?' Jessie agrees and Amit tells her that he'll call her back. He tries to ring Hershel's cellphone, but the line just rings and rings. One way or another, Hershel lied to him. It doesn't mean anything, but if he's still working for *ClearVista*, he could have stopped this. Amit tries to assemble the reasons in his mind, but he can't. Nothing adds up. Hershel isn't a mastermind: he's a surfer, a stoner; he's just naturally good with numbers.

★ ★ ★

Jessie emails the one contact who replied to her. She asks him to tell her everything he remembers about Thomas Hershel.

He was brains trust, he replies. *He was on the actual assembly of the thing. Had some formula of his own, to do with understanding trends. You know, social trending, like Twitter and Facebook and whatever. He worked all that in. Brass loved him.*

Jessie asks him to explain that more. *I don't know much about how the algorithm works,* she writes.

Join the club, he replies. *Three branches. Data mining (which was my side, where we're looking at getting information about you from every possible source we can); the questionnaire stuff (where they tried to work out your likely responses to certain scenarios, and outcomes of those responses); and then Hershel and his team were in charge of understanding how the algorithm worked with the rest of the world, basically. None of the rest of us understood that stuff. That was the last stage, actually figuring that out, taking into account everything else. So, in Walker's case – because I'm guessing that's what this is all about – they'll have been looking at the mood about the election, about how people have voted before, what they're looking for in a candidate. How the house swings. Everything. How they're talking about Laurence on social media. Basically, the other two departments were focused and personal, but Hershel's stuff tried to take into account everything in the entire world. Not a big ask.* ☺

And Thomas Hershel – he seemed like a good guy?

Sure, her contact replies. *I mean, we were all good guys. He was quiet, I remember that much.*

Were you friends? she asks.

We were work friends, so not close enough to give a damn what happened to the guy after we all left. He was there longer than me, anyway. His department: first in, last out. They'll have been the ones left to shut the lights off.

What do you mean?

Figure of speech, he writes.

Amit hands his credit card over to the man at the check-in desk. He types numbers and checks Amit's driving licence as proof that he is who he says he is, and then he cranes backwards and makes a noise. It's a sucking of air through his teeth, part whistle, part sigh.

'This has been declined,' he says. 'Do you have another?' That's the campaign money, Amit knows, all gone. He takes out his personal card.

'Try this,' he says, knowing that there isn't enough cash in his account, but hoping that his overdraft can bear the brunt. It does, and the ticket is sent to his phone.

'Did you not want to run the algorithm?' the man asks him.

'I'm fine. I trust you.'

'Have a good flight,' the man says.

'I'll do my best.' He runs to the gate, and the guards see him, the last man to arrive. They ask why he's running, and he says that he's late.

'This side, sir,' they say. They send him through the full-body, and they ask him to take off his jacket and his shoes and they run them through and scan them, and they use little knives to prise apart the plastic of the heel of the shoe, slightly; enough that they can peek inside, splitting the glue and checking that there is nothing in there. They open his wallet and take it apart, pulling all the cards out, even the fluff from the lining; and they turn his phone upside down and plug it in and check that it works. Then they hand everything back. 'Thank you,' they say. They've held the flight for him. He gets on board and everybody stares at him, as if it was *his* choice to delay this. He sits down and tries to call Deanna again, and Hershel, but there's no answers. Then they ask everybody switch off their phones for take off. He has a window seat, and he watches the world strip away: the cities, the streets, the woods, the lakes.

Deanna managed to sleep. She doesn't know how, but she did. She is in their room, because this is where Laurence told her she should sleep, and he told her that this room – the only pictures on the walls the ones that came with the place – this room is where he had thought of for her. He said that he assumed they would take this room for their own, if they actually moved in. He said that he wasn't tired. He said he had been asleep for long enough, and he wanted to stay outside and watch the sun rise. So she lay on the bed, which creaked with every slight movement on it; and she tried to ignore the house's new inhabitants, spiders and beetles and ants, who took over the place when the Walkers decided that they couldn't come back here. The girls had been sleeping – or, rather, not sleeping – in the room next door, another double bed between them, but she went in and got them in the night when she heard them talking, their voices coming through the walls. She heard Alyx ask about the house, and why they stopped coming here. They never told her how Sean died, and Lane danced around the answer.

'Sometimes a place just isn't the same as it used to be,' she told her sister, who asked why, and she said, 'because there are memories, and they change everything. And you can't escape them, not completely; so you escape them where you can.' Deanna thought that was as good a reason as any.

'What's wrong with Daddy?' Alyx asked then, and that's when Deanna got out of bed and went to them. She wanted to diffuse that question; she didn't want Lane to have to answer it. It was easier to let that question fade into the house itself. They went into Deanna's room, because it was slightly warmer, and the window didn't look out onto the lake, which was something; and they all slept in her bed, craned around one another, relishing each other's warmth. The girls were asleep within five minutes, and Deanna five minutes later. As she went to sleep, she was thinking of Laurence; of him diving in and pulling Sean's body out of the water.

So now, awake, the girls still gently sleeping next to her, she looks around the room. There are no curtains in here, not yet. The only night that they had stayed here before, Deanna stared at the moon and Laurence said that it was perfect; and they had all slept in the same room, the five of them, sleeping bags around the place. It was like camping, Sean said.

She gets out of bed and creeps towards the door and Lane opens her eyes and looks at her but doesn't say anything. It's like they both know. Deanna wants to see where Laurence is, because she's hoping that he's asleep. If he is, maybe she can get the girls into the car and go. Now isn't the time for wondering what's right or wrong. It's the time for asking what's best.

At the end of the hall is a window, and she can see the lake through it. The house faces east, catching the sun rising up above the water. The first time that they stayed here they all watched it the next morning; the reflection of it in the still mirror below, looking as if it were rising from the deepness in the far off, splitting into two as it went. She listens for anything coming from below: the sound of him sleeping or, worse, of him awake, ready for the day, waiting for the rest of them to stir. There is nothing, though. Not a single murmur from anywhere. She makes it to the bottom of the stairs and then sidles through to the living room, and then the kitchen. She stops in front of the door to cellar, wondering if Laurence might be down there. She cracks the door slightly and listens, but it's silent; only the slightest echo of a dripping, of water into water.

She looks on the counter for his wallet and keys – every house that they have lived in, that's been his routine, put the wallet and keys on the kitchen counter or a mantle or a table, whichever's most convenient – but she can't see them. She can't see his jacket either, which would be the next most likely place. His bag is here. She opens it, praying that the keys – or, next best, the gun – might have been left inside it. But there's nothing of any use: a shirt, a vest, a change of underwear, and his wash bag. Everything he might need for a stopover on the campaign trail. She opens the back door, sliding it to one side, steps out onto the decking. Plant boxes line the sides, built from the same wood, overgrowing with nothing that looks as if it's actually meant to be inside them. And the dock, or what they called the dock. The same wood as the deck. Where the ground drops away, a steep incline from the grass to sand, the dock stays level, two foot above the water. It's perfect for a small boat, Laurence once said. Think of the summers we can have when all of this is over.

It's incredible how still the water is. Every step makes the wooden struts move slightly and ripples come from them, like a finger breaking the surface. She reaches the end of the dock and looks down and sees the reeds below, and the creepers, like hands.

Everything reflects when the water is finally completely still; even Deanna, as she peers into the darkness below her.

She leaves the dock and heads around the side of the house, to the car. She prays that he's left the doors open and the keys inside it. Then she sees him, asleep in the passenger seat. It's jacked backwards as far as it can go and his eyes are shut. He is a sentry, waiting at the only road out of this place. But there are fields, and there are woods – other ways out of here – and if he doesn't see them, maybe they will have a chance.

She goes back inside and up the stairs, worrying less about the noise. It's still so early and, if they're lucky, Laurence will be asleep a good while yet. She tells the girls to get out of bed.

'What's happening?' Alyx asks, rubbing her eyes.

'We're leaving,' Deanna says. 'We have to be very quiet though.' She looks out of the window here at the side of the house. If they can get to the woods, they can make it back to town. It will only take them an hour or so. She gets them dressed, and she doesn't make a game out of this or pretend that there's anything other than escape occurring. There's no point, not now. She packs everything into the bag; but actually, she thinks, she should leave the bag, because when he wakes up and looks for them, that will be a distraction. It will make him think that they're there still. She looks through to see if there's anything that she needs, and there's the phone; the broken shell, cheap shattered plastic, the innards visible and the battery rattling inside. She leaves it with the clothes. All of this, now, is detritus.

'Down the stairs,' she says. They rush down, and there he is.

'You're all up early,' he says.

'Yes,' she tells him.

'I fell asleep,' he says. 'I was out there, on the dock, and I just went off. I was watching in the night and I saw a light across the way; I was trying to work out what it was, because maybe there was something on the other side of the lake. I don't think there were people living there when we were here before. But now, I could see it; at least, reflecting in the water, I saw it. I think I saw it in the air as well. But then I fell asleep. I think it's the sound of the lake. It laps, you know, against the beach. I hadn't thought.'

Deanna thinks about how still the water was when she was out there. The lake is landlocked. There's no tide.

'So I lay back and I listened to it and I watched the light. I haven't done anything like that in years and years. Just let myself relax, you know. Then I got cold, so I slept in the car.' He looks at the girls. 'I feel better here,' he says. 'We should eat something. There's bread in the freezer. Lots of other stuff as well. And jars in the pantry. Jelly and peanut butter.' He waits at the bottom of the stairs. 'Then I'm going to go swimming.'

They eat because they feel that they should, and because Deanna makes eyes at them. When their father is in the pantry, Alyx asks if they're still going, her voice low, buried by the background noise.

'Not now,' Deanna whispers. When Laurence comes back he has got his boxer shorts on, his shirt pulled off. Deanna cannot look at him; he is so thin she can see through his skin, almost. His bones look almost as if they are on the outside. He puts the suit on the sofa, laid out like an empty man, and he opens the back door.

'Come and watch me,' he says. He opens the back door and laughs, as if this is the most natural thing in the world. 'I'll bet the water is freezing,' he says. 'Oh my God.'

They can see him through the windows, as he struts onto the dock. He raises both arms above his head into a perfect dive pose, his ribs a ladder up the length of his body. 'Okay,' he says, and he breathes in, a suck of air that makes his chest swell; and he almost draws back for a second before going forward, a one and a two and then up into the air. Then down into the water, and the ripples spread out as he goes deeper. From where Deanna is standing she can't see him; only the water rushing out in lapping waves. She thinks about what happens if he doesn't resurface; if he calls for her help.

There's a gasp, and then a scream; and then he laughs. 'It's so cold!' he says. 'That is the coldest.'

He swims around and then climbs out, hoisting himself up, his skin blue from the water and from how cold he is; and then he does it again, and again.

He tells Deanna that they need food. He says, 'You should go and get it, I think.' He sits at the table, dressed again, his suit on. She sees his hand playing with the pocket of the jacket, the weight of the gun inside it pulling it down. He throws her the car key and he looks at the girls. 'Get enough food for a few days,' he says. 'Then we can work out where we're going to go after this.' He hands her money, crumpled banknotes. She wonders if he knows how threatening this is, or if this is all accidental. Maybe he just trusts her; or maybe the children are a bargaining chip. They're insurance.

'Okay,' Deanna says. She's fine while she goes to the car and gets in and adjusts the seat and the mirrors; and then all the way down the dirt path, and through the woods. It's not until she gets in view of their old house that she stops the car and screams to herself, and beats the steering wheel and cries.

There's a crowd of cars outside *Henderson's*. People doing their shopping, trying to avoid trekking to *Walmart* (or, if they're feeling sanctimonious and daring, *Whole Foods*). As people load their cars they look at her, but she doesn't make eye contact. She wonders what she should do here; because he has the gun, and her daughters. There's a television in the corner of the shop, mounted up on the wall. It's showing the news. She thinks, All of this is inevitable. Even seeing this now. There's a snippet of Laurence's video, the first one, from *ClearVista*. The newsreaders don't seem to even talk about it afterwards, as if it's a commercial being shown out of context. They say that Laurence is wanted for questioning. This is just a part of their daily programming schedule. Laurence, the newsreader says, should be considered armed and dangerous. They use a screen grab of him as the main image, rather than an older publicity photograph; it's slightly off angle, as he looks away from his video family. It all feels inevitable. Homme recreated his video to fulfil a prophecy and Laurence is a crashing airplane, a collapsing building of a man.

She turns away, and she sees Trent Henderson watching her from behind the counter. He leans over, both hands flat on the wood – he made this shop's fittings himself, he tells anybody who will listen, chopped and whittled and sanded and made appropriate for the purpose – and he bends forward.

'Deanna, are you okay?' he asks. He speaks quietly, so that he can barely be heard.

'I'm fine,' she says. 'Just getting some food.'

'Of course,' he says. 'So do you need help?' He suggests so much. Just tell me, his voice says, and

I can do whatever you like. I can call the police. I can have them come here. Deanna hesitates, which she knows is a mistake; it's what will get him wondering. Treat him as a man who said what he did about your husband. Remember that you love Laurence, and act it.

'I know where everything is,' she says. She picks up a box of cookies, as proof of this, and puts it into the basket she's carrying around the shop.

'Of course,' he says. 'Didn't mean to imply otherwise.' He nods. She turns away and goes to the chilled section at the back, picking up burgers and chicken fillets and mince for chili, and she gets vegetables to go with it all. This is all for show: five a day, protein and vegetables, playing house. She takes chips and cookies and other things that will keep, because she doesn't know how long they'll be there. Bagels, milk. All the stuff they might need. She takes the basket to the counter and heaves it up, and Trent starts unpacking it. 'Need bags?' he asks.

'Yes,' she says. He whips a paper bag through the air, sending air into it, inflating it, and he stands it on the counter. He looks closely at her, and he takes the items out of the basket and puts them straight into the bag, not running them through. He speaks quietly and she notices that it is barely moving his beard, that's how subtle he's being.

'I don't know if he's watching,' he says, 'but I will help you, Deanna. I can help. We can do

390

something.' He moves his head to make eye contact with her. 'This isn't your fault, and there is no guilt here. You hear me?'

'Okay,' she says. She nods. She nearly bites, but only nearly. He keeps filling the bags. 'You haven't put them through the till.'

'Oh,' he says, as if he hasn't noticed. 'So you listen to me, and answer me this: where are you staying? In the Roadtel?'

'No,' she says.

'Somebody was in here yesterday saw you out that way.'

'We were there,' she says.

'So now you're back at home.'

'No,' she says. She looks at the television, and she sees the video again. She can't even be sure it's on the screen there and then; that this isn't an echo, a memory of it. Lights tracing in the darkness. 'We're at the lake,' she says. Everything rushes: relief and panic, all in one. He nods and reaches out his hand, and he squeezes her hand.

'Okay,' he says. 'Don't worry.' She doesn't tell him what she wants, or what to expect. He will tell the police, and they will turn up at the lake house, likely; and they will take Laurence away. It will be the end of this. 'You take this stuff and we'll worry about it later.'

'I have to give you the money,' she says, and she takes out the money from her pocket and passes it to him.

'Whatever you want,' he says. He stands and

watches her load the car and then drive away, his arms folded across his chest. He stays there until she has gone completely from view.

When she gets back, Laurence runs out to help her carry the bags in. He is still in his suit. He leans in to pick up the bags, and he moves to her sharply, kissing her cheek.

'It's good to have you back,' he says.

CHAPTER 15

Amit queues to leave the airport for some reason, a train of people lined up to show their ID cards and get themselves verified. He is inspected, and he is asked his intentions in the Great State of California. He says that it's pleasure, because that's so much easier than even attempting to explain any of this. Because he doesn't *know* what this is, he thinks. He's here to go to *ClearVista*. He's here to try and track down Hershel. He's here to get an answer about how this happened, and maybe get something resembling an end to this. That's all he wants, he thinks. Closure.

The cab driver asks him where he's going. It's getting late, too late to do anything tonight, and so he asks for the nearest hotel he has a chain membership of. Might as well start spending the points, he thinks. There's no campaign trail to worry about now.

The hotel is what he expects. They hand him a warmed cookie with his key, and they say the same phrase as always to him. The room itself is the perfect temperature, and it's quiet. The television is on, tuned to the channel that he most watched in his last few stays. It's predictable, and predictive.

He takes everything out of his satchel, and he streams all the videos to the TV one last time. They've become even more unsettling to him, escalating in their terror, in the violence that they show. He orders room service, a burger that arrives and tastes the same as every other burger he's ever eaten in one of these hotels; and he watches TV, the paid channels that he doesn't pay for at home because he's never there. He is drifting off, the TV show in the background a shouted soundtrack to whatever it is he's thinking of as he goes, when his phone rings. It's Jessie.

'So: Thomas Gabriel Hershel the second. Arrested for gambling scams in Vegas, June 2013. Arrested for – wait for it – blackmail in August of 2015. Ran some scam, sending letters to a government representative out of New Orleans. Didn't do time, but paid out large.'

'He didn't tell me about that.'

'I'm not done. Arrested again, November 2016, running an online gambling scam. He did some time in Virginia State, came out, went back to working for *ClearVista*; and then he purchased it a month later.'

'Purchased it?'

'He bought out the shareholders.'

'With what?'

'He had a portfolio, that much is clear. He was

probably running things that he wasn't caught doing. You know how it is.'

'Yes.'

'So,' Jessie asks, 'big question is, why make the video he did?'

'You think he made it?'

'You think he didn't?' She's exasperated. 'Amit: blackmail, scams. He's a criminal.'

'That black and white?'

'That black and white, yes. Certainly.'

'Why would he do that?'

'Publicity? Look how much screen time *ClearVista* has gotten out of this. Look at what the Homme campaign has achieved. He's basically the next president of the United States, and all because he paid a hundred grand for some bullshit video.'

'It doesn't change anything.'

'Of course it does!'

'I knew him.' Amit looks up at the ceiling. He realizes that this hotel is different. A tiny, tiny thing. The others have plain, smooth ceilings with in-set light fittings. Nothing breaks the line of the room. This one, there's a pattern in the paint. Like you see in old houses, in older hotels, soft lines drawn into it, into concentric circular patterns.

'What are you going to do?' Jessie asks.

'Go to *ClearVista*, see if he's there. Try and talk to him.'

'You give me the story when you're done?'

'You clear Laurence's name, it's all yours.' He doesn't mean Laurence any more, he thinks.

He means Deanna and the kids. He wants them to have a life again, because this could ruin them. And himself; he wants to know that he was validated. That he didn't back the wrong horse.

'I'm one of the good guys,' Jessie says.

'So was Hershel.'

He sleeps. He dreams of something, and wakes up drenched in sweat, again and again; turning over, finding a cool part of the bed, sleeping again, and then repeating himself.

Breakfast is a croissant smeared with jelly and two thick espressos thrown down his throat. He orders a cab and waits outside in the sun, hopelessly ill-prepared for the weather here. He didn't bring his sunglasses or his lighter suit, so he takes his jacket off and rolls up his shirt sleeves and he lets himself sweat, surrounded by planted palm trees and pale burnt cacti. He tries to call Deanna again, but there's nothing; and he searches *Twitter* for Laurence's name. The cycle hasn't moved on yet. Everybody in political office around the country is doing their best to disown him if they're feeling kind, or smear his name if not. Some claim to have known what he was like; telling stories about the kind of man that they believed him to be. People who were photographed with Laurence, who thanked him for his contributions or support, who shook his hand before, and now they're jumping ship. Amit sees an interview with the Texan investor. He says that he never met with Laurence, because there was always an excuse. *Man like that, you can't trust. He had demands, and he wanted money and support. But he couldn't look me in the eye and tell me that he was a good person. I didn't contribute, in the end. Didn't trust Senator Walker, not one little bit.* Amit's name has been left out of all this. He's barely mentioned. This was all Laurence, it seems; a lone operator, gone rogue, accountable for his own actions and nothing else.

The cab pulls in and takes Amit down the highway. He winds the window down and moves his head close to the window, and he feels the wind – the rush – of California going past. This was part of the dream, once. A month after Texas, this was where they were going to be, drumming up support. It's red state heartland, so both Laurence and Homme were desperate to get its support. Nothing else mattered so much: a knock-down, drag-out fight between the two men to take this state's support and likely the nomination with it. Now, Amit can't fathom being here for that.

The view turns from trees and slickness to more run-down buildings, and then to desert, briefly; and then, in the distance, the shimmering silver and glass of the corporations and tech companies. They glimmer like a mirage in the distance, reflecting the sun. The cab driver turns on the GPS and says, '*ClearVista*,' and the computer adjusts and points them down street after street of buildings that tower over them. Amit doesn't see another human being. Instead, there are signs advertising low-cost lease options; padlocked doors; empty parking lots. Then the GPS says that they are approaching their destination, and Amit spots it on a junction ahead. They likely wouldn't have missed it, Amit thinks. It's curved, a filled-in archway of dark-mirrored glass, the company logo deep-set into the glass. On the floor, the same glass surrounds it, making a circular base that reflects the building and the sky both. Everything reflects itself. Amit pays the driver with his card, praying it'll go through – in his worst nightmares he is suddenly stranded, relying on his wiles, which feel worn away and too tired by far – and it does. The driver asks if he should stay.

'It's fine,' Amit says. He takes his number, in case he needs picking up, and he watches the cab leave. He turns and walks up the path, and then he's walking on the glass. It's immaculate, and the sun's reflection bounces off it, so bright that he can barely stand to look.

It's hard to see the door at first, until Amit spots a handle moulded from the same glass as the rest of the building. It's unlocked and he steps inside. It's freezing cold in the building. There is a desk here, and then staircases rising from either side, entwined, a helix. Above the lobby, a sign hangs. *ClearVista: the numbers don't lie.* Underneath it, a giant video screen showing the *ClearVista* advertorial. Here is the woman getting the job she desired. Here's the couple with their new baby.

Everything here is so simple, so easy to explain away. *ClearVista* leads to happiness and contentment, and the answer that you want. They're selling a vision of a future that you want to will into being. They can add Homme's video to this, Amit thinks, and barely skip a beat. Here's a man who is under-qualified, somehow proving himself by default; and then here's Laurence, buried in the annals of history. Hoist on his own petard.

There is nobody at the desk, but there is a button and a screen. He presses it. The screen clicks to life, with a face. A poorly animated face, like the ones in their promotional videos, but this one a somehow beautiful but generic woman. She is an amalgam and he finds it impossible to place her ethnicity. She reminds him of so many actresses, but isn't like any of them, not when you focus.

'Please state your name,' she says. Her voice is clipped. He recognizes it; the voice from the telephone service.

'Amit Suri,' he says.

'Please hold,' she says. She closes her eyes. She looks peaceful, Amit thinks. It's a trick; an exaggerated visual representation that she is doing something. She opens her eyes again. 'You're here to see Mr Hershel,' she says. His name is the only part of the sentence that sounds perfect, unclipped.

'Yes,' Amit says.

'Please hold. I will send for him.' Amit looks around, but there are no chairs. The face folds itself away, disappearing to a fixed point on the screen, and the screen goes blank. Amit walks around, looking behind the desk. There's no movement, so he waits, and he looks through the glass, and up the stairs. The building goes on and on, but he can't see any rooms, or doors, or people. There's only the building itself.

He waits and waits, and there's no sign, so he presses the button again. The face comes back and asks him for his name. He says it again, and again it rolls its eyes back in false thought.

'I will tell Mr Hershel of the urgency of your enquiry. Please hold.' Amit shakes his head and walks back. In the distance he hears the footsteps of somebody approaching. They echo throughout the building, because there is no other noise. He looks up the stairs, craning his neck to see expensive black shoes, tan slacks, and a man in a blue jacket coming down the stairs. Amit knows him; he saw him in the airport, way back. After Laurence's first incident, when they first received the report. Laurence said that he kept seeing him and Amit didn't believe him.

'He's waiting upstairs for you,' the man says. He seems resigned to something; that his being here isn't his choice.

'Who are you?' Amit asks.

'I told you before: I'm really nobody,' the man says. 'He's waiting.' He stands to one side of the staircase, to let Amit through. Amit walks past him, and up the glass staircase. The first floor stretches back, and finally there are rooms here, brushed-silver walls and darkened glass doors. He opens them, one by one, but there is nothing inside them. No furniture, no staff. There's no sign that there has ever been anything else here. Up the next flight of stairs, and then the stairs end. The building stretches up, but there are no more floors. There are more rooms here, but Amit knows where he's going. At the far end is a boxed-off room, larger than the others, and he can see a wall of computers lining the back wall. Lying on the floor in front of them is Hershel. He has his eyes open, and he stares at Amit.

'I'm sorry,' he says, before Amit can hear it. But he can see his lips form the words.

Hershel looks like shit, Amit thinks. He's a wreck. Protein bar wrappers are tucked in the room's solitary trashcan, and empty tins of soda. He pushes himself to his feet as Amit opens the room's solitary door. It's freezing inside. Amit sees little jets of air pumping out by the servers, the banks of blinking lights and whirring hard drives kept artificially cooled. Hershel stands in front of them, unsteady on his feet.

'Look,' he says. There's a crack in his voice. 'This wasn't meant to happen.'

'You did this?'

'No! The algorithm did.'

'You made it, Hershel.'

'Amit,' Hershel says, 'you don't understand. I'm

serious, here. This isn't something I intended. You think I knew?'

'I think you've conned people before. I think you've blackmailed and cheated, and I think you've found another way to do it.'

'No. I didn't ask you for money, did I? I didn't . . . I didn't blackmail you. I could have done. *ClearVista* could have done.'

'And how much press has *ClearVista* had because of this? You released this shit into the world. It's a pox, and you unleashed it!'

'I didn't release anything.' He puts his hand on the servers. 'They're not doing anything now, you know. It runs the equation and then it sleeps. It answers the phone and diverts the calls, and then it sleeps. It runs this entire business, and then it sleeps. You think it's insidious, but it's not. It's not an AI. It doesn't *know*. It just does what we told it to do before, and it's carried on doing it. It sees equations, and it fills them.'

'You told it to show Laurence like it did.'

'No! Jesus no.'

'So why did it? Why did it think he couldn't be President? Why did it make that video?' Hershel looks away, staring through the glass of the inside wall, and the outside. The view is warped.

'Okay,' Hershel says. 'I'll explain.'

'This all began about a decade ago. The stock markets have been using algorithms for years and years now, to predict and control their numbers.

It's a science, not an art. But sometimes things go wrong. Back at the start of the last decade, the New York stock exchange's algorithms just went haywire. Died. Over a period of thirty minutes, the markets suffered the largest crash in their history. Nobody could explain it – and everybody panicked. It was their algorithms. The software found a glitch and it compensated. Fucked the markets entirely. Know how they fixed it? They switched it off and then switched it on again.

'The algorithm that I helped build isn't all that different to what they use. It's mostly data mining and compositing information. It's taking sources and trying to make them work in conjunction. I was here from the start. They hired me – you remember that – after I dropped out: *because* I dropped out, probably. Paid me to do this, and they built a team from the ground up. I did the stuff where it drags data from the rest of the world and makes it work for the algorithm. So, let's say you come to *ClearVista* and you ask it about . . . fuck, I don't know. Whether you'll get a loan from a bank. It takes everything. It takes who you are, but it takes everything else. Loan rates, who applies for loads, what job you do, your credit rating, whether people with your credit rating get loans, whether they pay them back. All that stuff. I built the software that did that and then, when I was done, they offered me another role. Supervising the algorithm's day-to-day behavior. Watching it. Here's the thing; it grows. Not like it's intelligent, nothing like that, but it *learns*. It's designed to, and it can't help it, because the Internet tells it everything it needs to know. But sometimes shit goes wrong, and they needed somebody to make sure it didn't. So I took the job, and they gave me shares, and they paid me a wage. I could monitor the thing from home – it's an algorithm, doesn't need any managing or anything like that – so I did. Seemed easier.

'Then I thought about using it myself. I like gambling, dude, and the market was going to fall out of it. Look at it now! Soon as this became commercial, I knew there wasn't going to be any gambling on anything. Nothing would be a risk any more. So when it was just me, I made a few bets on things – sports, mostly, the Superbowl and some soccer games – and I started winning. Not every time. It's not infallible. But it picked up a lot, and I was teaching the algorithm more and more. Really getting to those bits of the Internet – of data – that it wasn't reaching before. It used everything: the type of grass on the fucking pitch, the wind-speed, the health of the players. I couldn't do big numbers, because I was being watched. I'm not allowed to gamble, but I am allowed to work for *ClearVista*. And that's a joke in itself.

'The algorithm didn't work every time. It works based on things that it can determine, but there are margins. Human error. Bet on the Kentucky Derby? Can't do that. Horses fall, and you can't call it. Laurence . . . He's like a horse. He's a loose variable. I didn't have anything to do with

Laurence's prediction. You can't alter it or trick it. Do you know how many people work here now? Me. Just me. Everybody else is a shareholder or silent partner. No staff, because the algorithm runs the phones. Plugins do the rest. Customer service? All that is automated and the servers self-maintain. The orders come in; the money follows; the numbers do the rest. That's how your video was generated. I saw it, and everything's automated after that. I didn't want it to get crazy; but it was new, you know, something worth checking out.

'So, I hired somebody to watch Laurence – the guy you met downstairs. He works for *ClearVista*. Used to be security. Now . . . oh, I don't know. I wanted to make sure that I knew how Laurence reacted. Because I had a theory. Let's say you want to use *ClearVista* before you go to a bank for a loan, so you ask the algorithm if you're likely to get one. The people who apply for the loan; what if they were in a social group likely to apply for a loan? And what if that social group was also likely to ask *ClearVista* for a result before they went through the paperwork? If they're unsure enough to ask *ClearVista*, the algorithm will know that. Do you see what I mean? It takes itself into account. Homme, he was the first potential nominee to ask the questions that he did. He got there first, Amit, and he asked what would happen, and *ClearVista* did what it could. As soon as somebody else asked if they would be president, the algorithm adapted. It worked out that he would ask that question, and it knew that it existed. It knew how this would work. If Homme's odds were 62%, Laurence was going to lose. The algorithm works in absolutes. If Laurence lost, he was going to have a breakdown, because everything said that he would: his medical results, his son's death, and the fact that he was in therapy. Don't ask me how, but the algorithm gets results we can't. Private records. It knows everything. *Everything*. So, the video was going to show Laurence having a breakdown. That's his end result, and the first video it booted out, right? But then you asked for a second video, after the plane; after he'd seen the first video. It knew he had watched the first, because this was a rework, and so the breakdown – the only inevitable part of this, if he lost the race, which he was now going to do, absolutely, no fucking question – was going to be worse. It drew on everything. Gun licenses. It knew that would come into play, because he was a soldier, and because he owned one. It made its own myth, Amit. It's self-aware, but not in the way that people think of computers as being. It can't think on its own, but it knows that it exists; so the algorithm cannot help but reflect itself now in everything that it does.

'And the worst thing? It released the video itself. The algorithm sent it to the news, because they were the ones who hated Laurence; and Laurence's breakdown was inevitable. It wrote itself into the prediction, and then all it could do was fulfil it. That's logic; that's the algorithm we built.

'This ends with a gunshot, Amit. It can't end any other way, now.'

Amit rubs at his face. 'How sure are you?' he asks.

'Positive. I mean, there's math to back it up. I could show you the breakdowns of where the decisions were made.'

'It's not been tampered with?'

'No. It's impossible to fuck with this.' Hershel stands up and paces. 'I keep thinking about whether I should feel guilty for this. Because I helped make this, you know? And it's the reason that this is happening. If the algorithm didn't work . . . I don't know. Maybe I'm wrong. But this gets worse. You didn't show Laurence the video I sent you, did you?'

'No,' Amit says. 'I don't know how he would react.'

'Yes you do,' Hershel says. 'I lied to the system. I asked for another go, and another. I've got videos that take this further and further.' He turns and brings them up on the screen; so many windows, and all of them showing Laurence. Amit glances at the frozen frames, and then looks away. They're worse than anything; in some of them, things that he would never wish to see. 'I could be wrong about all of this, but there's one thing that I can't change; Laurence was always going to have a breakdown. He was *never* going to be president.' He minimizes the windows. 'I could be wrong, of course.' He smiles slightly, because he knows that he isn't.

'I have to go,' Amit says. He opens the door. 'You got a car?'

'Outside, but I'll be—'

'The least you can do is give me the keys to your fucking car, Hershel!'

Hershel nods and pulls them from his pocket.

'I'm sorry,' he says. 'Tell the Walkers that I'm sorry as well, will you?' Amit doesn't stop. He keeps going, through the glass building, down the glass stairs, past the man in the blue jacket and out of the glass doors, into the thick, grimy heat.

He syncs his phone with the car and calls Jessie, and he explains to her about the algorithm. 'There's nothing to clear Laurence's name,' he says, 'no conspiracy, nothing underhand. Laurence has a got a gun, and he's dangerous.'

'Then we go on the air with the story as it is. A misunderstanding. Laurence Walker, a man on the edge. He can come on and explain.' She pauses. 'People love a comeback.'

'There's no comeback from this,' he says. He tries to call Deanna, but there's still no answer. There's nothing he can do. He pounds the steering wheel with his hands, leaving welts across his palms. The sun is setting, night coming. He sees the horizon as he approaches the freeway, and then there it is, in the distance; drooping as it folds behind the mountains.

★ ★ ★

The next flight to Syracuse is full, Amit discovers, and the one after that. Next closest would be a flight to JFK, leaving just before midnight, getting him there sometime in the middle of the night. It would be faster to do that and drive than wait for the morning Syracuse planes, the assistant tells him; so he uses his air miles for a ticket on that flight, and he walks through the airport, back and forth. The shops shut, and the cleaners come out, and the only people waiting are those who he's booked onto a flight with. They sit in the departure lounge, some of them on their computers, some reading, some sleeping; and then they're called to the plane and they queue slowly. Amit is sitting by himself in a row and once they're in the air he puts the arms up and lies flat across the seats; he pulls the complimentary blanket over himself and tries to sleep. The plane rumbles beneath him, and every so often a beep comes from somewhere else in the cabin and it makes him sit up, thinking that they are about to land; but then he looks out of the window and sees the blackness below, occasionally the threaded veins of lights that mean there are cities and towns and roads; and then they all drop away and he doesn't know if it's because there is nothing there, or just a cloud beneath him, obscuring his vision. He lies back and tries to sleep, but then he pictures the videos in his mind; and then there's that beep in the cabin, and it keeps happening to him, over and over, scaring him that something is about to happen.

409

CHAPTER 16

Laurence stands at the barbecue on the decking and he sprays fuel onto the coals. He lets it splash, because he loves the showmanship of this: the only time that he can cook and it be a display. He wears an apron that he found in the basement, left here in a box of things by the previous owners – it's black and dusty, water damage up the side of it, and was likely used for manual labor rather than cooking, by the looks of it – but it's all the same when covered in the splashes of the fat from the burgers. He steps back.

'Nearly got me,' he says. Deanna, Lane and Alyx wait inside, setting the table, putting salad into a bowl.

'I want to go home,' Alyx says, and she starts crying, so Deanna holds her and tells her that they will, soon enough.

'Don't lie to her,' Lane says.

'I'm not,' Deanna replies. They all sit and wait for the food, and then they eat, but it's overcooked, charred so much as to almost be inedible; but Laurence eats it all. His, and then Lane's, when she pushes it to one side in favor of the leaves and chopped tomatoes. When he's finished he talks to them all, looking at them one by one.

'This is going to be okay,' he tells them. 'I know it looks bad now, but we will recover. That's what we do. Pick ourselves up, dust ourselves off. We rebuild.'

'Why are you wearing the suit?' Deanna asks. He looks down at himself, pulling the apron to one side. Maybe he didn't realize.

'It's a good suit,' he says.

'It was. Why don't you change?'

'I don't want to.' He's almost affronted in his tone, Deanna thinks.

'It's what you were wearing in the video, Laurence. Maybe you should change it.'

He laughs, a spit of noise. 'You think that means something? No, Deanna. I'm wearing it because it's comfortable, and because it's what I want to wear. It's a fucking suit. It's not anything more than that. You think, what, that I am going to . . .? Like the video?'

'You've got the gun,' she says. She knows that it's dangerous, because it's true; but the girls are here, and they're terrified of him.

'Don't do this,' he says. 'All I want is to protect you.'

'Then let me take the girls home,' Deanna says.

'There was a time that I wanted to call this place home, you remember? We were prepared. We loved it here.'

'*You* loved it here,' she says, 'and then Sean died,

411

and . . .' She doesn't know how to finish the sentence. She doesn't know where they go from here. He stands up and he pulls the apron off.

'I think we're done for the night,' he says. It's dark outside now, and he walks to the back doors. He stands outside, but beneath the netting. 'You should all go to bed, I think. Get some sleep. If you aren't happy here, we'll leave in the morning. We'll find somewhere else.' He doesn't look back.

'What are you going to do?' Deanna asks. 'Aren't you going to sleep?'

'When I was out here last night I saw the strangest light,' he says. 'I want to see it again.' He walks out to the dock and he sits on the end of it, his feet dangling. Deanna walks to the door and looks out. The moon is there, underneath the water; somehow almost clearer to see there than it is in the sky.

Upstairs, they all take the larger bedroom again, and the same bed between them. Deanna tells them to get ready for bed, to clean their teeth. Lane has somehow gone back in years. If Deanna ever worried that she was growing up too fast, she needn't worry now: her little girl is back. And Alyx is quiet, like she was after Sean died. Nothing can be done about that now, Deanna thinks. When they're past this, therapy can start back up again. Maybe it will help clear up what's happened. Deanna supposes that the therapy will be different depending on how this ends. If Laurence walks out of here with them, that brings issues; and if he doesn't, a whole other set. Deanna doesn't know now which she would prefer. She just wants this to be easy, when it's over; and she assumes that it will be over. She doesn't want to think about the worst ending. Not yet.

She sits at the foot of the bed and takes the remnants of the cellphone out of her bag, and she puts them on the blanket. The battery is loose and the plastic case has mostly snapped off, but the screen, strangely, is nearly intact and still attached to the board inside it. She pulls the case to pieces. Some shards of it are inside, on the board, where the battery should go, so she pulls them out gently. She thinks of pulling grit from the wounded knees of her children. When it's done she tucks the battery in, so that it's touching the conductors, and she puts the case back and holds the whole thing tightly, to keep it as one. She presses the power button and the screen sputters into life. It jangles, a start-up tone, and she yanks the blanket over it to muffle the noise. It seeks reception, and finds it, and the deluge begins. Notifications and texts and missed call alerts. Amit has tried to call her, over and over. There's only one email. It's from her agent, telling her that the publishers who offered for the book sent a message through. They're desperate for it; they love it. There's a note from the editor, about how it made her cry. They have run prediction software, and they can tell that it will hit with the audiences that they want it to; that readers will respond to the story that Deanna has told. Deanna writes a reply. She tells her agent to take the offer. She wants to see the book out with this publisher. This is all part of a different life that she once had. She presses send, watching the little animation of the envelope, and then she tries to call Amit. The call beeps off, going to his answering machine, and so she tries again. She doesn't know what to say. She tells him not to call; that she's got the phone working, barely. She'll call back. She tells him where they are, because it might help if he were here.

She wondered if Trent Henderson might not have told the police, because they haven't come. No descending fleet of squad cars, no helicopters searching the woods for her fleeing husband; not even the sheriff, driving by to check that everything is all right in the house.

She tries Amit one more time and then switches her phone off. Thirty percent battery left. She doesn't know when she might need it, or what she might need it for.

The girls sleep. It's a miracle, Deanna thinks, how easily they can. They both breathe heavily next to her; and their breathing seems to fall in line with each other's. It's calming, to lie between them and feel it coming at her through the bed. It works its magic on her, despite her thinking that sleep is something she can't find – and, as she's trying, will never find again.

She dreams of Sean. Why would she dream of anything else?

She wakes up needing to use the bathroom, and as she gets out of bed there's a noise from outside; a rustling in the woods, foxes or deer or something. There's no hunting this close to the town, so the wildlife grows. Nature tries to take hold.

She walks to the bathroom and sits down. She can see out of the window from here, looking back towards town. There's a glow in the distance; what must be one of the shops, or the bar, or a restaurant. She doesn't know what time it is, but it's early in the morning. The black sky has a hint of the sun to it and she wonders who could be up at this time.

When she's done, she listens for Laurence. He is nowhere. She thinks about yesterday's plan. Maybe today. Second time's the charm. She goes downstairs and looks for him. He is on the decking, still; and still sitting up. She thinks about all the things that she could do. In the kitchen there is a knife, that they used to prepare dinner; and there is a weight to hold the door open, wrought iron, with one flat edge. She wonders how quiet she could be, creeping up behind him, and the thought of doing that – of having to do that in the first place – makes her feel sick to her stomach. She knows that she can't escape, not now. He's awake. She steps outside, instead. Maybe there is a way.

'What light?' she asks. He turns, surprised. Maybe she would have been quiet enough after all.

'You're awake,' he says.

'What light did you see?'

'Across the water. Out there, somewhere over the water. Closer to the other side.'

'One of the houses?'

'No. It almost as if it was floating there, away from the coast.'

'Like *Gatsby*.'

He smiles. 'I suppose, yes.' He looks back. 'I can't see it now. Couldn't see it all night. How can you miss something that you have only seen so briefly before?'

'How does this end, Laurence?' she asks. She sits on a chair at the back of the decking. She can't bring herself to walk out onto the dock itself; not with him there.

'I don't know,' he says.

'Let me take the girls away.'

'No,' he says. 'I did this for us. Remember? I was doing this for our future.'

'I remember,' she says. 'I don't think you're thinking of that now.'

'I am,' he says. He hits the decking with his hand. 'I am. Deanna, it is all that I can think of. It's everything to me, now. Making sure that we're all together.' He leans and looks down. 'I haven't forgotten what happened here,' he says. 'You might think that I have, but I can't. I never can. I know what it felt like for him, that second where he dived off here. Do you see that? I taught him to fucking swim! I taught him to dive! And I have swum these waters, I have swum where he died. I have been down there, Deanna, so I *know*.'

'No,' she says, 'you don't. Because you came up, and you took your next breath. *You* are still alive.'

'But maybe I'm not,' he says. He tilts his head. 'Can you see that?' he asks. He can see something, it seems, in the distance. Deanna stands up and looks.

'What are you looking at?' she asks.

'There's a light. In the water.'

'I told you, I can't see it.'

'Not that one,' he says. 'This is . . . It's coming from behind us. A reflection.' She catches a glimpse; something yellow, and dulled.

'What is it?' she asks. And then she hears a noise, coming from behind them; coming from the road. She turns and looks towards the car, and she sees the light that she thought was coming from the town now closer, and coming closer still, the dull light of a flame, cutting through the branches of the woods. And not just one, three of them, two smaller than the first. The noise, a static of feet on leaves, cracking branches as they go. No voices in the darkness. This is meant to be a surprise.

She sees a man at the top of the road; a hat and a beard and a cane, and she knows that it is Trent Henderson, and that this is what she has done.

They are coming like a swarm; everybody from the town, armed with their guns if they have them. Hunting rifles and shotguns and pistols, no doubt, and they wear clothes more befitting a hunting trip than a visit to see some of their neighbors. Deanna watches them come over the hill in the distance. They are only a few minutes away.

'Get inside,' Laurence says.

'We should find out what they're here for,' Deanna says. She knows, already, and so does he.

'Get inside,' he says. He stands behind her and ushers her. 'Are the girls awake?'

'No,' she says.

'Okay,' he tells her. 'Go and wake them and make sure that they're safe.'

'What are you going to do?' she asks.

'Deanna, please!' he shouts. He bares his teeth, and she sees the whiteness of his gums; the roots of his teeth, the thin lines of the muscles around his neck and jaw as he stretches to his shout. He's barely even physical. He walks to the door and opens it, and he stands outside. 'Stay in here,' he says. He pulls the door shut behind him.

She thinks about other ways of escape: maybe getting into the lake, diving into it, off the end of the dock and swimming. She can't do it, she's sure, but that doesn't stop her thinking of it, imagining it. She looks out of the back window at the stillness of the water and then rushes to the window at the foot of the stairs.

Deanna watches Laurence as he stands at the edge of the house's porch. He puts one hand onto the strut that holds the arch up above the doorway

418

and waits for them to get closer, watching them all. Trying to not make eye contact, so much, but sizing them up. There are twenty of them, maybe thirty. Deanna counts five guns, their black glinting. Here, the porch light is on, so she knows that they will be able to see Laurence. But the gulf between them is just wide enough to fall into darkness. She looks at her husband – strange to call him that, because the name, the title, they feel almost absent, almost moot – and his eyes are tipped down. He isn't looking at them. She wonders if he is scared.

'Can I help you?' he asks. His voice is muffled through the wood; a house this old, the sound carries in through the gaps between the boards that make up the walls, but it's not quite enough. Deanna opens the window slightly. He waits, because maybe they don't hear him; maybe he wasn't speaking loudly enough. They come closer, the gulf thinning. 'I asked if I could help you. You're on private property.'

They stop walking. Trent Henderson steps forward. He holds a torch in one hand; a decorated pistol in the other, the handle made of ivory, a pattern curled on it in metals. He speaks for the group.

'Laurence, we've known each other how long now?'

'Years.'

'Would you say that I have known the flavor of your character?'

'Yes,' Laurence says.

'So when I say that I am here for your benefit, you know that I have no reason to lie to you.'

'You've brought guns.'

'That's how you parlay. Those're the rules, Laurence: bring to the talk that which your fellow man brings.' He holds the gun up, closer to the flame light, showing it off. 'Listen, we can end this now. You put down your gun and come to us, and we take you in.'

'Why should I trust you?'

'Why would we lie?' From behind Henderson, Deputy Robards steps forward.

'Laurence, we're here for the good of your family. That's it. Nothing more.' Henderson turns one hand towards Laurence, and opens it. To show how transparent he is, and how he can be trusted. He rubs his chin. 'All we want to do is chat with you. Maybe get you some help.'

Laurence steps backwards. 'Go home,' he says. 'Take yourselves back to town. We'll leave here and we won't trouble you again. But you leave us alone.'

'Or what?' Robards asks.

'Or you know how this ends,' Laurence says.

She has never heard him speak like that before. Deanna watches as he pulls the gun from his pocket, and the posse – because that is what it is – shift their postures, preparing. She sees the men at the back of the pack lit by the torches, men who have a reputation, raise their guns and check them as if they might have lost bullets in that exchange. One pops his shotgun open and pulls shells from his pocket, loads them into the barrels. That gun, Deanna is sure, is not used for hunting. It likely wouldn't leave enough of the animal to claim as a trophy. Laurence steps inside and shuts the door behind him; he turns his back to it, as if they are going to rush at him and he has to keep it standing.

Deanna goes to the girls and wakes them up, kissing them on their foreheads. 'Okay,' she says, 'you have to stay in here, no matter what you hear from downstairs, okay?'

Lane sits up. 'Is it dad?'

'There are some people here to talk to him, is all. They're angry.'

'Because he won't let us go?' Lane asks. Deanna looks at her and Alyx and doesn't answer.

'Just stay here.' She pulls the cellphone from her pocket and she shows Lane how to hold it so that the battery stays against the connectors, giving it enough power to turn on. 'Keep this here,' she says. 'And if you need to, call the police.' She thinks about Robards out there with them, treacherously claiming that he is there to protect Laurence. 'No. Call Amit. His is the last dialled number. Tell him what's happening and he'll help, okay?'

'You want me to call the police?' Lane asks.

'They're already here,' Deanna says.

★   ★   ★

She stands in the stairwell. She thinks how easy this would be if she heard a gunshot now, before she even got down to the ground floor. How then, this would be over.

At least, she thinks, that would be an ending.

He trembles in the room. He leans against the glass and he looks out to where Sean was. Everything pauses; the moment seems to hang as if it's broken. It is, Deanna thinks, almost as if Sean is here. He is watching this and wondering what might have been, or could have been. Different things.

'Why won't you let us go?'

'Why do you want me to?'

'Because we're so scared.' Of you, she doesn't say, and of what is outside. We are terrified of it all. She stands by the front door. Laurence has always been reasonable. That's been a part of who he is. But he is not the same man, Deanna reminds herself; he hasn't been for over a year now. 'The girls are frightened, Laurence.'

'And you?'

'*I'm* frightened.'

He nods. 'When all I am trying to do is protect you.' He puts both hands on the glass of the door and he stretches out, pushing back against it. 'I mean, this isn't for me. None of this is for me, Deanna. This is for us. All of us. You, me, Lane, the twins. All of us.'

'Not the twins,' she says. 'This is not for Sean.'

It is as if he forgot, for a second; and now, he looks out over the dock and the water, lit by the moon's reflection as if from below, and he makes a noise that Deanna has never heard before. It's not quite a laugh or a howl, but something else, something from below them. He beats the glass of the door with both hands and it cracks; a sliver at first, coming from below his right fist, but that sliver grows and creaks outwards, rushing to create a cobweb of cracks. The glass fights itself and falls outwards, onto the decking, a crash, a shattering. Laurence doesn't jump backwards. Instead, he lets the pieces fall, and he stands there, in his suit. A shout comes from outside, carrying through the whole house.

'What's happening in there?' Trent Henderson asks.

'Nothing,' Laurence says, too quiet to be heard. He pulls the gun from his pocket, and he holds it; but his grip is loose, and unconvincing.

'Please,' Deanna asks. 'Let me get the girls out of here. They shouldn't be around this. I'll stay, and we can work this out.'

'We're a family,' he says. 'That's always been the point. A family is a whole, and we have been apart.' He is softening. She knows; she sees it.

'Laurence,' she says. His finger is on the trigger, but it is not cocked. This can be done, she thinks. 'We have to go,' she tells him.

'You can't,' he says, but he sounds unconvincing and unconvinced. Maybe, Deanna thinks, he sees the end himself. She steps forward; she wonders if she can reach for the gun, and take it, and maybe—

A crackle of glass behind him; a boot crunching it underfoot. It's unexpected, and Laurence turns to look. It's Robards. He has his pistol drawn, and he's caught because he's clumsy. He looks confused, blindsided. He drops his mouth to an O and he raises his gun at Laurence. He looks as if he is going to pull the trigger, but he doesn't get the chance. Laurence does first, and the noise fills the room; a clap like thunder. Deanna thinks for a second that it will bring the house down around them, it's so loud. Robards falls backwards onto the decking. He isn't dead; instead, he rolls to his stomach and he tries to crawl away, over the broken glass.

'What happened?' Henderson shouts through the wood. He is somewhere near them, right up next to the house. It's as if his voice is in there with them. Laurence doesn't say anything. He looks at Robards, pulling himself to the shore and the water, the trail of thick red that follows him. Like a slug, Deanna thinks. 'You shout out now who pulled that trigger, or we are coming in.'

'It was me,' Laurence screams. 'You sent him in here and he was going to put us all in danger. He was a threat.' The shouts sound as if they are coming from a voice that Deanna has never heard, a man that she has never known.

There's another shot, but this time from outside. Deanna screams and ducks down, curls herself into a ball. There is a hole in the wall the size of a billiard ball, light coming through it, and Laurence is gasping, clutching at his left shoulder. Blood runs over his fingers. He falls to one knee. 'Fuck,' he says. 'Oh fuck.' He tries to stand, but even that seems to hurt him, everything pulling against his arm. Deanna watches as the light at the hole is extinguished. Someone – multiple someones – is looking through at them.

'He's still alive,' Henderson shouts, and then there's another shot, another bullet, another hole. Deanna doesn't see them coming. A plate shatters in the kitchen. Laurence gasps, but he isn't shot again. He stands up.

'Go to the girls,' he says. Deanna stands up and runs upstairs, finds them both standing at the top. Lane watches her, but Alyx is facing away, her face pressed against Lane's chest.

'It's okay,' Deanna says.

'It's not,' Lane tells her. Alyx pulls away and hugs her mother. 'Why won't he let us go?' Lane shouts. She storms downstairs towards him, and he holds out his arms for her, as if this is going to make it all better.

'I can't, Laney,' he says.

'You're fucking crazy,' she tells him. Her voice is low and measured; even as she says this, she sounds calm and controlled. He stumbles towards her and she lashes out. Somehow he catches her top in his hands and pulls it away from her neck, and her tattoo is exposed. The four of them, their names, freshly inked; only his, at the bottom, the strongest, the support, is scratched and tarred. Lane has taken a knife to it and it's barely recognizable as Laurence's name. 'Why won't you let us go?' Lane screams, and she snaps his hand away from her and runs back upstairs to her mother. He stands at the foot fo the stairs, stock-still and static, and then shakes his head, almost, to rid himself of the thought. It's as if it never happened. There's another gunshot, and Deanna sees, through the window, the mob move towards them.

They are coming.

CHAPTER 17

Amit's plane lands, and he holds his cell-phone in his hand the entire time he walks through the airport. The New York airports cell-blank everything now and so he has no signal until he's past the final security checks and out into the main part of the terminal. He calls Jessie as he runs to the rental car place, to get something – anything – that can take him to the Walkers.

'What's changed?' he asks.

'We've just heard from the teams on the ground, at the Walker house. They say there are lights in the distance – and gunshots.'

'Gunshots? Coming from where?'

'Down by the lake.'

It hits Amit, then. He was there, but only once. The second day they owned it; delivering a contract for Laurence to sign. He had almost forgotten that they owned it. But the algorithm wouldn't have. It would have known. 'The holiday house.'

'I'm driving there,' Jessie says. 'I'm on call still, and I'm taking the story.'

'Can you do that?'

'I don't give a damn if I can't. It's done now.'

'Where are you?'

'An hour out, maybe, but the crews from the house will be there soon.'

Amit clicks his fingers at the guy behind the desk, who is watching the TV that hangs on the wall, and he looks.

'Can you turn it over?' Amit half whispers, and the guy hands him the remote. Amit flicks to Jessie's channel, and there is it: the pale wood, framed by the lake. Any other time, this would be beautiful: lit by flame torches, the light dancing. This is nature at its finest. But there is a crowd, and the camera stays back. A reporter whispers something that Amit cannot hear. 'They're there already,' he says to Jessie. 'I'm looking at it right now.'

'What does it look like?' she asks.

'It's a mob,' he says. There's another crack, and another gunshot. The cameraman ducks. 'Just get there,' he says. She hangs up; he calls her back.

'Yes?' she asks.

'Be careful,' he tells her.

He orders a car. They try to find him one that he likes, to match his previous choices, but he shouts, asks for whatever they have that's closest to the terminal and they hand him the keys and he runs to find it. He doesn't know what he'll do when he gets to Staunton. He thinks that he can talk to Laurence, maybe. Tell him what happened; how the video came to show what it did. Explain that it's not as bad as it seems; that Laurence isn't

428

the man that the world thinks he is. Except, Amit knows, he could be. This isn't all *ClearVista*'s fault. This was always, to some extent, inevitable.

He notices a message on his phone and he plays it as he steps into the car and starts the engine. It's Lane, telling him where they are. Explaining what's happened. They're trapped, and Laurence won't let them leave, and they are scared. He saves the message, the first time he hasn't deleted something from his server in what feels like years, and he drives.

'You let them out, Laurence,' Henderson says. He is against the door, speaking through the cracked glass window that's set halfway up. Laurence sits on the bottom stair, out of Henderson's view. It's still dark enough outside that they can't see in through their holes, but it won't be that way for long. 'You let them out, and we deal with you on our own.' The pretense of arresting him is gone, Deanna can hear, the idea that maybe this will be fine in the end. It was promises of arrest and therapy, and now it's something else entirely.

Deanna holds the girls, the three of them sitting at the top of the staircase. She can see her husband's head; the sharp jut of his spine from his neck down and the lines on the back of his skull. His hair, which is thinned more than it's ever been. Or, maybe, she thinks, it's just seeing him from here, from this angle. The girls are quiet, because she has begged them to be.

'We're a family,' Laurence says, 'and I cannot trust you. Look at what you did.' He glances back to where he shot Robards. He has the gun in his hand, and he keeps clicking the hammer, then letting it breathe, setting it back to neutral. 'Trent, how long have you known me? How long have you known us?' He doesn't look up, and he keeps his voice quiet. He doesn't want them to be able to pinpoint him from the outside. Deanna can tell: he doesn't want them to be able to do what they will. His shoulder bleeds, still, but he has stopped paying attention to it. The jacket is torn and split on the front and back both, the bullet having passed through. There are spatters of blood on the tie.

'I have known you long enough,' Henderson says. 'Long enough to know what family means to you.'

'Then you'll understand.'

'If you don't let them go, I most certainly will not.' He sounds disappointed, Deanna thinks. Laurence turns to look at his shattered family, sitting above him. He smiles a strained smile.

'Let us go,' she asks him. He shakes his head, and he looks at her sadly. As if there is something that she simply doesn't understand. She stands up and looks outside. There are more people now. In the crowd she sees bulky equipment, the glint of reflective lenses. Camera crews.

She knows this will all be over soon.

Jessie parks behind the vans which are blocking the small track like a barricade and she runs down the hill towards the group of people. The sun is coming up over the hills, across the lake, and she doesn't stop until she reaches the reporters. She knows some of them and finds her team easily.

'I've been told to run this,' she says.

'Nothing to run,' they tell her. 'There's a standstill. The man at the door, a Trent Henderson, he's trying to talk Walker into letting his family go.'

'Let them go?'

'This is a hostage situation.'

'Where are the police?' Jessie looks for them, but there are no uniforms, no badges. 'Aren't they controlling it?'

'They're here. One of them is dead. Walker shot him.'

'What?'

'Back of the house. The others are here, somewhere.'

'You haven't got any statements?'

'Nobody to get statements from. Look at this.' Jessie does. It's terrifying, she thinks; a group of people who would usually never look as if they would hurt anybody, threaten anything. And here they are, guns at the ready, in the name of protection. There's something archaic about it, Jessie thinks; something that feels wrong, desperate and reactionary.

'We have to stop this,' she says, but her crew ignores her and keeps filming the action below. She sees it on the screen at the back of the camera; the picture is zoomed in on Trent Henderson's face, his teeth gritted, his eyes sad; and then there's a pan down to his hand, and the gilt trim of his pistol's handle.

'I don't know what to do,' Laurence says.

He stands next to the door, and he holds the gun at the level of the window. It's as if he could just point it and pull the trigger and take out Trent Henderson where he stands. At the back of the house, the glass is catching the start of the sun's rays and the blood that Robards left on the decking shines like oil. His body, alive or dead, is nowhere to be seen. Deanna wonders if it is on the beach; or if he tried to swim, and found out what happens when you try that. She stands at the bottom of the stairs now, her back to the girls. This way she can see what's coming.

'You could let us leave,' she says to him.

He is broken, she knows. He cannot be fixed, she doesn't think. Maybe there's something just gone wrong now; or maybe it went wrong as soon as Sean died, when they lost that part between them. She went to group therapy, where grieving families sat in a circle and spoke about the loss of a child. They were all further along the path than Deanna and Laurence were, and they all said that one of two things happened: either it brought you together, united in your grief, or it did the opposite. It ruined you.

'You coming out, Walker?' Trent Henderson

shouts. 'You come out, or we drive you out. That's how this goes now.'

'I don't think we can leave,' Laurence says. He stands up and walks to the back of the house, taking his eyes off his family.

Deanna moves. She runs back up the stairs, into each room, and looks out of the windows. The girls ask what she's doing.

'Nothing,' she says.

Out of the bathroom, the window looks onto a smaller roof down below, a porch at the side of the house. It would be a drop, and the roof is sloped – no guarantees how that would end – but a broken ankle, she thinks, is better than the alternative. Nothing can happen from that fall that can't heal. And even if it doesn't, maybe that's still better. She flicks the catches and tries to force the window up but it's stuck, the wood refusing to move against itself. Swollen, most likely; the moisture from the lake getting inside everything, all the wood susceptible to rotting. Or maybe it's splintered inside there. Either way, it's not moving. She doesn't pause or flinch, hurling her elbow at the glass. She's never broken a pane before and doesn't know how this will work. It shatters into thick slabs of glass that fall around her. There's no large crash, no sound effect. She picks at the few shards that hang there in the dry fixative, putting them down carefully on the nightstand, and then the frame is clear.

'Come on,' she says to the girls. 'We're going

out this way.' She looks down. The drop isn't that bad. If she could, she would signal to the crowd and try to get them to help, but they're not looking this way. They're slightly out of sight.

She picks up Alyx and nods at Lane. 'You go first,' she says. 'You get down there and catch your sister, okay?' Lane goes to the frame.

'Oh my God,' she says. 'Mom, I can't.

'You can,' Deanna says. She can taste the air outside. It's so close.

'Come back inside,' Laurence says from behind her. 'Don't do that.'

Deanna turns, and he has the gun pointed at them. No, Deanna thinks; it's pointed squarely at her.

Jessie calls Amit. 'Where are you?' she asks.

'Middle of fucking nowhere,' he says. 'What's happening?'

'They're talking about how to drive Walker out.'

'What's he doing?'

'Nobody knows.' She looks out over the people. 'It's like Waco or something.'

'It's not,' Amit says. 'Laurence isn't insane. You try talking to him.'

'He won't listen to me.'

'How long have I got?'

'Not long,' Jessie says. 'I don't think there's long at all.'

'If I'm not stopped by the cops for speeding the shit out of these roads, I'll see you soon,' he says.

*　　*　　*

434

Laurence brings his family downstairs, away from the windows. He takes them to the kitchen, which has the most protection: cupboards and appliances, and the stairwell to the cellar. Alyx won't look at him, and Lane has her eyes down, a sad look on her face. Deanna keeps eye contact.

'You would break us up?' he asks. He whispers it, because he doesn't want Henderson to hear. He knows that he's not at the door any more, because they're huddled in a crowd, talking something over. But still, better safe than sorry, he reasons.

'No,' Deanna says. 'I would get the fuck away from you. You're scaring us, Laurence. Look at the girls.'

'Don't you fucking understand? I am not who they say I am.'

'Then who are you? Who *are* you? They say you would kill. They say you would threaten your family. Who are you, Laurence?'

'I am protecting you!' he roars. It's incredible, guttural and vulgar. He waves the gun around. 'They want to kill me. Do you even get that? They want to drag me out of this house and tie me up and fucking murder me.' He paces the kitchen, circling his family. 'They have said this all along. They have said who I am. They have *made* me, Deanna!'

'You made yourself,' she says.

She sees him flinch, raise his hand. He's never hit her before, not even once; but now she sees him contemplate it. There's nothing in his eyes.

★　　★　　★

435

'Walker,' Trent Henderson shouts through the door. 'You have one minute to send that family of yours out.'

'No,' Laurence says. He leans against the kitchen worktop, pushing at the soft wood with the barrel of the gun.

'Then you let us talk to them. You send them out here and we can see that they're all right.'

'You think that I'm stupid?'

'No, Laurence, I do not think that.'

'Deanna, tell him that you're fine.' He looks at her.

'No,' she says.

'Don't push me,' he says. 'Tell him that you're all fine.'

'No.'

'Then go out there. Show him.' He pauses. 'You could tell them to leave us alone. Say that we're happy here.'

'Laurence, your time is running out,' Henderson says.

'Go and fucking talk to him!' Laurence shouts at Deanna's face.

'I am not leaving my daughters,' she says. She stands in front of them and she faces up to him. She won't move. Laurence raises and points the gun at her. So much power in such a small thing . . . 'No,' she says again. He clicks the hammer. 'Who *are* you?' she asks.

'Laurence?' Henderson shouts. 'This is your last chance. You let them talk or we force you out of there.'

'Please,' Laurence says. The hand holding the gun goes slightly limp; the barrel pointing slightly more towards the floor, looser in his hand. 'Please, Deanna.'

'You let us go and I'll tell them that we were perfectly safe the entire time.' She steps towards him, closer to the gun. 'Maybe they'll let you off easier if I do.'

'No,' he says. 'You know that I can't. You know that I can't do that.'

'Time's up,' Henderson says. They hear his footsteps on the porch decking as he walks away.

'What are they going to do?' Lane asks.

'I don't know,' Laurence says. He softens. He starts to cry. 'I don't know what they're going to try to do to us.'

'Can we go?' Alyx asks. She cries as well, and the words come out huffed and inhaled.

'No, Pumpkin,' Laurence says. 'We're going to stay together.' His hand stiffens; the gun raises itself again.

Jessie sees one of the men rush off, running back through the woods. She thinks that he is like a wolf; he throws himself into the trees, staying off the path. He's run this route before, must know these woods like the back of his hand. The camera traces him for a second but then it's back to the house, a standoff where nothing seems to be happening but the tension is building. As the sun comes up, as this all becomes illuminated, that's more and more apparent. Everything is golden; this will be done before the sun is fully in the sky, Jessie knows.

There's a noise from the crowd, a scream and a shout. They've seen something, at the side of the house. It's Robards, crawled around to the dock. He was trying to escape but couldn't and he's there now, lying in the nascent morning rays. Maybe this is the first time that the reality of this has hit them. People will die. It happened on their watch, on their mission. The cameras all zoom in to pick up the body. It's a close-up, grotesque and marked in red. The group of leaders – Trent Henderson and the others from the town all stand and talk, trying to work out how to do this best. They need a plan.

The man who ran off comes back. He's got a container of gas with him. Jessie watches him haul it to the front of the crowd and Henderson shouts at him to stop, but he doesn't listen. He pulls the cap off and hurls it up at the house; over the porch, over the decking. It collides with the house and almost explodes, sending a shower of fuel all over the side of it. Henderson shouts at him, but he's passionate. He yells, and everybody hears it, that Robards was his friend, that he wants to get that asshole Walker out of the house now. Henderson says something about putting the children in danger. The man doesn't care. He pushes Henderson back. The other man – Templeton, somebody says his name, a Deputy – runs around to the side of the house, close to Robards' body, and he grabs Robards by the armpits, and leads his friend back towards the crowd. When he's done he picks up Trent Henderson's smoldering torch from the ground, and he doesn't say a word. He hurls it in the same arc as he threw the canister.

The flames seem to catch before the torch even hits the wood, as if the fumes might be enough. They rip around the house, swallowing the old gray wood. They cover all that can be seen in seconds, as if this house was always meant to be burned.

Inside the house, Deanna hears the water; it sounds like a gentle wave, a tide, lapping against the house. It cannot be that, because she knows that there is no tide. Then comes the heat from the flames and she realizes what has happened. The house starts succumbing almost immediately. She hears the crackle of the wood, and the creaking of it as it begins to buckle.

'No,' Laurence says. 'No!' The flames start to come inside. The gaps between the planks themselves, and the spaces underneath the doors, and the windows, and the small round bullet holes. The flames lick their way inside and Laurence crouches in the middle of the floor. 'Oh, no,' he says. 'No!' He rams the floor with the gun, over and over, as if he could just fire into the wood, and then he stands up. 'We go upstairs,' he says.

'The house will collapse,' Deanna tells him. 'We'll all die.' He nods, as if that's an acceptable outcome, and then it hits him, like inspiration.

'Down, then. The cellar. That's stone. We can survive the fire there.'

'And what happens—'

'Just fucking listen to me!' he screams. 'Just fucking listen! I am trying to save you, don't you see that? I am trying to save us all!' He crosses to the cellar door and opens it. He looks into the darkness; there is no bulb in the fitting down there and he'll want to close the door, but it's cold old stone walls and a stone ceiling and stone floors, and it will be safe. Even if it's only for a short while. 'Get downstairs,' he says, 'in the cellar.' He holds the door open for them.

The TV in Amit's dash tells him about the fire and he struggles to not watch it, to keep his eyes on the road. The house burns, a red and orange and yellow thing against the backdrop of the lake, and the sun in the distance, coming over the hills at the far side. It's almost the same color. On the small screen it looks like they're bleeding into each other. The whole house is somehow engulfed.

The GPS tells him that he's twenty minutes away. He wants to be able to see the town in the distance and he looks, to find a glow of gold, because if he can see it burning he will know that he is getting closer.

It's pitch black and they can't see anything. There is no adjusting to the light, because there's nothing to adjust to, nothing coming in from anywhere.

The cellar is like a bunker, like somewhere you would drag your family to escape the terrors of nuclear war. Built like a safe room, only without a lead-lined door; and with no way of looking out, of seeing if the world outside is safe or not. Deanna can't see Laurence, but she can hear him pacing around, his legs swirling the water around his ankles. She can feel her daughters, because they're all clinging to each other, and she puts her hand out to feel the back wall. It's cold, maybe even damp, and she feels her way along it, trying to get as far away from Laurence as possible. He murmurs, standing by the water main. She doesn't care what he's trying to say now.

'Why have you done this?' she asks.

'I. Have. Done. Nothing,' he replies. He pauses between his words as if he cannot catch his breath; as if he has been running and he's come back and she has tried to have a normal conversation. He struggles.

'We could die down here.'

'You could die up there! Didn't you see? They wanted to burn us down, Deanna.'

'Not us,' she replies. He stops moving, and she suddenly becomes aware that she's lost him. In this darkness, he is silent. He is holding his breath. 'They wanted *you*, Laurence. Not the girls.'

'I didn't want this,' he says. 'You think that I did? You think that I ever imagined that this would be the way that this would go? I was going to be president. Do you remember that? It feels like such a long time ago, doesn't it, that once that was the dream? Better for me, and for our family, and for the whole country. I mean, what even *was* that? Because, apparently, I was never going to be that man. Apparently, fuck you, Laurence Walker. Fuck you, because you're just a fucking joke. You're a man with a gun and we'll treat you like a fucking murderer and you will—I mean, I am not a bad man, Deanna. Girls. I am not. I have tried so hard; you know that. But what did I do? What did I *do*?' He's silent. He waits in the quiet, and he breathes.

'I don't know,' she says. She doesn't say anything more and there is no sound. The silence is broken by the sobbing of one of their daughters, but honestly, in this darkness, Deanna cannot tell which one it is.

Jessie watches as the house begins to crumble; she hears the creak of wood breaking in on itself. The townsfolk stand and watch, but they aren't proud. They don't want blood on their hands. Or, they don't want the wrong blood. She knows what they would have done to Laurence – and everybody would have stood aside. This would have been in self-defense. She can hear the headlines. He was a violent man, an unstable man, a terrifying man. He wasn't who he seemed to be. We were told that he couldn't be trusted. He killed a police officer. He was insane.

Jessie pushes through the crowd, trying to get to the front. She thinks about shouting to Laurence what has happened, but doesn't think he'll hear her. If he does, he won't listen. Deanna might. So she tries, but the townsfolk look at her and close ranks. She is held back. *My name is June,* one woman's badge reads, and she puts her hands on Jessie's shoulders and looks her square in the eyes.

'This is ours,' she says, as if Jessie is trying to kill Laurence herself. She pushes Jessie back, so she tries shouting out the things that Amit has told her, but they're lost to the crowds of people and the sound of the world waking up. The sun is in the sky and the birds are wide awake. It's morning.

'When did this happen?' Laurence asks.

'What?'

'This. My decline.' He spits the words, stolen from whatever TV show he heard them in. They are not his own. 'It hasn't always been like this, has it? Have you always been afraid of me?'

'No,' Deanna says. 'Not always.'

'We were happy. Girls, your mother and I, we were always happy. This is only recent, whatever this is.'

'Laurence,' she says, as if she is going to plead with him to spare them again; as if maybe she has an excuse, a reason that he should let them go. But, she realizes, if the simple fact that they would be alive isn't enough, what can she say?

'I know,' he says. 'What are they so scared of? Because there are worse things than this. There are certainly worse things than me.' Above them, there is the crash of something falling onto something else, wooden floorboards and walls beginning to tear themselves apart, no longer able to sustain the weight. Deanna can't tell what it is, but those wrought-iron beds will outlast the floors they're standing on; and the glass of the windows, the ceramics of the bathrooms. They'll all fall down on top of them. There's another crash, another shattering of something. She wonders how long they have because, one way this ends is with Laurence too afraid to do anything, too cowardly, if that's what it is; and Trent Henderson will still get to him in the end, walking across the charred ashes of the house and hauling him from this pit. Maybe she just has to wait it out. Maybe. 'I won't let you leave,' he says, 'because this is the only way. I was there, in that video, Deanna. I was there with you all, and with the gun.'

'It wasn't always the same video. In the beginning it was different. It wasn't as bad.'

'No,' he says. 'It wasn't.' She hears his suit rubbing against itself, the shirt against the jacket collar. He is nodding, and she can picture it; agreeing when he doesn't really agree. 'But look at us now!' He sounds almost amused. 'It was always a truth, wasn't it?'

'Homme posed for his video. He recreated it.'

'That is still a truth.'

'It was *manufactured*.'

'Everything is. Nothing is accidental, Deanna. I

don't know that it's ever been.' He shuffles. 'All of you: can I hold you all again?'

'No,' Lane says. It's abrupt, and her voice cuts through the darkness, as if it has to get used to it.

'I understand,' Laurence says. 'Pumpkin? What about you?'

'No,' Deanna says. 'Lane, keep a hold of your sister.' She feels behind her; they are both there, both as safe as she can possibly keep them. 'You can hold *me*, Laurence.' If it protects them, she thinks, if it stops him getting to them. Maybe she can do something.

'Thank you,' he says. He steps towards her and she feels his hot breath as he does and his arms around her. She puts hers around him and she feels him – every part of him – underneath them. He feels as if he is made from paper. She could crush him, she thinks. She feels it, though; the cold shape of the gun on her back, the flat of the metal pressed against her.

'That's enough,' she says. 'Now let us go.'

'Not until it's done,' he says.

Amit drives through Staunton. He hears something in the distance that he thinks could the be faint whirr of a helicopter's blades, the police or the press. When they arrive, this will all be over, and he will have no chance at all of impacting anything – so he drives faster, pushing the engine as much as he can. He nearly misses the turning and ends up cutting the corner, the tires on the car snagging on something. He hears something buckle and the flap of the tire tearing on it. He can't stop, he knows.

All along the dirt road down towards the woods: thwap, thwap, thwap. And then he sees the smoke rising above the trees. No light other than the sun, but the smoke is thick and black with the old wood of the house, like a cloud rising from behind the trees, from the lake itself.

The house is like origami, almost, folding inwards. What was there is now something else, a mess of angles waiting to be flattened. The flames are gone, because it burned so brightly and so quickly, and now there's red cinder and dark, blackened wood, and that smell, and the smoke which is so dark that it can barely be seen through. Jessie wonders why they didn't leave the house, if Walker kept them there and let it swallow them. She can barely breathe. She shouts something, but so too, it seems, does everybody else.

Amit's phone rings. He answers.

'Is this my fault?' Hershel asks. 'I'm watching on the news. Is this really actually my fault?'

'I don't know,' Amit says. Through the woods he goes, the car on the dirt.

The whole thing falls around them, the wood and the fixtures and the fittings raining down. There is a crack, and a joist in the room – the one holding up the ceiling, Deanna suspects – snaps and splinters. The room groans. She backs against the far wall and she feels the ceiling, the bricks.

'We'll die in here,' she says. Laurence is silent. She feels something, then, around her ankles. Ripples. 'Stop moving,' she says to the girls, and everybody is motionless. Still, the water ripples around her ankles. The level is rising, but the lapping is coming from somewhere.

'I want to go,' Alyx cries.

'I know, Pumpkin,' Laurence tells her. She cries more at that. Deanna bends down and feels the wall. There's a hole, now underneath the waterline. This is where the flood damage came from. Where Sean was.

'The water,' Laurence says. 'It's rising.'

'We're being flooded.' She leaves the girls where they are – everything is complicit and they don't make noise when she does; they understand that she's doing this for them – and she crouches into the water, feeling for the hole. She presses between the stones, her finger finding its way along the concrete, and it flakes away with the water.

'What are you doing?' Laurence asks.

She presses the stone and it shifts, a loose tooth in a gum. The water becomes a torrent. There is light, from the hole, pouring in: this is the lake, the part underneath the dock. This, she realizes, is the water that Sean died in. It brings light in with it, enough to see the shapes of her family.

'What did you *do*?' Laurence shouts.

Deanna pulls another block out, and another. It's big enough to climb through, she thinks, certainly big enough for Alyx.

'Let us go!' she yells.

'No,' he says. He runs up the stairs and tries the door, but it's stuck fast. The house is blocking them. She pulls the girls towards the hole. The room will flood, and then it will collapse. She looks at Laurence. He is where he stood and he has the gun by his side. He cocks the trigger. He doesn't look at her. 'But we're together,' he says. The water is up to her waist, and they are next to the hole, lined up and terrified. The hole is where Sean was, along with whatever's at the bottom of the lake. She cannot wait.

'Swim through,' she says to the girls.

'Don't leave me,' Laurence tells her. 'Deanna, I am not that man.'

More water. A brief pause, and a look in Laurence's eye. He—

Amit comes over the hill. He pulls the handbrake and throws the door open, runs down the track towards the smoking remnants of the house. The whole thing is gone, or will be. Fizzled out, the dying embers of a hearth. Around the shoreline the water is chopped into waves, moving back and forth; it's murky, reflecting the smoke above it, as if it is full of mud, or ash, or ink.

He sees the crowd. Faces from the town and from the Walkers' life, from the news companies,

Jessie in the middle, searching for him as he runs. He knows he's too late.

This is how the video ends.

From the house he hears a bang, the crack of a pistol; and then Alyx's voice screams through the darkness.

It echoes through the trees. The sound is caught on camera and broadcast, and everybody outside the remains of the house stares. Amit runs down the path, through the people, pushing them aside. At the edges of the smoldering ashes of the house he shouts their names. The water of the lake is like a sea.

Everybody stands still, to see what happens next.

EPILOGUE

Laurence opens the door to the outside, to the decking, to the fledgling sun that is rising in the distance.

'Look at that,' he says. He points into the distance, to the far side of the lake. 'Can you see that?' he asks Sean, but his son isn't listening. 'This is what it should be like. This is what our life, when we get a chance, should be.' He picks up Sean and he laughs, and Sean laughs, and Laurence threatens to throw him into the water, running and laughing with him. He stops, and they both collapse with giggles.

'Go in,' he says, 'get used to it. Then I'll show you.'

Sean pads down the bank and into the water, Laurence right behind him. It's freezing, and Laurence bends away from it when it hits his waist. Sean starts swimming, this half breaststroke, half doggy-paddle thing that he picked up from his friends, and then Laurence follows, howling with the cold.

'Holy crap!' he yells and Sean laughs at the curse word. 'This is so cold!' He goes under, soaking his hair and face. 'Now this is the best part. Come on!' he shouts, beckoning Sean towards him. They both climb out and up onto the dock, and then Laurence explains what they are going to do. The water drips off them and onto the wood, and the dock seems to move slightly. The lake is no longer still.

He explains how this works: that you have to trust in the water and in your own body. You have to step back, take a little run up. Sean is scared, but Laurence reassures him.

'We'll do it from the end,' he says. They stand with their toes at the lip of the wood, and Laurence poses for his son, to show him; arms up, outstretched to a point. And then you tip forward, and you break the water, and you're underneath so you start kicking to back up. Take a breath before you dive, and hold it. You have to remember to hold it.

'I'm scared,' Sean says.

'It's okay,' Laurence says. 'You won't be when you've done it once. Then you'll want to do it over and over. Remember the rollercoaster at Disney?' Sean nods. 'This is like that. It's *good* scary.'

'Okay,' Sean says. They stand there in the same pose. Sean is so thin, his skin almost translucent in this light.

'One. Two. Three!' Laurence says. He puts his hand gently on Sean's back, helping the boy tip forward; and he watches him go into the water, breaking the surface and then kicking out, half in panic and half in pleasure. Laurence smiles, and then he steps back and he launches forward in turn, up and into the air; and then down, following his son underneath the waves that they themselves have made.